Mary Balogh is a *New York Times* bestselling author. A former teacher, she grew up in Wales and now lives in Canada.

Visit her website at www.marybalogh.com

Slightly Wicked

Mary Balogh

piatkus

PIATKUS

First published in the United States in 2003 by
Bantam Dell, a division of Random House, Inc.
First published in Great Britain in 2007 by Piatkus Books Ltd
This edition published in 2007 by Piatkus Books
Reprinted 2008, 2009, 2011, 2014

Copyright © 2003 by Mary Balogh

The moral right of the author has been asserted.

A CIP catalogue record for this book
is available from the British Library.

ISBN 978-0-7499-3754-6

Data manipulation by Phoenix Photosetting, Chatham, Kent
www.phoenixphotosetting.co.uk
Printed and bound by CPI Group (UK) Ltd, Croydon, CR0 4YY

Papers used by Piatkus are from well-managed forests
and other responsible sources.

Slightly Wicked

CHAPTER I

MOMENTS BEFORE THE STAGECOACH OVER-
turned, Judith Law was deeply immersed in a
daydream that had effectively obliterated the
unpleasant nature of the present reality.

For the first time in her twenty-two years of existence
she was traveling by stagecoach. Within the first mile or two
she had been disabused of any notion she might ever have
entertained that it was a romantic, adventurous mode of
travel. She was squashed between a woman whose girth
required a seat and a half of space and a thin, restless man
who was all sharp angles and elbows and was constantly
squirming to find a more comfortable position, digging her
in uncomfortable and sometimes embarrassing places as he
did so. A portly man opposite snored constantly, adding
considerably to all the other noises of travel. The woman
next to him talked unceasingly to anyone unfortunate or
unwise enough to make eye contact with her, relating the
sorry story of her life in a tone of whining complaint. From
the quiet man on the other side of her wafted the odors of
uncleanness mingled with onions and garlic. The coach

rattled and vibrated and jarred over every stone and pothole in its path, or so it seemed to Judith.

Yet for all the discomforts of the road, she was not eager to complete the journey. She had just left behind the life-long familiarity of Beaconsfield and home and family and did not expect to return to them for a long time, if ever. She was on her way to live at her Aunt Effingham's. Life as she had always known it had just ended. Though nothing had been stated explicitly in the letter her aunt had written to Papa, it had been perfectly clear to Judith that she was not going to be an honored, pampered guest at Harewood Grange, but rather a poor relation, expected to earn her keep in whatever manner her aunt and uncle and cousins and grandmother deemed appropriate. Starkly stated, she could expect only dreariness and drudgery ahead—no beaux, no marriage, no home and family of her own. She was about to become one of those shadowy, fading females with whom society abounded, dependent upon their relatives, unpaid servants to them.

It had been extraordinarily kind of Aunt Effingham to invite her, Papa had said—except that her aunt, her father's sister, who had made an extremely advantageous marriage to the wealthy, widowed Sir George Effingham when she was already past the first bloom of youth, was not renowned for kindness.

And it was all because of Branwell, the fiend, who deserved to be shot and then hanged, drawn, and quartered for his thoughtless extravagances—Judith had not had a kind thought to spare for her younger brother in many weeks. And it was because she was the second daughter, the one without any comforting label to make her continued presence at home indispensable. She was not the eldest—Cassandra was a year older than she. She was certainly not the beauty—her younger sister Pamela was that. And she was not the baby—seventeen-year-old Hilary had that dubious distinction. Judith was the embarrassingly awkward one, the ugly one, the always cheerful one, the dreamer.

Judith was the one everyone had turned and looked at when Papa came to the sitting room and read Aunt Effingham's letter aloud. Papa had fallen into severe financial straits and must have written to his sister to ask for just the help she was offering. They all knew what it would mean to the one chosen to go to Harewood. Judith had volunteered. They had all cried when she spoke up, and her sisters had all volunteered too—but she had spoken up first.

Judith had spent her last night at the rectory inventing exquisite tortures for Branwell.

The sky beyond the coach windows was gray with low, heavy clouds, and the landscape was dreary. The landlord at the inn where they had stopped briefly for a change of horses an hour ago had warned that there had been torrential rain farther north and they were likely to run into it and onto muddy roads, but the stagecoach driver had laughed at the suggestion that he stay at the inn until it was safe to proceed. But sure enough, the road was getting muddier by the minute, even though the rain that had caused it had stopped for a while.

Judith had blocked it all out—the oppressive resentment she felt, the terrible homesickness, the dreary weather, the uncomfortable traveling conditions, and the unpleasant prospect of what lay ahead—and daydreamed instead, inventing a fantasy adventure with a fantasy hero, herself as the unlikely heroine. It offered a welcome diversion for her mind and spirits until moments before the accident.

She was daydreaming about highwaymen. Or, to be more precise, about a highwayman. He was not, of course, like any self-respecting highwayman of the real world—a vicious, dirty, amoral, uncouth robber and cutthroat murderer of hapless travelers. No, indeed. This highwayman was dark and handsome and dashing and laughing—he had white, perfect teeth and eyes that danced merrily behind the slits of his narrow black mask. He galloped across a sun-bright green field and onto the highway, effortlessly controlling his powerful and magnificent black steed with one hand, while he pointed a pistol—unloaded, of course—at the heart of the coachman. He laughed and joked merrily with the passengers as he deprived them of their valuables, and then he tossed back those of the people he saw could ill afford the loss. No . . . No, he returned *all* of the valuables to *all* the passengers since he was not a real highwayman at all, but a gentleman bent on vengeance against one particular villian, whom he was expecting to ride along this very road.

He was a noble hero masquerading as a highwayman, with a nerve of steel, a carefree spirit, a heart of gold, and looks to cause every female passenger heart palpitations that had nothing to do with fear.

And then he turned his eyes upon Judith—and the universe stood still and the stars sang in their spheres. Until, that was, he laughed gaily and announced that he *would* deprive *her* of the necklace that dangled against her bosom even though it must have been obvious to him that it had almost no money value at all. It was merely something that her . . . her *mother* had given her on her deathbed, something Judith had sworn never to remove this side of her own grave. She stood up bravely to the highwayman, tossing back her head and glaring unflinchingly into those laughing eyes. She would give him nothing, she told him in a clear, ringing voice that trembled not one iota, even if she must die.

He laughed again as his horse first reared and then pranced about as he brought it easily under control. Then if he could not have the necklace *without* her, he declared, he would have it *with* her. He came slowly toward her, large and menacing and gorgeous, and when he was close enough, he leaned down from the saddle, grasped her by the waist with powerful hands—she ignored the problem of the pistol, which he had been brandishing in one hand a moment ago—and lifted her effortlessly upward.

The bottom fell out of her stomach as she lost contact with solid ground, and . . . and she was jerked back to reality. The coach had lost traction on the muddy road and was swerving and weaving and rocking out of control. There was enough time—altogether too much time—to feel blind terror before it went into a long sideways skid, collided with a grassy bank, turned sharply back toward the road, rocked even more alarmingly than before, and finally overturned into a low ditch, coming to a jarring halt half on its side, half on its roof.

When rationality began to return to Judith's mind, everyone seemed to be either screaming or shouting. She was not one of them—she was biting down on both lips instead. The six inside passengers, she discovered, were in a heap together against one side of the coach. Their curses, screams, and groans testified to the fact that most, if not all, of them were alive. Outside she could hear shouts and the whinnying of frightened horses. Two voices, more distinct than any others, were using the most shockingly profane language.

She was alive, Judith thought in some surprise. She was also—she tested the idea gingerly—unhurt, though she felt considerably shaken up. Somehow she appeared to be on top of the heap of bodies. She tried moving, but even as she did so, the door above her opened and someone—the coachman himself—peered down at her.

"Give me your hand, then, miss," he instructed her. "We will have you all out of there in a trice. Lord love us, stop that screeching, woman," he told the talkative woman with a lamentable lack of sympathy considering the fact that he was the one who had overturned them.

It took somewhat longer than a trice, but finally everyone was standing on the grassy edge of the ditch or sitting on overturned bags, gazing hopelessly at the coach, which was obviously not going to be resuming its journey anytime soon. Indeed, even to Judith's unpracticed eye it was evident that the conveyance had sustained considerable damage. There was no sign of any human habitation this side of the horizon. The clouds hung low and threatened rain at any moment. The air was damp and chilly. It was hard to believe that it was summer.

By some miracle, even the outside passengers had escaped serious injury, though two of them were caked with mud and none too happy about it either. There were many ruffled feathers, in fact. There were raised voices and waving fists. Some of the voices were raised in anger, demanding to know why an experienced coachman would bring them forward into peril when he had been advised at the last stop to wait a while. Others were raised in an effort to have their suggestions for what was to be done heard above the hubbub. Still others were complaining of cuts or bruises or other assorted ills. The whining lady had a bleeding wrist.

Judith made no complaint. She had chosen to continue her journey even though she had heard the warning and might have waited for a later coach. She had no suggestions to make either. And she had no injuries. She was merely miserable and looked about her for something to take her mind off the fact that they were all stranded in the middle of nowhere and about to be rained upon. She began to tend those in distress, even though most of the hurts were more imaginary than real. It was something she could do with both confidence and a measure of skill since she had often accompanied her mother on visits to the sick. She bandaged cuts and bruises, using whatever materials came to hand. She listened to each individual account of the mishap over and over, murmuring soothing words while she found seats for the unsteady and fanned the faint. Within minutes she had removed her bonnet, which was getting in her way, and tossed it into the still-overturned carriage. Her hair was coming down, but she did not stop to try to restore it to order. Most people, she found, really did behave rather badly in a crisis, though this one was nowhere near as disastrous as it might have been.

But her spirits were as low as anyone's. This, she thought, was the very last straw. Life could get no drearier than this. She had touched the very bottom. In a sense perhaps that was even a consoling thought. There was surely no farther down to go. There was only up—or an eternal continuation of the same.

"How do you keep so cheerful, dearie?" the woman who had occupied one and a half seats asked her.

Judith smiled at her. "I am alive," she said. "And so are you. What is there *not* to be cheerful about?"

"I could think of one or two things," the woman said.

But their attention was diverted by a shout from one of the outside passengers, who was pointing off into the distance from which they had come just a few minutes before. A rider was approaching, a single man on horseback. Several of the passengers began hailing him, though he was still too far off to hear them. They were as excited as if a superhuman savior were dashing to their rescue. What they thought one man could do to improve their plight Judith could not imagine. Doubtless they would not either if questioned.

She turned her attention to one of the unfortunate soggy gentlemen, who was dabbing at a bloody scrape on his cheek with a muddy handkerchief and wincing. Perhaps, she thought and stopped herself only just in time from chuckling aloud, the approaching stranger was the tall, dark, noble, laughing highwayman of her daydream. Or perhaps he was a real highwayman coming to rob them, like sitting ducks, of their valuables. Perhaps there *was* farther down to go after all.

A<small>LTHOUGH HE WAS MAKING A LENGTHY JOURNEY</small>, L<small>ORD</small> Rannulf Bedwyn was on horseback—he avoided carriage travel whenever possible. His baggage coach, together with his valet, was trundling along somewhere behind him. His valet, being a cautious, timid soul, had probably decided to stop at the inn an hour or so back when warned of rain by an innkeeper intent on drumming up business.

There must have been a cloudburst in this part of the country not long ago. Even now it looked as if the clouds were just catching their breath before releasing another load on the land beneath. The road had become gradually wetter and muddier until now it was like a glistening quagmire of churned mudflats. He could turn back, he supposed. But it was against his nature to turn tail and flee any challenge, human or otherwise. He must stop at the next inn he came across, though. He might be careless of any danger to himself, but he must be considerate of his horse.

He was in no particular hurry to arrive at Grandmaison Park. His grandmother had summoned him there, as she sometimes did, and he was humoring her as he usually did. He was fond of her even apart from the fact that several years ago she had made him the heir to her unentailed property and fortune though he had two older brothers as well as one younger—plus his two sisters, of course. The reason for his lack of haste was that, yet again, his grandmother had announced that she had found him a suitable bride. It always took a combination of tact and humor and firmness to disabuse her of the notion that she could order his personal life for him. He had no intention of getting married anytime soon. He was only eight and twenty years old. And if and when he *did* marry, then he would jolly well choose his own bride.

He would not be the first in his family to take on a leg shackle, though. Aidan, his elder brother, had succumbed and married abruptly and secretly a mere few weeks ago in order to fulfill a debt of honor to the lady's brother, his fellow officer in the Peninsula. By some strange miracle the hasty marriage of convenience seemed already to have developed into a love match. Rannulf had met Eve, Lady Aidan, for the first time just two days ago. He had ridden from their house this morning, in fact. Aidan had sold his commission and was settling into the life of a country gentleman with his wife and her two foster children, the besotted idiot. But Rannulf had liked his new sister-in-law.

Actually it was a relief to know that it *was* a love match. The Bedwyns had a collective reputation for wildness and arrogance and even coldness. But they also had a tradition among themselves of remaining scrupulously faithful to their spouses once they did marry.

Rannulf could not imagine loving one woman for the rest of his life. The thought of remaining faithful for a lifetime was distinctly depressing. He just hoped his grandmother had not said anything about the projected match to the woman concerned. She had done that once and he had had the devil of a time convincing the woman, without appearing to do so, of course, that she really did not want to marry him.

His thoughts were diverted suddenly by the appearance of a black dot ahead of him denser than the prevailing mud and hedgerows. At first he thought it was a building, but as he rode a little closer he realized that it was actually a collection of people and a large, stationary coach. An overturned coach, he soon realized, with a broken axle. The horses were out on the road as well as a few of the people. Most, though, were huddled on the grassy verge above the wreck of the coach, keeping their feet out of the worst of the mud. Many were shouting, waving, and gesticulating in his direction as if they expected him to dismount, set his shoulder to the ruined vehicle, heave it to the road again, magically repairing the axle in the process, and hand them all inside once more before riding off into the proverbial sunset.

It would be churlish, of course, to ride on by without stopping merely because he could not offer any practical assistance. He drew rein when he was close to the group and grinned when almost everyone tried to talk to him at once. He held up a staying hand and asked if anyone had been seriously hurt. No one, it seemed, had been.

"The best I can do for you all, then," he said when the hubbub had subsided again, "is ride on with all the speed I can muster and send help back from the nearest village or town."

"There is a market town no more than three miles ahead, sir," the coachman told him, pointing off along the road. A particularly inept coachman, Rannulf judged, to have so completely lost control of his coach on a muddy road and not to have thought of sending a postilion on one of the horses to fetch assistance. But then the man showed distinct signs of having been keeping himself fortified against the damp and the chill with the contents of the flask that was clearly visible inside a gaping pocket of his greatcoat.

One of the passengers—a woman—had not joined the others in greeting him. She was bent over a muddy gentleman seated on a wooden crate, pressing some sort of makeshift bandage to his cheek. He took it from her even as Rannulf watched, and the woman straightened up and turned to look at him.

She was young and tall. She was wearing a green cloak, slightly damp, even muddied at the hem. It fell open down the front to reveal a light muslin dress and a bosom that immediately increased Rannulf's body heat by at least a couple of degrees. She was bareheaded. Her hair was disheveled and half down over her shoulders. It was a glorious shade of bright red-gold such as he had never before seen on a human head. The face beneath it was oval and flushed and bright-eyed—the eyes were green, he believed—and quite startlingly lovely. She returned his stare with apparent disdain. What did she expect him to do? Vault down into the mud and play hero?

He grinned lazily and spoke without looking away from her.

"I could, I suppose," he said, "take one person up with me. One lady? Ma'am? How about you?"

The other women passengers were having their say about his offer and his choice, but Rannulf ignored them. The red-headed beauty looked back at him, and he fully expected from the scorn on her face that she would reject his offer. He was certain of it when one of her fellow passengers, a thin, reedy, sharp-nosed individual who might have been a clerical gentleman, gave his opinion, uninvited.

"Strumpet!" he said.

" 'ere," one of the other women said—a large, buxom woman with apple-red cheeks and a redder nose, "you watch 'o you are calling a strumpet, my man. Don't think I 'aven't noticed the way you been eyeing 'er for the past 'alf a day 'cos I 'ave, you old lecher, squirming around in your seat so you could feel 'er up surreptitious like. And you with a prayer book in your 'ands and all. You should be ashamed of yerself. You go with 'im, dearie. I would if 'e arsked me, which 'e wouldn't do on account of the fact I would dent 'is 'orse in the middle."

The redhead smiled at Rannulf then, an expression that grew slowly even as the color deepened in her cheeks.

"It would be my pleasure, sir," she said in a voice that was warm and husky and crawled up his spine like a velvet-gloved hand.

He rode over to the side of the road, toward her.

H E WAS NOTHING LIKE THE HIGHWAYMAN OF HER DAY-dream. He was neither lithe nor dark nor handsome nor masked, and though he smiled, there was something mocking rather than carefree in the expression.

This man was solid. Not fat by any means, but . . . solid. His hair beneath his hat was fair. It looked wavy and it was certainly overlong for fashion. His face was dark-complexioned, dark-browed, and big-nosed. His eyes were blue. He was not at all handsome. But there was something about him. Something compelling. Something undeniably attractive—though that did not seem quite a powerful enough word.

Something slightly wicked.

Those were the first thoughts that flashed through Judith's head when she looked up at him. And of course he was no highwayman but merely a fellow traveler offering to ride on for assistance and to take someone with him.

Her.

Her second thought was one of shock, indignation, outrage. How dared he! Who did he think she was that he expected she would agree to mount a horse with a stranger and ride off alone with him? She was the daughter of the Reverend Jeremiah Law, whose expectations of strict propriety and morality from his flock were exceeded only by what he expected of his own daughters—especially her.

Her third thought was that within a very short distance—the coachman had said three miles—there was a town and the comfort of an inn, and that perhaps both could be reached before the rain came tumbling down. If she availed herself of the stranger's offer, that was.

And then she remembered her daydream again, the foolish, lovely fantasy of a dashing highwayman who had been about to carry her off on some unknown, glorious adventure, freeing her of all obligation to her family and her past, freeing her from Aunt Effingham and the dreary life of drudgery awaiting her at Harewood. A dream that had been shattered when the coach overturned.

She had a chance now to experience a real adventure, even if it was just a tiny little one. For three miles and perhaps as long as an hour she could ride up before this attractive stranger. She could do something as scandalously improper as leaving the safety and propriety of numbers to be alone with a gentleman. Her papa would shut her into her room with bread and water and her Bible for a week if he ever heard of it, and Aunt Effingham might well decide that even a month was not long enough. But who would ever know? What harm could possibly come to her?

And then the bony man called her a strumpet.

Strangely she did not feel indignant. The accusation was so absurd that she almost laughed. Yet it acted like a challenge to her. And the plump woman was encouraging her. Could she be such a sorry creature that she would turn down this small chance of a lifetime?

She smiled. "It would be my pleasure, sir," she said, hearing with some surprise that she was not speaking with her own voice but with that of a fantasy woman who would dare do such a thing.

He rode closer to her, holding her eyes with his own as he came, and leaned down from the saddle.

"Take my hand and set your foot on my boot, then," he instructed her.

She did both and suddenly it was too late to change her mind. With a seemingly effortless strength that left her breathless rather than alarmed, he lifted her and turned her so that almost before she knew she had left the ground she was sitting sideways before him, his arms bracketing her and giving her the illusion of safety. There was noise all about them. Some people were laughing and encouraging her while others complained about being left behind and begged the stranger to hurry and send back help before the rain came down.

"Is one of those portmanteaux yours, ma'am?" the stranger asked.

"That one." She pointed. "Oh, and the reticule beside it." Although it contained only the very small amount of money Papa had been able to spare her for tea and perhaps some bread and butter during her one-day journey, she was horrified at her carelessness in almost leaving it behind.

"Toss it up here, man," the horseman instructed the coachman. "The lady's portmanteau can be fetched with the others later."

He touched his whip to the brim of his hat after she had her reticule and nudged his horse into motion. Judith laughed. Her great, pathetically small adventure of a lifetime had begun. She willed the three miles to stretch to infinity.

For a few moments she was preoccupied with the fact that she was far from the ground on horseback—she had never been much of a horsewoman—and that the ground itself was a sea of oozing mud. But it did not take her long to become more aware of the startling intimacy of her position. She could feel the warmth of the stranger's body all down her left side. His legs—they looked very powerful encased in tight breeches and supple top boots—were on either side of her. Her knees touched one of them. She could feel the other brushing her buttocks. She could smell horse and leather and male cologne. The dangers of travel paled beside these other wholly unfamiliar sensations.

She shivered.

"It *is* rather chilly for a summer day," the horseman said, and he wrapped one arm about her and drew her sideways until her shoulder and arm were leaning firmly against his chest and she had no choice but to let her head fall against his shoulder. It was shocking indeed—and undeniably thrilling. It also made her suddenly remember that she was not wearing her bonnet. Not only that—with a quick sideways swivel of her eyes she noticed that at least some of her hair was loose and untidy about her shoulders.

What must she look like? What must he think of her?

"Ralf Bed—ard at your service, ma'am," he said.

How could she announce herself as Judith Law? She was not behaving at all true to her upbringing. Perhaps she should pretend to be someone else entirely—a fantasy self.

"Claire Campbell," she said, slapping together the first names that came into her head. "How do you do, Mr. Bedard?"

"Extremely well at the moment," he said huskily and they both laughed.

He was flirting with her, she thought. How scandalous! Papa would depress his impertinence with a few withering words—and then doubtless punish *her* for flaunting herself. And this time he would be justified. But she was not going to spoil her precious adventure by thinking of Papa.

"Where are you bound?" Mr. Bedard asked. "Pray do not tell me there is a husband waiting somewhere to lift you down from the coach. Or a sweetheart."

"Neither," she told him, laughing again for no particular reason except that she felt lighthearted. She was going to enjoy her brief adventure to the very last moment. She was not going to waste time, energy, or opportunity in being shocked. "I am single and unattached—the way I like it." Liar. Oh, liar.

"You have restored my soul," he assured her. "Who, then, is awaiting you at the end of your journey? Your family?"

Inwardly she grimaced. She did not want to think about

the end of her journey. But the good thing about adventures was that they were neither real nor lasting. For the remainder of this strange, brief one she could say and do—and be—whatever took her fancy. It was like having a dream and some reality all at the same time.

"I have no family," she told him. "None that would own me, anyway. I am an actress. I am on my way to York to play a new part. A leading role."

Poor Papa. He would have an apoplexy. And yet it had always been her wildest, most enduring dream.

"An actress?" he said, his voice low and husky against her ear. "I might have known it as soon as I set eyes on you. Such vivid beauty as yours would shine brightly on any stage. Why have I never seen you in London? Can it be because I rarely attend the theater? I must certainly mend my ways."

"Oh, London," she said with careless scorn. "I like to *act*, Mr. Bedard, not just be ogled. I like to choose the parts *I* wish to play. I prefer provincial theaters. I am well enough known in them, I believe."

She was, she realized, still talking in that voice she had used at the roadside. And, incredibly, he believed her story. It was evident in his words and in the look in his eyes—amused, appreciative, knowing. Branwell, after he had first gone away to university and into the great wide world, had once told his sisters—in the absence of Papa—that London actresses almost always supplemented their income by being mistresses to the rich and titled. She was wading in dangerous waters, Judith thought. But it was for only three miles, for only an hour.

"I wish I could see you onstage," Mr. Bedard said, and his arm tightened about her while the backs of his leather-gloved fingers raised her chin.

He kissed her. On the mouth.

It did not last long. He was, after all, riding a horse over treacherous roads with a passenger hampering both his own movements and those of his horse. He could ill afford the distraction of a lengthy embrace.

But it lasted long enough. Quite long enough for a woman who had never been kissed before. His lips were parted, and Judith felt the moist heat of his mouth against her own. Seconds, or perhaps only a fraction of one second, before her brain could register either shock or outrage, every part of her body reacted. Her lips sizzled with a sensation that spread beyond them, through her mouth, into her throat, and up behind her nostrils. There was a tightening in her breasts, and a powerful ache down through her stomach and her womb and along the insides of her thighs.

"Oh," she said when it was over. But before she could express her indignation over such an insolent liberty, she remembered that she was Claire Campbell, famous provincial actress, and that actresses, even if not the mistresses of the rich and titled, were expected to know a thing or two about life. She looked into his eyes and smiled dreamily.

Why not? she thought recklessly. Why not live out her fantasy for this short little spell to discover where it might lead? This first kiss, after all, would probably also be her last.

Mr. Bedard smiled back at her with lazy, mocking eyes.

"Oh, indeed," he said.

CHAPTER II

WHAT THE DEVIL WAS HE DOING GETTING involved—*very* involved—in a kiss while with every step it took Bucephalus was in danger of skidding and breaking a leg and tossing its two riders to a bumpy, muddy landing? Rannulf mentally shook his head.

She was an actress who claimed to prefer acting worthy parts to being ogled in a fashionable theater. Yet she was displaying all that artfully disarranged hair, which—if his eyes did not deceive him—was her natural color, and showing no apparent reluctance to be pressing all those warm, voluptuous curves against his front. The flush of color in her cheeks was natural too. She had a way of partially lowering her dark-lashed eyelids over her remarkable eyes—they *were* green—in a look of pure invitation if ever he had seen one. And her voice still caressed him like a velvet-gloved hand.

He was playing the game, was he? Well, *of course* he was playing the game. Why else had he given her a false name? Why would he not, especially when it had offered itself so unexpectedly, at a time when he had been contemplating a chaste few weeks with his grandmother? He had lusty appetites and was not about to turn down an invitation such as she was clearly offering. But even so—kissing on horseback? On a dangerously muddy road?

Rannulf chuckled inwardly. This was the stuff of fantasy. *Delicious* fantasy.

"What is *your* destination?" she asked him. "Are you going home to a wife? Or a sweetheart?"

"To neither," he said. "I am single and unattached."

"I am glad to hear it," she told him. "I would hate to think of your having to confess that kiss to someone."

He grinned at her. "I am on my way to spend a few weeks with friends," he said. "Are those buildings I see up ahead? Or do my eyes deceive me?"

She turned her head to look. "No," she said. "I believe you are right."

It was going to start raining again any second. It would be good to get off the muddy road and inside a building. It was certainly necessary to report the wrecked carriage as soon as possible so that help could be dispatched. Nevertheless, Rannulf felt some regret that the town was coming upon them so soon. However, all might not be lost. It was going to be impossible for either of them to journey on today, close though he was to his own destination.

"Within a few minutes, then," he said, lowering his head until his mouth was close to her ear, "we should be safe at an inn and help will have been sent to those poor stranded passengers. You will be relaxing in one warm, dry room and I in another. Will you be glad?"

"Yes, of course," she said in a brisk voice that was unlike the one she had been using so far in their acquaintance.

Ah. He had mistaken the signs, had he? A mild flirtation on horseback was one thing, but anything further was not in her plans? He lifted his head and concentrated upon guiding his horse the final few yards to what looked like a sizable posting inn on the edge of a small town.

"No," she said a few moments later, her voice low and throaty again. "No, I will not be glad."

Ah.

I T WAS WARM AND DRY INSIDE THE INN, AND FOR THE FIRST time in several hours Judith felt physically safe. But the inn was crowded. The yard outside had been bustling, and people were milling about inside, some of them at windows watching the sky, others clearly having decided to stop for the night.

She had a problem. She did not have enough money to pay for a room. But when she had mentioned that fact to Mr. Bedard, he had merely smiled that mocking smile at her and said nothing. Now he was standing at the reception desk speaking with the innkeeper while she stood a few feet away. Was it possible that he intended to pay for her room? Would she allow it? How would she ever pay him back?

She wished and wished that her brief, glorious adventure had not ended so soon. She wanted more. She would relive the past hour over and over in the coming days and weeks, she knew. She would relive that kiss perhaps forever. Poor forlorn spinster, she thought, giving herself a mental shake. But her spirits seemed to be flattened against the soles of her rather muddy half boots. She felt more depressed now than she had an hour ago, before he rode into her life.

He was a tall man and solidly built. His hair, she could see now that he had removed his hat, was indeed wavy. It was also thick and fair and almost touched his shoulders. If one mentally added a beard and a horned helmet, one could imagine him standing at the prow of a Viking ship directing an attack on a hapless Saxon village. With herself as a brave, defiant villager . . .

He turned away from the desk and closed the distance between them. He stood rather close to her and spoke low.

"A number of travelers have already taken refuge here,"
he said. "And the passengers from the stagecoach are going
to need rooms too. The inn will be overflowing tonight.
There is, however, a smaller, quieter inn farther into the
town, by the market green. It is used primarily on market
days, but I have been assured that it is perfectly clean and
comfortable. We could leave two rooms vacant here by removing there."

There was a look in his eyes that was not exactly amusement and not exactly mockery. She could not interpret it
though it sent shivers down to her very toes so that she
found herself curling them involuntarily inside her half
boots. She licked her lips.

"I have told you, Mr. Bedard," she said, "that I do not
have more than a few coins on me, having expected to journey straight through to York without stopping. I will remain
here. I will sit in the dining room or in the window here until another stagecoach arrives to take me on my way." Actually, she thought, she was probably not very far from
Harewood Grange. They were in Leicestershire already,
were they not?

His eyes smiled at her with that expression that was not
quite mockery. "The innkeeper will have your portmanteau
sent over as soon as it arrives," he said. "The coach has a
broken axle. The wait for another may be a long one, certainly an overnight one. You might as well wait in comfort."

"But I cannot afford—" she began again.

He set one finger over her lips, startling her into silence.

"Ah, but I can," he said. "I can afford the price of *one*
room, at least."

For a moment of utter stupidity she did not understand
him. And then she did. She wondered that her face did not
flame with such heat that she would set his finger on fire.

She wondered that her knees did not buckle under her while she collapsed into a deep swoon. She wondered that she did not scream and slap his face with all the force of her outrage.

She did none of those things. Instead she hid behind the worldly mask of Claire Campbell while she felt the full force of temptation. She felt an almost overwhelming yearning to continue her adventure, her stolen dream. He was suggesting that they share a room at the other inn. He must surely intend too that they share a bed. He must intend that they have marital relations there—though *marital* was quite the wrong word, she supposed.

Today. Tonight. Within the next few hours.

She smiled Claire Campbell's smile and was aware as she did so that no other answer was necessary. She was absolved of having to make any real decision or any verbal commitment. But nonetheless she *had* made a certain decision, otherwise Claire could not have smiled. Just once in her life she needed, she *desperately* needed, to do something gloriously outrageous and shocking and daring and . . . out of character.

She might never have another chance.

"I will go rescue my horse before he settles too comfortably into a stall," he said, taking a step back from her, looking her over quickly from head to toe, and then turning in the direction of the outer door.

"Yes," she agreed.

After all, nothing was final. She would not really go through with the whole scheme. When the time came, she would simply excuse herself and explain to him that he had misunderstood, that she was not that kind of woman. She would sleep on the floor or on a chair or *somewhere* he was not. He was a gentleman. He would not force her. She was merely extending her adventure by agreeing to go with him. She would not be doing anything irreversibly depraved.

Oh, yes, you will be, a small voice inside her head told

her, unbidden. *Oh, yes, you will be, my girl.* It spoke in the brisk tones of Judith Law at her most sensible.

T HE RUM AND PUNCHEON WAS A SMALL MARKET INN. IT was empty of guests though the taproom was crowded enough. Mr. and Mrs. Bedard were received with jovial hospitality and given the best room in the inn, a square, clean chamber that soon had a fire crackling in the hearth, a welcome buffer against the rain that was pattering against the windows, and a pitcher of hot water steaming on the washstand behind the screen. They would be served their dinner, they were assured, in the small dining parlor that adjoined their bedchamber. They would be cozy and private there, the innkeeper's wife informed them, beaming at them as if she fully believed them to be a married couple.

Claire Campbell pushed back the hood of her cloak when they were alone together in their room and stood looking out the window. Rannulf tossed his cloak and hat onto a chair and looked at her. Her hair had lost even more of its pins and was looking considerably disheveled. Her green cloak was dark with damp at the shoulders, slightly muddied at the hem. His intention had been to tumble her into bed as soon as they arrived so that they might slake the first rush of their appetite. But the time did not feel right. He was a lusty man but not one of unbridled passions. Sex, after all, was an art as well as a necessary physical function. The art of sex needed atmosphere.

All evening and all night stretched before them. There was no hurry.

"You will wish to freshen up," he said. "I will have a pint of ale in the taproom and come back up when dinner is ready. I'll have a pot of tea sent up to you."

She turned to him. "That would be kind of you," she said.

He almost changed his mind. The color was high in her

cheeks again, and her eyelids were slightly drooped in invitation. Her hair was rumpled, as though she had just risen from bed. He wanted to put her back there, himself on top of her and between her thighs and deep inside her.

Instead he made her a mocking bow and raised one eyebrow.

"Kind?" he said. "Now kindness is something I am not often accused of, ma'am."

He spent all of an hour in the taproom, drinking his ale while a group of townsmen included him hospitably in their circle and asked his opinion of the weather and his observations on the state of the roads while puffing on their pipes and drinking deep from their tankards and agreeing sagely with one another that now they were going to pay for all the hot summer weather they had been enjoying for the past several weeks.

He went up to the private dining parlor when the landlady informed him that the food was about to be carried up. Claire was there, standing in the doorway between the two rooms, watching a maid set the table and then bring in the food and set it down.

"It is steak-and-kidney pie," the girl said with a smile and a curtsy before she left the room and closed the door behind her. "The best for ten miles around, I do declare. Enjoy it. Ring when you want me to remove the dishes."

"We will. Thank you," Claire said.

Rannulf had been almost afraid to look at her until they were alone together. He had had only glimpses of the muslin dress beneath her cloak. Now he could see that it was a simply styled garment, unexpectedly modest for a woman of her profession. But she had been traveling by stage. She had probably needed to wear something that would not attract too much attention. The dress did nothing to hide the glories of the body beneath it, though. She was not slender even though her long limbs gave that initial impression. She was lusciously curved, her waist small, her hips flaring invitingly. Her breasts, full and firm, were every man's dream come true.

She had not dressed her hair up. She had brushed it back from her face, and it fell in shining ripples over her shoulders and halfway down her back. It was a glorious, almost shocking shade of red with gold highlights that glinted in the late daylight. Her long, oval face had lost its flush of color and was as pale and delicate as porcelain. Her eyes looked startlingly green. And—yes, by Jove—there was something unexpected about the face, something that drew her down into the realm of mortality. He closed the distance between them and ran a finger lightly over her nose, from one cheek to the other.

"Freckles," he said. The merest dusting of them.

Some of the color returned to her cheeks. "They were the bane of my childhood," she said. "And alas, they have never completely disappeared."

"They are charming," he said. He had always admired goddesses. He had never bedded one. He liked his women made of flesh and blood. He had almost feared when he first came into the room that Claire Campbell was a goddess.

"I have to cover them with a great deal of paint when I am onstage," she told him.

"Almost," he said, his gaze lowering to her mouth, "you have robbed me of my appetite for food."

"*Almost,*" she said in that brisk voice he had heard once before. "But not quite. How foolish, Mr. Bedard, when your dinner awaits you on the table and you are hungry."

"Ralf," he said. "You had better call me Ralf."

"Ralph," she said. "It is time for dinner."

And later they would indulge in dessert, he thought as he seated her at the table and took his place opposite her. A sweet delight that they would savor all night long. His blood hummed in anticipation of good sex. He had no doubt that it would be very good indeed. In the meantime she was right—his body needed to be fed.

He talked of London at her request since it appeared that she had never been there. He talked about the social scene during the Season—about the balls and routs and concerts, about Hyde Park and Carlton House and Vauxhall Gardens. She spoke about the theater at his urging, about the parts she had played and those she longed to play, about her fellow actors and about the directors she had worked with. She described it all slowly, with dreamy eyes and a smile on her lips as if it were a profession she thoroughly enjoyed.

They ate well. And yet it surprised Rannulf about an hour after they had begun to look down at the table and see that most of the large quantities of food were gone and that the bottle of wine was empty. He could hardly remember the taste of anything, though he had a feeling of general well-being—and a constant spark of anticipation.

He got to his feet, crossed to the fireplace, and pulled on the bell rope. He had the dishes cleared away and another bottle of wine brought up.

"More?" he asked Claire, tilting the bottle above her glass.

She set one hand over the top of it. "Oh, I really ought not," she said.

"But you will." He looked into her eyes.

She smiled. "But I will." She removed her hand.

He leaned back in his chair after filling their glasses and taking a sip. Now was perhaps the moment. The meager light of day was finally fading beyond the windows. The rain pelting against them and the fire crackling in the hearth added an atmosphere of coziness and intimacy, unusual for summer. But there was something else.

"I want to see you act," he said.

"*What?*" Her eyebrows rose and her hand, holding the wineglass, paused halfway to her mouth.

"I want to see you act," he repeated.

"Here? Now?" She set the glass down on the table. "How absurd. There is no stage, there are no props, no other actors, no script."

"A talented, experienced actress surely does not need a script for some parts," he said. "And no stage or props either. There are any number of famous soliloquies that do not require other actors. Perform one for me, Claire. Please?"

He raised his glass and held it up to her in a silent toast.

She stared at him, the flush back in her cheeks. She was embarrassed, he thought in some surprise. Embarrassed to put on a private performance for a man who was about to become her lover. Perhaps it was difficult to think one's way into a dramatic role under such circumstances.

"Well, I could do Portia's famous speech, I suppose," she said.

"Portia?"

"*The Merchant of Venice*," she explained. "Surely you know the 'Quality of Mercy' speech?"

"Remind me."

"Shylock and Antonio were in court," she said, leaning slightly across the table toward him, "for it to be decided if Shylock had the right to take a pound of flesh from Antonio. There was no doubt that he had such a right—it was stated clearly in the bond they had both agreed to. But then Portia arrived, intent on saving the dearest friend and benefactor of Bassanio, her love. She came disguised as a lawyer's clerk and spoke up in Antonio's defense. At first she appealed to Shylock's better nature in the famous speech about mercy."

"I remember now," he said. "Do Portia for me, then."

She got to her feet and looked around. "This is the courtroom," she said. "It is no longer an inn dining parlor but a courtroom, in which the very life of a noble man hangs in the balance. It is a desperate situation. There would seem to be no hope. They are all here, all the principal players of the drama. Shylock sits in that chair." She pointed at the chair Rannulf was occupying.

"I am Portia," she said. "But I am disguised as a young man."

Rannulf pursed his lips in amusement as she looked around again. She lifted her arms, pulled back her hair, twisted it, and knotted it at the back of her neck. Then she disappeared for a moment into the bedchamber and came back buttoning his caped cloak about her. She still looked about as different as it was possible to be from any man. And then she had finished doing up the buttons and looked up directly into his eyes.

Rannulf almost recoiled from the hard, controlled expression on her face.

" 'The quality of mercy is not strained,' " she told him in a voice to match the expression.

For a moment, foolishly, he thought that it was she, Claire Campbell, who was addressing him, Rannulf Bedwyn.

" 'It droppeth as the gentle rain from heaven / Upon the place beneath,' " she continued, coming closer to him, her expression softening slightly, becoming more pleading.

Devil take it, he thought, she was Portia, and he was that damned villain, Shylock.

" 'It is twice blest.' "

It was not a very long speech, but by the time she had finished it, Rannulf was thoroughly ashamed of himself and ready to pardon Antonio and even go down on his knees to grovel and beg pardon for having considered cutting a pound of flesh from his body. She was bending over him, tight-lipped and keen eyed, waiting for his answer.

"By Jove," he said, "Shylock must have been made of iron."

He was, he realized, half aroused. She was very good. She could bring a role alive without any of the fancy theatrics he associated with all the most famous actors and actresses he had ever seen onstage.

She straightened up and smiled at him, unbuttoning his cloak as she did so.

"What else can you do?" he asked. "Juliet?"

She made a dismissive gesture with one hand. "I am two and twenty," she said. "Juliet was about eight years younger and a pea-goose at that. I have never understood the appeal of that play."

He chuckled. She was not a romantic, then.

"Ophelia?" he suggested.

She looked pained. "I suppose men like watching weak women," she said with something like contempt in her voice. "They do not come any weaker than that silly Ophelia. She should simply have snapped her fingers in Hamlet's face and told him to go and boil his head in oil."

Rannulf threw his head back and shouted with laughter. She was looking pink and contrite when he lifted his head again.

"I'll do Lady Macbeth," she said. "She was foolish and could not sustain her wickedness, but she was no weakling for all that."

"Her sleepwalking scene?" he asked. "Where she is washing her hands of blood?"

"There. You see?" She looked contemptuous again as she gestured toward him with one arm. "I suppose most men like that scene best. Wicked woman finally breaks down into madness because typical woman cannot be eternally strong."

"Macbeth was hardly sane either by the end," he reminded her. "I would say Shakespeare was impartial in his judgment of the relative strength of the male and female spirit."

"I'll do Lady Macbeth persuading Macbeth to murder Duncan," she said.

And he, Rannulf supposed, was to be a silent Macbeth.

"But first," she said, "I will finish my wine."

Her glass was two-thirds full. She drained it in one gulp and set down the empty glass. Then she undid the knot of hair at her neck, and shook her hair free.

"Macbeth has just told his wife, 'We will proceed no further in this business,'" she said. "He is backing out of the planned murder; she is spurring him on."

Rannulf nodded, and she turned her back for a moment and stood quite still. Then he watched her hands ball slowly into fists and she turned on him. He almost got up from his chair and retreated behind it. The green eyes pierced him with cold scorn.

"'Was the hope drunk / Wherein you dress'd yourself?'" she asked him quietly. "'Hath it slept since, / And wakes it now, to look so green and pale / At what it did so freely?'"

Rannulf resisted the urge to speak up in his own defense.

"'From this time / Such I account thy love,'" she told him.

She spoke his lines too, leaning over him to do so and speaking in a low voice, giving him the impression that he was saying the words himself without moving his lips. As Lady Macbeth she whipped into him with her energy and contempt and wily persuasions. By the time she had finished, Rannulf could fully understand at last why Macbeth had committed such an asinine deed as murdering his king.

She was panting by the time she came to the end of her persuasions, looking cold and triumphant and slightly mad.

Rannulf found himself near to panting with desire. As her identification with the role she had played faded from her eyes and her body, they stared at each other, and the air between them fairly sizzled.

"Well," he said softly.

She half smiled. "You must understand," she said, "that I am somewhat rusty. I have not acted for three months and am out of practice."

"Heaven help us," he said, getting to his feet, "if you were *in* practice. I might be dashing off into the rain to find the nearest available king to assassinate."

"So what do you think?" she asked him.

"I think," he said, "that it is time for bed."

For a moment he thought she was going to refuse. She stared at him, licked her lips, drew breath as if to say something, then nodded.

"Yes," she said.

He bent his head and kissed her. He was quite ready to tumble her to the floor and take her there and then, but why put them to that discomfort when there was a perfectly comfortable-looking bed in the next room? Besides, there were certain bodily realities to consider.

"Go and get ready," he said. "I'll wander downstairs for ten minutes."

Again she hesitated and licked her lips.

"Yes," she said and turned away. A moment later the bedchamber door closed behind her.

The next ten minutes, Rannulf thought, were going to feel like an uncomfortable eternity.

Devil take it, but she could act.

CHAPTER III

JUDITH STOOD WITH HER BACK AGAINST THE BED-
chamber door after she had shut it, and closed her eyes.
Her head was spinning, her heart was thumping, and she
was breathless. There were so many reasons for all three
conditions that she could not possibly sort through them all
to regain her customary composure.

Primarily, she had drunk too much wine. Four glasses in
all. She had never before drunk more than half a glass in one
day, and even that had happened only three or four times in
her life. She was not drunk—she could think quite coher-
ently and walk a straight line. But even so, she *had* consumed all that wine.

Then there had been the intoxicating excitement of acting before an audience—even if it *had* been an audience of
only one. Acting had always been a part of her very secret
life, something she did when she was quite, quite sure she
was alone and unobserved. She had never really thought of
it as *acting*, though, but as the bringing alive of another human being through the words the dramatist had provided.
She had always had the ability to think her way into

another person's body and mind and know just what it felt like to be that person under those circumstances. Sometimes she had tried to use that ability to write stories, but it was not in the written word that her talent lay. She needed to create or re-create characters with her very body and voice. When she acted the part of Portia or Lady Macbeth, she *became* them.

But tonight acting had been more intoxicating than the wine she had drunk. She had played for her audience of one better than she had ever played before. He had been both Shylock and Macbeth, and yet he had been Ralph Bedard too, and she had been strangely excited, exhilarated by him. It had seemed as if the very air between them were sizzling with invisible energy.

She opened her eyes suddenly and hurried toward the screen at the far side of the room. She had only ten minutes in which to get ready—less than ten now. Her portmanteau had arrived and been brought up, she saw with relief. She would have a nightgown to wear.

But she stopped abruptly even as she bent down to open the bag. *Get ready?* For what? He had just kissed her again. He was coming in ten minutes' time—less—to take her to bed. To do *that* to her. She was not even fully aware, except in the vaguest, most sketchy of ways, just what *that* was. Her knees felt unsteady. She felt breathless and lightheaded again. She was not going to let it happen . . . was she?

It was time to end the adventure. But it had been—it *was*—such a very splendid adventure. And there would be no others. Not ever. She knew that women who fell into poverty and lived as unpaid poor relations in the homes of their wealthier family members stood little or no chance of ever changing the condition of their lives. There was only now, today. And tonight.

Judith tore open the portmanteau in haste. She was wasting precious time. How embarrassing it would be if he returned to find her in her shift or before she had relieved herself or washed herself or brushed her hair! She would think later about *it,* about how she would avoid it. There was a wooden settle in the other room. With a pillow and her cloak and one of the blankets from the bed, it would make a tolerable sleeping place.

He must surely have stayed away for longer than ten minutes. She was standing in front of the fire, clad decently in her cotton nightgown, brushing her hair, when his knock came at the door and it opened before she could cross the room to it or call out any summons. She felt suddenly naked. She also knew that she must be more inebriated than she had realized. She felt a rush of longing rather than the horror she knew she ought to be feeling. She did not *want* to end the adventure. She wanted to experience *that* before her youth and her life came to an effective end. She wanted all of it—with Ralph Bedard. He was breathtakingly attractive—she wished there were a more powerful word than that for his appeal.

He stood looking at her with narrowed eyes, his lips pursed, his eyes moving slowly down her body to her bare feet.

"Is it your profession or your instinct," he said at last, his voice low, "that has taught you to understate your appearance? White cotton, with not a frill or a flounce! You are very wise. Your beauty speaks loud and clear for itself."

She was ugly. She knew that. People—even her own mother—had always compared her hair to carrots when she was a child, and it had never been a compliment. Her skin had always been too pale, her face too disfigured with freckles, her teeth too large. And then, by a horrible cruelty of fate, just when her hair had begun to darken a shade and the worst of her freckles had begun to disappear and her face and mouth had started to fit her teeth, she had begun to shoot up into something resembling a beanpole. She had grown as tall as Papa. She had felt only temporary relief when the beanpole had begun to take on the shape of a woman. To add insult to injury, that shape had come to include very full breasts and wide hips. She had always been an embarrassment to her family and worse than that to herself. Papa had been forever instructing her to dress more modestly and to cover her hair, and he had been forever blaming her for the leering glances men tended to send her way. It had always been a severe burden to be the ugly one of the family.

But tonight she was willing to accept that for some strange reason—probably the wine, since he had drunk more of it than she had—Ralph Bedard found her attractive.

She smiled slowly at him without removing her eyes from his. Wine had a strange effect. She felt a degree removed from reality, as if she were observing herself rather than up front *being* herself. She could stand in a bedchamber in her nightgown with a man, knowing that he intended taking her to bed within the next few minutes, and yet smile at him with slow invitation without feeling quite responsible for what she did. The observer was doing nothing to intervene on the side of virtue and respectability. And Judith did not want her to.

"I suppose you have been told a thousand times how beautiful you are," he said, his voice sounding wonderfully husky.

There! He really was drunk.

"A thousand and one now," she said, still smiling. "And I suppose you have been told a thousand and one times how handsome you are."

It was a lie. He was not handsome. His nose was too prominent, his eyebrows too dark, his hair too unruly, his skin too swarthy. But he was overpoweringly attractive, and attractive seemed ten times more appealing than handsome at this precise moment.

"A thousand and two now." He came toward her and she knew the moment of decision was upon her. But instead of grabbing her, he stopped a foot away from her and held out his hand. "Give me the brush."

She handed it to him, expecting him to toss it over his shoulder before proceeding to business. Would she allow him to proceed? Her breathing quickened.

"Sit down," he told her. "On the side of the bed."

Sit? Not lie? Were there still a few moments left to enjoy, then, before she must put an end to it all? The bed had been turned down neatly for the night while they were still in the dining room, just as the fire had been built up and her portmanteau and fresh water placed behind the screen.

She sat down, her feet side by side on the floor, her hands clasped in her lap, watching him strip off his form-fitting coat, his waistcoat, and his neckcloth. He sat on a chair and pulled off his boots before standing up in his stockinged feet.

Oh, dear, she thought, she ought not to be watching this. But it was so very enjoyable a sight. He was a large man, but she would swear there was not one ounce of unnecessary fat on him. He was broad-shouldered but far slimmer of waist and hip. His legs were long and powerfully muscled. He showed to distinct advantage wearing only his shirt and breeches.

He picked up her brush again and walked around to the other side of the bed. She felt his weight depress the mattress behind her. She did not turn to look. This was the moment when she should get to her feet. Ah, but she did not *want* to. And then she could feel his body heat against her back even though he did not touch her.

Then he did—with the brush. He settled it just above her forehead—she could see the white of his shirtsleeve from the corner of her right eye—and drew it backward through the length of her hair. He was kneeling behind her for the purpose of brushing her hair! As soon as she realized the innocence of his intention, she tipped back her head and closed her eyes.

She almost swooned from the delight of it. The brush set her scalp to tingling. She could hear her hair crackle. Occasionally she could feel his free hand moving her hair back over her ear or behind her shoulder. It was surely the most delicious feeling in the world, having one's hair brushed by someone else—by a man. She could feel his heat and smell his cologne. She could hear his breathing. Soon she felt relaxed and languorous and yet strangely stimulated and alert at the same time. Her breasts felt tight. An aching pulse was beating pleasurably between her legs.

"It feels good?" he asked her after a while, his voice low and husky.

"Mmm." She could not muster the energy for a more eloquent reply.

He continued drawing the slow, rhythmic strokes through her hair until finally he tossed aside the brush. She heard it thud to the floor at the foot of the bed. And then she was aware that he had moved closer to her. He had spread his knees and moved them to either side of her so that if she wished she could move her hands outward to rest on them. His chest came against her back, and his hands slipped beneath her arms and cupped the undersides of her breasts. She heard him draw a slow, audible breath.

She almost jumped to her feet in panic. Not her breasts. They were *so* embarrassing. But her slight inebriation slowed both her shock and her reactions. His hands were warm and gentle. And his thumbs were brushing over her nipples, which were strangely hard and tender. Yet he was not hurting her. Instead, his touch was sending raw aches shooting up into her throat and spiraling down between her legs and she was throbbing—inside.

He did not seem to be finding her breasts grotesque.

She closed her eyes again and tipped her head back to rest against his shoulder. Just a little more. Just a few moments longer. She would end it soon. His thumbs were gone from her nipples then, and she could feel his fingers opening the buttons down the front of her nightgown and folding the edges back so that she must be exposed from shoulders to navel. When his hands came back to circle the naked flesh of her breasts, to lift them and fondle them, to pinch and rub and pulse against her nipples, she knew that finally her adventure, her stolen dream, was perfect.

This was what she had always wanted. This. Ah, just this ever since she had become a woman. To feel a man touch her and see her and not judge her inadequate. To allow the touch. To revel in it without shame or fear. She willed the moment never—ah, please, never—to end.

"Stand up," he murmured against her ear, and though she was reluctant to move away from his touch, she obeyed and opened her eyes to watch her nightgown slip away to the floor. She felt curiously unembarrassed even though the fire was still burning and two candles were flickering on the mantel, and she had always hated looking at herself in a mirror. She sat down again.

She was aware of him pulling his shirt off over his head and tossing it to join her brush on the floor. And then his bare chest was warm and solid against her back, and his arms were beneath hers again. He rubbed his hands hard over her breasts and then spread them flat over her ribs and moved them down over her waist and abdomen. She set back her head and closed her eyes again and moved her shoulders and back to rub against him. His chest was lightly furry. He slid his hands down her legs to her knees and back up again. She spread her arms and set them along his outer thighs, cupping his knees with her hands.

It was at the next moment that she knew she had passed

the point at which she might have stopped what was to happen. But she did not care. She *did* not. Common sense and
propriety and morality would show her the full extent of the
error of her ways in the glaring light of tomorrow, but
though she knew it, she simply did not care. This was the
night that would give light and warmth and meaning to all
the rest of her days. She knew that just as certainly. Fallen
woman—who would ever know? Who would ever care?

His right hand had moved down between her legs to the
warm, secret place. She should have been horrified. Yet she
heard herself make a low sound of approval deep in her
throat, and she opened her legs a little to allow him freer
access.

She was very warm there. She could tell that by the contrasting coolness of his fingers. She feared she might also be
wet. But he did not recoil. His fingers explored her, parting
folds, rubbing lightly between them, finding the innermost
reaches and sliding up a little way inside. She could hear the
sounds of wetness but was beyond embarrassment. It did not
take her long to understand that he knew exactly what he
was doing. Desire throbbed through her entire being. And
then he did something with his thumb, something so light
that she could not even tell exactly what he did. Except that
desire suddenly crashed into pain and beyond pain even before she could feel it. She arched her back, every muscle in
her body tensing, and cried out before collapsing, panting
and trembling, back against him.

What . . . what on earth had *happened*?

"Yes," he was whispering against her ear, a note of exulta-
tion in his voice. "Ah, yes. Magnificent!"

Her breath was shuddering audibly out of her.

"Lie down," he told her.

"Yes." She no longer even considered *not* lying down
with him. Her head was spinning, but whether from the

effects of the wine or from what had just happened, she did not know.

She lay down between the sheets while he got to his feet, and watched him strip away the rest of his clothes. He looked even more magnificent without them, all hard muscles and flat abdomen, and . . . For a few moments she wondered if she should feel frightened after all, but she wanted it, she realized. She desperately wanted it. She wanted *him*.

He came down directly on top of her, pressing his knees between hers as he did so and pushing her legs wide—very wide. She bent them at the knees and set her feet flat against the mattress to brace herself. He lifted himself from the waist up, bracing himself on his forearms, and lowered his head to kiss her. His mouth was open, and soon hers was too as he licked through the seam of her lips and explored the soft flesh behind. When she parted her teeth he pressed his tongue into her mouth, clashing with her own, stroking over the sensitive roof, arousing the rawness of desire in her again.

When he lifted his head again, he was smiling his rather mocking smile at her.

"I am afraid," he said, "that I may explode as soon as I mount, quite as speedily as you just did. But we have the rest of the night in which to play at our leisure. Am I excused in advance?"

"You are excused." She smiled back at him, though in truth she did not understand what he was saying.

He came down fully on her again and she felt his hands come beneath her buttocks to hold her firm. She felt him hard and probing at her entrance, but before she could draw a steadying breath he had plunged into her. There might have been pain. She was not at leisure to notice. There might have been shock. There was no time to absorb it. There was only a wondering surprise that a man could be so large and so hard and yet fit fully inside her. And then he moved in her, almost withdrawing and plunging deep again, over and over, faster and harder until he strained deep, cried out, and collapsed all his weight on her. She wrapped her arms about him. He was hot and slick with sweat.

She felt the shock then. Her virginity was gone. Just like that. And with the shock came knowledge. Knowledge not only of what happened between a man and a woman, but of what it felt like. It had been disappointing. And yet not entirely so. Part of her exulted. She had mated with a man. She would not go through life without that most primal of human experiences. She had mated. She still lay beneath him, her breasts pressed to his chest, her thighs hugging his powerful legs, his . . . that part of him inside her.

She was not sorry. And if it was the wine telling her that, then she would tell the wine the same thing tomorrow. She was *not* sorry. She never would be. He had touched her and delighted her and made her feel feminine and beautiful as no one had ever done before—quite the contrary, in fact. And she had mated with him and satisfied him. He was sleeping, she realized. He was heavy. She was having difficulty breathing. Her legs were going to cramp soon. She would surely be sore inside. But she willed him not to wake up. She hugged her splendid, stolen dream to herself.

A FTER RANNULF WOKE UP AND ROLLED OFF HER, APOLO-gizing for squashing every bone in her body, Claire Campbell excused herself. He could hear her washing herself behind the screen, and grinned, lacing his fingers behind his head. A fastidious lover. He would soon have her wet and smelling of sex again.

She was magnificent. Her body and her hair were enough to keep any red-blooded male in a state of constant arousal, but there was more to her than just those attributes. There were her eyes with their drooping, come-hither eyelids when she was aroused, and her perfect teeth, and her low, seductive voice. There were her acting skills and her smiles and laughter. And there was her knowledge of the game.

An actress of her allure and experience might well have tried to lead the way, and their first sexual encounter might have become a clash of wills and expertise, each trying to establish mastery and control. He would have enjoyed it—how could one not enjoy any sexual encounter with someone like Claire Campbell?—but not as much as the game he had set out to play and she had complied with. The game of slow, quiet seduction.

She had sat on the bed like a prim virgin while he had brushed the red glory of her hair and felt desire course through him like an ever-building flood that would sweep all before it when it burst its dam. She had allowed him to lead every step of the way though he had felt her growing heat and seen her peaked nipples and felt the wetness of her desire. Her orgasm had been powerful and flattering. So many women faked it and imagined that their lovers did not realize. The genuineness of her release had given him permission to take his own swiftly without feeling inadequate, like a randy schoolboy.

She appeared from beyond the screen and came around to the empty side of the bed. His mouth turned dry at the sight of her. His big regret was that this was a one-night-only encounter. He would need a month or more to explore all the delights of her body and slake his appetite for her.

"Don't lie down," he told her. "Kneel on the bed."

She did so, facing him, and gazed inquiringly down at him. The fire had been reduced to mere glowing embers, but the two candles still flickered across the room.

"Let's play," he said, reaching out and touching her hand.

"Very well," she said gravely.

He chuckled. "Little Miss Prim has already been done," he said. "Exquisitely, I might add. I do promise you that I am not usually so . . . frenzied in my mount. That was merely the effect your quiet compliance had on me. I had my way with you that time. It is your turn now. What would you like to do?"

She stared down at him for a long time. Even her stillness and her steady look could stir arousal in him.

"I do not know," she said at last.

"Is your arsenal so vast, then?" He grinned at her. "I wish the night were a month long so that you could try the whole of it on me. Would a month be long enough, though? Make your choice. I am all yours. Your slave if you will. Have your way with me. Make love to me, Claire. Have sex with me." He spread his arms and his legs on the bed.

She knelt there for a long time not moving. But her eyes were roaming over him, he saw, watching her, and her eyelids drooped over them. Once she licked her lips, the tip of her tongue moving slowly from one corner to the other.

She was very clever and clearly far more experienced than he had expected. He had anticipated that she would fall on him and subject him to any number of blatant, exquisite sex tortures to drive them both into a precoital frenzy. He had observed that her manner of dress was understated. But so was her behavior. He grew pleasantly warm under her slow gaze, tingling with anticipation.

And then she leaned over him and touched him with her fingertips, cool from the water with which she had just washed herself. She touched his forehead, sliding her fingers up through his hair. She feathered her fingers down over his face, running her forefinger down the hooked length of his nose—a family legacy that he shared with most of his brothers and sisters—and then very lightly over his lips, and set her palms on his shoulders while she lowered her head and kissed him on the mouth. Curtained by her red hair, he felt her tongue move across his lips, and when he opened his mouth she stretched her tongue inside. He resisted the desire to suck on it. His role was a passive one for some time to come—for a long time, he hoped. He did not know what she was about, but he was liking it very well so far. Perhaps she was doing to him what he had done to her—slowly seducing him. And succeeding. His toes curled with pleasure.

Her hands and her mouth—and her tongue and her teeth—moved slowly down his body, pausing whenever he gave the slightest indication of pleasure. The witch! As if she did not know very well every one of a man's pleasure spots. She suckled his nipples, rubbing her tongue lightly over them as she did so until he almost reared up and ended her game before it had even approached the climax she must intend. He lay still, concentrating on his breathing.

She covered every inch of his body with her light, cool, erotic touch except for the part that had stirred into life again and stiffened into its full hard length well before she was finished. She skirted all around it, the tease. He was finding it more difficult to breathe quietly.

And then she did touch him there, taking him in her two cool hands, at first so lightly that he almost exploded, and then with more assurance, closing her hands about him, stroking him, rubbing her thumb over the sensitive tip.

"Does that feel good?" she asked him in a low, throaty voice that just about hurtled him over the edge.

"Too damned good," he said.

She turned her head and smiled at him and kneeled upright and pushed her hair behind her shoulders with both hands. She stayed that way for a long time, looking down into his eyes.

"I do not want to do the rest of it alone," she said.

Released from the rules of the game, he reached for her with both hands, closing them about her waist and lifting her over him, to straddle him. He held her there, smoothing his hands lightly over her shapely hips while she continued to kneel upright, her legs wide now.

"Come, then," he said. "Put me inside and we will ride together. A good long ride this time, I promise. You like to ride?"

Her expression was strangely, arousingly grave. "I like to ride with *you*," she said after a few moments of silence.

The witch! As if he were someone special to her. But her words had their desired effect.

She was a consummate tease. Or perhaps she knew that pauses could have as much erotic effect as movement. Several more seconds passed before she took him lightly in one hand, brought herself into position, removed her hand, and pressed firmly down until she was fully impaled on him. He watched and heard her draw a deep breath. With any lesser woman he might have suspected a deliberate intent to compliment him on his size. With her he suspected genuine pleasure.

She leaned over him then, supporting herself on her hands, curtaining him with her hair once more. She gazed into his eyes, and he spread his hands more firmly over her hips.

"Ride me, then," he said. "I will be the obedient steed beneath you. I will ride to your rhythm and at your pace. You may set the destination and the distance before we arrive. Let it be a long distance."

"A hundred miles," she said.

"A thousand."

"More."

She rode him slowly at first, feeling him, adjusting her position in the saddle, tightening her inner muscles about him to create just the right angle. And then she rode more steadily, her rhythm less shallow, more assured. He had never encountered such apparently artless expertise in any other woman. She might well spoil him for all others, he thought, reading her pace, matching it, thrusting into her descent, withdrawing to her ascent, rocking and twisting to keep her steady and increase her pleasure, his hands spread over her hips. She was hot and invitingly wet. Soon he could hear the erotic sucking sounds of their ride—and their labored breathing. She knew just how to make use of her inner muscles, exciting him, drawing him closer to climax without catapulting him over too soon.

He waited for her. He waited a long time—he could wait forever if necessary. It was a slow, exquisite game she had chosen to play, and he could play it all night stroke for stroke with her. But she straightened up eventually, all her weight on her knees and lower legs, her eyes closed, her fingertips touching his stomach. He watched her and understood that she was close to the edge, had been for some time, but could not find her way over. Unlike many other women, she would not feign release as a compliment to him or as an excuse to be finished with him.

He took one hand from her hip, moved it down between them, slid one finger down until he found the spot, and rubbed it lightly.

Her head went back, her hair falling in a golden red cloud down behind her, tensed in every muscle, and cried out. He grasped her hips firmly and drove up into her once, twice, with powerful strokes and growled out his own release.

"At least a couple of thousand miles," he said when she raised her head again and gazed down at him as if for the moment she did not know quite where she was.

"Yes," she said, and he took hold of her, turned with her, and set her down on the bed beside him. He bent his head and kissed her warmly, deeply.

"Thank you," he said. "You are magnificent."

"So are you," she said. "Thank you, Ralph."

He grinned at her. He liked the sound of his name on her lips.

"I think," he said, "that you have earned a sleep."

"Yes," she agreed. "But not for long."

"Not?"

"I want to play more," she said.

Had he not been so exhausted, he might have had another erection there and then. Instead he chuckled.

"Now on that score," he said, "I am always ready to oblige, ma'am. Well, *almost* always. But first we must sleep or there will be nothing to play with."

She laughed softly and he gathered her into his arms, pulled the bedcovers up over them, and went immediately to sleep with a smile on his lips. The last thing he noticed was that the rain was still hammering against the window.

CHAPTER IV

R AIN WAS PELTING AGAINST THE WINDOW. IT
had not stopped all night. Travel would surely be
impossible this morning. Perhaps there would be a
little more time after all.

Judith did not open her eyes. She was lying half on her
back, half on her side on the bed, a warm arm beneath her
neck, its partner draped heavily across her waist. Her legs
were all tangled up with two others. He was breathing
deeply, still asleep. He smelled of cologne and sweat and
man. It was a curiously pleasant smell.

She really had been inebriated last night, else surely she
would never have come even close to doing what she had
done. This morning she was sober with a slight headache as
an aftermath of drinking more than she ought. This morning she could understand the enormity of what she had
done. It was not just that she was now a fallen woman—that
did not matter one iota to her in light of her imminent fate
as a dependent relative and fading spinster. It was more that
she now knew what was going to be missing from all the rest

of her life. Last night she had thought that the memories would be enough. This morning she was not so sure.

And this morning she had thought of something else too—oh, she really must have been *very* drunk. She might have been got with child during any one of last night's four separate encounters. There was panic in the thought, which she tried to quell by concentrating on her breathing. Well, she would know soon enough. Her courses were due within the next few days. If nothing happened . . .

She would think of that later.

It had been a glorious night indeed. His belief that she was an actress and an experienced courtesan had spurred her on into role-playing as nothing ever had before. Those four glasses of wine had helped too, no doubt. She could hardly believe the things she had done, the things he had done to her, the things they had done together, the sheer fun of it all. And the exquisite sensual delights.

She had never suspected that Judith Law was capable of overcoming a lifetime of strict moral training to become a wanton. She listened to the rain and willed it not to stop. Not yet.

Ralph sighed against her ear and then stretched lazily without untwining himself from her.

"Mmm," he said. "I am delighted to discover that all that was not just a delectable dream."

"Good morning." She turned her face to him and then flushed at the absurd formality of her words.

"Good indeed." He regarded her with lazy blue eyes. "Is that rain I hear against the glass?"

"I daresay," she said, "no coach will dare attempt travel on the open highway while it continues. Will you risk your horse's safety or your own?"

"Neither." His eyes smiled. "I suppose that means we are stranded here for today and probably tonight again, Claire. Can you imagine a more dreadful fate?"

"If I tried very hard I might," she said and watched the smile spread to his lips.

"We are going to be killed by boredom," he said. "However are we going to fill in the time?"

"We will have to set our minds to the problem," she told him, her voice deliberately grave. "Perhaps together we will find a solution."

"If nothing else occurs to us," he said with a sigh, "we will have no choice but to remain in bed and while away the weary hours here until the rain stops and the roads begin to dry."

"How very boring," she said.

His eyes held hers. *"Boring,"* he said, his voice pitched low. "Yes, indeed."

She understood his meaning suddenly, flushed, and then laughed. "The pun was unintentional," she told him.

"What pun?"

She laughed again.

"However," he said, drawing his arm from beneath her head and rolling away from her to sit up on the side of the bed, "the boring part of the day is going to have to be delayed. I am for my breakfast. I could eat an ox. Are you hungry?"

She was. Very. She wished she had more money. He had paid for the room and their dinner and was presumably prepared to do the same tonight. She could not expect him to continue footing the bill for her all day long.

"A cup of tea will do for me," she said.

He got out of bed and turned to look down at her, stretching as he did so, apparently quite unself-conscious about his nakedness. But then, why would he be? He was splendidly formed. She could not stop herself from feasting her eyes on him.

"That is not very flattering," he said, looking down at her

with his rather mocking smile. "Good sex is supposed to make one ravenous. But all you want is a cup of tea?"

That word—*sex*—had never been spoken aloud at the rectory or in any company of which she had been a part. It was a word she had always skirted around even in her thoughts, choosing euphemisms instead. He spoke the word as if it were part of his everyday vocabulary—as it probably was.

"It *was* good." She sat up, careful to keep the blankets over her bosom and beneath her arms, and clasped her knees. "You know that."

He looked closely at her for a few moments. "How empty *is* your purse?" he asked her.

She could feel herself flushing again. "I did not expect to have to stop on the road, you see," she explained. "I brought only what I thought I would need for a nonstop journey. There is always the danger of highwaymen."

"How can an actress of your caliber be out of work for three months?" he asked her.

"Oh, I was not out of work," she assured him. "I took time off deliberately because I was—because I was tired of being constantly from home. I do that occasionally. And I *do* have money. I just do not have it with me."

"Where is home?" he asked her.

Their eyes clashed.

"Somewhere," she said. "It is private. My own retreat. I never tell anyone where it is."

"Let me guess," he said. "You are a proud, independent woman, who does not allow any man to protect and support you."

"That is right," she said. *If only it were true.*

"This occasion will have to be something of an exception, then," he told her. "I will not offer to pay you for your services. I believe our desire for each other and our pleasure in satisfying that desire have been mutual. But I will pay your keep for as long as we are here. You do not have to starve yourself on tea and water."

"Can you afford it?" she asked him.

"I have always believed," he said, "that any highwayman who chose to attack me would have to be soft in the head and that if he was not, he certainly would be by the time I had finished with him. I do *not* travel with an empty purse. I can afford to buy you breakfast and all your other meals too for as long as we remain here."

"Thank you." She could not suggest that she pay him back at some future date. She would never have enough money.

"Now," he said, "tell me that I was good enough last night to make you hungry this morning."

"Ravenous." She smiled at him. "You were *very* good, as you know full well."

"Aha," he said, leaning a little closer, "another human trait. You have a dimple beside the right corner of your mouth."

That sobered her. The triumvirate of childhood plagues— a freckled carrottop with a dimple.

"It is utterly charming," he said. "I am going to wash and dress and go downstairs, Claire. You can follow me down when you are ready. We might as well eat in the public dining room this morning and see something of the world. It is going to be a long day."

Judith hoped it would be an eternity long. She hugged her knees tightly as he disappeared behind the screen.

I T STRUCK RANNULF THAT FATE HAD DEALT HIM A PRETTY fair hand. Normally being stranded at a small town inn by inclement weather would have been the stuff of nightmares. Under any other circumstances he would have been chafing at the bit and scheming to find a way to get himself and his horse safely to his grandmother's despite the danger. He realized that he was no farther than twenty miles from Grandmaison Park.

But these were not other circumstances, and it helped to know that his grandmother did not even realize that he was on his way, though she always expected him to come promptly when summoned. He could delay his arrival for a week or more if he wished without every constable in the land being called out to search for him.

When she appeared in the downstairs dining room, Claire Campbell was dressed in a pale green cotton dress, even simpler than yesterday's muslin. She had brushed her hair back severely over the crown of her head and braided and coiled it at the back of her neck. He had become accustomed to the way she understated her charms. This was an actress with class, he decided, rising and bowing to her.

They ate a hearty breakfast at a leisurely pace, conversing about inconsequentials until the innkeeper brought them more toast and stayed to discuss the farming situation and the blessing the rain would be after weeks of hot, dry weather. Then his wife brought freshly boiled water to heat up their tea and stayed to talk about the nasty weather and all the extra work it gave the women, who had to be constantly scrubbing their floors because their men and children *would* insist upon going outside in the rain, even when they did not have to, and traipsing all the wet and all the mud across clean floors no matter how often one scolded them or chased them with a broom. Indeed, she said, chasing them only made the matter worse, because then they would flee farther *into* the building than out of it, and even if they did run out, eventually they came back in and the whole business started again.

Claire laughed and commiserated.

Before many minutes had passed, the innkeeper and his wife had pulled up two chairs, the wife had poured herself a cup of tea while the innkeeper had fetched himself a tankard of ale, and they settled in for a lengthy chat.

It considerably amused Rannulf that he was sitting at a table in an inn that no stretch of the imagination could describe as fashionable, fraternizing with the servants. Bewcastle, his brother, the duke, would have frozen them into two icicles with a single glance. He would have quelled their pretensions with the mere lifting of one finger or one eyebrow. But then one look at Bewcastle and no one below the rank of baron at the very least would dream of even raising his gaze from the floor unless invited to do so.

"Why," the innkeeper asked suddenly, "was Mrs. Bedard on the stagecoach, sir, while you was on horseback?"

"We been wondering," his wife explained.

Rannulf met Claire's eyes across the table. Her cheeks had turned pink.

"Oh dear," she said, "*you* tell them, Ralph."

She was the actress. Why could she not come up with a suitable tale? He gazed at her for a few moments, but she was looking back at him as expectantly as the other two were. He cleared his throat.

"I did not take the delicacy of my wife's sensibilities into account at our wedding breakfast," he said without taking his eyes off her. "Some of our guests had imbibed too much of the wine, and a few of them—my own cousins, in fact—made some risqué remarks. Embarrassed though I was, I laughed. My bride did not. She excused herself, and it was only later that I discovered she had fled her own wedding night."

The color had deepened in her cheeks.

"See?" the innkeeper's wife said, poking her husband in the ribs with one large elbow. "I told you they was newlyweds."

"I finally caught up to her yesterday," Rannulf continued and watched her catch her lower lip between her teeth. "I am happy to report that I have been forgiven for my inappropriate laughter and all is now well."

Her eyes widened.

The innkeeper's wife turned her head to beam tenderly at Claire.

"Don't you mind none, ducks," she said. "The first time is the worst. I didn't hear no sobbings, mind, and I don't see no trace of tears this morning, so I daresay it was not so bad as you feared. I expect Mr. Bedard knows how to do it right proper." She laughed conspiratorially and Claire joined her.

Rannulf glanced sheepishly at the innkeeper, who glanced sheepishly back.

They went outside after breakfast, Rannulf and Claire, though he was surprised when she asked to join him. He wanted to see his horse, to make sure it had taken no harm yesterday and had been properly tended. He wanted to rub it down and feed it himself this morning. Claire put on her half boots and her cloak with the hood up, and they made a dash for it across the open yard, trying to step on tufts of grass as they went and avoid the worst of the mud and manure.

She sat on a clean pile of hay while he worked, her hood back, her hands clasped about her knees.

"That was some story," she said.

"About you as skittish bride? I thought so too." He grinned at her.

"The landlady is going to tidy our rooms herself and make sure fresh fires are laid in the hearth in both rooms," she said. "It must be a great honor to have her personal services instead of those of the maid. It seems hardly fair so to deceive them, Ralph."

"You would rather we told the truth, then?" he asked. His horse was looking none the worse for wear, though it was doing some restless snorting. It wanted to be out and moving.

"No," she said. "That would not be fair either. It would lower the tone of their house."

He raised his eyebrows but made no comment.

"What is your horse's name?" she asked.

"Bucephalus," he said.

"He is a beauty."

"Yes."

They were quiet then until he had finished brushing the horse down, forking the old hay out of the stall and spreading fresh, feeding and watering the animal. It was surprising really. Most women of his acquaintance liked to chatter, with the notable exception of his sister Freyja. But then Freyja was an exception to almost all rules. The silence was a comfortable one. He did not feel at all self-conscious at her quiet scrutiny.

"You love horses," she said when he was finished and leaned back against a wooden beam and crossed his arms. "You have gentle hands."

"Do I?" He half smiled at her. "You do not love horses?"

"I have not had much to do with them," she admitted. "I believe I am a little afraid of them."

But before they could become more deeply involved in conversation, a stable lad appeared to inform them that the innkeeper's wife had a pot of chocolate awaiting them in the dining room, and they made their way back across the yard, running and dodging puddles again. The rain seemed to be easing somewhat.

They sat and talked for two hours until their midday meal was ready. They talked about books they had both read and about the wars, newly over now that Napoléon Bonaparte had been defeated and captured. He told her about his brothers and sisters without telling her exactly who they were. He told her about Wulfric, the eldest; about Aidan, the cavalry officer who had recently come home on leave, married, and decided to sell out; about Freyja, who had twice been almost betrothed to the same man but who had lost him to another woman last year and had been spitting mad ever since; about Alleyne, his handsome younger brother; and about Morgan, the youngest, the sister who bade fair to being lovelier than anyone had any right to be.

"Unless," he added, "she were to have fire-gold red hair and green eyes and porcelain skin." And the body of a goddess, he added silently. "Tell me about your family."

She told him about her three sisters, Cassandra, older than herself, Pamela and Hilary younger, and about her younger brother, Branwell. Her parents were both still alive. Her father was a clergyman, a fact that explained why she was estranged from her family. What had impelled the daughter of a clergyman into a life of acting? He did not ask the question and she did not volunteer the information.

By the time they had finished the midday meal, the rain had eased to a light drizzle. If it were to stop within the next hour or so, the roads should be passable by tomorrow. The thought was somewhat depressing. The day seemed to be going far too fast.

"What is there to do for amusement in this town?" he asked the landlady when she came to remove their dishes—they had been deemed far too important for the services of the maid, it seemed. That wench was busy serving a few townsmen their ale in the adjoining taproom.

"There isn't nothing much on a day like this," she said, straightening up, setting her hands on her hips, and squinting in concentration. "It's not market day. There is just the church, which isn't nothing much as churches go."

"Any shops?" he asked.

"Well, there is the general shop across the green," she said, brightening, "and the milliner's next to it and the blacksmith's next to that. Not that you would have any need of *his* services."

"We will try the general shop and the milliner's," he said.

"I have a mind to buy my wife a new bonnet since she ran away without one."

Claire's—the only one she had brought with her—had been lost inside the stagecoach, she had told him earlier.

"Oh, no!" she protested. "Really, you must not. I could not allow—"

"You take wotever he is offering, ducks," the innkeeper's wife said with a wink. "I daresay you earned it last night."

"Besides which," Rannulf said, "wives are not supposed to question how their husbands spend their money, are they?"

"Not so long as it is spent on them." The woman laughed heartily and disappeared with the dishes.

"I cannot let you—" Claire began.

He leaned across the table and set a hand over hers. "It is altogether possible," he said, "that every hat in the shop is an abomination. But we will go and see. I want to buy you a gift. There is no question of your having earned it. A gift is simply a gift."

"But I do not have enough money with me to buy you one," she said.

He raised one eyebrow and got to his feet. She was a proud woman indeed. She would drive a large number of potential protectors to madness if she were ever to descend upon any of the green rooms in London.

ALL OF THE BONNETS ON DISPLAY AT THE MILLINER'S SHOP were indeed abominations. But any hope Judith had entertained about avoiding the embarrassment of having a gift bought for her was dashed when Miss Norton disappeared into the back of the shop and came out with another bonnet lifted on the back of her hand.

"This," she said with an assessing glance at Ralph, "I have been keeping for a special customer."

Judith fell in love with it on sight. It was a straw bonnet

with a small brim and russet ribbons. About the upper side of the brim, where it joined the rest of the bonnet, was a band of silk flowers in the rich colors of autumn. It was not a fussy bonnet, nevertheless. Its simplicity was its main appeal.

"It suits madam's coloring," Miss Norton observed.

"Try it on," Ralph said.

"Oh, but—"

"Try it on."

She did so, helped by the fluttering hands of Miss Norton, who tied the wide ribbons for her to the left side of her chin and then produced a hand mirror so that Judith could see herself.

Ah, it was so very pretty. She could see her hair beneath it, both at the front and at the back. Every bonnet she had ever owned had been deliberately chosen by Mama—though with her full acquiescence—to hide as much of her carroty hair as possible.

"We will take it," Ralph said.

"Oh, but—" She whirled around to face him.

"You will not regret it, sir," Miss Norton said. "It complements madam's beauty to perfection."

"It does," he agreed, taking a fat-looking purse out of a pocket inside his cloak. "We will take it. She will wear it."

Judith swallowed awkwardly. A lady was simply not permitted to accept a gift from a gentleman who was not her betrothed. And even then . . .

How absurd! How utterly absurd after last night to be thinking of what a lady would do. And the bonnet was prettier than anything she had owned before in her life.

"Thank you," she said and then noticed just how many bills he was handing to Miss Norton. Judith closed her eyes, appalled, and then felt all the contradictory pleasure of being the owner of something new and expensive and lovely.

"Thank you," she said again as they left the shop and he

hoisted over their heads the large, ancient black umbrella the landlord had insisted upon lending them for their sortie across the rather boggy green between the inn and the shops. "It is terribly pretty."

"Though quite overshadowed by its wearer," he said. "Shall we see what the general shop has to offer?"

It had a little bit of almost everything to offer, most of the wares cheap and garish and in execrable taste. But they looked at everything, their heads bent together, stifling their laughter at a few of the more hideous items. Then the shop-keeper engaged Rannulf in a discussion of the weather, which was beginning to clear up at last. The sun would be shining by the morning, the shopkeeper predicted.

Judith took her purse out of her reticule and hastily counted up her coins. Yes, there was just enough. She would have to hope that the stagecoach tomorrow would get her to her aunt's without any more delays, for there would be nothing left for any refreshments. But she did not care about that. She picked a small snuffbox off a shelf and took it to the counter. They had laughed at it because it had a particularly ugly carving of a pig's head on the lid. She paid for it while Ralph was wrestling the umbrella tightly closed since they would have no need of it on the return journey across the green.

She gave him the gift outside the shop doors, and he opened the paper that had been wrapped around it and laughed.

"*This* is the measure of your esteem for me?" he asked her.

"May you remember me every time you enjoy a good sneeze," she said.

"Oh," he said, opening his cloak and placing the snuffbox carefully into his pocket, "I will remember you, Claire. But I will treasure your gift. Did you spend your very last coin on it?"

"No, of course not," she assured him.

"Liar." He drew her arm through his. "It is halfway through the afternoon, and boredom has not yet driven us to bed. But I believe it is about to. *Will* we find our time there tedious, do you suppose?"

"No," she said feeling suddenly breathless.

"That is my feeling too," he said. "The landlord and his good lady have been feeding us well. We will somehow have to build up an appetite to do justice to the dinner they are doubtless preparing for us. Can you think of a way we can do that?"

"Yes," she said.

"Only one?" He clucked his tongue.

She smiled. She felt pretty in her new bonnet, her gift to him was lying in his pocket, and they were on their way back to the inn to go to bed again. There was all the rest of the afternoon left, and there was all night ahead of them. She would make it an eternity.

She glanced up at the sky, but already there were breaks in the clouds and blue sky showing through. She would not look. There were hours left yet before morning came.

CHAPTER V

"LOOK AT IT," SHE SAID, HER VOICE FILLED WITH soft wonder. "Have you ever seen a more glorious sight?"

She was at the open window of their private sitting room, both elbows resting on the sill, her chin cupped in her hands, watching the sun set beneath an orange, gold, and pink sky. She was wearing a striped silk dress of cream and gold in what he was coming to recognize as her characteristic simple yet elegant style. Her hair, loose down her back, seemed dark in contrast.

He was constantly surprised by her. Who would have expected an actress to marvel at a sunset? Or to show such bright-eyed delight in a bonnet that was exquisitely pretty but by no means either ostentatious or costly? Or to giggle over a cheap, ugly snuffbox and spend the last penny of her traveling allowance on it? Or to make love with such obvious personal enjoyment?

"Ralph?" She turned her head and reached out one hand to him. "Come and look."

"I *was* looking," he told her. "You were part of the picture."

"Oh, you do not need to keep on flattering me," she said. "Come and look."

He took her hand in his and moved up beside her at the window. The trouble with sunsets was that darkness followed quickly upon their heels. Just as the trouble with autumn was that winter was not far behind. And what was making him so maudlin?

"The sun will be shining tomorrow," she said.

"Yes."

Her hand tightened about his. "I am glad it rained," she said. "I am glad the stagecoach overturned. I am glad you did not take shelter at the last town."

"So am I." He slipped his hand from hers and draped his arm loosely about her shoulders. She leaned in against him, and they watched the sun disappear over the edge of a distant field.

He wanted to bed her again. He fully intended to do so, as many times during the night as his energy would allow. But tonight he did not feel the urgency he had felt last night or the lusty exuberance he had felt this afternoon. Tonight he felt almost—melancholy. It was not a mood he was accustomed to feeling.

They had indulged in two energetic bouts of sex after returning from the shops—on clean sheets, he had observed. They had slept a while and then dined in private. She had acted the parts of Viola and Desdemona for him. And then she had noticed the sunset.

It was getting late. Time was running out, and he felt regret that he could not pursue their affair until it reached its natural conclusion, perhaps in a few days, perhaps not for a week or longer.

She sighed and turned her head to look at him. He kissed her. He liked the way she kissed, relaxing her mouth, opening it for him, responding to him without demanding mastery. She tasted of wine even though she had drunk only one glass this evening.

It was while he was kissing her that he conceived his idea. His brilliant idea. His *obvious* idea.

"I am coming with you tomorrow," he said, lifting his head.

"What?" She gazed back at him, heavy-eyed.

"I am coming with you," he repeated.

"On the stagecoach?" She frowned.

"I'll hire a private carriage," he said. "There must be one available here somewhere. We will travel in comfort. We—"

"But your friends," she said.

"They will not send out any search parties," he told her. "They do not even know exactly when to expect me. I'll come with you to York. I have a burning desire to see you act on a real stage with other actors. And we are not finished with each other yet. Are we?"

She stared at him. "Oh, no," she said. "I could not so inconvenience you. A private carriage would cost a fortune."

"My purse is fat enough," he said.

She shook her head slowly, and he had a sudden thought.

"Is there someone waiting for you?" he asked her. "Another man?"

"No."

"Anyone else, then?" he asked. "Anyone who is likely to be offended by my accompanying you?"

"No."

But she continued the slow head shaking. He considered another rather lowering possibility.

"*Are* we finished with each other?" he asked her. "Or will we be after one more night together? Will you be glad to be free again and on your way alone tomorrow?"

The head shaking continued, he was relieved to see.

"I want more of you, Claire," he said. "More of your body,

more of *you*. I want to see you act. I will not stay forever, only for a week or so until we are both satisfied. You are an independent woman who does not like to be tied to one man—I can see that. I am a man who enjoys brief affairs and then is content to move on. But tomorrow is too soon. Besides, you really cannot be looking forward to climbing into a stagecoach again and taking your place beside another bony holy man."

Her head was still. For a moment she half smiled.

"Tell me you want more of me," he said, moving his mouth closer to hers.

"I want more of you."

"Then it is settled." He kissed her swiftly. "We will leave here together tomorrow. I will come to York and see you act. We will spend a few more days in each other's company, perhaps a week. Maybe longer. As long as it takes."

She half smiled again and touched her fingertips to his cheek.

"That would be very lovely," she said.

He set his hand over hers and kissed her palm. Who would have thought yesterday morning when he left Aidan's, bound for Grandmaison, that he was riding straight into the arms of a new mistress and a hot affair? He had cursed the mud and the threatening rain, but both had turned into blessings.

"Ready for bed?" he asked.

She nodded.

He was feeling rather weary. Four times last night and twice this afternoon had taken some toll on his stamina and doubtless on hers too. But now tonight need not be as frantic as he had expected. They need not stay awake all night, taking full advantage of every moment. They had days and nights ahead of them, as many as they needed.

"Come, then." He took her hand again and led her in the

direction of the bedchamber. "We'll enjoy long, slow love-making and then sleep, shall we?"

"Yes," she said, her voice low and husky and curling about him with a warm, sensual promise.

I T WAS ALREADY LIGHT OUTSIDE THOUGH IT WAS PROBABLY still very early. The stagecoach was to leave from the posting inn at half past eight, the landlord had reported last evening, though he had assumed that Mr. and Mrs. Bedard would not be traveling on it.

They would not. But Judith Law would if she possibly could.

She could not go with Ralph. Where would they go?

The adventure was over. Her stolen dream was flat and empty. Dull pain settled like a heavy hand on her chest. Soon she must wake him and suggest without seeming too urgent about it that he go out to hire a private carriage. She did not have the courage to tell him the truth or even another lie. She was too much of a coward to tell him no, that she would not go with him, that she would continue her journey alone and by stage instead.

Telling him the truth would be the honorable thing to do and perhaps the kinder.

But she could not bear to say good-bye to him.

He had slept deeply all night long after they had finished making slow, almost languorous love. She had lain beside him all night, staring upward, occasionally closing her eyes but not sleeping, watching the window for signs of daylight, willing the night to last forever to prolong her agony.

It was hard to believe that just two mornings ago she had been the Judith Law she had known all her life. Now she no longer knew who Judith Law was.

"Awake already?" he asked from beside her, and she

turned her head to smile at him. To drink in the sight of him, to store memories. "Did you sleep well?"

"Mmm," she said.

"Me too." He stretched. "I slept like the proverbial log. You certainly know how to wear a man out, Claire Campbell. In the best possible way, of course."

"Will we make an early start?" she asked him.

He swung his legs over the side of the bed and crossed to the window.

"Not a cloud in the sky," he reported after pulling back the curtains. "And hardly a puddle left in the yard down there. There is no reason to delay. Perhaps I should go out in search of a carriage as soon as I have dressed and shaved. We can breakfast afterward, before we leave."

"That sounds like a good plan," she said.

He disappeared behind the screen and she could hear him pouring water from the pitcher into the bowl. She willed him to hurry. She willed time to stand still.

"Have you ever had sex in a carriage, Claire?" he asked. She could hear laughter in his voice.

"I certainly have not." Just two days ago the question would have shocked her beyond words.

"Ah," he said, "then I can promise you a new experience today."

A few minutes later he appeared again, fully dressed in shirt, waistcoat, and coat with buff riding breeches and top boots, his damp hair brushed back from his freshly shaven face. He strode over to her side of the bed, bent over her, and kissed her swiftly.

"With your hair all over the pillow like that and your shoulders bare," he said, "you are enough to tempt even the most ascetic of saints—of which number I am not one. However, business first and pleasure after. A carriage makes a very . . . interesting bed, Claire." He straightened up, grinned at her, turned, and was gone.

Just like that.

Gone.

The silence he left behind him was deafening.

For a moment Judith was so devastated that she could not move. Then she sprang into action, jumping out of bed, darting behind the screen, dragging her clothes with her. Less than fifteen minutes later she was descending the stairs, carrying her reticule in one hand, her heavy portmanteau in the other.

The innkeeper, who was washing off a table in the tap-room, straightened up and looked at her, his eyes focusing on her portmanteau.

"I need to catch the stagecoach," she said.

"Do you?" he asked.

And then his wife came through a doorway to Judith's left.

"What has happened, ducks?" she asked. "Been rough with you, has he? Spoken harsh words, has he? Never you mind about them. Men always speak without thinking. You got to learn to wheedle your way back into his good graces. You can do it like nothing. I seen the way he looks at you. Fair worships you, he does."

Judith pulled her lips into a smile. "I have to leave," she said. But she had a sudden thought. "Do you have paper, pen, and ink I can use?"

Both of them stared at her in silence for a few moments, and then the innkeeper bustled behind the counter and produced all three.

She was wasting precious minutes, Judith thought, her stomach muscles knotting in panic. He might return at any moment, and then she would have to speak the words to him. She could not bear to do that. She *could not*. She scribbled hurriedly, paused a moment, and then bent her head to add one more sentence. She signed her name—Claire—hurriedly, blotted the sheet, and folded it in four.

"Will you give this to Mr. Bedard when he comes in?" she asked.

"I will that, ma'am," the innkeeper promised her as she bent to pick up her portmanteau. "Here, I'll send the lad from the stables with you to carry that."

"I have no money to pay him," Judith said, flushing.

The landlady clucked her tongue. "Lord love you," she said, "we will add it to *his* bill. I could take a rolling pin to his head, I could, frightening you like this."

More precious moments were lost while the stable lad was summoned, but finally Judith was hurrying away in the direction of the posting inn, her head—clad in her new bonnet—bent low. She hoped and hoped—oh, please God—she would not run into Ralph on the way.

And yet half an hour later, as the stagecoach—a different one with a different driver and mostly different passengers—pulled out of the inn yard and onto the road north, she pressed her nose to the window and desperately looked about her for a sight of him. She felt sick to her stomach. Yesterday morning's headache had returned with interest. She was so depressed that she wondered if this was what despair felt like.

RANNULF RETURNED TO THE INN FORTY MINUTES AFTER leaving it, having arranged for the hire of a tolerably smart carriage and two horses at an exorbitant price. They were to be ready for him within the hour. There would be time for breakfast first. He was ravenously hungry again. He hoped Claire was not still in bed—he was also feeling lusty and she had looked very inviting when he left their room.

He took the stairs two at a time and threw the door wide. The bed was empty. She was not behind the screen. He opened the door to the private dining room. She was not there either. Dash it all, she had not waited for him but had gone down to breakfast already. But when he got to the top of the staircase he stopped suddenly, frowned, and turned back. He stepped inside their bedchamber and looked around.

Nothing. No clothes, no hairpins, no reticule. No portmanteau. His hands curled into fists at his sides and he felt the beginnings of anger. He could not pretend to misunderstand. She had slipped away and left him. Without a word. She had not even had the backbone to tell him that she was going.

He went back downstairs and came face to face with both the innkeeper and his wife, the one staring at him with apparent sympathy, the other with compressed lips and angry glare.

"I suppose," Rannulf said, "she has gone on the stage-coach."

"Skittish," the landlord said. "A new wife, see. Some of them are like that, until they are properly broken in."

"Wives are not horses," his wife said severely. "I suppose you quarreled, and I suppose you said some nasty things. I just hope you did not hit her." Her eyes narrowed.

"I did not strike her," Rannulf said, hardly believing that he would stoop to defend himself to servants.

"Then you had better ride after the coach and eat some humble pie," she advised. "Don't you scold her, mind. You tell her you are sorry and you will speak gentle to her for the rest of your natural-born life."

"I will do that," he said, feeling remarkably foolish—and furiously angry deep down. She had not had the decency . . .

"She left a note for you," the landlord said, tossing his head in the direction of the counter.

Rannulf turned his head to see a folded piece of paper lying there on the bare wood. He strode across the taproom, picked it up, and unfolded the paper.

"I cannot go with you," the note read. "I am sorry I do not have the courage to say so in person. There *is* someone else, you see. Respectfully yours, Claire." She had underlined the one word three times.

So he had been bedding and making merry with someone else's mistress, had he? He nodded his head a couple of times, a mocking smile playing about his lips. He supposed it *had* been naive of him to believe that a woman of her looks and profession was without the protection of some wealthy man. He crumpled the note in one hand and stuffed it into a pocket of his coat.

"You will be wanting your horse, sir," the innkeeper informed him. "To go after her."

Dammit all, he wanted his *breakfast.*

"Yes," he said. "I will."

"It is all ready," the man informed him. "I took the liberty after your good lady left of—"

"Yes, yes," Rannulf said. "Give me your bill and I will be on my way."

"And her a new bride just two nights ago," the landlord's wife said. "I changed the bedding, sir, as you may have noticed. You did not want to be laying on bloody sheets last night, did you, now?"

Rannulf was facing the counter, opening his purse, his back to her. For a moment he froze.

Bloody sheets?

"Yes, I did notice," he said, pulling out the required sum plus a generous vail. "Thank you."

He recited every obscenity, every profanity he could think of as he rode away from the inn a few minutes later, supposedly in pursuit of his skittish, high-strung wife.

"Bugger it," he said aloud at last. "She was a damned *virgin.*"

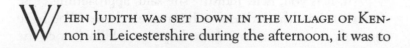

WHEN JUDITH WAS SET DOWN IN THE VILLAGE OF KENnon in Leicestershire during the afternoon, it was to the unsurprising discovery that no gig or cart or servant from Harewood Grange was awaiting her. The house was three miles away, she was informed, and no, there was no safe place to leave her portmanteau. She must take it with her.

Tired, hungry, and heartsick, Judith trudged the three miles, taking frequent stops to set her portmanteau down and switch hands. She had brought very little with her— there was not a great deal to bring—but it was amazing how heavy a few dresses and shoes and nightgowns and brushes could be. The sun beat down on her from a cloudless sky. Soon thirst became even more pressing than hunger.

The driveway up to the house seemed interminably long, winding as it did beneath dark overhanging trees, which at least provided some welcome shade. The house itself, she could see when it finally came into sight, was something of a mansion, but then she had expected it to be. Uncle Effingham was enormously wealthy. It was why Aunt Effingham had married him—or so Mama had once said when cross over a letter she had perceived as condescending.

A servant answered Judith's knock at the front door, looked at her down the length of his nose as if she were a slug the rain had brought out, showed her into a salon leading off the high, marbled hall, and shut the door. She waited there for well over an hour, but no one came or even brought her any refreshments. She desperately wished to open the door and ask for a glass of water, but she was foolishly awed by the size of the house and the signs of wealth all around her.

Finally Aunt Effingham came, tall and thin, with improbable black curls framing the underside of the brim of her bonnet. She looked very little different than she had eight years ago, when Judith had last seen her.

"Ah, it is you, is it, Judith?" she said, approaching close enough to kiss the air next to her niece's cheek. "You have certainly taken your time. I was hoping for Hilary since she is the youngest of you and would probably be the most bid-dable. But you will have to do instead. How is my brother?"

"He is well, thank you, Aunt Louisa," Judith said. "Mama sends her—"

"Gracious heaven, child, your hair!" her aunt exclaimed suddenly. "It is quite as gaudy as I remember it being. What a dreadful affliction and what a trial for my brother, who has always been the soul of propriety and respectability. What was your mama thinking of to buy you that bonnet when it merely draws attention to your hair? I will have to find you another. Did you bring caps to wear indoors? I shall find you some."

"I do have—" Judith began, but her aunt's gaze had moved below the offending bonnet and hair to her niece's cloak, which had been opened back for some coolness. Her eyebrows snapped into a horrified frown.

"*What*," she exclaimed, "was my sister-in-law thinking of to send you to me dressed like *that*?"

Beneath her cloak Judith was wearing her plain muslin dress with its modest neckline and fashionably high waist. She glanced down at herself in some unease.

"*That dress*," her aunt said in thunderous tones, "is *indecent*. You look like a *trollop*."

Judith could feel herself flushing. For two nights and the day in between she had been made to feel both beautiful and desirable, but her aunt's words brought her crashing back to reality. She was ugly—embarrassingly ugly, as Papa had al-ways made clear to her though he had never used words quite as cruel as Aunt Effingham's. But perhaps she really *did* look like a trollop. Perhaps that was why Ralph Bedard had found her desirable. It was an excruciatingly painful thought.

"I will have to inspect your clothes," Aunt Effingham said. "If they are all like this, I will have to have them taken out at the seams and somehow made more modest. I hope

Effingham is not going to be forced to pay for new dresses for you. Not this year, at least, when he has already been put to the expense of Julianne's presentation to the queen and come-out Season, and we fully expect the additional expenses of a wedding and bride clothes for her."

Julianne was Judith's eighteen-year-old cousin, whom she had also not seen for eight years.

"How is Grandmama?" Judith asked.

Her grandmother lived with Aunt Effingham. Judith had not seen her since she was a child. She had only vague memories of a gaudily clad, jewel-bedecked lady, who had talked a great deal, laughed loudly, hugged her grandchildren at every excuse, and told them stories and listened to their prattle. Judith had adored her until it had become obvious to her that her mama and papa found Grandmama a trial and something of an embarrassment.

"With a large number of houseguests expected here within the next few days you will be able to make yourself useful keeping her company," Aunt Effingham said briskly. "You will not have much else to do since you have never been brought out or introduced to fashionable society and would feel uncomfortable joining in the activities of the house party. And you will, of course, wish to do all in your power to show your gratitude to Effingham for offering you a home here."

Judith had hardly needed the reminder that she had been brought to Harewood as a poor relation to serve the family in whatever capacity they decided upon. She was to be her grandmother's companion, it seemed. She smiled and thought she would surely faint soon if she did not have something to eat or drink. But how could she ask even for a glass of water?

"You may come up and pay your respects to her," Aunt Effingham said. "She has already had her tea in her own rooms since Julianne and I were out paying calls. We were all expecting you to arrive days before this, though we were hoping for Hilary, of course. I cannot imagine why my brother delayed so long in sending you and thus releasing himself from one financial burden."

"The stagecoach I was on overturned in the mud two days ago," Judith explained. "I was then delayed by the rain."

"Well, it has been very inconvenient not to have you here just when you could have been making yourself most useful," her aunt said.

The door opened again before her aunt had reached it, and a very pretty young girl came into the room. Eight years had transformed Julianne from a pale, rather uninteresting child to a small, slender but shapely young lady with a heart-shaped face, large blue eyes, and soft blond curls.

"Which one is it?" she asked, looking her cousin over from head to toe. "Oh, you are Judith, the one with carroty hair. I was hoping Uncle would send Hilary. We expected you days ago. Mama was dreadfully annoyed because Tom had been sent into the village to fetch you and did not return home for all of four hours. Mama accused him of drinking inside the inn but he denied it quite vehemently. Mama, I want my tea. Are you *never* going to come? One of the servants can take Judith up to Grandmama."

I am happy to see you too, Julianne, Judith thought silently. It was also evident to her that she was not being included in the plans for tea.

Her new life, it seemed, was going to be very much as she had pictured it.

R ANNULF HAD STOPPED FOR BREAKFAST AND AGAIN FOR luncheon. It was during the latter meal that his baggage coach and his valet finally caught up with him. It was late afternoon by the time he rode through the gates of

Grandmaison Park, past the empty dower house just inside, and along the straight, wide driveway to the main house. He was shown up to his grandmother's private sitting room. She got to her feet and looked him over as he strode into the room, still in his riding clothes.

"Well," she said, "and about time too, Rannulf. Your hair needs cutting. Give me a hug." She held her arms open.

"I was held up for two days by the infernal rain," he informed her. "My hair grew four inches in the damp air while I waited. Are you sure I will not crush every bone in your body?"

He wrapped his arms about her tiny waist, lifted her off her feet, and kissed her cheek with a loud smack before setting her back down.

"Impudent boy," she said, straightening her dress. "Are you dying of hunger and thirst? I have given instructions that food and drink are to be brought up within five minutes of your arrival."

"Hungry as a bear," he told her. "And I could drink the sea dry, though not, I hope, even a single cup of tea." He rubbed his hands together and looked her over. As usual she was looking as neat as a pin. She seemed smaller, though, and more slender than ever. Her hair, in its elegant coiffure, was as white as her lace cap.

"And how," she asked him, "are your brothers and sisters? I have been informed that Aidan has married a coal miner's daughter."

Rannulf grinned. "But even if you were to look ever so closely, Grandmama, with the aid of a lorgnette," he said, "you would not be able to detect one speck of coal dust beneath her fingernails. She was raised and educated as a lady."

"And Bewcastle?" she asked. "Does he show any sign of taking *anybody's* daughter to the altar?"

"Wulf?" he said, "Not him. And pity help the woman he

decided to offer for. He would freeze her between the bed-sheets."

"Ha!" his grandmother said. "That is all *you* know of the appeal of men like Wulfric, Rannulf. And is Freyja still pining for that viscount?"

"Ravensberg? Kit?" he said. "She socked me in the jaw when I suggested that she was, but that was a year ago, when his betrothal to Miss Edgeworth was new, before he married her. Kit and his viscountess are in expectation of an interesting event within the next few months, which may or may not be a painful thing for Freyja. But she does not wear her heart on her sleeve."

"And how is Alleyne?" she asked. "As handsome as ever?"

"The ladies seem to think so," he said, grinning.

"And Morgan? Wulfric will be having her brought out soon?"

"Next year when she is eighteen," he said. "Though she declares she would rather die first."

"Foolish girl," she said and paused while a maid carried a tray into the room, curtsied, and withdrew.

The drink was *not* tea, Rannulf saw with some satisfaction. He helped himself and resumed his seat after his grandmother with one raised hand indicated that she would neither eat nor drink. Ah, the moment of truth had come, he thought with an inward sigh of resignation, sensing that the preliminary courtesies were at an end and she was about to get down to business.

"Aidan is the wise one," she said, "even if he *has* chosen a coal miner's daughter. He must be thirty years old, and it is high time he started setting up his nursery. And you are eight and twenty, Rannulf."

"A mere fledgling, Grandmama." He grinned at her.

"I have found someone very eligible for you," she said. "Her papa is only a baronet, it is true, but it is an old, respected family and there is no shortage of money there. She is as pretty as the day is long and has just been presented this past spring. She is ready to make an advantageous match."

"Just been presented?" Rannulf frowned. "How old is she?"

"Eighteen," his grandmother said. "Just the right age for you, Rannulf. She is young enough to be easily molded to your will, and she has most of her breeding years ahead of her."

"Eighteen!" he said. "A mere infant. I would rather choose someone closer to my own age."

"But that age has grown so advanced," she said tartly, "that any woman close to it will be at least halfway through her breeding years. I want to be assured that my property will be secured in you and your line, Rannulf. You have brothers, all of whom I hold in deep affection, but I decided long ago that you were the one."

"I have years left in which to oblige you," he said. "You are just a spring chicken, Grandmama."

"Saucy boy." She clucked her tongue. "But I do not have forever, Rannulf. Far less than forever, in fact."

He looked keenly at her, his glass halfway to his lips. "What are you saying?" he asked her.

"Nothing to concern yourself with unduly," she said briskly. "Merely a little trouble that will doubtless take me eventually, perhaps a few years earlier than if I were forced to wait for old age to take me off."

His glass was down and he was on his feet before she could hold up a very firm staying hand.

"No," she said. "I want no sympathy, no soft words, no comfort. It is my life and will be my death and I will deal with both myself, thank you very much. I merely want to see you well married before I go, Rannulf. And perhaps, if you are *very* dutiful and I am very fortunate, I will see your first son in his cradle before I go."

"Grandmama." He raked the fingers of one hand through his hair. He hated to think of his own relatives as mortal. The last time it had been his father, when he was only twelve years old. He closed his eyes as if to shut out what she had clearly implied. *She was dying.*

"You will like Julianne Effingham," she said. "She is a pretty little thing. Just your type, I would guess. I know you came here fully intending to shrug off my matchmaking attempts, Rannulf, as you have always done in the past. I know you believe yourself to be quite unready for matrimony. But give it a try, will you, this possibility of a suitable match? For my sake? I ask only that you promise to try, not that you promise to marry her. Promise me?"

He opened his eyes, looked down at her, surely far thinner than she had been when he last saw her, and sighed.

"I promise," he said. "I'll promise you the earth and the sun and moon too if you wish."

"The promise to meet and court Miss Effingham is quite sufficient," she said. "Thank you, my boy."

"You must promise me one thing too," he said.

"What?" she asked.

"Not to die anytime soon."

She smiled fondly at him.

CHAPTER VI

JULIANNE EFFINGHAM'S COME-OUT HAD BEEN DE-
clared a resounding success by her mama. It was true that
she had failed to achieve that pinnacle of all young
ladies' dreams—the attachment of a rich and handsome
husband during her very first London Season. But the situation was by no means desperate. She had attracted a whole
host of admirers, several of them very eligible young gentlemen indeed, and she had cultivated the friendship of several
young ladies of a superior social rank to her own.

The list of friends and admirers had been carefully pored
over by Julianne and her mama, a dream list of houseguests
had been drawn up, and invitations had been sent out to attend a two-week-long house party at Harewood Grange. Almost half had accepted, and the desired number had easily
been achieved by sending out invitations to a new list of
second choices and then third choices. The guests were due
to arrive four days after Judith.

It was no coincidence, as she soon realized. Even apart
from the fact that her usefulness in looking after her grandmother's needs must have been the prime, long-term motive

for sending for her, there were also a thousand and one other ways in which her hands and feet could be kept busy during the frantic days before everyone arrived.

Aunt Effingham and Julianne spoke of nothing else but the house party and beaux and marriage prospects. Uncle George Effingham spoke of nothing at all and rarely opened his mouth except to put food and drink into it or to answer a question directed specifically at him. Judith's grandmother spoke a great deal on a wide range of topics, and she was very ready to laugh at anything that slightly amused her. It was soon evident to Judith, though, that apart from herself, no one appeared to take much notice of what her grandmother said.

She was a great deal plumper than Judith remembered, and more indolent. She complained of a host of maladies, both real and imaginary. She passed the mornings in her own rooms, much of the time spent on decking herself out in elaborate coiffures, not-so-subtle cosmetics and perfumes, brightly colored clothes, and masses of jewelry. She moved to the drawing room for the afternoons and evenings, rarely went outside unless it was to visit her neighbors and friends by closed carriage, and overate, her particular indulgence being cream cakes and bonbons. Judith loved her from the first moment. She was good-natured and genuinely delighted to see her granddaughter.

"You are here at last," she had cried that first day, enfolding Judith in a warm, violet-scented hug, the silver bangles on both her wrists jangling as she did so. "And it is *Judith*. I was so hoping it would be you. But I have been worrying myself sick that all the rain would wash you away. Let me have a good look at you. Yes, yes, Louisa, you may go down for your tea. But have Tillie bring a tray up for Judith, if you would be so good. I daresay she did not eat a great deal during her journey. Oh, my love, you have grown into a rare beauty, as I knew very well you would."

Grandmama was demanding even though her smiles and apologies and thanks and hugs made all the unnecessary errands less annoying than they might otherwise have been. Whenever she was upstairs she needed something from downstairs. When she was down, she needed something from her rooms. When she was five feet from the cake plate or bonbon dish, she needed someone to fetch her the food since her legs were particularly bad today. It was easy to understand why Aunt Effingham had been willing to take in one of her brother's daughters when Papa had written to her about his straitened circumstances.

True to her word, Aunt Effingham examined every garment Judith had brought with her and whisked away almost all her dresses in turn. A maid who was clever with her needle let out the side seams so that the garments hung loosely about her, disguising her voluptuously curved figure and making her look simply plump and shapeless. Judith had brought two caps with her, since her mama had always been insistent that she wear one even though Cassandra, one year older than she, still went bareheaded most of the time. Aunt Louisa found her another for wear during the daytime, a matronly bonnet cap that tied beneath her chin and hid every strand of her hair and, together with her altered dresses, made her look thirty years old at the very least.

Judith made no protest. How could she? She was living at Harewood on her uncle's charity. Her grandmother protested, and Judith humored her by sometimes removing the cap when they were alone together in Grandmama's sitting room.

"It is because you are so beautiful, Judith," her grandmother said, "and Louisa has always been afraid of your kind of beauty."

Judith merely smiled. She knew better.

Much of the family conversation during the days before the guests arrived was for her edification, she soon realized, even though she was very rarely addressed by name. Some of the expected guests were titled or the offspring of titled gentlemen. All were socially prominent. Most were wealthy and those who were not had birth and breeding to recommend them instead. Most of the gentlemen who were coming were head over ears in love with Julianne and very close to declaring themselves. But Julianne was not at all sure she would have any of them. She thought she might well have someone else instead—if he met with her approval.

"Lord Rannulf Bedwyn is brother to the Duke of Bewcastle, Mother," Aunt Louisa explained in the drawing room the second evening. "He is a third son but still the second heir since neither the duke nor Lord Aidan Bedwyn has yet sired a son. Lord Rannulf is the second heir to a dukedom."

"I saw the Duke of Bewcastle in London this spring," Julianne said. "He is dignified and haughty and everything one would expect of a duke. And just imagine! His brother is coming to visit Lady Beamish, his grandmother and our neighbor."

Since Aunt Louisa, Uncle George, and Grandmama must have been well aware of the fact that Lady Beamish was their neighbor, Judith gathered that she was the intended recipient of this startling information. Lady Beamish, presumably the maternal grandmother of the Duke of Bewcastle, lived close by.

"I know she is looking forward to Lord Rannulf's arrival," Grandmama said, lifting one sparkling, heavily ringed hand from the arm of her chair. "She told me so when I called on her a few days ago. May I trouble you to pass the cakes again, Judith, my dear? Cook has made them unfortunately small today. You really ought to have a word with her, Louisa. Three bites and they are gone."

But Julianne had not finished her recital. "And Lady Beamish particularly wishes to present Lord Rannulf to *me*," she said. "She eagerly accepted Mama's suggestion that he participate in the activities of the house party. She has invited me and our houseguests to Grandmaison for a garden party."

"Of course she has, my love," Aunt Effingham said, smirking with pride. "Lord Rannulf Bedwyn is Lady Beamish's heir as well as being in possession of a sizable fortune of his own. It is natural that she should wish to see him make a good match, and what more suitable choice could she make than a pretty young lady of birth and fortune who is also her neighbor? It will be a splendid match for you, will it not, Effingham?"

Uncle George, who was reading a book, grunted.

"And you can see now, Julianne," her mother continued, "why it was wise of you to take my advice not to encourage the addresses of the first gentleman or two who would have offered for you in London."

"Oh, yes," Julianne agreed. "I might have married Mr. Beulah, who is a bore, or Sir Jasper Haynes, who is not even handsome. I *may* not marry Lord Rannulf Bedwyn, either. I will see how I like him. He *is* rather old."

Judith was sent upstairs at that point to return her grandmother's jeweled earrings to her jewelry box because they were pinching her earlobes as they always did if she wore them for longer than an hour at a time, and to bring down the heart-shaped ruby ones instead.

Hearts! Her own was heavy indeed, Judith thought as she trudged up the stairs. She had been released mercifully soon from her worst anxiety—her courses had begun the day after her arrival at Harewood. But nothing, she suspected, was going to release her from deep depression for a long time to come. She could think of nothing but her day and a half and two nights with Ralph Bedard, reliving every moment, every word, every touch and sensation, unwilling to let go of the memories for a single moment lest they fade away entirely, wondering if it would not be kinder to herself to let them do just that.

Sometimes she felt that her heart would surely break. But she knew that hearts did not literally break merely because their owners were unhappy—and foolish. How dreadfully foolish she had been. Yet she clung to the memories as to a lifeline.

Late on the morning of the day before the houseguests arrived, while Tillie was curling her grandmother's gray hair into its usual elaborate style and Judith was mixing her morning medicine, the one that ensured her ankles did not puff up too badly, Julianne burst into the dressing room, fairly bubbling with excitement.

"He is come, Grandmama, Judith," she announced. "He arrived a few days ago and is to call here this afternoon to pay his respects." She clasped her hands to her bosom and pirouetted on the carpet.

"That will be delightful," Grandmama said. "A little higher on the left, I believe, Tillie. *Who* is coming?"

"Lord Rannulf Bedwyn," Julianne said impatiently. "Lady Beamish sent word this morning announcing her intention of calling on us this afternoon for the purpose of presenting Lord Rannulf. Eight and twenty is not so *very* old, is it? Do you suppose he is handsome, Grandmama? I do so hope he is not downright ugly. *You* can have him if he is, Judith." She laughed merrily.

"I daresay that if he is a duke's son he will look distinguished at the very least," Grandmama said. "They usually do, or did in my day, anyway. Ah, thank you, Judith, my love. I am feeling rather short of breath this morning, a sure sign that my legs are going to swell up."

"We must all be sure to be in the drawing room, wearing our very best," Julianne said. "Oh, Grandmama—a *duke's* son." She bent her head to kiss her grandmother's cheek and darted lightly back across the room to leave. But she stopped with her hand on the doorknob. "Oh, Judith, I nearly forgot. Mama says you must be sure to wear the bonnet cap she gave you. You had better not let her see you bareheaded like that."

"Do hand me the bonbons, Judith, if you will be so good," Grandmama said after Julianne had left. "I never can abide the taste of that medicine. Louisa must have windmills in her head, insisting that you wear caps when you are a mere child. But I daresay she does not want your hair outshining Julianne's blond curls. She need not worry. The girl is pretty enough to turn any foolish male head. What shall I wear this afternoon, Tillie?"

A short while later Judith changed into her pale green muslin dress, one of her favorites, though it now hung loose and almost waistless about her person, and tied the narrow strings of the bonnet cap beneath her chin. Goodness, she looked like someone's spinster aunt, she thought with a grimace before turning firmly away from the mirror. No one was going to be interested in looking at her this afternoon anyway. She wondered if Julianne would have Lord Rannulf Bedwyn even if he turned out to be a three-foot-tall hunchback with a gargoyle face. Her guess was that her cousin would not be able to resist the lure of becoming Lady Rannulf Bedwyn no matter how he looked or behaved.

R ANNULF HAD SPENT THE WHOLE OF HIS FIRST DAY AT Grandmaison in his grandmother's company, talking with her, strolling with her in the formal gardens, where she refused the support of his arm, telling her more about the recent activities of his brothers and sisters, sharing his first impressions of Eve, Lady Aidan, his new sister-in-law, answering all her questions.

He noticed that she was slower than she had been, that she seemed tired much of the time, but that pride and dignity held her upright and active so that she did not once complain or accept his suggestion that she retire to rest.

He dressed with care for the visit to Harewood Grange, allowing his valet to heft him into his tightest, most fashionable blue coat with its large brass buttons, and to create one of his elaborately folded neckcloths. He wore his buff, form-fitting pantaloons and his white-topped Hessian boots. Since his hair was too long for a fashionable Brutus or any other style currently in vogue, he had it tied back at the nape of his neck with a narrow black ribbon, ignoring his valet's pained comment that he looked like something escaped out of a family portrait from two generations ago.

He was going courting. He winced at the mental admission. He was going to view his prospective bride. And he did not see how he was going to get out of it this time. He had promised his grandmother. She was definitely ill—it was no trick she was playing on him. Besides, she had asked him to promise only that he would consider the girl, not that he would marry her. She had been as fair to him as she could be.

But he knew he was trapped. Trapped by his own sense of honor and his love for her. He would give her the sun and moon if she wanted them, he had told her. But all she wanted was to see him eligibly married before she died, perhaps with a child in his wife's womb or even in the cradle. He would not be looking at the girl just to see if she might suit him. He would be courting her. Marrying her before the summer was out if she would have him. There was not much doubt in his mind that she would. He had no illusions about his eligibility, especially to the daughter of a mere baronet of impeccable lineage and sizable fortune.

He rode in an open barouche to Harewood Grange beside his grandmother, wishing for once in his life that she had not passed over Aidan as her heir simply because Aidan had had a well-established career in the cavalry. But the main problem, he knew, was that he loved her. And she was dying.

And to think that he had almost delayed his arrival here by a week or more. If Claire Campbell had not deserted him, he would be in York with her now, indulging in a hot affair with her, while his grandmother waited, every day bringing her closer to the end. He still could not think of Claire without anger and humiliation and guilt. How could he not have noticed . . .

But he turned his thoughts firmly away from her. She had been part of a very slight incident in his past. And as it had turned out, she had done him a favor by running away as she had.

"Here we are," his grandmother said as the barouche drew free of dark trees overhanging a long, winding driveway. "You will like her, Rannulf. I promise you you will."

He took her hand in his and raised it to his lips. "I fully expect to do so, Grandmama," he said. "I am already half in love with her merely because *you* recommend her."

"Foolish boy!" she said briskly.

A few minutes later they had entered a spacious, marbled hall, had climbed an elegant, winding staircase, and were being announced at the drawing room doors by a stiff, sour-faced butler.

There were five people in the room, but it was not at all difficult to pick out the only one who really mattered. While Rannulf bowed and murmured politely to Sir George and Lady Effingham and to Mrs. Law, Lady Effingham's mother, he noted with some relief that the only young lady present, to whom he was introduced last, was indeed exquisitely lovely. She was tiny—he doubted the top of her head reached even to his shoulder—and slender, blond, blue-eyed, and rosy-complexioned. She smiled and curtsied when her mother presented her, and Rannulf bowed and looked fully and appreciatively at her.

It was a strange feeling to know with some certainty that he was looking at his future bride—and not too far in the future either.

Damn it! Damn it all!

There followed a flurry of laughter and bright conversation, during the course of which Mrs. Law presented both him and his grandmother to her companion, whom he had not even noticed until she did so—Miss Law, presumably a relative, a plump, shapeless woman of indeterminate age, who hung her head and repositioned her chair slightly behind that of the old lady when they all sat down.

Mrs. Law invited Lady Beamish to sit near her on a sofa so that they could indulge in a comfortable coze together, as she phrased it, and Rannulf was offered the seat beside his grandmother. Miss Effingham took her place strategically close on an adjacent love seat, the tea tray was carried in, and the visit began in earnest. Lady Effingham did most of the talking, but whenever she invited her daughter to tell Lord Rannulf about some event she had attended in London during the Season, the girl obliged, her manner neither too forward nor too shrinking. She spoke fluently in a low, sweet voice, her smile always at the ready.

She was quite agreeable to having him, Rannulf could see before ten minutes had passed. So was the mother. He must represent the catch of a lifetime to them, of course. He smiled and conversed amiably and felt the shackle close about his leg. Effingham, he noticed, made almost no contribution to the conversation.

The tea tray had been set on a table close to where Rannulf sat. The plate of dainty cucumber sandwiches had been passed around once as had the plate of cakes. Second cups of tea had been poured, after which the maid had been dismissed with a nod from Lady Effingham. But Mrs. Law's appetite had not been satisfied, it seemed. Her silk dress rustled about her plump form and the jewels in her necklace and earrings and on her rings and bracelets sparkled in the sunlight as she half turned to the woman behind her.

"Judith, my love," she said, "would you be so obliging as to bring the cakes again? They are particularly good today."

The drab, shapeless companion got to her feet and came behind the sofa on which Rannulf sat and picked up the plate. His attention was on a list of expected houseguests Mrs. Effingham was reciting for his edification.

"Oh, do pass them around, my love, if you will," the old lady said as the companion began her return path behind the sofa. "Lady Beamish did not take one the last time. But you have all the exertion of the journey home to face, Sarah."

"We are expecting my stepson too," Lady Effingham was saying to Rannulf, "though one can never be quite certain with Horace. He is a charming young man and is in constant demand at all the summer house parties."

"No, thank you, Miss Law," his grandmother said softly, waving away the cake plate. "I really have eaten enough."

Rannulf lifted his hand to make the same gesture of refusal as the woman moved in front of him and offered the plate, her head bowed so low that the brim of her cap hid her face from his view. Not that he looked up into it anyway. He did not afterward know what it was that made him suddenly pause. She was simply one of the invisible female creatures with which the households of the wealthy tended to abound. One simply did not notice them.

However it was, he did pause, and she lifted her head just a fraction. Enough that their eyes met. And then she lowered her head hastily again and moved on even before he could complete his dismissive gesture.

Green eyes. A nose very lightly dusted with freckles.

Law. Miss Law. Judith. Judith Law.

For a moment he felt completely disoriented.

Claire Campbell.

"Er, I beg your pardon?" he said to Lady Effingham. "No. No, I do not believe I have the pleasure of his acquaintance, ma'am. Horace Effingham. No, indeed. But I may well know him by sight."

She had set down the plate, moved behind him again—this time he *felt* her as she passed—and resumed her seat, though first she moved it even farther behind the old lady's.

He dared not even glance at her, though he felt no doubt whatsoever that he had not mistaken. It was not as if he had been searching for green eyes and freckled noses wherever he went after all. He had not. He had not wanted to see her again, had not expected to do so. Besides, he had been firmly convinced that she was in York.

Even so, the evidence of his senses had presented him with too bizarre a truth.

There was no such person as Claire Campbell, actress, then? Even *that* had been a clever deception? She was Judith Law, some relative of the family. A *poor* relation by all appearances. Hence her empty purse when she had traveled—and hence too the stagecoach as her mode of travel. She had allowed herself a sensual fling with him when it had offered itself. She had recklessly sacrificed her virtue and her virginity and risked all the dire consequences.

The consequences.

Rannulf did not know what was said to him or what he replied during the five minutes that passed before his grandmother got to her feet to take her leave. He rose too, somehow said all that was proper to the occasion, and found himself in five minutes more back in the barouche, having handed in his grandmother ahead of him. He set back his head and closed his eyes, but only for a brief moment. He was not alone.

"Well?" she asked as the carriage rocked into motion.

"Well, Grandmama," he said, "she is indeed remarkably pretty. Even prettier than you led me to believe."

"And quite prettily behaved too," she said. "If there is any excess, it is mere youthful folly and will soon mature under the demands of matrimony and motherhood and the patience of a good husband. She will be a good match for you, Ralf. Not brilliant, perhaps, but I believe even Bewcastle will not protest too loudly."

"It was never understood," he said, "that Wulf would choose my bride, Grandmama."

She chuckled. "But I would be willing to wager on it," she said, "that he was near to having an apoplexy when he discovered that Aidan had married a coal miner's daughter."

"After that shock," he said, "I am confident that he will approve of someone as eligible as Miss Effingham."

"You will seriously court her, then?" she asked, setting one hand on his sleeve. He noticed how the skin stretched thin and pale over the bones, and covered it with his own hand.

"I agreed to go back tomorrow for dinner, after the houseguests have arrived, did I not?" he reminded her.

"You did." She sighed. "I expected you to be far more difficult. You will not be sorry, I promise you. Bedwyn men have always been reluctant to marry, but they have invariably made marriages that turned into love matches, you know. Your poor dear mama never did recover her health after Morgan's birth and died far sooner than she ought, but she was very, very happy with your papa, Rannulf, and he doted on her."

"I know," he said, patting her hand. "I know, Grandmama."

But his head was pounding with thoughts about Judith Law, alias Claire Campbell. How the devil were they going to avoid each other during the coming weeks? At least now he could understand why she had fled. He had wanted to go with her so that he could see her *act*, not realizing that everything he had seen of her from the first moment on had been nothing but an act.

He was no less furious with her now. She had deceived him. For all the excesses of his life, he would never have dreamed of seducing a gently nurtured woman. And that was exactly what he felt like—a seducer of innocence. A damned lecherous villain.

Life had certainly taken several turns for the worse since his grandmother's letter had reached him in London.

H E IS SO VERY *LARGE,* MAMA," JULIANNE SAID, NEVERTHE-less clasping her hands to her bosom as if in ecstasy.

Uncle George had gone downstairs to see Lady Beamish and Lord Rannulf Bedwyn on their way and had not returned to the drawing room.

"But a fine figure of a man," Aunt Effingham said. "There is no padding in *his* clothes, I declare, nor does there need to be."

"He is not at all handsome, though, is he?" Julianne said. "He has such a big nose."

"But he has blue eyes and good teeth," her mama said. "And all the Bedwyns have that nose, Julianne, my dearest. It is what is known as an aristocratic nose. Very distinguished."

"His hair!" Julianne said. "It is *long,* Mama. He had it *tied back.*"

"That is a little strange, I must confess," Aunt Effingham said. "But hair can always be cut, dearest, especially when a lady for whom he cares requests it. At least he is not *bald.*"

She and Julianne tittered merrily.

"In my day, Julianne," Grandmama said, "long hair on men was still all the rage, though many of them shaved their heads and wore wigs. Not your grandpapa, though. His hair was all his own. Long hair is very appealing, in my opinion."

"Ugh!" was Julianne's comment. "What did *you* think of Lord Rannulf Bedwyn, Judith? Do you think he is handsome? Shall I have him?"

Judith had had more than half an hour in which to compose herself. She had thought she would surely faint when he first came into the room. It could not be, it just *could* not be, she had thought for the merest moment. Her eyes and her mind must be playing tricks on her. But it was unmistakable and indisputable—Ralph Bedard and Lord Rannulf Bedwyn were one and the same. All the blood had drained out of her head, leaving it cold and clammy, dimming sounds and making everything before her eyes sway and swim in a strange unreality.

Ralph—Rannulf. Bedard—Bedwyn. Close, but different enough to keep his true identity from a potentially demanding and ambitious actress. And different enough that she had not even noticed the similarity before being confronted by the man himself. She had fought not to swoon and thus draw unwelcome attention to herself. But she still felt unsteady enough to faint if she allowed herself.

"Handsome?" she said. "No, I don't think so, Julianne. But he is, as Aunt Louisa says, distinguished looking."

Julianne laughed, jumped to her feet, and pirouetted as she had done in Grandmama's dressing room earlier.

"He was very attentive, was he not?" she said. "He listened to every word I spoke and did not look superior or bored as so many gentlemen do when one speaks. Shall I have him, Mama? Shall I, Grandmama? Do you not wish you were in my place, Judith?"

"He will have to make Papa an offer first," Aunt Effingham said, getting to her feet. "But he was clearly very taken with you, dearest, and it is clear too that Lady Beamish fully intends to promote the match. She must have considerable influence over him. I believe we can be optimistic."

"Judith, my love," Grandmama said, "would you be so

good as to help me to my feet? I do not know why I am so sluggish these days. We will have to have the physician again, Louisa. He must give me more medicine. We will go upstairs and you must summon Tillie for me, Judith, if you will. I believe I will lie down for an hour."

"Ah, then you will be free, Judith," Aunt Effingham said. "You will join me in the library in a few minutes' time. There are place cards to be written for dinner tomorrow and numerous other little tasks to be accomplished. You must not remain idle. I am sure your papa has told you about the devil finding work for idle hands."

"I will come down as soon as I have seen Grandmama settled," Judith promised.

"Julianne, dearest," her mother said, "you must go and rest and not overexert yourself. You need to be looking your prettiest tomorrow."

Judith's mind was still whirling. He was *Lord Rannulf Bedwyn*, and he had come here to court and to marry Julianne. At least, that was what her aunt and cousin believed. She would surely see him every day for the next two weeks. She would see them together.

Did he know? Had he recognized her? Why, oh why, had she looked up when his hand had lifted to refuse a cake and then paused? Why had she not simply anticipated his gesture and moved on? Their eyes had met. She had lowered her head again before she had seen any recognition in his eyes, but she had sensed it.

He had recognized her? The humiliation of being seen thus, of being known for who and what she was, was just too much to bear. But if he had not recognized her this afternoon, then surely he would sometime during the next two weeks. She could not hide from him for all that time. She had overheard Grandmama arranging to call on Lady Beamish tomorrow afternoon while all the houseguests were arriving at Harewood. Would she, Judith, be required to go too? Would *he* be there?

She had thought life could not possibly get worse. But she had been wrong. She felt raw with pain. Dreams and reality were not supposed to mingle. Why had this dream—the most glorious one of her life—come crashing into her present reality? Perhaps because it had not been a dream at all?

"I'll take your arm, Judith, if it is not too much trouble," Grandmama said, leaning heavily on it. "Did you notice how Louisa forgot to introduce you to Lady Beamish and Lord Rannulf? I saw you hang your head in mortification and was indignant on your behalf, I do not mind telling you. You are her own niece, after all, and Julianne's first cousin. But that is the way of people who have set themselves to climbing the social ladder, never looking back at those who are on lower rungs lest they be dragged downward themselves by association. Louisa was always foolish in that way. Have you lost weight since you came here, my love? Your dress is hanging on you today and not showing your lovely figure at all to advantage. We must ask Tillie if she can take in the seams, and I must watch to see that you eat properly. Look, my feet have swelled after all. Perhaps the medicine you mixed this morning was not strong enough."

"You have had a busy afternoon, Grandmama," Judith said soothingly. "You will feel better after lying down and putting your feet up for a while."

She could not bear what had just happened, she thought. *She simply could not bear it.*

CHAPTER VII

THE CARRIAGE THAT CONVEYED MRS. LAW TO Grandmaison Park the following day was a closed one, and every window was tightly shut despite the fact that the day was sunny and hot. A draft might bring on one of her chills, she explained to Judith, who was seated beside her, convinced that both of them would surely melt in the heat. Her grandmother was in high spirits, nevertheless, and chatted the whole way. Lady Beamish had been her closest friend since she had moved to Harewood almost two years ago, she explained. It was good occasionally to get away from the house, where Louisa was forever in a cross mood over something.

Judith had been kept constantly busy during the morning, running errands to and from the kitchens and various other rooms and to the stables and carriage house as Aunt Effingham tried to ensure that she had not forgotten a single detail of the preparations for the arrival of the houseguests. Julianne meanwhile, who possessed the same number of hands and feet as her cousin, spent the morning twirling about in exuberant pirouettes whenever she was not dashing to the windows to see if anyone was arriving early or running upstairs to change her slippers or sash or hair ribbons, and generally wearing herself to the bone, as her mother said in fond warning.

But Judith's hope that she would not be called upon to accompany her grandmother on the afternoon visit had been dashed when her aunt looked at her late in the morning, observed with annoyance that her niece's cheeks were unbecomingly flushed, that her eyes were unnaturally bright, and that a piece of her hair was showing beneath her cap at the back. Julianne had chosen that moment to speak to her mother.

"Lady Margaret Stebbins is not prettier than I, Mama, is she?" she had asked, suddenly anxious. "Or Lilian Warren or Beatrice Hardinge? I *know* Hannah Warren and Theresa Cooke are not even though they are very sweet girls and I love them to distraction. But I *will* be the prettiest here, will I not?"

Aunt Effingham had rushed to hug her daughter and assure her that she was ten times lovelier than any of her dear friends who would be arriving during the afternoon. But her stern eye had alighted on Judith even as she spoke and on the errant lock of hair that her niece was tucking back beneath her cap.

"You really need not be here this afternoon when our guests arrive, Judith," she had said. "There will be nothing useful for you to do, and you will only be under everyone's feet. You may accompany Mother to Grandmaison, and Tillie will stay here instead, where I can put her to good use."

"Yes, of course, Aunt Louisa," Judith had said, her heart sinking while Julianne focused her eyes curiously upon her.

"Poor Judith," she had said, "never to have had a comeout Season even though you are years older than I. How inconvenient and distressing for you not to be able to mingle freely in fashionable society. Mama says your case might not be so desperate if Uncle had made a more advantageous marriage. How fortunate you are to have been invited to live here, where you will at least be able to rub shoulders with people of superior breeding."

Judith had not answered. She had been given no chance to even had she thought it worth expressing her indignation on her mother's behalf—Julianne had turned to Aunt Louisa with an anxious plea for an opinion on her choice of dress.

But now she was riding in the carriage beside her grandmother, fanning her against the heat. Gentlemen surely did not dance attendance upon elderly ladies very often, especially when another elderly lady was coming to visit. Lord Rannulf Bedwyn would surely not be with his grandmother this afternoon.

She was to be proved wrong.

After descending from the carriage and entering the hall of Grandmaison, they were shown into a spacious, high-ceilinged sitting room on the ground floor, its ivory-colored walls and gilded trimmings reflecting light and spelling expensive elegance. Landscape paintings in gilded frames added depth and beauty. The long French windows at the far side of the room were opened back so that it seemed filled with birdsong and the fragrance of flowers. Judith might have fallen in love with the room at a glance if she had not been instantly aware of the presence in it of two people instead of one.

Lady Beamish was rising to her feet from a chair beside the empty hearth. Lord Rannulf Bedwyn was already standing before the fireplace. Judith lowered her chin and ducked half behind her grandmother as they proceeded across the room. She wished she could be anywhere else on earth but where she was. She felt utterly humiliated and even uglier than usual, clad as she was in one of her newly altered striped cottons with the bonnet cap and a plain, large-brimmed bonnet that Aunt Louisa had let her have because she had no further use for it herself.

"Gertrude, my dear," Lady Beamish said warmly, kissing Grandmama's cheek. "How are you? And you have brought Miss Law with you. How pleasant. She is one of your son's daughters of whom you have spoken to me?"

"Yes, Judith," Grandmama said, beaming fondly at her. "The second one and always my favorite granddaughter. I hardly dared hope that Jeremiah would send her instead of one of her sisters."

Judith darted her a surprised glance. Grandmama surely did not know them nearly well enough to have favorites.

"How do you do, Miss Law?" Lady Beamish said kindly. "Do have a seat."

Lord Rannulf meanwhile was making his bow to Grandmama and then to Judith, murmuring her name as he did so. She curtsied without looking up and sat down on the nearest chair. But as she removed her gloves she realized how abjectly she was behaving and how impossible it was to hide her identity from him for much longer—if indeed he had not already discerned it. She lifted her head and looked directly at him.

He was looking back, his eyes narrowed. She tilted her chin a little higher even as she felt color flood both cheeks.

Polite conversation occupied the next few minutes. Lady Beamish asked after the health of Judith's family and Grandmama asked after that of Lord Rannulf Bedwyn's. The expected arrival of the houseguests at Harewood that very afternoon was spoken of as well as the fact that Lord Rannulf intended to ride over for dinner. And then Lady Beamish spoke more briskly.

"Gertrude and I are old friends, Rannulf," she said, "and love nothing better than an hour together prosing on about matters that would interest no one else but our two selves. You are excused from the tedium of being polite. Why do you not take Miss Law outside and show her the formal gardens? Perhaps after that she would enjoy a quiet sit in the rose arbor while you go about your business."

Judith's hands clenched in her lap.

"It would seem that we are merely in the way here, Miss Law," he said, taking a few steps toward her and half bowing to her while one arm indicated the French windows. "Shall we step outside?"

"Perhaps, Lord Rannulf," her grandmother said as Judith got reluctantly to her feet, "you would be so good as to shut the windows as you leave—if you have no objection, that is, Sarah. I do believe one of my fevers is threatening to come on. Judith had to fan my face all the way here."

Judith ignored the arm that was offered her. She hurried toward the French windows and out onto the cobbled terrace beyond. She was on a path that bisected the center of the formal gardens before she stopped to hear the French windows close behind her. Where was she running to? And why would she run? But surely she had never in her life felt more embarrassed than she did at this precise moment.

"Well, Miss *Judith Law*," he said softly, and she realized with a start that he had come up close behind her. There was quiet venom in his voice.

She clasped her arms behind her and turned, looking boldly up into his face—horrifyingly close and just as horrifyingly familiar.

"Well, *Lord Rannulf Bedwyn*," she said.

"Touché." He looked back at her, a familiar mocking gleam in his eyes. He indicated the path ahead with one arm. "Shall we stroll? We are fully visible from the sitting room where we stand now."

The formal gardens had been set out with geometric precision, Judith could see, straight cobbled paths leading like spokes of a wheel to a fountain at the center, a marble Cupid standing on one foot in the center of a marble basin, water shooting out of the end of the arrow fixed to his bow and spraying about him back into the basin. Low, neat box hedges lined the paths and enclosed flower beds that provided a feast of color and bloom to the eyes and sweet scents to the nose.

"You deceived me," he said as they walked.

"And *you* deceived *me*." Her hands took a firmer grip on her forearms behind her back. She wished she had never discovered his true identity. *Why* had this had to happen? Of all the possible destinations in England, they had been headed for homes that were no more than five miles apart. And he was, in effect, going to be a part of the house party at Harewood.

Was he really going to marry Julianne? Had he planned it even before his journey north?

"I wonder," he said, his voice pleasant and conversational, "if your grandmother and your aunt and uncle would be interested to learn that you are an actress and a courtesan."

Was he threatening her? Was he afraid, perhaps, that *she* would expose *him*?

"I wonder," she said tartly, "if they would be equally interested to learn that the man they are courting for my cousin Julianne engages in casual affairs with strangers on his travels."

"You show your ignorance of the world, Miss Law," he said. "The Effinghams are undoubtedly well aware that gentlemen have certain, ah, *interests* that they pursue at every opportunity both before and after marriage. Are you an honored guest in your uncle's home?"

"Yes. I have been invited to live at Harewood," she said.

"Why are you not there this afternoon, then, to meet all the houseguests as they arrive?" he asked.

"My grandmother had need of my company," she told him.

"You lie, Miss Law," he said. "Indeed, you lie a great deal. You are a poor relation. You have come to Harewood in the nature of an unpaid servant, primarily to relieve your aunt of the necessity of catering to the demands of your grandmother, if my guess is correct. Did your father not make as advantageous a marriage as your aunt?"

They had reached the fountain and stopped walking. Judith could feel droplets of spray cool against her cheeks.

"My mother," she said testily, "was of perfectly good family. And my father, as well as being a clergyman, is a man of means."

"Of means," he repeated, mockery in his voice. "But not of fortune? And the means have been depleted to the degree that your parents have been forced to farm out one of their daughters to wealthier relatives?"

Judith moved around the fountain to the path on the other side of it. He circled around the other way and then was beside her again.

"Your interrogation is impertinent," she said. "My circumstances are none of your business. Neither are my father's."

"You are a gentleman's daughter," he said softly.

"Of course I am."

"You are also angry," he said.

Was she? Why? Because it was humiliating to be seen and known for who she really was? Because her one stolen dream, which would have sustained her through the rest of a lonely life, had been shattered? Because he was so poised and unaffected by this horrible coincidence? Because he mocked both her and her parents? Because Julianne was young and pretty and rich? Because Branwell had wasted away Papa's small but carefully nurtured fortune? Because life was not fair? Who had ever said it was supposed to be?

"And a coward," he added after a short silence. "You did not even have the courage to look me in the eye and spin your yarn about there being another man. You did not have the courage to say good-bye to me."

"No," she admitted. "No, I did not."

"And so," he said, "you made me look a pretty fool. I was scolded by the innkeeper's wife for mistreating you and advised to ride after you and eat very humble pie."

"I am sorry," she said.

"Are you?" He looked down at her and she realized they had stopped walking again. "I would have taken you even if you had told me the truth. Did you realize that? I would have set you up as my mistress. I would have kept you, looked after you."

She was furiously angry then and knew exactly the reason why. *Why* had the one great dream of her life had to die such an ignominious, *painful* death? She hated him suddenly, despised and hated him for forcing her to see the essential sordidness of what had happened between them.

"Let me see." She tapped one finger against her lips and looked upward as if thinking. "I believe that was to have been for a few days, perhaps even a week. Until we tired of each other, which, being translated, meant, I believe, until *you* tired of *me*. No, thank you, Lord Rannulf. I had my pleasure out of our encounter. It filled in a potentially dull few days while we waited for the rain to stop. I had already tired of you by that time. It would have been unkind to say so, though, since you had said you still needed a few more days or even a week of me. And so I slipped away while you were gone. Forgive me."

He stared at her for several silent moments, the look in his eyes quite unreadable.

"If you will show me where the rose arbor is, I will sit there until my grandmother sends for me," she said.

He spoke abruptly, ignoring her suggestion. "Are you with child? Do you even know yet?"

If a black hole had just been obliging enough to open at her feet, she would gladly have jumped into it.

"No!" she said, her cheeks hot. "Of course I am not."

"Of course?" With raised eyebrows he looked mocking and haughty and aristocratic. "Babies do result from such activity as we indulged in, Miss Law. Did you not know that?"

"Of course I knew it!" If it was possible to feel more embarrassed, she could not imagine the circumstances. "You do not believe, do you, that I would have allowed—"

One raised hand stopped her. "Please, Miss Law," he said, sounding infinitely weary, "do drop the worldly-wise act. It *is* an act as surely as your Viola or your Lady Macbeth was. *Do* you know for sure?"

"Yes." Her lips were suddenly stiff and would barely form the word. "I am quite sure. Where is the rose arbor?"

"Why are you dressed so hideously?" he asked her.

She stared at him with compressed lips. "That is hardly a gentlemanly question to ask," she said when he waited for her answer.

"You were not dressed thus when you were traveling," he said, "though I blame myself for not seeing that you were a simple country girl playing at being an actress and a courtesan. You are good—at both. But where did the bonnet come from, and the ridiculous cap and the ill-fitting dress?"

"Your questions are insolent," she said.

But his eyes and his half-smile mocked her—quite viciously.

"My guess," he said, interrupting her again, "though I fancy it is more conviction than guess, is that your aunt took one look at you when you arrived at Harewood, realized in some chagrin that you far outshone her daughter, and devised as heavy a disguise for you as she could muster. Am I right?"

Of course he was not right. Was he *blind*? Aunt Louisa was merely insisting, even more than Papa had done, that she hide her uglier features.

"Or was even your hair a part of the act?" he asked, his

mouth lifting at one corner into further mockery. "Are you bald beneath the cap, Miss Law?"

"You grow both tedious and offensive, Lord Rannulf," she said. "Indicate the way to the rose arbor, if you please, or I shall find a gardener who will."

He stared at her for a moment longer, his nostrils flared in an expression that might have been anger, and then he clucked his tongue, looked away from her, and began to stride back the way they had come, along the path, halfway about the fountain, and off along an adjacent path that led—she could see it now—toward rose-draped trellises that must be the outer boundaries of the arbor.

It was breathtakingly lovely—or would be under other circumstances. Enclosed on three sides by high trellises to protect it from the wind, it descended over four wide terraces to a bubbling stream below. There were roses everywhere, all shades and colors, all sizes and types. The air was heavy with their perfume.

Judith seated herself on a wrought-iron seat on the top tier and folded her hands in her lap.

"You need not remain to keep me company," she said. "I will be quite happy alone in such surroundings."

He stood beside her for what seemed a long while, saying nothing. She did not look up to see whether he looked at her or whether he was merely admiring the view, but she could see the toe of one of his Hessian boots beating out a tattoo on the cobbles beside her. She willed him to go away. She could not bear his closeness. She could not bear reality or the knowledge that her stolen dream was ruined forever.

And then he went without a word and she felt bereft.

R ANNULF WENT STRAIGHT UP TO HIS ROOM. AND PACED. She was a gentleman's daughter.

Damn it all to hell! She had had no business being sent off to travel alone, without even a maid to offer respectability. Her father deserved to be shot for allowing it. She had had no business accepting a ride with him, using that husky voice, pretending to be an actress. *Flirting* with him. Allowing him to steal a kiss from her without whacking his head right off his shoulders for his impertinence.

She must know the rules of genteel behavior as well as he did.

He knew the rules.

He leaned both hands on the windowsill, drew a deep breath, held it, and let it out slowly. He peered downward. A footman was skirting about the formal gardens on his way back to the house. The glass of lemonade Rannulf had ordered sent out to her had been delivered then.

She had had no business accepting his outrageous suggestion that they move from the posting inn to the quieter one by the market green. Or agreeing to share a room with him. Or dining alone with him. Or fanning his lust with that acting—where the devil had she learned to act like that? Or wearing that Siren's hair all down over her shoulders.

She had had no damned business bedding with him.

She must know the rules.

He knew the rules.

He pounded the edge of one fist against the windowsill and cursed between clenched teeth.

He knew the rules, dammit all to hell. His father had raised headstrong, unruly sons who flouted convention and public opinion at every turn. He had also raised honorable sons, ones who knew the rules that could not be broken.

He had told her he would have taken her with him even if he had known the truth about her. He would have made her his mistress, he had said. Would he have? Probably not—undoubtedly not.

She was a gentleman's daughter.

Deuce take it, but she probably did not know yet if she

had escaped the worst of all possible fates. She was an accomplished liar. She had probably lied about that too. She might be giving birth to his bastard child in a little less than nine months' time.

He pounded a fist on the windowsill once more and then turned away from the window to pace his room again, his hands clenched into fists at his sides.

Damn, damn, damn.

Finally he tore open the door and strode out into the corridor beyond without stopping to close the door behind him. Without stopping to think further.

She was sitting where he had left her, her hands one on top of the other, palm up, in her lap, the glass of lemonade, with perhaps an inch drunk, standing on a small wrought-iron table that the footman must have drawn up beside her. She was staring toward the stream and only half turned her head when he came through the trellised arch from the terrace.

"I have been pacing my room," he said, "trying to convince myself that you were entirely to blame for what happened. It is simply not true. I am as much to blame."

Her head came about entirely then, and he found himself staring into wide, surprised green eyes.

"What?" she said.

"You were an innocent, inexperienced young lady," he said. "I am far from either innocent or inexperienced. I should have known. I should have seen through the act."

"You are blaming yourself for what happened between us?" she asked him, sounding quite astonished. "How foolish! There is no question of blame on either side. It was something that was mutually entered into. It is over and best forgotten."

If only it were that easy!

"It is not over," he said. "I had your virginity. You are now, to put it crudely and bluntly, damaged goods, Miss Law, and you cannot be so innocent that you have not realized that fact."

Her cheeks flamed, her head whipped around to face front again, and she stood up abruptly.

"What makes you think—" she began.

"Oh, not my own observations," he told her. "I was somewhat inebriated, both by the wine I had consumed and by your acting performances and your charms. After you had fled, the landlady explained to me why she had changed the sheets on our bed after our first night together. There was blood on the ones she removed, she was charmed to report."

Her back visibly flinched.

"You are a gentlewoman, Miss Law," he said, "though not of a socially prominent or wealthy family, it is true. You are from a class well below any from which my family or my peers would expect me to choose a bride, but my hand has been forced. *Not* that I blame you. I blame myself for being so blind to reality. But it is too late to regret that now. Will you do me the honor of marrying me?"

Her back did not flinch this time. It stiffened. For several moments he thought she was not going to answer him. But she did speak eventually.

"No," she said, her voice quite steady and firm. And she walked away from him, down over each wide terrace, past all the roses until she came to a stop at the water's edge.

Perhaps he should have presented his offer with softer words, gone to stand in front of her, taken her hand in his. Instead, he had paid her the compliment of speaking the bald truth to her. She surely would have recognized falsehood from him anyway. In her guise as Claire Campbell she had struck him as an intelligent woman. He went after her.

"Why not?" he asked her.

"I am no one's problem, Lord Rannulf," she said. "I will be a salve to no one's guilty conscience. But your guilt is unnecessary. I went with you willingly and I—I lay with you willingly. It was an experience I wished to have and decided to take when the chance offered itself. You are quite right about the reason for my coming to Harewood. There is not much likelihood that a woman in my circumstances will ever be found out as a fallen woman or *damaged goods*. Women like me remain spinsters all their lives. I suppose the chance of marrying after all should be tempting. I could be Lady Rannulf Bedwyn and rich beyond my dreams. But I will not be married because your hand has been forced or because it is too late to extricate yourself from the trap you perceive me to be. I would not be married because honor forces you to offer such an unequal and imprudent match. You would not feel honored if I married you but martyred."

"I beg your pardon," he said. "I did not mean to imply—"

"Oh, no," she said, "you implied nothing. You *stated* it. For which of several possible reasons did you expect me to leap at your offer, Lord Rannulf? Because you are a duke's son and enormously wealthy? Because my hopes of making any other marriage are dim indeed even if I still had my *virginity*? Because propriety dictates that I must marry my seducer since he has seen fit to offer for me—though of course you did *not* seduce me, did you? Because you told me I would *honor* you by accepting? My answer is no."

Relief warred with incredulity and continued guilt. It was the grudging manner of his offer that had offended her. If he had asked her properly, would she have done the proper thing?

"Forgive me," he said. "I believed you would scorn smooth, flattering words. Allow me to—"

"No." She turned to face him and her eyes gazed fully into his. "It was a fleeting experience, Lord Rannulf. It was never meant to last. I was curious, my curiosity was satisfied, and I was satisfied. I had no wish to continue the liaison, and I certainly have no wish to marry you. Why should I? I am not so innocent or so ignorant that I do not know what men of your rank are like. I had proof of it on the road, and your words today have confirmed what I already knew. You are neither innocent nor inexperienced, you said with pride. Anyone who knows what is what, you said, would understand that such behavior is to be expected of you both before and after marriage. Even if I wished for marriage to you I would not marry you. Why would I knowingly become a wife married unwillingly and left to wilt in some quiet, respectable corner while her husband carries on with his life of philandering and debauchery just as if she did not exist? I wanted you for experience, not for a husband, and I was satisfied with the experience, which I feel no desire to repeat. How fortunate for you! Now you will not have to face the scorn of your peers and the displeasure of your brother, the Duke of Bewcastle, after all. Good day to you."

Strangely, despite her fluent, scornful words and her barely suppressed anger and her drab, ill-fitting clothes, she was suddenly appealing to him again and he remembered the consuming sexual attraction he had felt for her during their day and a half and two nights together. Until now it had been hard to realize that she could possibly be the same woman.

"This is your final word?" he asked her.

"Which of the ones I have spoken do you not understand, Lord Rannulf?" she asked, still staring directly at him.

But before he could say anything more, he became aware of someone else in the arbor. He looked up to see the same footman as before standing just inside the arch, clearing his throat. Rannulf raised his eyebrows.

"I have been sent to summon Miss Law to the sitting room, my lord," he said.

"Thank you," Rannulf said curtly. But as he turned to offer his arm to Judith Law, she hurried across the lowest terrace and up to the next, holding her skirt up with both hands and totally ignoring his very existence.

He did not follow her. He stood looking after her, heady with relief. Though why he should feel relieved he did not know. He suddenly remembered that one way or another he was going to have to marry *someone* this summer.

He was feeling ruffled. And still plagued with guilt. And more than half aroused, dammit.

CHAPTER VIII

HAREWOOD GRANGE WAS BUZZING WITH NOISE and activity when the carriage set Judith and her grandmother down on the terrace. All the expected guests had arrived, they discovered. Most were already in the drawing room, taking tea with Aunt Louisa, Uncle George, and Julianne. Only a few latecomers were still in their rooms, changing their garments. Many of their numerous trunks and bags and hatboxes were still strewn about the terrace, servants and strange valets darting about to take them as quickly as possible to their relevant rooms.

"I am far too fatigued to put in an appearance, Judith," her grandmother said. "I feel one of my migraines coming on. But you must not miss joining the gathering. You may help me up to my room if you would be so good and then run and fetch a cup of tea for me and perhaps a little cake or two—the ones with the white icing, my love. After that you must put on a pretty dress and join Louisa and Julianne in the drawing room and be presented to all the guests."

Judith had no intention of doing any such thing. She spied the opportunity for her first hour of real freedom since her arrival at Harewood, and she would not squander it. She hurried to her room after Tillie had been summoned to settle Grandmama in her bed for an afternoon sleep, changed quickly into one of the few dresses that had not yet been subjected to alteration, an old lemon-colored cotton that she was attached to, threw off her cap and replaced it with her own straw bonnet, and hastened down the back stairs, which she had discovered during several errands to the kitchen in the past few days. She slipped out through the back door and found herself facing the kitchen gardens, vegetables on one side, flowers on the other. Beyond, grassy lawns stretched away to a tree-dotted hill. Judith walked toward it and then lengthened her stride, raising her face to the sun and to the light breeze, which felt good lifting the hair at her brow and her neck, which were usually covered by her cap.

Was she quite, quite mad to have turned down a marriage proposal? From a man who was titled and wealthy? From a man with whom she had lain? Whom she found achingly attractive? With whose memory she had expected to fill every dream for the rest of her life? Marriage was every woman's ultimate goal, her dearest hope being that marriage would bring her security and children and a tolerable measure of comfort, perhaps even companionship.

For the past few years Judith had waited patiently to meet a man willing to marry her, someone acceptable to Papa and tolerable to herself. She had very sensibly never expected her dreams of romance to become reality. Yet today—a little more than an hour ago—she had refused *Lord Rannulf Bedwyn.*

Was she *mad?*

The hill was not a high one. Even so, it provided picturesque views across the surrounding countryside. From the top she could see in all four directions. The breeze was a little stronger up here. She faced into it, closed her eyes, and tipped back her head.

No, not mad. How could she have accepted when he had not even tried to hide his resentment at being forced into offering for her? When he had made his contempt for her lowly social standing so obvious? When he had quite openly confessed that what had happened between them was no unusual occurrence for him . . . and that such encounters would continue even after his marriage?

How could she marry a man she actively despised?

Even so, she thought, spying water below the hill on the far side and making her way down toward it, there had been some sort of reckless madness in her refusal—pride overriding common sense. Common sense now reminded her that even if marriage to Lord Rannulf *had* led to being hidden away in some forgotten corner while he continued with his life of philandering, it would at least have *been* marriage. She would have become the respected mistress of her own home.

Instead of which she was a dependent of Uncle George, who hardly knew she existed, despised by Aunt Louisa and at her constant beck and call for endless years into the future. Only her grandmother made life tolerable for her at the moment. She gave herself a mental shake when she caught the self-pitying drift of her thoughts. There were worse fates. She could be married to a man who cared not the snap of two fingers for her and neglected her and was unfaithful to her and . . .

Well, there were worse fates.

The lake at the bottom of the hill was lovely and secluded. It was surrounded by long grass and wildflowers and a few trees. It looked quite neglected and was surely never used or even visited.

Perhaps, she thought, it could become her own private little retreat in the days and months and years ahead. She kneeled on the bank and trailed a hand in the water. It was fresh and clear and not nearly as cold as she had expected. She cupped some in her hands and lowered her flushed face into it.

She was crying, she realized suddenly. She almost never wept. But her tears were hot in contrast to the coolness of the water, and her bosom was heaving with sobs she seemed powerless to control.

Life really *was* unfair at times. She had reached out just once in her life and stolen a brief and magnificent dream. She had neither expected nor demanded that it be prolonged. She had wanted only the memory of it to last her the rest of her life.

Clearly it had been too much to ask.

Now it was gone, all of it. The memories were sullied—all of them. Because now he knew that she was not the bright star, the flamboyant actress he had found attractive despite her physical defects. And because she now knew that he was a man to be despised.

Yet he had just offered her *marriage*.

And she had refused.

She got to her feet and made her way back up the hill. She must not be missed. If she were, Aunt Louisa would surely make sure that she had no future chance for idleness.

Someone, she discovered when she arrived back at the rear of the house, had locked the back door. It would not open to all her efforts and a knock drew no response. She made her way around to the front, fervently hoping that everyone was still gathered in the drawing room so that she could slip up to her room undetected.

Two horses were being led off toward the stables as she rounded the corner to the front terrace, and a mountain of baggage was being lifted out of a baggage coach. Two gentlemen stood with their backs to Judith, one of them directing operations in impatient, imperious tones. She shrank back and would have disappeared back around the corner, but the other gentleman half turned his head so that she could see him in profile. She stared, unbelieving, and then hurried toward him, her reluctance to be seen forgotten.

"Bran?" she cried. "Branwell?"

Her brother turned toward her, his eyebrows raised, and then he grinned and hurried to meet her.

"Jude?" he said. "You are here too, are you? Famous!" He swept off his hat, gathered her up into a bear hug, and kissed her cheek. "Are the others here as well? I like the bonnet— very fetching."

He was dressed in the very height of fashion and looked handsome and dashing indeed, his fair hair blowing in the breeze, his eager, boyish, good-looking face smiling fondly into her own. For a moment she forgot that she wanted to visit exquisite torture on every part of his body, down to the last toenail.

"Just me," she said. "One of us was invited, and I was the one chosen."

"Famous!" he said.

"But what are *you* doing here, Bran?" she asked.

Before he could answer her, the other gentleman came up to join them.

"Well, well, well," he said, looking her over with the sort of bold scrutiny that would have had Papa scolding *her* afterward if he had been here to witness it. "Present me, Law, will you?"

"Judith," Branwell said. "My second sister. Horace Effingham, Jude. Our stepcousin."

Ah, so he *had* come, Uncle George's son from his first marriage. Aunt Effingham would be gratified. Judith had never met him before. He was a few years older than Branwell's twenty-one and a couple of inches shorter—he was about on a level with her own height. He was a little stockier than Bran too and darkly handsome in an almost pretty way. His smile revealed very large, very white teeth.

"Cousin," he said, reaching out a square, smooth hand for hers. "This is a pleasure indeed. Suddenly I am delighted that I succumbed to my stepmama's persuasions and came to what I expected to be certain tedium. I brought your brother with me to help alleviate the boredom. I will take the liberty of calling you Judith since we are close relatives." He carried her hand to his lips and held it there longer than was necessary.

"Effingham is a fine fellow, Jude," Branwell said eagerly. "He has taken me to the races and given me useful tips on picking a winner, and to Tattersall's and advised me on how to choose the best horseflesh. He took me as a guest to White's Club one evening and I took a turn at the tables and won three hundred guineas before losing three hundred and fifty. But still, only fifty guineas lost when other fellows around me were losing hundreds. And at *White's*. You should just see it, Jude—but of course you can't because you are a woman."

She had recovered from the first surprise of seeing him, and from the first delight too. Branwell, the only boy among four sisters—handsome, eager, sunny-natured Bran—had always been the darling of them all. He had gone away to school at great expense to Papa and had come home with very mediocre reports. But he had excelled on the playing fields and was everyone's best friend. Then he had gone to Cambridge and scraped through every examination by the skin of his teeth. But he had not been interested in a career in the church or in law or in politics or the diplomatic service or the military. He did not know what he wanted to do. He needed to be in London, mingling with the right people, discovering exactly where his talents and abilities could be put to best use to earn him a fortune.

In the year since he had come down from Cambridge, Branwell had spent everything their father had set aside for him—and then everything that had been allotted to his daughters as modest dowries. Now he was eating into the very substance of Papa's independence. Yet he was still the darling boy, who would soon be finished sowing his wild oats and would then proceed to rebuild the family fortune. Even Papa, who was so very strict with his girls, could see no wrong in Branwell that time and experience would not mend.

"I am pleased to make your acquaintance, Mr. Effingham," Judith said, withdrawing her hand from his as soon as she was decently able. "And I am delighted to see you again, Bran. But I must hurry inside. Grandmama will be waking from her sleep, and I must see if she needs anything."

"Grandmama?" Branwell said. "I had forgotten the old girl was here. An old tyrant, is she, Jude?"

She did not like the disrespect with which he spoke.

"I am remarkably fond of her," she said, quite truthfully. "You may wish to pay your respects to her as soon as you have freshened up, Bran."

"If Judith is going to be with her, I'll come with you, Law," Horace Effingham said with a laugh.

But Judith was hurrying away, contrasting her situation with her brother's. She was here in the nature of an unpaid servant, while Bran was just arriving as a guest. Yet he was the cause of all her woes. *All* of them. If it were not for Bran she would not have been on that stagecoach. She would not be here.

But there was absolutely no point in falling back into self-pity.

She noticed in some relief that the hall and stairs were still deserted. As she hurried upward she could hear the hum of voices coming from the drawing room.

R ANNULF, JUST LIKE THE REST OF HIS FAMILY, HAD NEVER been much enamored of social gatherings, whether in

London during the Season or at Brighton or one of the spas in the summer or at house parties any time of the year. The house party at Harewood was going to be particularly insipid, he could see almost immediately. Yet he could not escape it. He must spend the next two weeks determinedly dancing attendance on Miss Effingham. During those two weeks or soon after he was going to have to propose marriage to her.

Two proposals to two different women, both within a month of each other. But from the second he could expect no reprieve.

It was made embarrassingly obvious from the moment of his arrival at Harewood for dinner that he was the honored guest, even though he was not staying at the house as all the others were. Not only honored guest, but most favored suitor for the hand of Miss Julianne Effingham. The mother led him about the drawing room after his arrival to introduce him to those guests he did not already know—most of them, in fact—and invited her daughter to join them in their progress. Then she had him lead the girl into the dining room, and he found himself seated beside her through dinner.

He was interested to discover that one of the guests was Branwell Law, a fair-haired, good-looking lad, who was presumably the brother of Judith Law—had not Claire Campbell named him? Of Judith herself and Mrs. Law there was no sign, for which fact he was enormously thankful. To say that he felt embarrassed after their encounters in the garden, especially the second one in the rose arbor, would be to understate the case. *She had refused him.*

Miss Effingham seemed absurdly young and alarmingly empty-headed. She talked about nothing but the parties she had attended in London and how this one and that one— mostly titled gentlemen—had complimented her and wished to dance with her when she had already promised all her dances to other gentlemen. She really thought dances should come in sets of two instead of three so that there could be more of them during an evening and more gentlemen could dance with the lady of their choice. What did Lord Rannulf think?

Lord Rannulf thought—or *said* he thought—that was a remarkably intelligent suggestion and should be brought to the attention of some of London's more prominent hostesses, particularly those of Almack's.

"How would *you* feel," she asked him, gazing at him with wide blue eyes, her spoon suspended over her pudding, "if you wanted to dance with a lady, Lord Rannulf, and she was engaged for every set to other gentlemen even though she wanted *desperately* to dance with you?"

"Kidnap her," he said and watched her eyes widen still further before she laughed with light, trilling merriment.

"Oh, you never would," she said. "*Would* you? You would cause a shocking scandal. And then, you know, you would be forced to offer for her."

"Not so," he said. "I would have borne her off to Gretna Green, you see, and married her over the anvil."

"How *romantic*," she said with an excited little gasp. "Would you really do that, Lord Rannulf? For someone you admired?"

"Only if she had no dances left to offer me," he said.

"Oh." She laughed. "If she knew that ahead of time, she would make very sure that there were none. And then she would be whisked off . . . But you would not really do such an outrageous thing, would you?" There was a small cloud of doubt in her eyes.

Rannulf was weary of the silly game. "I always make sure," he said, "that if there is a lady I particularly admire, I arrive at a ball early enough to engage her for at least one dance."

Her mouth turned down at the corners. "Are there very many ladies you admire, Lord Rannulf?" she asked.

"At the moment," he said, fixing his gaze on her, "I can see only one, Miss Effingham."

"Oh."

She must surely know that she looked her prettiest with her mouth pouted just so. She held the expression for a moment, then blushed and looked down at her dish. Rannulf took the opportunity to turn to Mrs. Hardinge, mother of Miss Beatrice Hardinge, at his other side and to address a remark to her. Soon after, Lady Effingham rose to signal the ladies that it was time to follow her to the drawing room while the gentlemen settled to their port.

The first person he saw when he entered the drawing room half an hour later was Judith Law, who was seated by the hearth close to her grandmother. She was wearing a pale gray silk dress which looked to be as shapeless as the striped cotton she had worn to Grandmaison earlier. She was also wearing a cap again. It was slightly prettier than this afternoon's though it covered her hair just as completely. She was holding a cup and saucer for the old lady, he could see, while the latter held a plate and made short work of the cream cake on it.

He ignored the two ladies after nodding genially to Mrs. Law, who smiled and nodded back. It was intriguing to notice that for everyone else in the room Judith Law might as well have been invisible—as of course she had been to him just yesterday when he had first been introduced to her. All her vivid, voluptuous beauty was quite effectively masked.

Sir George Effingham offered him a place at a table of whist, but Lady Effingham took him firmly by the arm and bore him off in the direction of the pianoforte at which Lady Margaret Stebbins was favoring the company with a Bach fugue.

"It is your turn next, Julianne, dearest, is it not?" her

mother said even before Lady Margaret had finished. "Here is Lord Rannulf come to turn the pages of your music."

Rannulf resigned himself to an evening spent charming and flattering a gaggle of giggling young ladies and matching wits with a group of foolishly posturing young gentlemen. He felt a hundred years old.

Judith Law, he could not help noticing, was kept busy by her grandmother. She was constantly going back and forth between her seat and the tea tray. Twice she was sent from the room. The first time she came back with the old lady's spectacles, which were set down and never used. The second time she returned with a cashmere shawl, which was then folded and set over the arm of the old lady's chair and forgotten. Nevertheless, he noticed that the two of them were talking to each other and smiling and apparently enjoying each other's company.

He smiled and complimented Miss Effingham, who had finished her second piece on the pianoforte and was clearly angling for a request for an encore. Meanwhile the Honorable Miss Lilian Warren and her sister awaited their turn at the instrument.

And then there was a commotion from the direction of the tea tray. Judith Law had apparently been pouring a cup of tea when someone—it was Horace Effingham, Rannulf could see—must have jogged her elbow. The tea had spilled all down her front, darkening the gray of her dress, making it half transparent, and molding it to her bosom. She had cried out, and Effingham had produced a handkerchief and was attempting to mop her down with it. She was pushing his hand away with one of hers while with the other she was attempting to pluck the wet fabric away from her bosom.

"Judith!" Lady Effingham cried in awful tones. "You awkward, clumsy girl! Remove yourself immediately."

"No, no, it was all my fault, Stepmama," Effingham called. "Allow me to wipe you dry, Cousin."

There was laughter in his eyes, Rannulf saw—lascivious laughter.

"Oh dear," Miss Effingham murmured, "Judith is making *such* a cake of herself."

Rannulf found himself clenching his teeth and striding across the room to grab the shawl from under Mrs. Law's elbow. He hurried toward the tea tray and tossed the garment about Judith Law's shoulders from behind without actually touching her. She looked around, startled and grateful, even as her hands grasped the ends and drew it protectively about her.

"Oh," she said. "Thank you."

Rannulf bowed curtly. "Are you burned, ma'am?" he asked. Had no one considered the fact that it was *hot tea* she had spilled down herself?

"Only a little scalded," she said. "No, really, nothing." She turned to hurry from the room, but he could see that she was biting her lower lip hard.

Rannulf found himself eye to eye with Horace Effingham, whose leering expression came very close to a wink.

"How gallant," he said, "to find a shawl to hide the lady's, er, *embarrassment.*"

It had been deliberate, Rannulf realized suddenly, narrowing his gaze on the other man. By God, it had been deliberate.

"She might have been badly burned," he said curtly. "It would be advisable to be more careful around tea trays in future."

And then Effingham *did* wink as he murmured very low. "*I* am burned, even if she is not," he said. "As are you too, Bedwyn, I'll wager. Quick witted of you to find an excuse to hurry closer."

But Lady Effingham had raised her voice again, though now she was laughing and pleasant. "Carry on as before, everyone," she said. "I do apologize for that unfortunate and undignified interruption. My niece is unaccustomed to mingling in polite society and has become all thumbs, I am afraid."

"Oh, I say, Aunt," young Law said, "Jude has never been clumsy. It was just an accident."

"Lord Rannulf." Mrs. Law tweaked his sleeve, and he could see when he turned toward her that the incident had upset her. "Thank you so very much for being the only one with the presence of mind to help Judith and to save her some embarrassment. I must hurry upstairs to see how badly hurt she is."

She set two plump hands on the arms of her chair to support herself.

"Allow me, ma'am," he said, offering his hand.

"You are most kind." She leaned heavily on him as she hoisted herself to her feet. "I believe it must be the summer heat that has caused my ankles to swell and that is making me so breathless all the time."

He thought it was more likely to be all the cream cakes she seemed to consume and her generally indolent lifestyle.

"Allow me to escort you, ma'am," he said.

"Well, I will if it is not too much trouble," she said. "I did not even really want that cup of tea, you know, but I wanted Judith to move from my side and mingle with the guests. She is very shy and even insisted upon taking her dinner with me tonight since I was too weary to come down to the dining room. I thought perhaps someone would engage her in conversation and all would be well. I *am* vexed with Louisa for forgetting to introduce her to the guests after dinner. I daresay she has too much else on her mind."

Rannulf did not intend to take her farther than the top of the stairs. But she leaned so heavily on him that he took her all the way to her room. At least, he assumed it was her room until she raised one heavily ringed hand and knocked.

The door opened almost immediately, and Rannulf was

trapped by the burden on his arm. Judith had removed both her dress and her cap. Her hair, still pinned up, had nevertheless pulled loose in several places so that long locks of bright red hair hung over her shoulders and temples. She was wearing a loose dressing gown, which she was holding closed with one hand. Even so, a large V of bare flesh was visible from her shoulders to the top of her cleavage. For a few inches above the latter her skin was a fiery red.

"Oh." Soon her cheeks matched the scald mark. "I—I thought it was someone bringing the salve I asked to be sent up." She focused her gaze on Mrs. Law, but Rannulf knew she was very aware of him. Her hand clutched the robe closer.

"You *are* burned, Judith, my love," Mrs. Law cried, relinquishing her hold on Rannulf's arm and hurrying forward far faster than he had ever seen her move before. "Oh, my poor child."

"It is nothing, Grandmama," Judith said, biting her lip. But Rannulf saw tears spring to her eyes and knew she was in pain.

"Allow me," he said, "to find the housekeeper and make sure the salve is sent up without further delay. In the meantime, Miss Law, a cold wet cloth held against the burn may take away some of the sting."

"Thank you," she said, her eyes meeting his. For a moment their glances locked, and then she turned away and the old lady set an arm about her shoulders.

Rannulf hurried away, entertaining himself with pleasing visions of bathing Horace Effingham in something a great deal hotter than tea.

CHAPTER IX

J
UDITH REMAINED IN HER OWN ROOM FOR TWO DAYS, nursing a painfully sore chest. Her grandmother, who forgot her own maladies now that there were someone else's to occupy her mind, visited her often, bringing her books and bonbons and news from the rest of the house and admonitions to lie down and sleep if she could. And Tillie, on Grandmama's orders, brought food trays to Judith's room and came every few hours to apply more of the soothing salve.

Horace Effingham sent up a bouquet of flowers with Tillie and a note explaining that he had picked the blooms with his own hands and wishing her a speedy recovery.

Branwell came in person to see her.

"Are you enjoying the house party?" she asked him when he had inquired after her health.

"Oh, I am having the greatest good time," he said. "We went riding to Clynebourne Abbey this morning. There are just a few old ruins there, but it is very picturesque. We rode over to Grandmaison first to invite Bedwyn to join us. I think Julianne fancies him, but she is looking to have her heart broken, if you were to ask me. The Bedwyns are all enormously high in the instep. Bewcastle—the Duke of Bewcastle, that is, head of the family—is known as a thoroughly cold fish and would be very unlikely to approve of an alliance with the daughter of a mere baronet."

"I am glad you enjoyed the ride." Judith smiled. What would Branwell have to say, she wondered, if he knew that Lord Rannulf Bedwyn had offered to marry *her* just yesterday?

"I say, Jude." He got up abruptly from the chair on which he had been seated and paced across to the window of her bedchamber to stand looking out, his back to her. "You would not be able to lend me a few pounds by any chance, would you? Maybe thirty?"

"No, I most certainly would not," she said. "I doubt I could scrape together a shilling even if I were to turn my purse inside out and upside down and squeeze it. Why do you need thirty pounds?" It seemed like a vast sum to her.

He shrugged and turned to face her with a sheepish grin. "It is not important," he said. "It is a trifling sum, and Effingham did tell me not to worry about it. But I hate to be in his debt. I hated to have him pay all the expenses of my journey, but Papa has turned remarkably tight-fisted lately. Is he sickening for something?"

"The journey here cost *thirty pounds*?" Judith asked, considerably shocked.

"You do not understand what it means to be a gentleman moving in the company of other gentlemen, Jude," he said. "One has to keep up with them. One cannot look like a country bumpkin with ill-fitting coats and breeches and boots that look as if they were made by an apprentice to a country cobbler. And one needs fashionable digs and a decent horse to get about on. And unless one struts one's stuff all alone, one must do what other gentlemen do and go where they go—the clubs, the races, Tattersall's."

"Bran," she asked, not really sure she wanted to hear the answer, "do you owe other people money too?"

He waved a dismissive hand and grinned at her, though there was something sickly in the expression.

"Everyone owes money," he said. "A gentleman would be thought queer in his attic if he did not owe half a fortune to his tailor and his bootmaker and his haberdasher."

"And do you have gambling debts, too?" she asked before she could stop herself. She really did *not* want to know.

"Trifling ones." Again he flashed her his sickly grin. "Nothing like some fellows, who owe thousands. Some men lose whole estates, Jude, on one turn of a card. I never wager what I cannot afford to lose."

She was too cowardly to ask him the extent of his gaming debts.

"Bran," she asked, "when are you going to decide upon some career?"

"Actually," he said, laughing and looking his sunny-natured self again, "I have been thinking of marrying a rich girl. It's a pity Julianne has her eye on Bedwyn—though she does not have a hope in a million of snaring him, I daresay. But the Warren sisters have a papa who is as rich as Croesus, or so I have heard, and they are both passably pretty girls. I do not suppose their papa would give me the time of day, though, would he?"

He spoke as if the whole idea were just a lighthearted joke, but Judith was not sure it was. He was obviously deep in debt—again. She did not know if their father could extricate him this time without completely ruining himself. And then what would happen to Mama and their sisters?

"Oh, come now, Jude," Branwell said, getting to his feet and possessing himself of both her hands, "don't look so grim. I'll come about. You must not worry about me. Did you burn yourself *very* badly?"

"I will be better in a day or two," she told him.

"Good." He squeezed her hands. "If you *do* happen to come by a few pounds within the next week or two, perhaps when Papa sends you your allowance, could you see your way to lending me some of it? I am good for it, as you must know, and there cannot be much for you to spend money on here, can there?"

"I am not expecting any money," she told him.

"I say." He frowned. "You did come just for a visit, did you not, Jude? Papa did not send you here to live and depend upon Uncle George's bounty, did he? That would be the outside of enough. What is *happening* to Papa lately?"

You have been happening to him, Bran, she thought—*and to all of us*. But though she was suddenly angry and would surely have ripped into him and told him a few home truths of which he seemed remarkably ignorant, she was prevented from doing so by the arrival of Tillie with more salve and a dose of laudanum.

"You are going to have to excuse me now, Bran," Judith said. "I must rest for a while."

"Of course." He raised one of her hands to his lips and smiled one of his sweetest smiles. "Look after yourself, Jude. You cannot know how pleasant it is to have one of my sisters here. I miss you all, you know."

If only he had someone to take him in hand, she thought, he might yet turn out well. However, she was not at leisure to brood on the matter. She was in pain. Whoever would have thought that a mere cup of tea could be so lethal?

ON THE THIRD DAY JUDITH VENTURED DOWNSTAIRS after luncheon. She hoped to avoid intruding upon the houseguests and find her grandmother. But as fortune would have it, the first person she saw as she descended the stairs was Horace Effingham, and he came hurrying to meet her, all smiles.

"Judith!" he exclaimed. "You are recovered at last. I apologize most profusely for my clumsiness the other evening. Do come to the drawing room. We are trying to decide what to do this afternoon now that last night's drizzle and the morning clouds have cleared off. Come and have your say."

He was offering her his arm.

"I would really rather not," she said. "I do not know anyone in there. Do you know where Grandmama is, Horace?"

"You do not *know* anyone?" he said. "You astonish me. Has no one thought to introduce you to all the guests?"

"It really does not matter." She shook her head.

"Ah, but it does," he said. "I cannot have you running away again after waiting patiently for three days for you to reappear. Come."

She took his arm reluctantly and found herself immediately drawn indecorously close against his side as he led her toward the drawing room. But it was, she conceded over the next few minutes, just as well that someone had thought to introduce her to all the guests. She was not quite a servant, after all, and it would be awkward over the next week and a half to be constantly running into people to whom she had not been formally presented. She *looked* almost like a servant, of course. Branwell grinned at her and asked her how she did, Mrs. Hardinge commiserated with her on her unfortunate accident, and Julianne told her she was glad to see her up again so that she could save the rest of them from Grandmama's tedious conversation and constant demands. Most of the guests, however, though polite in their acknowledgment of the introductions, made no attempt to engage her in conversation.

Judith would have made her escape as soon as all the introductions had been made, but she was forestalled, at least for a few moments, by the arrival of Lady Beamish and Lord Rannulf Bedwyn.

"Ah, two more introductions to make, Cousin," Horace said, leading her toward them.

"I have already had that pleasure," she told him, but she was too late to prevent a face-to-face encounter.

"Miss Law," Lord Rannulf said, bowing to her, "I hope I see you well again?"

She curtsied and tried not to remember the last time she had seen him—outside the door of her bedchamber with Grandmama, giving her advice on how to treat her burn and looking at her with genuine concern in his eyes before striding off to hasten the arrival of a servant with the salve she had asked for. After what had happened earlier in the day, she had wanted only to despise him and forget him.

"Rannulf told me about the unfortunate accident," Lady Beamish said. "I trust you have taken no permanent harm from it, Miss Law?"

"No, indeed, thank you, ma'am," Judith assured her. "I am quite well again."

Julianne was clapping her hands for everyone's attention. She was glowing and pretty in a dress of daffodil yellow muslin, her blond curls bouncing about her heart-shaped face as she moved.

"It has been decided," she announced, "that we are to stroll in the wilderness walk for an hour and then have a picnic tea on the lawn. Now that Lord Rannulf Bedwyn has arrived, we need delay no longer." She smiled radiantly at him, and Judith, glancing at him despite herself, saw him bow his acquiescence as he looked her cousin over with appreciative eyes.

It hurt. Stupidly, stupidly, it hurt.

"We must fetch our hats and bonnets and be on our way," Julianne said.

Her plans appeared to meet with general approval. There was bright chatter as most of the room's occupants hurried away to get ready for the outing.

"I must go and find Grandmama," Judith murmured, sliding her hand free of Horace's arm at last.

But her grandmother had appeared at the drawing room door with Aunt Effingham, and Grandmama had heard her.

"You must not bother yourself with me, my love," she said, beaming fondly at Judith. "I will have Sarah for company. Now that you are up again, you must run along and enjoy yourself with the other young people."

"The fresh air will do you good after a few days of confinement indoors, Miss Law," Lady Beamish said kindly.

Aunt Effingham had other ideas, of course. "I can certainly make use of your help, Judith," she said briskly. "It has been most unfortunate that your own carelessness resulted in such a lengthy spell of idleness."

"But Stepmama," Horace protested, smiling ingratiatingly at Aunt Effingham, "*I* have dire need of Judith's help too—help in saving me from the fate of being a wallflower. Perhaps you had not noticed that the gentlemen outnumber the ladies at this house party."

"It is because you did not inform me that you were definitely coming, Horace," she said, looking somewhat chagrined. "Or that you were going to bring Branwell with you."

"Judith." Horace bowed to her. "Run along and fetch your bonnet."

Life at Harewood was proving to be even more trying than she had expected. Although Mama had always kept her girls busy at home and Papa had strict expectations of their behavior, nevertheless she had never felt totally powerless there. Or without any freedom whatsoever. At least her preferences and opinions had often been solicited there. Here they were not. Everyone might have been surprised to learn that she would have far preferred to be put to work by her aunt than allowed the dubious pleasure of strolling along the wilderness walk feeling like an intruder and paired with Horace—and in full view most of the time of Julianne and Lord Rannulf Bedwyn, who walked arm in arm while she chattered brightly and he bent his head closer to hear her. A few times they laughed together and Judith was unwillingly reminded of the times when he had laughed with *her*, most notably outside the village shop when he had unwrapped his snuff box.

The wilderness walk wound its way through the trees to the west of the house and had been planned with some care for maximum beauty. Wildflowers grew within sight of the path, and there were occasional seats and small grottoes, most of them placed at the top of rises in the path and affording pleasing prospects of the house and the rest of the park. It was a path designed to shelter the walker from the heat of the summer sun and the chill of an autumn wind.

Judith was unable to appreciate its loveliness, though she thought that perhaps it would become another quiet retreat for her down the years, whenever she had an hour to spare.

She was not enjoying *this* hour. Horace was ignoring everyone else and concentrating all his attention on her. But far from being flattering, his attentions were distressing. He tried to take her arm through his, but she clasped both arms firmly behind her back. He tried to slow their steps so that they would fall behind the rest of the group, but she determinedly increased the pace every time a noticeable gap developed. His eyes were on her rather than the scenery most of the time, mostly on her bosom, which even her loose dress could not entirely hide. He commented upon how the wet tea had molded her dress to her and revealed a figure that should be dressed far more becomingly than it was.

"But I daresay Stepmama has something to do with your dresses," he said, "and your caps. She is determined to marry Julianne off this summer, preferably to Bedwyn. Have you noticed how my half-sister is many times prettier than all the other girls who have been invited here?" He chuckled.

"Stepmama cannot countenance competition at such a crucial stage of Julianne's career. Least of all from a cousin."

Judith could think of no reply to make to such a speech and so made none. She lenghened her stride to close the gap between them and Mr. Peter Webster and Miss Theresa Cooke, the nearest couple ahead of them. But then Horace exclaimed with annoyance and stopped walking altogether. There was a stone wedged in the heel of his boot, he explained, and he set a hand against the tree trunk on the other side of Judith and lifted his foot to dislodge the stone, effectively boxing her in between himself and the tree.

"Ah, done," he said after a few moments and returned his foot to the ground and lifted his head to smile at Judith.

He was uncomfortably close, and by now they had fallen well behind the others.

"You know, Judith," he said, his eyes flitting over her face but coming to rest on her bosom, "I could make you very comfortable indeed at Harewood. And I could be induced to visit here far more often than I have been in the habit of doing."

One of his hands lifted with an obvious destination. She batted at it and moved forward in order to get around him, but since he did not step back, she only succeeded in bringing herself closer to him.

"I am quite comfortable enough here as I am," she said. "We are being left behind."

He chuckled low and his hand found its target, closing around one breast. But only for a brief moment. He lowered the hand and took a short step back as the crunching of twigs heralded the return of one of the walkers. She could have almost cried with relief when she saw Branwell.

"Oh, I say," he said cheerfully, "a problem, is there?"

"I almost had to have your sister haul my boot off," Horace said with a chuckle. "I had a stone lodged in the heel and it was devilish difficult to get rid of it."

"Ah," Branwell said, "Bedwyn was wrong, then. He sent me back here because he thought perhaps Jude was not feeling quite the thing and might need to be escorted back to the house. The stone has gone, has it?"

"I wrestled it free," Horace said, offering his arm. "Judith? Shall we restore Branwell to whichever lady was fortunate enough to win his escort? Did you know that your brother has become the darling of all the ladies?"

But Judith was not going to miss the opportunity that had been presented to her on a platter, so to speak.

"Do go on without me," she said. "Both of you. I do not need an escort, but I *do* feel rather weak after spending the last two days in my room. I shall go and sit with Grandmama and Lady Beamish. Or perhaps I will go and lie down."

"Are you sure, Jude?" Branwell asked. "I am quite willing to come with you."

"Quite sure." She smiled.

A few minutes later she had found her way out of the walk and was hurrying toward the safety of the house. She felt as if her flesh was crawling. His hand had felt like a snake, or what she imagined a snake would feel like. He had been offering to make her his *mistress*. Were all men alike?

But it was Lord Rannulf who had sent Branwell back to her, she remembered. Had he really thought she was ill? Or had he guessed the truth? But how was it he had even noticed that she and Horace had disappeared from the back of the group?

She could not return to the house yet, she realized suddenly. Even if she could reach the privacy of her room she would feel too confined. But the chance was strong that she would not even get there before being seen by either her grandmother or Aunt Effingham. She was feeling too agitated to encounter either the affectionate kindness of the one or the tart irritation of the other.

She turned toward the back of the house and a minute or

two later was hurrying through the kitchen gardens and across the back lawn and up the slope of the hill. She had intended to sit there, allowing the air and the wide view to soothe her agitated spirits. But the lake looked invitingly cool and secluded. She shuddered, feeling that hand close about her breast again. She felt *dirty*.

AFTER NEARLY THREE DAYS OF BEING ALMOST CON-stantly in the company of Miss Effingham and her houseguests, Rannulf was longing for the quiet sanity of Lindsey Hall, the ducal seat where he still made his home for most of each year. There were never house parties there, and most guests were chosen with care as people who were likely to have something sensible to say. Freyja and Morgan, his sisters, might be unconventional and headstrong and difficult and quite untypical of other young ladies of their class, but Rannulf would take them any day of the week over the likes of the Honorable Misses Warren, Miss Hardinge, Miss Cooke, and Lady Margaret Stebbins. They were all bosom bows of Miss Effingham, who was flaunting him before them like a newly acquired and prized lapdog.

He simply could not do this, he thought at least once an hour when in her company. He could not marry her and shackle himself to her pretty silliness for the rest of his life. He would be stark raving mad within a year. Freyja and Morgan would make mincemeat of the girl, and Bewcastle would freeze her with one disdainful glance.

But at least once each hour, following directly upon the heels of that thought, came the memory of his promise to his grandmother that he would at least try to consider her as a bride. He had spent enough time in his grandmother's company to see that she was indeed ill. She would be dreadfully disappointed if he did not become at least betrothed this summer. And it was a disappointment she might well take to the grave. He simply could not do it to her.

And so he perservered, playing Miss Effingham's silly flirtation games with her, charming her friends, jollying along all the young gentlemen who continued to make him feel like an octogenarian at the very least even though he was only a few years older than most of them.

He had firmly set aside his guilt over Judith Law. What had happened between them had *not* been seduction, and she had gone to some lengths to deceive him. He had done what was proper and made her an offer. She had refused. There was no more reason for feeling responsible for her. But he knew Horace Effingham's type. And he knew that tea-spilling incident had been deliberate on Effingham's part. Rannulf had guessed that the man would pursue his lecherous intent at the earliest opportunity.

It had become quickly apparent to him on the wilderness walk both that Effingham was maneuvering to get her alone and that she was resisting his efforts. And then they disappeared altogether. Fortunately Branwell Law was within hailing distance and was easily persuaded to go back to attend his ailing sister.

A few minutes later Law was back, Effingham with him, announcing that his sister was indeed feeling weak but that she had insisted upon returning to the house alone. And yet, Rannulf observed a couple of minutes after that as they strolled past another seat and view down to the house and park, she was not going to the house—or looking either weak or weary. She was hurrying away from the back of the house.

A picnic tea was set out on the front lawn when they left the wilderness walk. Everyone milled about, mingling and laughing and wandering off in groups. Rannulf took the opportunity to be free of Miss Effingham's empty, boastful chatter for at least a short while and withdrew with his plate to the terrace, where his grandmother and Mrs. Law were seated side by side.

"I wonder where Judith is," Mrs. Law said, searching for a sight of her granddaughter.

"Did Branwell Law not inform you, ma'am?" Rannulf asked. "She was feeling somewhat weary after a while and returned to the house for a rest. She would not let him accompany her."

"But she is missing her tea," Mrs. Law said. "I must have Tillie take a tray up to her. If you would be so good, Lord Rannulf—"

He held up a staying hand. "If I may make so bold, ma'am," he said, "may I suggest that it might be better to allow Miss Law to rest in quiet for a while longer?"

"Yes, indeed," she agreed. "You are quite right. May I trouble you to fetch that plate of pastries, Lord Rannulf? Your grandmama did not take one, but I am quite sure she must wish to try them."

He brought the plate, offered it to his grandmother, who shook her head, and to Mrs. Law, who took three, and returned the plate to the table. No one's attention was on him, he noticed with a quick glance around. Lady Effingham was talking with Mrs. Hardinge, and Miss Effingham was in a laughing group with Miss Hannah Warren, Lord Braithwaite, and Jonathan Tanguay.

Rannulf slipped around the corner of the house before someone could notice him and around to the back. There was no sign of her. Where had she gone? he wondered. Had she returned yet? Perhaps she really was resting in her room by now. There was a tree-dotted hill in the near distance. He squinted ahead to it but could not see her there. It looked like a quiet place to go anyway. He lengthened his stride and made his way toward it.

She must indeed have returned to the house, he thought a few minutes later as he climbed the last few feet to the top

of the hill and looked around appreciatively at the view.
And it was just as well. He had not really been hoping to
meet her, had he? For what purpose? He had not thought of
asking himself that until this moment.

There was a lake down below. It looked neglected and
overgrown but rather lovely nevertheless. He was surprised
it had not been connected to the wilderness walk. He was
trying to decide whether to go down there or not when he
saw her. She had just appeared from beneath the overhanging branches of a willow tree. Swimming. She was on her
back, kicking lazily, her hair spread about her like a dark
cloud.

Ah. She had come here to be alone.

He should respect her privacy.

But he found that his legs were carrying him down the far
side of the hill nonetheless.

CHAPTER X

I T WAS A FEELING RATHER THAN ANYTHING SHE SAW
or heard—a feeling that she was no longer alone. She
opened her eyes and turned her head with some dread,
fully expecting that Horace had somehow followed her
here.

For a moment she felt intense relief when she saw that it
was Lord Rannulf Bedwyn who was sitting beside the pile of
her clothes under the willow tree, one leg stretched out before him, the other bent with one arm draped over his knee.

Her clothes! She moved swiftly until she was treading
water, only her head above the surface. She lifted her arms
to sleek her hair back over her head and then, seeing them
bare, returned them hastily to the water, spreading them out
below the surface to balance herself.

How foolish, *foolish* of her to risk swimming here in her
shift.

"I am *not*," he said quietly though his voice carried
clearly across the water, "going to run off with your clothes.
Or force myself on you."

"What do you want?" she asked him. She was intensely

embarrassed even though they had spent a day and two nights . . . But that seemed like more than a lifetime ago. It seemed like something that must have happened to someone else.

"Some quiet time," he said. "Did he harm you?"

"No." Except that she had splashed around for several minutes, trying desperately to get herself clean.

"I would come and join you," he said. "But alas, my absence will appear ill-mannered if it is too lengthy. Why do you not come here and join me?"

She was amazed—and alarmed—at how very tempting the suggestion was. They had nothing more to say to each other and yet . . . and yet he had saved her from a potentially nasty situation on the wilderness walk. And despite his admission a few days ago that he was a philanderer, she knew somehow that she could trust him not to force unwelcome attentions on her. He had just said so.

"Is it the fact that I will see you in your shift?" he asked when she did not immediately approach the bank. "I have seen you in less."

If she told him to go away, would he go? She believed he probably would. Did she want him to go? She swam slowly toward him. No. If she was perfectly truthful with herself, the answer was no.

She set her hands on the bank and hoisted herself up, setting a knee on the grass when she was able. Water streamed off her. Her shift clung like a second skin. She turned and sat, her feet still dangling in the water.

"Perhaps," she said without turning, "you would be good enough to hand me my dress, Lord Rannulf."

"You would only get that wet too," he said, "and be no better off than you are now. It would be wiser to leave it until you are ready to return to the house and then remove the shift first."

"Are you suggesting—" she began.

"No, I am not," he told her. "I did not come here to seduce you, *Miss Law*."

Why had he come? For some quiet time, as he had
claimed? Was it pure coincidence that he had found her
here?

She was aware of him getting to his feet and shrugging out
of his coat. A moment later it landed, wonderfully heavy and
warm, about her shoulders. And then he sat down beside her,
crossing his legs and looking both informal and relaxed.

"Has he bothered you between three evenings ago and
this afternoon?" he asked.

"No." She shook her head. "And I do not expect him to
bother me again. I believe I made myself clear today."

"Did you?" She was aware that he was gazing at her profile even though she did not turn her head to look at him.
"Why did you not make yourself clear to *me*?"

"Just now?" she said. "You told me—"

"When I offered you a ride," he explained. "When I suggested that we take a room together at the inn by the market
green."

She could not think of a suitable answer even though he
waited for her to speak. She drew her feet out of the water,
clasped her arms about her raised knees, and lowered her
head to rest her forehead against them.

"That was different," she said lamely at last. But *how* was it
different? Perhaps because she had sensed from the very first
moment that if she had said no he would not have pressed the
point? But how had she known it? And was it true? "I wanted
the experience." But it was a dream she had wanted.

"You would have taken that experience with Effingham,
then, if *he* had come riding along instead of me?" he asked.

She shivered. "No, of course not."

He did not speak again for a while and when he did, he
changed the subject.

"Your brother is a fashionable young gentleman," he said,

"and moves in fashionable circles. Even *fast* circles, if one may judge from his friendship with Horace Effingham. He is enjoying the idle life of a guest while you are here as a type of glorified servant. Do I detect a story behind those contrasting details?"

"I do not know," she said, lifting her head and staring across the water. "*Do* you?"

"Is he the black sheep of the family?" he asked. "But do you love him nevertheless?"

"Of course I love him," she said. "He is my brother, and it would be very hard to dislike Bran even if he were not. He was sent away to school and university for a gentleman's education. It is only natural that he would wish to mingle with other gentlemen on a basis of equality. It is only natural that he be somewhat extravagant until he discovers what he wants to do with his life and settles to some career. He is not vicious. He is just . . ."

"Thoughtless and self-absorbed?" he suggested when she could not think of a suitable word. "Does he know that he is responsible for your being here?"

"He is not—" she began.

"You do altogether too much lying, you know," he said.

She turned her head to look indignantly at him.

"It is not your business, Lord Rannulf," she said. "Nothing to do with my life or my family is your business."

"No, it is not," he agreed. "By your choice, Miss Law. Have your sisters suffered a similar fate to your own?"

"They are all still at home," she said, feeling such a wave of homesickness suddenly that she had to dip her forehead against her knees again.

"Why you?" he asked her. "Did you volunteer? I cannot imagine anyone was eager to come here to suffer the kindly affection of your aunt."

She sighed. "Cassandra is the eldest," she said, "and our mother's right hand. Pamela is the third of us and the beauty of the family. She could not have borne to leave, not to be the center of everyone's admiration—not that she is unduly vain about her looks. And Hilary is too young. She is only seventeen. It would have broken her heart to have to leave our mother and father—and it would have broken all of our hearts too."

"But no one's heart will be broken by your absence?" he asked.

"One of us needed to come," she said. "And they did all shed tears over me when I left."

"And yet," he said, "you would defend that extravagant young puppy of a brother to me?"

"I do not need to," she said, "or to censure him. Not to *you*."

And yet she was not really angry with him for prying or for understanding the situation so well. It felt treacherously good to have someone interested enough in her life to ask questions about it. Someone who understood, perhaps, the extent of the sacrifice she had made voluntarily . . . though of course she would have been the chosen one even if she had not offered to come.

"Where did you learn to act?" he asked. "Does your family engage in amateur theatricals at the vicarage or rectory or wherever it is you live?"

"Rectory," she said, lifting her head again. "Oh, dear, no. Papa would have an apoplexy. He is fanatically opposed to acting and the theater and declares that they are the work of the devil. But I have always, always loved acting. I used to go off on my own into the hills, where I would be neither seen nor heard, and throw myself into different roles I had memorized."

"You seem to have memorized a great deal," he said.

"Oh, but it is not difficult to do," she assured him. "If you act a part as if you *are* that character, you see, then the words become your own, the only logical ones to speak under those particular circumstances. I have never consciously memorized a part. I have simply *become* various characters."

She fell silent, rather embarrassed by the enthusiasm with which she had just explained her passion for acting. She had wanted desperately to be an actress when she grew up until she had learned that acting was not a respectable career for a lady.

Lord Rannulf sat quietly beside her, one wrist draped over his knee, the other hand absently plucking at the long grass. She thought of him as he had looked earlier, his head bent over Julianne, listening attentively to her chatter.

"Does it amuse you," she asked, "to toy with Julianne's affections?" The words were out before she fully realized she was about to speak them aloud.

His hand stilled. "Does she have affections to be toyed with?" he asked in return. "I think not, Miss Law. She is after a titled husband, the richer and more socially prominent the better. I daresay a duke's son who is independently wealthy seems like a brilliant catch to her."

"You do not believe, then," she said, "that she looks for love or at least *hopes* for love? That she has some tender feelings? You must be a cynic."

"Not at all," he said. "Merely a realist. People of my class do not choose marriage partners for love. What would happen to the fabric of polite society if we started doing that? We marry for wealth and position."

"You *are* toying with her, then," she said. "My uncle is a mere baronet. His daughter must be far beneath the serious notice of a *duke's* son."

"There you are wrong again," he told her. "Titles do not tell the whole story. Sir George Effingham's lineage is impeccable, and he is a wealthy man of property. My grandmother believes that the alliance will be perfectly eligible."

Will be?

"You are going to marry Julianne, then?" she asked. She

had not fully believed it until this moment despite all Aunt Effingham and Julianne had said.

"Why not?" He shrugged. "She is young and pretty and charming. And well born and rich."

She did not know why her heart and her mind raced with such distress. She had been given her own chance to have him and had refused him. But of course she knew. She could not *bear* the thought of his being with Julianne. *She is young and pretty and charming.* And also empty-headed and vain and selfish. Did he deserve better, then? Everything he had told her about himself said no. And yet . . .

"Of course," he said, "Miss Effingham and her mama will be disappointed if they hope to see her a duchess one day. I am second in line now, but my elder brother married recently. In the nature of things it is altogether probable that his wife will be breeding soon. If she produces a boy, I will be pushed back into third spot."

She knew the look that would be on his face, and sure enough, when she glanced at him she saw the familiar mockery there.

"Perhaps," he said, "Lady Aidan will do her duty consummately well and produce twelve sons in as many years. That will leave me almost without hope. What is the opposite of hope? Despair? Each of Aidan's sons will plunge me deeper into despair."

She realized suddenly that his intent was not so much to mock either her or himself as to amuse her. And she *was* amused. What an absurd picture he painted. She laughed.

"How dreadfully sad for you," she said.

"And if you think *my* plight desperate," he said, "imagine that of Alleyne, my younger brother. Aidan busy begetting sons, me twenty-eight years old and in danger of taking a bride at any moment and doing some begetting of my own."

She laughed again, looking into his face as she did so.

"That is better," he said, a gleam of something that might

have been amusement in his eyes. "You need to smile and laugh more often." He lifted one hand to set his forefinger lightly along the length of her nose for a moment before withdrawing it, adjusting his position, clearing his throat, and gazing out across the lake.

She felt rather as if she had been branded with liquid fire.

"Will the duke not marry?" she asked.

"Bewcastle?" he said. "I very much doubt it. No woman is good enough for Wulf. Or perhaps that is not strictly fair. Since he inherited the title and everything that went along with it at the age of seventeen, his life has been devoted to performing his ducal duties and being head of the family."

"And what do *you* do, Lord Rannulf?" she asked him. "While your brother occupies himself with his duties, what is left for you to do?"

He shrugged. "When I am home at Lindsey Hall," he said, "I spend time with my brothers and sisters. I ride and hunt and fish with them and pay social calls with them. My closest friend, Kit Butler, Viscount Ravensberg, lives nearby. We are still close, despite a nasty quarrel a few years ago that left us both bruised and bloody and despite the fact that he is now married. I am on friendly terms with his wife too. When I am not at Lindsey Hall I like to be active. I avoid London whenever I can and soon tire of such places as Brighton, where all is frivolity and idleness. I went on a walking tour of the Scottish Highlands last year and of the Lake District earlier this year. The exercise and experience and company were good."

"Do you read?" she asked.

"Yes, actually." He looked at her with a lazy smile. "Surprised?"

She was neither surprised not unsurprised. She knew so little about him, she realized. And she should, of course, be content to let things remain that way.

"I suppose," she said, hugging her knees, "the sons of dukes do not have to work for a living."

"Not the sons of the duke who sired me," he said. "We are all indecently wealthy in our own right, not to mention Bewcastle, who owns large chunks of England and part of Wales too. No, we do not need to work, though of course there are traditional expectations of younger sons. Aidan as the second son was intended for a military life and did his duty without a murmur. He sold out only recently—after his marriage. Bewcastle had expected to see him a general in another year or two. I as the third son was intended for the church. I did *not* do my duty."

"Why not?" she asked. "Is your faith not strong enough?"

He raised his eyebrows. "I have rarely known faith to have much to do with a gentleman's decision to make the church his career," he said.

"You *are* a cynic, Lord Rannulf," she said.

He grinned. "Can you picture me climbing the pulpit steps of a Sunday morning, holding my cassock above my ankles, and delivering an impassioned sermon on morality and propriety and hellfire?" he asked her.

Despite herself she smiled back. She would hate to see him as a clergyman, sober and pious and righteous and judgmental and joyless. Like her father.

"My father had images of me wearing a bishop's miter," he said. "Perhaps even the Archbishop of Canterbury's. I would have disappointed him had he lived. I have disappointed my brother instead."

Was there a thread of bitterness in his voice?

"Do you feel guilty, then," she asked, "for not doing what was expected of you?"

He shrugged. "It is my life," he said. "Sometimes, though, one wonders if there is any shape, any meaning, any point to life. Do you demand such things of your life, Judith? What possible shape or meaning or point can you discern in what has happened recently to your family and to you as a result?"

She looked away from him. "I do not ask such questions," she said. "I live my life one day at a time."

"Liar," he said softly. "What is ahead for you here? Nothing and nothing and nothing again down the years? And yet you do not ask yourself why? Or what the point of going on with life is? I believe you do, every hour of every day. I have seen the real Judith Law, remember? I am not sure, you see, that that vivid, passionate woman at the Rum and Puncheon Inn was the act and that this quiet, disciplined woman at Harewood is the reality."

Judith scrambled to her feet, holding his coat about her with both hands.

"I have been here too long," she said. "I will be missed and Aunt Louisa will be annoyed. Will you leave first? Or will you—will you turn your back while I dress?"

"I will not peep," he promised, resting both wrists over his knees and lowering his head.

She dropped his coat to the grass beside him.

"It is damp inside, I am afraid," she said.

She peeled off her still-damp shift as fast as she could and pulled on her dress. She twisted her wet hair into a knot and hid it beneath her cap. She put on her bonnet and tied the ribbons firmly beneath her chin.

Nothing and nothing and nothing again down the years.

Her teeth chattered as she hurried to make herself look presentable.

"I am dressed now," she said, and he got to his feet in one fluid motion and turned toward her.

"I do beg your pardon," he said. "I upset you."

"No, you did not," she assured him. "I am a woman, Lord Rannulf. Women are accustomed to boredom, to futures that spread ahead of them without . . ."

"Hope?"

"Without any promise of change or excitement," she said. "Most women live dull lives, whether they marry or grow old as I will do, dependent upon the charity of their wealthier relatives. *This* is the real me, Lord Rannulf. You are looking at her."

"Judith." He strode toward her and possessed himself of her hand before she could even think of snatching it away. "I—"

But he stopped abruptly, looked down at the ground between them, sighed audibly, and released her hand after squeezing it painfully tightly.

"I do beg your pardon," he said again, "for making you maudlin when just a short while ago I had you laughing. I must get back too, Miss Law. I daresay my grandmother is ready to return home. I'll go around the hill and come at the front lawn from the side. You will go over the hill to the back of the house?"

"Yes," she said and watched him stride away without once looking back. Soon he was out of sight. She drew a deep breath and released it slowly. She really had not wanted to start knowing him as a person. She had not wanted to find anything likable about him. Her prospects were dreary enough without regret being added to them.

Regret! Did she regret the answer she had given him three days ago, then? No, she did not. Of course she did not. He had made clear today the sort of woman who would suit him as a bride, and she did not qualify on any of the counts. Besides, when he married, it would be only for the purpose of producing sons to carry on his name. He would reserve all his charm, all his energy, all his passion for such women as the nonexistent Claire Campbell.

No, she did not regret her decision. But her feet felt as heavy as her heart as she made her way back to the house.

CHAPTER XI

As usual Rannulf had been invited to go to Harewood the following afternoon, by which time some plan would have been devised for his entertainment and everyone else's. However, fairly early in the morning a veritable cavalcade of carriages was seen to be approaching Grandmaison. The butler came to the morning room to warn Lady Beamish, who was at her escritoire, writing letters, and Rannulf, who was reading letters, one predictably short one from his friend Kit, the other a longer one from his sister Morgan.

A footman was sent from the leading carriage to invite Lord Rannulf Bedwyn to join the Harewood party on a day's excursion to a town eight miles away. But by the time he had knocked on the door, Rannulf was already in the hall and striding outside and able to receive the invitation at greater length from Miss Effingham herself, who had descended from the carriage with the Honorable Miss Lilian Warren and Sir Dudley Roy-Hill. The other three carriages were also emptying themselves of passengers, all of whom appeared to be in high spirits.

Judith Law was not among them, Rannulf saw at a glance. Horace Effingham was.

"You simply must come with us, Lord Rannulf," Miss Effingham told him, stepping forward and stretching out both hands to him. "We are going to shop and spend all our money. And then we are going to take tea at the White Hart. It is very elegant."

Rannulf took both hands in his and bowed over them. She was looking very fetching indeed in a spring-green carriage dress and straw bonnet. Her big blue eyes sparkled in anticipation of a day of adventure. As far as Rannulf could see, Mrs. Hardinge, in the fourth carriage, was the only chaperon of the group.

"We will grant you ten minutes to get ready, Bedwyn," Effingham called cheerfully. "Not a moment longer."

"I have kept a place for you in my carriage," Miss Effingham added, in no hurry to withdraw her hands from his, "though both Mr. Webster and Lord Braithwaite vied for it."

The day loomed mentally ahead of Rannulf. A couple of hours in the carriage both this morning and during the return trip—all in close company with his intended bride. A few hours shopping with her and taking tea seated beside her at the inn. And doubtless a return to Harewood afterward, where he would be seated beside her at dinner and maneuvered into turning the pages of her music or sitting beside her or partnering her at cards in the drawing room afterward.

His grandmother and her mother would be ecstatic over the happy progress of the courtship.

"I do beg your pardon." He released the girl's hands, clasped his own behind him, and smiled apologetically at her and the group at large. "But I have promised to spend today with my grandmother, planning the entertainments for tomorrow." Tomorrow was the day of the garden party at Grandmaison, an occasion he had not spared a single thought for until now.

Miss Effingham's face fell and she pouted prettily at him. "But *anyone* can plan a garden party," she said. "I am sure your grandmama will spare you when she knows where we are going and that we have all come deliberately out of our way in order to invite you."

"I am honored that you have done so," he said. "But I really cannot break a promise. Have a pleasant day."

"I will go and speak to Lady Beamish myself," Miss Effingham said, brightening. "She will spare you if *I* ask."

"Thank you," he said firmly, "but no. I simply cannot leave today. Allow me to hand you back into your carriage, Miss Effingham."

She looked openly dejected and he felt a moment's pang of remorse. He had doubtless ruined her day. But even as she placed her hand in his and arched him a look that he could not immediately interpret, she called out along the terrace.

"Lord Braithwaite," she called gaily, "you may sit up here with me after all. It seemed only polite to reserve a place for Lord Rannulf, did it not, but he is unable to come."

Rannulf was amused to observe, as he stood back after handing her in and waited politely for the cavalcade to resume its journey, that she did not once look at him again but smiled dazzlingly at Braithwaite, placed a hand on his sleeve, and proceeded to converse animatedly with him.

The silly chit was trying to make him jealous, he thought as he made his way back into the house. His grandmother was just coming into the hall.

"Rannulf?" she said. "They are leaving without you?"

"They have a full day's excursion planned," he said, hurrying toward her and drawing her arm through his. She would not use a cane, but he knew that she often needed to lean on something as she walked. "I did not wish to leave you that long."

"Oh, nonsense, my boy," she said. "However do you think I manage when you are not here—which is most of the time?"

He led her in the direction of the stairs, assuming she was retiring to her own apartments. He reduced the length of his stride to fit hers.

"Have I been a disappointment to you, Grandmama?" he asked her. "Not going into the church as a career. Not coming here more often even though it is years since you named me as your heir? Not showing any interest in my future inheritance?"

She looked at him sharply as they climbed. He noticed how she had to take each stair separately, her left foot leading each time.

"What has brought on this crisis of conscience?" she asked him.

He was not sure. The talk with Judith Law yesterday, maybe. The things she had said about the idleness of gentlemen, his own admission that he had not done his duty, as Wulf and Aidan had. He had refused to become a clergyman. But he had done nothing else instead. He was no better than that jackanapes, Branwell Law, except that he had the money with which to live an idle life. He was twenty-eight years old and bored and directionless, the accumulation of his life's wisdom leading him only to the cynical conclusion that life was meaningless.

Had he ever tried to *give* life meaning?

He answered his grandmother's question with one of his own. "Have you ever wished," he asked, "that I would come here more often, take an interest in the house and estate, learn how they work, perhaps oversee them and reduce your responsibilities? Get to know your neighbors? Become an active member of this community?"

She was rather breathless when they reached the top of the stairs. He paused to give her a chance to catch her breath.

"Yes to all your questions, Rannulf," she said. "Now, would you care to tell me what this is all about?"

"I am considering matrimony, am I not?" he said.

"Yes, of course." She preceded him into her private sitting room and motioned him toward a chair after he had helped seat her in her own. "And so the prospect is awakening your latent sense of responsibility, as I had hoped it would. She is a sweet little thing, is she not? Rather more flighty and frivolous than I realized, but nothing that time and a little maturity will not erase. You feel an affection for her, Rannulf?"

He considered lying outright. But affection was not a prerequisite for the marriage he had promised to consider.

"That will come in time, Grandmama," he said. "She is everything you say."

"And yet," she said, frowning, "you have just rejected the chance to spend a whole day in her company."

"I rather thought," he said, "that I might search out your steward, Grandmama, and see if he has the time to take me around the home farm and explain a thing or two to me. I am remarkably ignorant about such matters."

"The end of the world must be coming," she said. "I never thought I would live to see the day."

"You will not think me presumptuous, then?" he asked her.

"My dear boy." She leaned forward in her chair. "I have dreamed of seeing you not only a married man and a father in my lifetime, but also a grown up, mature, happy man. You have been a lovable boy for as long as I have known you, but you are twenty-eight years old."

He got to his feet. "I'll go mend my ways, then," he said, grinning at her, "and leave you to rest."

There was a new spring in his step as he made his way back downstairs. It amazed him that he had not thought of this before but had been content to idle away his life at Lindsey Hall, which was Bewcastle's home, not his, and wherever else he could expect to derive a few days or weeks of amusement.

And yet for years he had known that he would eventually be a landowner. There was much to do, much to learn if, when the time came, he was going to be able to give to the land as well as take from it.

Yet it was all to be done with Julianne Effingham at his side. His mind shied away from the prospect. He would think of that another time.

JUDITH WOULD HAVE LIKED TO JOIN THE SHOPPING EXCURsion, especially when Branwell specifically asked her. But when Aunt Effingham intervened quite firmly to declare that she needed her niece at home, she made no objection. She had no money to spend anyway, and shopping was no fun if one could not buy even the most trivial bauble to show for the day. Besides, Horace had been quick to second Bran's invitation. And if she went, she would have to look at Julianne and Lord Rannulf Bedwyn chattering and laughing together all day long.

She did not *love* him. But she was lonely and depressed, and foolishly—ah, foolishly—she had tasted another sort of life altogether . . . with him. She could not help remembering. Her *body* remembered, particularly during the times when her guard was most effectively down. She was starting to wake at night, her body aching for what it would never know again.

On the whole she was quite content to spend her day writing a pile of invitations to next week's grand ball and delivering some of them herself in the village, walking all the way there and back since the gig had not been offered her, and then cutting flowers from the kitchen garden and arranging them in fresh bouquets for each of the day rooms. She spent an hour in the drawing room, sorting through a bag of her aunt's embroidery threads, which had become horribly tangled together, patiently separating them and

winding them into soft silken skeins. Twice she had to inter-
rupt the task, once to run upstairs for her grandmother's
handkerchief and again to bring down the dish of bonbons
Grandmama particularly liked.

But her grandmother was at least good company. For as
long as Aunt Effingham was not with them, they chattered
brightly on an endless number of topics. Grandmama loved
to tell stories about Judith's grandfather, whom Judith had
never known, though she was seven years old when he died.
They both chuckled over anecdotes from home Judith told
purely for her amusement, like the one of the whole village
chasing madly after an escaped piglet through the churchyard and rectory garden until Papa had stepped outside from
his study, fixed the poor, terrified animal with his most severe clerical look, and stopped it in its tracks.

And then the butler interrupted them.

"I beg your pardon, ma'am," he said, looking from one to
the other of them, apparently not knowing quite which of
them to address, "but there is a, ah, *person* in the hall insisting upon speaking with Mr. Law. He refuses to believe that
the young gentleman is not here."

"He wishes to speak with Branwell?" Judith asked. "But
who is he?"

"You had better show him in here, Gibbs," her grandmother said. "Though why he would not believe you I do
not know."

"No." Judith got to her feet. "I'll go see what he wants."

The man standing in the hall was turning his hat around
and around in his hand and looking uncomfortable. His age
and his manner of dress immediately disabused Judith of any
notion that he might be a friend of Bran's who was in the
same part of the country and had decided to pay him a surprise call.

"May I help you?" she asked him. "Mr. Law is my
brother."

"Is he, miss?" The man bowed to her. "But I need to see the gentleman in person. I have something to deliver into his own hands. His sister's will not do. Send him to me if you will."

"He is not here," Judith said. "He is gone for the day. But Mr. Gibbs has already told you that, I believe."

"They always say that, though," the man said. "But it usually isn't true. I'll not be avoided, miss. I'll see him sooner or later. You tell him that. I'll wait till he comes."

Whatever for? she wondered. And why the persistence almost to the point of rudeness? However had he found Bran here? But she was not entirely foolish. She felt a prickle of apprehension.

"Then you must wait in the kitchen," she said. "If Mr. Gibbs will allow you there, that is."

"Follow me," the butler said, looking along his nose at the visitor as if he were a particularly nasty worm.

Judith looked after them, frowning, and then returned to the drawing room. But she could hear the sound of horses and carriages even before she had a chance to sit down again, and crossed to the window to look out. Yes, they had returned, far earlier than she had expected.

"They are back already?" Her grandmother's surprise echoed her own.

"Yes," Judith said. "They have made good time." They would not have had to make the detour to Grandmaison on the return journey, of course. They would have brought Lord Rannulf with them. Despite herself she found that she was leaning closer to the window to catch a glimpse of him as he descended from the carriage. But it was Lord Braithwaite who handed Julianne out, and they were followed by Miss Warren and Sir Dudley Roy-Hill. Aunt Effingham had gone outside to greet them.

"What did that man want with Branwell?" her grandmother asked.

"I have no idea," Judith said. "He is waiting to see him personally."

"I daresay he is a friend," her grandmother said.

Judith did not disabuse her. A moment later the drawing room door was flung open and Julianne hurried inside, looking cross and tight-lipped, her mother on her heels. Aunt Effingham closed the door behind her. Presumably, all the guests had gone straight to their rooms to freshen up after the day out.

"He could not come," Julianne said, her voice brittle and overloud. "He had promised to stay with Lady Beamish. But he would not let me persuade her to release him from his promise. He *would* not come. He does not like me. He is not going to offer for me. Oh, Mama, whatever will I *do*? I *must* have him. I will simply die if I have to settle for anyone inferior."

"You are home very early, Julianne," Grandmama commented. "Whatever is wrong?"

"There were no shops worth looking in," Julianne said petulantly. "All their wares look shabby after those on display in even the least fashionable shops in London. Yet everyone dragged about wanting to linger everywhere and exclaim in wonder at everything. I was fatigued to death within an hour. And whoever said the White Hart is elegant has clearly seen nothing that *is*. We had to wait ten whole minutes for warm tea and stale cakes. And if Hannah and Theresa tell you that *theirs* were hot and fresh, Mama, then they are lying. It was such a stupid idea to go there today. I am sure you had a divine day in comparison to mine, Judith."

Judith understood that it was Lord Rannulf's refusal to join the expedition that had doomed it to certain failure. Why had he refused to go?

"Of course he likes you, dearest," Aunt Effingham said soothingly. "Lady Beamish has been quite particular in promoting a match between the two of you, and Lord Rannulf has been most attentive. If he could not go with you today, you can be sure there was a good reason. You must not show that you are upset with him. Tomorrow is the day of the garden party at Grandmaison, and you know that we have been invited to stay for dinner too. All will be well tomorrow, as you will see. You must be your natural pretty, charming self, my love. No man is ever caught with a lady's anger."

"I bought two bonnets, though I do not like one of them above half," Julianne said, somewhat mollified, it seemed. "And the other is not a style that becomes me well, I fear. I bought some lengths of ribbon too. I could not decide which color I liked best so bought a length of each. Though really there was no color there that I really liked at all." She sighed deeply. "*What* an insipid day!"

Her grandmother decided at that point to withdraw to her own rooms, and Judith helped her to her feet and accompanied her there.

"These earrings pinch me," her grandmother said, pulling one off as they approached her room and wincing. "I always forget which ones do. But everything in my jewelry box is in such a jumble that I put my hand in and pull out whatever is closest to the top. I must push these to the bottom."

"I'll do it for you, Grandmama," Judith offered.

But when she saw the inside of the large, ornate wooden box in which all her grandmother's considerable collection of jewelry was piled, she could see that something drastic needed to be done about it.

"Would you like me to sort it all out?" she offered. "You see, Grandmama, the box is divided into compartments. If you used one for your rings, another for your earrings, and others for your brooches, necklaces, and bracelets, then everything would be much easier to find."

Her grandmother sighed. "Your grandfather was forever buying me jewels," she said, "because he knew that I liked them so much. I *do* keep the most precious pieces separate, as you can see." She pointed at a wine-colored velvet drawstring bag that was almost submerged under the clutter of everything else. "*Will* you sort everything out for me? How very good of you, Judith, my love. I have never been good at keeping things tidy."

"I'll take the box to my room," Judith suggested, "so that I will not disturb you as you rest."

"I do need to rest," her grandmother admitted. "I believe I must have taken a chill to the stomach while sitting outside with Sarah yesterday. I thought that perhaps my tea would settle it, but it did not. Tillie will give me a dose of something, I daresay."

Judith took the heavy box with her to her room and tipped everything out onto her bed. Grandpapa must indeed have been besotted with Grandmama, she thought, smiling, to have given her so many and such ostentatious jewels, many of the glittering pieces almost indistinguishable from one another.

She was sorting through the necklaces, the last pile to be dealt with, when there was a hasty tap on her door and Branwell opened it and came hurrying inside even as she was calling for whoever it was to come. He was looking as pale as a ghost.

"Jude," he said. "I need your help."

"What is wrong?" She suddenly remembered the persistent visitor. It must be he who had upset her brother. "What did that man want?"

"Oh." He tried to smile. "He was just a messenger. Damned impudence really. A fellow owes his tailor and his bootmaker and has to be pursued halfway across the country, as if his gentleman's word to pay up eventually is not sufficient."

"He was a tailor come to demand payment?" she asked him, a heavy sapphire necklace suspended from one hand.

"Not the tailor himself," he said. "They have fellows hired for just this sort of thing, Jude. I have two weeks to pay up, he told me."

"How much money?" she asked, her lips feeling suddenly stiff.

"Five hundred guineas," he said, his smile ghastly. "There are fellows who owe ten times more than that, but no one is pursuing *them*."

"Five hundred—" For a moment Judith thought she was going to faint. The necklace landed with a thud in her lap.

"The thing is," Branwell said, pacing to the window, "that Papa is going to have to cough up more of the blunt. I know this is a lot, and I know I cannot do it again. I must mend my ways and all that. But it is done this time, you see, and so Papa is going to have to get me out of it. But he will explode if I go and ask him in person or even if I write to him. *You* write to him for me, will you, Jude? Explain to him. Tell him—"

"Bran," she said, her voice seeming to come from a long way off, "I am not sure Papa has that much money to give you. And even if he does, he does not have anything more. He will be beggared. So will Mama and Cass and Pamela and Hilary."

He turned paler if that were possible. Even his lips were white.

"Is it that bad?" he asked. "Is it, Jude?"

"Why," she asked softly, "do you think I am here, Bran? Because coming to live with Aunt Effingham is my life's dream?"

"Oh, I say." He looked at her with frowning sympathy. "I am dreadfully sorry, Jude. I did not want to believe it. Is it really so, then? I have done this to you? Well, no longer. I'll come about, you'll see. I'll pay off my debts and restore the family fortune. I'll see to it that you are fetched home and that there are portions to attract husbands for all of you. I'll—"

"*How*, Bran?" Far from feeling touched by his outpouring of remorse, she was angry. "By playing for higher stakes at the races and the gentlemen's clubs? We would all be far happier if you settled to some respectable career and made a decent living for yourself."

"I'll think of something," he said. "I *will*, Jude. I'll think of something. I'll come about and without applying to Papa either. Good Lord." His eyes had been absently focused on the jewelry box. "Whose glitters are all those? Grand-mama's?"

"They were all jumbled together," she explained, "except for her most precious pieces in the bag here. I offered to sort them for her."

"There must be a *fortune* there," he said.

"Oh, no, you don't, Bran," she said grimly. "You will *not* apply to Grandmama to pay your debts. These are her jewels, her mementos of her life with our grandfather. Maybe they *are* worth a fortune, but they are hers, not mine and not yours. We have never even paid her much attention in our lives, have we, because Papa has always given the impression that she is not quite respectable, though I cannot imagine why. She can be tiresome in some ways, always forgetting things in another room, always complaining about her health, though she has done less of that recently. But I have grown remarkably fond of her. She is *fun* and loves to laugh. And I do not believe she has a mean bone in her body—which is more than I can say of her daughter or . . . or her son." She flushed at having said something so very disloyal about her father.

Branwell sighed. "No, of course I'll not ask the old girl for help," he said. "It would be humiliating to have to admit to her that I am in difficulties, for one thing. Good Lord, though, she would not even miss one or two or ten of those pieces, would she?"

She fixed him with a severe eye.

"I was *joking*, Jude," he said. "Do you not know me better than to believe I might consider robbing my own grandmother? I was *joking*."

"I know you were, Bran." She got to her feet and gave him an impulsive hug. "You are going to have to find your own way out of this difficulty. Perhaps if you call on the tradesmen involved, you can come to some agreement with them to pay them so much a month or—"

He laughed, a mirthless sound.

"I ought not to have bothered you with my troubles," he said. "Forget about them, Jude. They are not *your* troubles, after all. I'll come about. And as for you, I don't see why you should not attract a decent husband even though you are living here without any fortune. But you will not do it looking like that. I never understood why Papa always insisted that Mama keep you in caps when the other girls don't wear them half the time. I have never seen what is so dreadful about your hair. I have always thought red hair on women rather attractive."

"Thank you, Bran." She smiled. "I must finish off here and get this box back to Grandmama's room. I confess it makes me somewhat nervous to have all this wealth in my own keeping. I wish I could help you, but I cannot."

He grinned at her and looked more himself. "Never fear," he said. "Fellows go through this all the time. But they always come about. I will too."

It had become something of a catch phrase with him, Judith realized. *He would come about.* But she did not see how.

Papa would be dragged into it eventually, she thought, and Mama and the girls too. And she would be stranded forever and ever at Aunt Effingham's. She had not realized until this moment how a part of her had still held out hope of one day going back home, of everything being restored to normal again.

CHAPTER XII

THE WEATHER COOPERATED IN GRAND STYLE FOR
the garden party at Grandmaison. Despite a cloudy
morning that looked for a while as if it might have
been the prelude to rain, the afternoon was clear and sunny,
with just enough heat not to oppress the senses. The sitting
room was in use for anyone who felt more inclined to sit indoors than out, but the French windows were opened back
and most of the guests remained outdoors, walking the paths
of the formal gardens, sitting in the rose arbor, or strolling
over the lawns or down along the stream path. On the terrace, long tables covered with crisp white cloths were laden
with appetizing foods of all descriptions as well as tea urns
and large jugs of lemonade and punch.

Judith was determined to enjoy herself. She was wearing
what she had always considered her prettiest dress, the pale
green muslin, though like most of her dresses it had not escaped alteration. And she was wearing one of her own caps
beneath the bonnet Aunt Louisa had given her. She did not
feel pretty, but then she had never been under any illusions
about her looks. However, this afternoon she did not feel so

very different from a number of the other guests who had been invited from the neighborhood. Most of them did not look nearly as elegant or fashionable as the Harewood set. And Judith had the advantage of having made the acquaintance of some of them the day before when she had delivered invitations to the ball.

She spent the first half hour with the vicar's wife and daughter and believed that she might in time develop a friendship with them. They in turn introduced her to a few other people who spoke politely to her and did not look at her with disdain or—worse—turn immediately away as if she simply were not there. After an hour or so she went to join her grandmother in the sitting room and brought her a plate of food from the terrace. They sat there, comfortable together until Lady Beamish found them and bore them off to the rose arbor after persuading Grandmama that the air was warm and the breeze really close to being nonexistent.

She *was* enjoying the party, Judith told herself after leaving the two old friends together to chat with each other. All around her she could hear the sounds of laughter and merriment. It seemed as if the young people were all moving about in groups, sometimes in couples, looking youthful and exuberant, enjoying one another's company. Even all the older guests seemed to have *someone* with whom they belonged or felt thoroughly comfortable—as did she, of course. She had her grandmother.

Julianne was surrounded by the closest of her female friends and a few of the gentlemen from the house party. Lord Rannulf was at her side, as he had been almost all afternoon, and she was sparkling up at him though she must have said something to make the whole group laugh.

He really was going to marry Julianne.

Judith longed suddenly for solitude, having discovered—as she had never done at home—that it was possible to feel at one's loneliest in the midst of a crowd. No one was taking any notice of her at the moment. It was almost a certainty that the back of any grand home would be quiet. She took a path around the side of the house and found the expected kitchen gardens at the back. Fortunately they were deserted and immediately she breathed more easily.

She was going to have to get over this, she told herself sternly—this feeling of displacement, this loss of all confidence in herself, this self-pity.

The stables were at the far side of the house with a paddock behind them. She walked past the fenced-off area, looking at the horses grazing there, relieved that there were no grooms outside to see her and wonder what she was doing so far from the party.

Beyond the stables the ground fell away down a steepish grassy slope into a wooded area. Judith half ran down it and found herself among rhododendron bushes, surrounded suddenly by their heavy fragrance. And ahead of her, now that she was down, she could see a pretty little summerhouse and beyond it a lily pond.

The summerhouse was hexagonal and completely closed in beneath its pointed shingled roof though there were windows on all sides. She tried the door and it opened inward on well-oiled hinges to reveal a tiled floor and a leather-covered bench all around the wall. That it was sometimes used was obvious. It was clean. There were a few books strewn along one side of the bench. But surely it was not someone's completely private retreat. It was not locked.

She went inside, leaving the door open so that she could breathe the rhododendron-fragrant air and listen to the birds singing, and so that she could get an unobstructed view of the pretty, well-kept lily pond, its water dark green beneath the roof of tree branches, the lilies a startling white in contrast.

It was a little heaven on earth, she decided, sinking onto one of the benches, folding her hands in her lap, and allowing herself to relax for the first time all afternoon. She pushed aside homesickness, loneliness, and heartache. It was not in her nature to harbor negative feelings for long and these ones had oppressed her for altogether too many days. Here were peace and beauty to nurture her spirit, and she would accept the gift by opening herself to what was offered and giving it a chance to seep into her soul.

She inhaled deeply and then relaxed further. Her eyes closed after a couple of minutes, though she was not sleeping. She felt both happy and aware of being blessed. She lost track of time.

"A pretty picture indeed," a voice said softly from the doorway and she was jolted back to unpleasant reality just as if she really had been sleeping.

Horace was standing there, one shoulder propped against the door frame, one booted leg crossed over the other.

"Oh," she said, "you alarmed me. I came for a walk, found the summerhouse, and sat down to rest for a few moments. I must be getting back." She stood up and realized that the summerhouse was really not very large at all.

"Why?" he asked her without moving. "Because Stepmama may have some errands for you to run? Because your grandmama may need someone to fetch her more cakes? The garden party will continue for some time yet, and we Harewood guests will be staying even after everyone else leaves, you know. We are invited for dinner. Relax. You will not be missed for some time yet."

That was precisely what she was afraid of.

"It is all very picturesque, is it not?" she said brightly. *And very remote and secluded.*

"Very," he agreed without removing his eyes from her. "And would be even more so without its bonnet and cap."

She smiled. "Is that a compliment, Mr. Effingham?" she asked. "I thank you. Will you stay here a while? Or will you walk back to the house with me?"

"Judith." He smiled at her, revealing almost all his perfect white teeth. "There is no need to be skittish—or to call me Mr. *Effingham*. I saw you leave the party because you were feeling alone and neglected. You go unappreciated here, do you not? It is because Stepmama treats you like a poor relation and encourages the impression most of the guests have that you are your grandmama's companion. And because you have been forced to wear this heavy disguise. I am the only man here, apart from your brother, who has been privileged to catch a glimpse beyond it."

She silently reprimanded herself for dressing the way she had on that day he had arrived with Bran. He would have shown no interest in her if he had seen her only as she looked now. She could think of no sensible answer to his words.

"You are not *quite* unappreciated, though," he told her.

"Well." She laughed. "Thank you. But I really must go now." She took one step forward. Another would bring her into collision with him. But, as he had done on the wilderness walk, he stood his ground and did not move aside for her to pass. "Excuse me, please, Mr. Effingham."

"I daresay," he said, "you had a very strict and narrow upbringing at the rectory, did you, Judith? A little dalliance can be very entertaining, you know, especially when the party is so dull."

"I am *not* interested in dalliance," she told him firmly.

"That is because you have never experienced it," he said. "We will correct that gap in your education, Judith. And could we ask for more . . . picturesque surroundings for the first lesson?"

"Enough of this," she said curtly. She was truly alarmed now, since he seemed to be a man who would not take no for an answer even when it was firmly given. "I am leaving. And I would advise you not to try stopping me. Uncle George and Aunt Louisa would not be pleased with you if you did."

He chuckled and sounded genuinely amused.

"Little innocent," he said. "Do you really believe they would put any blame on me? And do you really believe you *would* tell?" He took one step forward and she took a half step back.

"I do not want this, Mr. Effingham," she said. "It would be ungentlemanly of you to come one inch closer to me or to speak any further on a matter that is thoroughly distasteful to me. Let me go now."

Instead of letting her go, he lifted one hand, pulled open the ribbons of her bonnet, and tossed both it and her cap onto the bench behind her before reaching for her. Half of her hair fell down over one shoulder, and she heard the sharp intake of his breath.

It was the last thing she consciously heard or saw for what seemed forever and was perhaps a minute, maybe two. She struck out at him blindly, flailing both fists, stamping with both feet, sinking her teeth into whatever came close to her mouth—but not screaming, she realized afterward. She had never been a screamer. Yet it was strange how, mindless as she seemed to be, a part of her took a step back and watched almost dispassionately as she struggled in a panic for her freedom and as Horace overpowered her quite effortlessly, laughing softly most of the time, cursing once or twice when she struck him.

And then her body was pressed to his, her dress half ridden up her legs, one of his wedged between them, her hands imprisoned against his chest, his horrid wet, open mouth seeking hers. It was the moment when her conscious mind returned. He fully intended to ravish her, and she was essentially powerless to stop him. But she would not go down meekly. She struggled on, panic returning as she became aware that her twistings and turnings were doing nothing to free her, but were only further amusing and inflaming him.

And then suddenly, without any warning, she *was* free,

gazing in terrified incomprehension at the great monster who had just lifted Horace bodily away from her and was still growling menacingly as it turned and flung him outside. The monster resolved itself into Lord Rannulf Bedwyn as he went outside after Horace, lifted him from the ground with one hand, and slammed his back against a tree.

Judith reached out blindly for the nearest windowsill and clung to it.

"Perhaps it escaped your notice," Lord Rannulf was saying—still in a harsh growl, "that the lady was unwilling."

"This is rather extreme, is it not, Bedwyn?" Horace said, trying unsuccessfully to brush off the hand that held him by both coat lapels. "She was being coy rather than unwilling. We both know that . . . Oofff!"

Lord Rannulf had drawn back his free hand and driven his fist into Horace's stomach.

"What we both know," he said in a voice that suggested his teeth were half clenched, "is that to call you a worm, Effingham, would be to dishonor the insect kingdom."

"If you fancy her yourself . . . Oofff!" Horace sagged forward as another blow landed to his stomach, but Lord Rannulf's left hand held him firmly in place.

"You can be thankful," he said, "that we are on my grandmother's land with a garden party in progress. It would otherwise give me the greatest pleasure to send Miss Law away and give you the thrashing you deserve. I guarantee that you would end up unconscious and bloody on the ground here, your features permanently rearranged on your face."

He dropped his hand and Horace, looking visibly shaken, stood away from the tree and started to restore his coat and shirt to rights.

"You think so, Bedwyn?" he said with studied nonchalance. "Dear, dear, and all over a wench who is simply panting for the attentions of anything in breeches."

Lord Rannulf clearly kept in mind that the scandal of a

fight must not ruin Lady Beamish's garden party. Not one of his blows was aimed at Horace's face. All were directed at his body above the waist. Judith clung more tightly to the windowsill and watched, only half noticing that Horace, though he waved his fists ineffectually a few times, did not land even one blow. It was not a fight, though Horace was free to make it into one if he so chose. It was punishment. It ended only when Horace was on his hands and knees on the ground, retching horribly into the grass between his hands.

"You may wish," Lord Rannulf said, his voice only slightly breathless, "to excuse yourself from staying for dinner, Effingham. It would make *me* sick to see you at my grandmother's table. You will stay away from Miss Law in the future, do you hear me? Even when I am not in the vicinity to observe you pursuing her. I will find out, and next time I will thrash you to within an inch of your life . . . *if* you are fortunate. Get out of my sight now."

Horace stumbled to his feet, clutching his stomach with one hand. He was pale to the point of greenness. But he looked at Lord Rannulf before turning and stumbling away.

"I'll get even with you for this," he said. He switched his gaze to Judith. "I'll get you for this." His eyes blazed with hatred.

And then, finally, he was gone, and Judith realized that her knuckles were white from the death grip she had on the windowsill and that her stomach was fluttering and her knees shaking. Lord Rannulf was straightening his clothes and then turning to her. It was only at that moment that she realized she should have been using the time to put herself to rights, but she still could not release her hold on the sill.

"I am sorry you were a witness to that violence," he said. "I should have sent you back to the house first, but you would not wish to be seen like this and have everyone knowing or guessing what had happened."

He came inside the summerhouse when she did not reply.

"You were putting up a fierce fight," he said. "You have spirit."

He took her hand from the sill then, prising her fingers gently away from it, took it on one of his, and chafed it with the other. His knuckles were reddened, she could see.

"It will not happen again," he said. "I know men like Effingham. They are bullies with women who will not worship and adore them and cowards with men who call them to account. I do assure you he fears me and will heed my warning."

"I did not invite any of that," she said, her voice shaking quite beyond her control. "I did not come here with him."

"I know," he said. "I watched you go around the side of the house, and then I saw him go after you. It took me a few minutes to extricate myself from the company I was in and to disappear without notice. I beg your pardon that I came so late."

She could see her hair—on both sides of her face. Her dress, she saw when she looked downward, had been pulled forward in the struggle so that its modest neckline now revealed the tops of her breasts. She lifted her free hand to pull it up and discovered that her hand was shaking so badly that she could not even grasp the fabric with it.

"Come." He took that hand in his too and lowered her to sit on the bench. He sat beside her, still holding one of her hands, his arm pressing reassuringly against her shoulder. "Never mind your appearance for a few minutes. No one else will come here. Rest your head on my shoulder if you wish. Breathe in the peace of the surroundings."

She did as he suggested, and they sat like that for five, perhaps even ten minutes, not speaking, not moving. How could two apparently similar men be so different? she wondered. Lord Rannulf had issued an invitation to her after the stagecoach accident, a most improper one, and had proceeded to act upon it. What made him different from

Horace, then? But she had answered the question already. And she still believed her own answer, perhaps now more than ever. He would have ridden on alone that day if she had said no. He would have left her at the posting inn if she had said no to the move to the one by the market green. He would have allowed her to sleep on the settle in the private dining room there if she had said no. No, actually he would have given her the bed and slept on the settle himself. She *knew* he would have. Lord Rannulf Bedwyn was quite prepared to flirt with and even sleep with a willing woman, but he would never *ever* force himself upon an unwilling one.

And yet he would dishonor marriage vows by taking mistresses? It did not fit what her instinct told her of him. But she was—oh, *of course* she was—in love with him, and so it was natural that she would idealize him. She must not begin to believe that he was perfect.

She lifted her head and drew her hand from his and leaned away from the support of his shoulder. He did not turn his head, she noticed gratefully, while she adjusted the bodice of her dress and, in the absence of a brush, smoothed her hair back as best as she could, secured it to the back of her head with as many hairpins as she could find, and shoved the whole mess beneath her cap and then her bonnet.

"I am ready to go back now," she said, getting to her feet. "Thank you, Lord Rannulf. I do not know how I am ever going to repay you. I seem always to be in your debt." She held out her right hand to him. It was quite steady, she was proud to see.

He took it in both his own again as he stood. "If you wish," he said, "you may excuse yourself from dinner and the entertainment afterward by saying you are indisposed. I will see to it that you are sent home in my grandmother's carriage and will even send a servant to stay with you if you fear you will be molested there. Just say the word."

Ah, it was tempting. She did not know how she would be able to sit down to dinner and retain her composure and converse with whoever was seated to either side of her. She did not know how she would be able to bear seeing Lord Rannulf seated beside Julianne, as he surely would be, talking and laughing with her. But she was a lady, she reminded herself. And though she was only a lowly member of Uncle George's family, she *was* a member nonetheless.

"Thank you," she said, "but I will stay."

He grinned suddenly. "I like that way you have of lifting your chin as if inviting the world to bring on its worst," he said. "It is at such moments that the real Judith Law steps onto the stage, I believe."

He lifted her hand to his lips, and for a moment she could have wept over the brief loveliness of the intimacy. Instead she smiled.

"I suppose," she said, "there *is* a little of Claire Campbell in Judith Law."

She would not take his arm, though he offered it. The occasion had drawn them close, but there was no more to their amity than that. He had saved her and comforted her because he was a gentleman. She must not refine on his behavior more than that. She must not cling to him. She clasped the sides of her skirt and plodded up the slope toward the stables.

"I will go back the way I came," she said when they reached the top. "You must go a different way, Lord Rannulf."

"Yes," he agreed. And he strode off toward the front of the stables, leaving her feeling unreasonably bereft. Had she expected him to argue?

She hastened past the paddock and the kitchen gardens, shuddering at the realization that she could be returning under vastly different circumstances if he had not noticed Horace following her. It did not bear thinking of.

But *why* had he noticed? She had been convinced that she had slipped away without anyone's seeing her. Yet Horace had seen and Lord Rannulf had seen. Perhaps after all she was not quite as invisible as she had begun to believe.

CHAPTER XIII

RANNULF WAS SEATED BETWEEN LADY EFFING-
ham and Mrs. Hardinge at dinner, his grandmother
having been more discreet in her table arrange-
ments than Lady Effingham was at Harewood. It was a relief
to him, even though the one lady talked about nothing but
the travails of having six daughters to bring out when one
would like nothing better than to remain on one's own
country estate all year long, and the other tittered and commiserated with him over the fact that he had to keep two
matrons company when he would doubtless far prefer to be
seated by someone younger and prettier.

"Might I even say," she suggested, arching him a sidelong
glance, "a *particular* someone?"

Miss Effingham, farther down the table, on the same side
as Rannulf, talked animatedly with Roy-Hill and Law, her
table companions. A few times Lady Effingham leaned forward and wanted to know the cause of a particular burst of
laughter.

"Lord Rannulf and I and everyone else feel very isolated

from the merriment, dearest," she said on one of those occasions.

Judith Law sat on the other side of the table and conversed quietly with her uncle on one side and Richard Warren on the other. Looking at her now, one would never guess that she had endured such a terrifying experience just a few hours ago. She was far more the lady than her aunt, despite the latter's elegance and surface sophistication. Like the other ladies from Harewood, she had changed in a room allotted to her upstairs. She was wearing the same cream and gold silk dress she had worn at the Rum and Puncheon on the second evening. He remembered it for its simple elegance, which at the time he had thought deliberately understated, like the rest of her garments. It now had panels of a well-coordinated darker cream fabric set into the sides, a band of the same material lining the neckline so that far less of her bosom was visible, and an almost nonexistent waistline. She wore a fine, lace-trimmed cap, which, quite predictably, covered her hair.

How many of those seated about the table, he wondered, though they had been acquainted with her for a week, realized that she was below thirty years of age? Or knew the color of her hair—or of her eyes for that matter?

One thing had become distressingly clear to him in the course of the day. He could not—he *really* could not—marry the Effingham chit. He would be insane within a week of their marriage. It was not just that she was silly and emptyheaded. It was more that she was vain and totally selfabsorbed. And her only reason for trying to attach his interest was that he was the son of a duke and a wealthy man. She had made no attempt whatsoever to get to know him as a person. She probably never would. He might spend fifty years married to a woman who would never know—or care—that he had spent the last ten years denying the guilt he felt over not doing his duty and entering upon a career in the church as his father had planned for him and instead had lived a life of aimlessness and occasional dissipation. Or that very recently he had decided to give his life direction and meaning by becoming a knowledgeable, involved, responsible, perhaps even progressive and compassionate landlord.

The dinner table conversation did not demand much of his brain. He was able to do a great deal of thinking at the same time.

He could not marry Miss Effingham.

Neither could he disappoint his grandmother. Was he the only one who could see the rigidity of her bearing and the deep lines on either side of her mouth, both indications of suppressed pain? Or the brightness of her eyes that masked bone-weariness? And yet this garden party extending into a dinner and entertainment for the Harewood guests had been her idea. Rannulf glanced several times at her with fond exasperation.

And there was Judith Law. He wondered if she realized that two men had panted equally for her this afternoon. To his infinite shame he had wanted her quite as desperately as Effingham had. Pale and disheveled and bareheaded, she had looked achingly appealing, and her trembling bewilderment had invited him to comfort her in other ways than the one he had chosen.

He had sat beside her in the summerhouse, imposing rigid control on his own urges, concentrating every effort of his will on giving her the quiet, passive comfort he had sensed she needed and castigating himself at every moment with the knowledge that he was not far different from Effingham.

He had always seen women as creatures designed for his personal pleasure and satisfaction, to be taken and used and paid and forgotten. Except for his sisters, of course, and other ladies, and all women of virtue, and even those few of questionable virtue who had said no to him.

The trouble for women as voluptuously gorgeous as Judith Law must be that men would almost always look on them with lust and perhaps never see the person behind the goddess.

His grandmother interrupted his rambling thoughts by rising from her place and inviting the other ladies to join her in the drawing room. It was tempting after they left to settle in to the port and congenial male conversation for an indefinite length of time, especially since he suspected that Sir George Effingham and a number of the other gentlemen would be quite happy to spend the rest of the evening at the table. However, duty called and he had promised himself that he would play host and lift some of the social burden from his grandmother's shoulders. He stood up after a mere twenty minutes, and the gentlemen followed him to the drawing room.

He had no intention of having the same few young ladies as usual entertain the gathering with their pianoforte playing, Miss Effingham inevitably keeping the instrument all to herself once she had occupied the bench, with him as her page-turner.

"We will take tea," he announced, "after which we will all entertain one another. *All* of us who are—let me see—all of us who are below the age of thirty."

There was a chorus of protests, most of them male, but Rannulf held up one hand and laughed.

"Why should the ladies be the ones expected to display all the talents and accomplishments?" he asked. "We all, surely, can do something that will entertain a gathering of this nature."

"Oh, I say," Lord Braithwaite cried, "no one would wish to hear me sing, Bedwyn. When I joined the choir at school, the singing master told me that the kindest comparison he could think of for my voice was a cracked foghorn. And there was an end to my singing days."

There was general laughter.

"There will be no exceptions," Rannulf said. "There are more ways to entertain than by singing."

"What are *you* going to do, Bedwyn?" Peter Webster asked. "Or are you going to exempt yourself on the grounds that you are the master of ceremonies?"

"You may wait and see," Rannulf told him. "Shall we say ten minutes for tea before we have the tray removed?"

He went first. It seemed only fair. He had learned a few conjuring tricks over the years and had been fond of entertaining Morgan and her governess with them. He performed several of them now, foolish tricks like making a coin disappear from his hand and then reappear out of Miss Cooke's right ear or Branwell Law's waistcoat pocket, and making a handkerchief suddenly transform itself into a pocket watch or a lady's fan. He had, of course, the advantage of being able to plan well ahead of time. His audience exclaimed in wonder and delight and applauded with enthusiasm, just as if he were a master of the art.

A few of the guests had to be coaxed and one of them— Sir Dudley Roy-Hill—refused categorically to make an idiot of himself, as he phrased it, but it was amazing over the next hour to discover what varied and sometimes impressive talents had lain hidden through the first half of the house party. Predictably, the ladies entertained with music, most either vocal or on the pianoforte, one—Miss Hannah Warren—on the drawing room harp that Rannulf could never remember hearing played before. Law sang a woeful ballad in a pleasant tenor voice, and Warren sang a Baroque duet with one of his sisters. Tanguay recited Coleridge's "Kubla Khan" with such passionate sensibility that the ladies burst into appreciative applause almost before the last word was out of his mouth. Webster did a creditable imitation of a cossack dance he had once seen on his travels, bending his knees and crossing his arms and kicking his feet and leaping and singing his own accompaniment and succeeding in convulsing both himself and his audience in helpless laughter before collapsing in an inelegant heap on the carpet. Braithwaite, perhaps encouraged by the reception of his choirboy story, told three more tall tales about his school days, all at his own expense, embroidering the details with humorous exaggeration until the ladies and even a few gentlemen were mopping at their eyes while still laughing.

"Ah," Lady Effingham said with a sigh when Braithwaite sat down, "that is everyone. I could continue watching and listening for another hour. But what a splendid idea, Lord Rannulf. We have all been royally entertained. Indeed I—"

But Rannulf held up a staying hand.

"Not so, ma'am," he said. "Not everyone. There is still Miss Law."

"Oh, I really do not believe Judith will wish to make a spectacle of herself," her fond aunt said hastily.

Rannulf ignored her. "Miss Law?"

Her head had shot up, and she was gazing at him with wide, dismayed eyes. This whole scheme of his had been designed for just this moment. It really had infuriated him that she had been made into an invisible woman, little more than a servant, all because that puppy of a brother of hers had thought he could live beyond his means and be funded by the bottomless pit of his father's fortune. She should become visible, even if just once, while all the guests were still staying at Harewood, and in all her greatest magnificence.

It had been a gamble from the start, of course. But it had been planned before the distressing events of this afternoon. All evening he had toyed with the idea of leaving her invisible.

"But I have no particular accomplishment, my lord," she

protested. "I do not play the pianoforte or sing more than tolerably well."

"Perhaps," he said, looking directly into her eyes, "you have some verse or some passage from literature or the Bible memorized?"

"I—" She shook her head.

He would leave it at that, he decided. He had done the wrong thing. He had embarrassed and perhaps hurt her.

"Perhaps, Miss Law," his grandmother said kindly, "you would be willing to *read* a poem or a Bible passage if we were to have a book fetched from the library. I noticed in conversation with you this afternoon what a very pleasant speaking voice you have. But only if you wish. Rannulf will not bully you if you are too shy."

"Indeed I will not, Miss Law." He bowed to her.

"I will read, then, ma'am," she said, sounding unhappy.

"Will you fetch something from the library, Rannulf?" his grandmother asked. "Something by Milton or Pope, perhaps? Or the Bible?"

So, he had succeeded only in embarrassing her, Rannulf thought as he strode toward the door. But before he reached it a voice stopped him.

"No, please," Judith Law said, getting to her feet. "Fetching a book and finding a suitable passage will only cause a long delay. I will . . . I will act out a little scene I have memorized."

"Judith!" her aunt said, sounding truly horrified. "I hardly think a gathering of this nature would appreciate being subjected to schoolgirl theatricals."

"Oh, yes, *yes*, Judith!" Mrs. Law exclaimed almost at the same moment, her heavily ringed hands clinking as she clasped them together, and her bracelets jangling. "That would be *wonderful*, my love."

Judith walked slowly and with obvious reluctance into the open area before the hearth that had been cleared for the nonmusical items of entertainment. She stood there for a few moments, the bent knuckle of one hand against her lips, her gaze on the floor. Rannulf, his heart beating in his chest like a large hammer, was aware of a few shufflings of discomfort from the guests. Several of them, he guessed, were looking full at her for the first time. She looked like someone's plain and overweight governess.

And then she looked up, timidity and embarrassment still in her face.

"I'll do Lady Macbeth's speech from the last part of the play," she said, her glance darting to Rannulf and away again. "The sleepwalking scene that you are all probably familiar with, the scene in which she tries constantly to wash the blood of the murdered King Duncan from her hands."

"Judith!" Lady Effingham said. "I really must ask you to sit down. You are embarrassing yourself and everyone else."

"Shhh!" Mrs. Law said. "Do be quiet, Louisa, and let us watch."

From the look of astonishment on Lady Effingham's face, Rannulf guessed that it was the first time in a long while that her mother had spoken thus to her.

But he had little attention to spare for anyone except Judith Law, who was looking quite, quite inadequate to the role she had just taken on. What if he had made a dreadful mistake? What if she was hopelessly overawed by the occasion and the company?

She turned her back on them. And watching her, he began gradually to relax. He could see her, even before she turned around again, work her way into another woman's body and mind and spirit. He had watched it before. And then she dipped her head forward, removed her cap and dropped it to the floor, drew out the pins from her hair, and dropped them too.

Her aunt gasped and Rannulf was half aware of a few of the other men in the room sitting up straighter.

And then she turned.

She was not Judith Law in any of her guises. Her loose dress had become a nightgown. Her hair had been messed up while she tossed and turned in bed trying to sleep and then sleeping restlessly. Her eyes were open, but they were the strange, vacant eyes of a sleepwalker. Yet her face was so filled with horror and revulsion that it bore no resemblance whatsoever to Judith Law's face.

Her shaking hands lifted slowly before her face, the fingers spread, looking more like serpents than fingers. She tried washing her hands, desperately rubbing them over each other, and then held them up again and gazed intently at them.

In the play there were two other characters—a doctor and a gentlewoman—to witness and describe her appearance and actions. Their words were not necessary tonight. She was unmistakably a woman in torment, a woman with both feet in hell, even before she spoke. And then she did.

" 'Yet here's a spot,' " she said in a low, dead voice that nevertheless carried clearly to the farthest corner of a room that seemed to hold its breath.

She touched the spot on her palm with the middle finger of her other hand, picked at it, scratched at it, gouged it, her actions becoming more and more frenzied.

" 'Out, *damned* spot! out, I say!' "

Rannulf was caught firmly in her spell. He stood close to the door, neither seeing nor hearing anything but her—Lady Macbeth, the sad, horrifying, guilty ruin of an ambitious woman who had thought herself strong enough to incite murder and even commit murder. A young, beautiful, misguided, and ultimately tragic woman whom one pitied to the depths of one's soul because it was too late for her to go back and apply newly acquired wisdom to past decisions. As perhaps it is *not* too late for those of us who are fortunate enough to have committed sins less irreversible, he thought.

And then finally she heard a knocking at the castle door and became panicked over the possibility of being caught literally red-handed over a murder committed long ago.

" 'Come, come, come, come, give me your hand,' " she told an invisible Macbeth, her hand a claw grasping his invisible arm. " 'What's done cannot be undone. To bed, to bed, to bed.' "

She turned then and even though she moved only a few steps in the confining space, it seemed that she hurried a great distance, panic and horror in every step. She ended, as she had begun, with her back to the audience.

There was a moment's complete hush . . . and then loud, genuine, prolonged applause. Rannulf felt himself sag with relief and realized in some astonishment that he was very close to tears.

Roy-Hill whistled.

Lord Braithwaite sprang to his feet. "Bravo!" he cried. "Oh, I say, bravo, Miss Law."

"Wherever did you learn to act like *that*, Jude?" her brother asked. "I had no idea."

But she was down on one knee on the floor, her back still toward the room, quickly pinning up her hair and stuffing it beneath her cap again. Rannulf crossed the room and offered her his hand.

"Thank you, Miss Law," he said. "That was a magnificent performance and a very fitting conclusion to our entertainment. I would not wish to be the one to try following that."

She was Judith Law again, her face aflame with embarrassment. She set her hand on his, but her head was dipped low as she hurried back to her chair beside Mrs. Law's without looking at anyone.

Mrs. Law, Rannulf noticed, was drying reddened eyes with her handkerchief. She grasped one of her granddaughter's hands and squeezed it tightly though she said nothing.

Rannulf moved away.

"But my dear Miss Law," his grandmother asked, "why at your tender age do you keep all that glorious, beautiful hair covered?"

Judith's eyes widened in surprise, Rannulf saw when he glanced back at her. He noticed in the same moment that the attention of *all* the gentlemen was riveted on her.

"Beautiful, ma'am?" she said. "Oh, I think not. The devil's own color, my papa always called it. My mama always described it as carroty."

The devil's own color! Her own father had said that?

"Well," his grandmother said, smiling, "I would compare it to a gold-tinged fiery sunset, Miss Law. But I am embarrassing you. Rannulf—"

"We have stayed rather late, Lady Beamish," Lady Effingham said firmly, getting to her feet, "my niece having decided to prolong the entertainment and make herself the center of attention. You have been most kind to her, for which condescension I thank you on her behalf. But it is time we took our leave."

The carriages had to be brought around and all the extra baggage necessitated by a change of clothes after the garden party loaded up with the valets and personal maids who had come from Harewood. But within half an hour the guests had all been seen on their way and Rannulf was able to escort his grandmother to her room. She was almost gray with fatigue, he saw, though she would not admit as much.

"That was all very pleasant," she said. "Miss Effingham looks particularly pretty in pink."

Had she been wearing pink? He had not noticed.

"But she has very little countenance," she added. "Of course, she has had only her mother's example to follow, and Lady Effingham has an unfortunate tendency to vulgarity. The girl was flirting at dinner and afterward with every gentleman within range of her, just because *you* were not beside her, I believe, Rannulf. It is regrettable behavior in a young lady I still hope will be your bride. You are pleased with her?"

"She is only eighteen, Grandmama," he said. "She is just a child. She will grow up, given time."

"I suppose so." She sighed as they reached the top of the stairs. "Lord Braithwaite has a comic genius. He can create hilarity out of the most ordinary circumstances and is not afraid to mock himself. But Miss Law! She has the sort of talent that makes one feel humble and honored in its presence."

"Yes," he said.

"Poor lady." She sighed again. "She is beautiful beyond belief and does not even know it. Her father must be a puritanical, joyless sort of clergyman. How could he possibly say such dreadful things of that glorious hair of hers?"

"I daresay, Grandmama," he said, "he has seen some of his male parishioners getting an eyeful of her and has concluded there must be something sinful about her appearance."

"Foolish man! It is a dreadful fate to be poor and female, is it not?" she said. "And to be offered the charity of someone like Louisa Effingham? But at least Miss Law has her grandmother. Gertrude is fast coming to dote on her."

What's done cannot be undone. That line she had spoken as Lady Macbeth kept running through Rannulf's head after he had seen his grandmother to her dressing room and had retired to his own room.

How very true. He could not go back and ride on alone for help after coming across the overturned stagecoach. He could not restore her virginity. He could not erase that day and a half or those two nights when they had talked and laughed and loved and he had been prepared to pursue her wherever she went, to the ends of the earth if necessary.

He could not go back and change any of that.

He had fallen somewhat in love with Claire Campbell,

he admitted to himself at last. Not just in lust. There had been more to his feelings than that. He was not in love with Judith Law, but there was something . . . It was not pity. He would have been actively repelled by her if he could do no more than pity her. It was not lust even though he definitely and ignominiously wanted to bed her. It was not . . . He simply did not know what it was or was not. He had never been much of a one for deep emotions. He had colored his world with faint, bored cynicism for as far back as he could remember.

How could he define his feelings for Judith Law when he had no frame of reference by which to measure them? But he thought suddenly of his quiet, morose, stern, always correct, always dutiful elder brother, Aidan, who had taken a commission in the cavalry on his eighteenth birthday, just as it had been planned all his life that he would. Aidan, who had recently married without telling anyone in his family, even Bewcastle, and had then just as abruptly sold out in order to live with the wife he had married only to keep a solemn vow made to her dying brother, a fellow officer in the south of France. Rannulf had accompanied Aidan home from London to his wife's property on the first stage of his own journey to Grandmaison and had met Lady Aidan for the first time—and the two young children she had fostered.

Rannulf had watched, transfixed, outside the house as the two children had come racing eagerly to meet Aidan, the little girl addressing him as Papa, and he had scooped them up and given them his fond attention just as if they were the most dearly loved products of his own loins. And then he had looked at his wife as she came more slowly after the children and enfolded her in his free arm and kissed her.

Yes, Rannulf thought, *that* was his frame of reference. Just that moment when Aidan had set his arm about Eve and kissed her and looked young and human and exuberant and vulnerable and invincible all at the same time.

There was only one word to describe what he had witnessed.

Love.

He strode impulsively into his dressing room and found his cloak in the wardrobe there. He dug around in the inside pocket until he found what he was searching for. He drew it out, unwrapped the brown paper from about it, and gazed down at the cheap little snuffbox with the ugly pig's head carved on its lid. He chuckled softly, closed his hand about the box, and then felt almost overwhelmingly sad.

CHAPTER XIV

JUDITH RETURNED HOME IN THE LAST CARRIAGE with her grandmother, who had been slower than everyone else getting ready to leave and had twice asked Judith if she would be so good as to run back up to the room in which she had changed to make sure she had not forgotten anything. It was very late by the time they arrived at Harewood. All the guests had retired to their rooms for the night.

Aunt Effingham was waiting in the hall.

"Judith," she said in awful tones, "you will assist Mother to her room and then attend me in the drawing room."

"I am coming too, Louisa," her mother said.

"Mother." Lady Effingham bent a stern gaze on the old lady though she attempted to soften her tone. "It is late and you are tired. Judith will take you up and ring for Tillie if she is not already there waiting for you. She will help you undress and get into bed and will bring you a cup of tea and a draft to help you sleep."

"I do not want my bed or a cup of tea," her mother said firmly. "I will come to the drawing room. Judith, my love, may I trouble you for your arm again? I daresay I sat too long in the rose arbor this afternoon. The wind has made all my joints stiff."

Judith had been expecting the scold that was obviously coming. She could hardly believe herself that she had had the temerity to *act* before an audience—Papa would surely have sentenced her to a full week in her room on bread and water if she had ever done such a thing at home. She had even taken her hair down. She had acted and she had *re-acted* to the audience, which had given her its total, undivided attention even though she had not been consciously aware of it. She had *been* Lady Macbeth. The audience had liked her and applauded and praised her. What she had done could not have been so very wrong. Everyone else had entertained the company, not all of them with music. She was a lady. She had been as much a guest of Lady Beamish as anyone else.

Lady Beamish had called her hair glorious and beautiful. How else had she described it? Judith frowned in thought as she climbed the stairs slowly with her grandmother while Aunt Effingham came behind.

I would compare it to a gold-tinged, fiery sunset.

Lady Beamish, though she had perfect manners, was not given to frivolous, flattering compliments, Judith suspected. Was it possible, then, that her hair could be seen that way? *A gold-tinged, fiery sunset . . .*

"These earrings pinch me almost as badly as those others," her grandmother said, pulling them off as they entered the drawing room. "Though I *have* been wearing them all evening, of course. Now where shall I put them so that they will not be lost?"

"Give them to me, Grandmama," Judith said, taking them from her and putting them safely inside her reticule. "I will put them away in your jewelry box when we go upstairs."

Horace was in the room, she saw at a glance, sitting on

the arm of a chair, a glass of some dark liquor in his hand, swinging one leg nonchalantly and looking at her with insolent malice. Julianne was there too, dabbing at her eyes with a lace-edged handkerchief.

"Are you feeling better, Horace?" Grandmama asked. "It is a great shame you were indisposed and had to miss dinner and the entertainment in the drawing room afterward."

"Indisposed, Grandmama?" Horace laughed. "It was the indisposition of boredom. I know from past experience how insipid evenings at Lady Beamish's can be."

Judith, her stomach knotted with revulsion, tried not to look at him or hear his voice.

"It was a horrid evening," Julianne said. "I was seated half a table away from Lord Rannulf during dinner, yet he did not protest the seating arrangement even though he was in his own grandmother's house. And I *thought* Lady Beamish was promoting a match between us. I daresay he persuaded her to keep me away from him. He does not like me. He is not going to offer for me. He did not even applaud my performance on the pianoforte any more than he did Lady Margaret's even though I played *much* better than she did. And he did not call for an encore. I have never been so humiliated in my life. Or so wretched. Mama, I hate him, I *hate* him."

"There, there, dearest," her mother said soothingly. But it was clear her mind was on other matters than her daughter's distress. Her bosom appeared to swell to twice its size as she turned on her niece. "Now, *Miss Judith Law*, you will kindly explain yourself."

"Explain myself, Aunt?" Judith asked as she seated her grandmother in her usual chair by the fire. She would not be cowed, she decided. She had done no wrong.

"*What*," her aunt asked, "was the meaning of that vulgar spectacle you made of yourself this evening? I was so ashamed I scarcely knew how to keep my countenance. Your poor uncle was speechless all the way home in the carriage and shut himself into the library the moment we returned."

"Oh, dear me, Cousin," Horace said, sounding mildly amused, "whatever have you been up to?"

But before Judith could form any reply to her aunt, her grandmother spoke up.

"Vulgar, Louisa?" she said. "*Vulgar?* Judith bowed to persuasion as all the other young people did to entertain the company. She acted out a scene, and I have never witnessed finer acting. I was amazed and delighted by it. I was moved to tears by it. It was by far the best performance of the evening, and clearly everyone else—*almost* everyone else— agreed with me."

Judith looked at her grandmother in astonishment. She had never heard her speak in half so impassioned a way. She was actually angry, Judith could see. Her eyes were flashing and there were two spots of color in her cheeks.

"Mother," Aunt Louisa said, "I think it would be best if you stayed out of this. A *lady* does not take her hair down in public and draw everyone's attention her way with such . . . theatrics."

"Oh, tut, tut," Horace said, lifting his glass in Judith's direction. "Did you do that, Cousin?"

"A lady *does* take her hair down at night," the old lady said. "When she goes sleepwalking she does not take the time to pin it up first. Judith was not herself tonight, Louisa. She was *Lady Macbeth*. It is what acting is all about, immersing oneself in the character, bringing that character alive for an audience. But I would not expect you to understand."

Judith was amazed that her grandmother did.

"I am sorry if I displeased you, Aunt Louisa," she said. "But I cannot apologize for offering some entertainment to the company when both Lord Rannulf Bedwyn and Lady Beamish urged me to do so. It would have been impolite to be coy. I chose to do what I thought I could do well. I do not understand why you feel such an aversion to acting. You are like Papa in that. No one else this evening appeared to be scandalized. Quite the contrary, in fact."

Her grandmother had taken one of her hands in both her own and was chafing it as if it were cold.

"I suppose, Judith, my love," she said, "your papa has never told you, has he? Neither he nor Louisa could quite forgive your grandfather for what he had done to them, and they have both run from it all their lives. Though neither of them would even *have* life if he had not done it."

Judith looked down at her with a frown of incomprehension.

"Mother!" Aunt Louisa said sharply. "Enough. Julianne—"

"Your grandfather met me in the green room at the Covent Garden Theater in London," the old lady explained. "He said he had fallen in love with me even before that, when he saw me acting onstage, and I always believed him even though all the gentlemen used to say that or something similar—and there were many of them. Your grandfather married me three months later and we had thirty-two happy years together."

"Grandmama?" Julianne was openly aghast. "You were an *actress*? Oh, this is insupportable. Mama, what if Lady Beamish discovers the truth? What if *Lord Rannulf* does? I'll die of shame. I swear I will."

"Well, well," Horace muttered softly.

Her grandmother patted Judith's hand. "I knew when I saw you as a child," she said, "that you were the one most like me, my love. That hair! It so horrified your poor papa and your mama too, suggesting as it did a flamboyance unfitted to a child from the rectory—and suggesting too that you might have inherited more than just that from your scandalous grandmama. When I watched you tonight, it was like looking at myself almost fifty years ago. Except that you are more beautiful than I ever was, and a better actress too."

"Oh, Grandmama," Judith said, squeezing the plump, ringed hand beneath her own. Suddenly so much of her own life made sense to her. *So much*.

"Well, I will not stand for it, miss," Aunt Louisa said. "You have shamed me and my young, impressionable daughter, before houseguests I selected from the very cream of society, before Lady Beamish and the son of a *duke* who is courting Julianne. I would remind you that you were brought here by the kindness and charity of your uncle. You will remain here for the next week, when I will need you to tend to your grandmother. Tomorrow I will write to my brother and inform him that I am severely displeased with you. I daresay he will not be surprised. I will offer to take one of your sisters instead of you. This time I will ask specifically for Hilary, who is young enough to learn her place. *You* will be going home in disgrace."

"Tut, tut, Cousin," Horace said. "After only a week."

Judith should have been feeling relieved, even euphoric. She was going *home*? But Papa would know all about the acting at Lady Beamish's. And Hilary was going to have to come to take her place.

"If Judith goes, I will go too," her grandmother said. "I will sell some of my jewels, Judith. They are worth a fortune, you know. We will buy a little cottage somewhere and be cozy together. We will take Tillie with us."

Judith squeezed her hand again. "Come, Grandmama," she said. "It is late and you are upset and tired. I'll help you up to your room. We will talk in the morning."

"Mama?" Julianne wailed. "You are not paying any attention to *me*! You do not care about me either, I daresay. What am I going to do about Lord Rannulf? I *must* have him. He almost ignored me this evening and now he may find out that I am the granddaughter of an *actress*."

"My dearest Julianne," her mother said, "there is more

than one way to catch a husband. You will be Lady Rannulf Bedwyn before the summer is out. Trust me."

Horace smiled nastily at Judith as she passed his chair, her grandmother leaning heavily on her arm.

"Remember what I said, *Cousin*," he said softly.

D URING THE FOLLOWING WEEK RANNULF SPENT HIS mornings, sometimes the afternoons too, with his grandmother's steward, learning some of the intricacies of the workings of an estate. He was surprised to discover that he enjoyed poring over account books and other business papers quite as much as he did riding about the home farm and tenant farms, seeing for himself and talking with a number of the farmers and laborers. He was careful about one thing, though.

"I am not offending you, Grandmama?" he asked her at breakfast one morning, taking her thin hand with its almost translucent blue-veined skin in his own and holding it gently. "I am not giving the impression that I am taking over as if I were already master here? I wish, you know, that you would live another ten years or twenty or longer."

"I am not sure I have the energy left with which to oblige you," she told him. "But you are brightening my final days, Rannulf. I did not expect this, I must admit, though I *did* expect that you would learn quickly and do a creditable job here after my time. You are a Bedwyn after all, and Bedwyns have always taken their duty seriously no matter what else one might say about them."

He raised her hand to his lips and kissed it.

"Now, if I could just see you well married," she said, "I would be entirely content. But *is* Julianne Effingham right for you? I so hoped she would be. She is a neighbor, her grandmother is one of my dearest friends, and she is young and pretty. What do *you* think, Rannulf?"

He had been hoping she would change her mind about pressing the match on him. At the same time he knew she would be bitterly disappointed if he did not marry soon.

"I think I had better keep on going over to Harewood each day," he said. "The house party will be over in another week. There is the ball still to come. I promised you I would seriously consider the girl, Grandmama, and I will."

But the trouble was, he discovered as the week progressed, he could not like Miss Effingham any better on closer acquaintance. She still pouted whenever he neglected to dance attendance upon her every hour of every day and still tried to punish him by flirting with all the other gentlemen. She still prattled on about herself and her various accomplishments and conquests whenever he was in her company and tittered at his flatteries. She bored him silly. And of course her mother made every attempt in her power to throw them together. They always sat beside each other if he was at Harewood for dinner, as he was most evenings. They always rode together in a carriage whenever he joined any of the numerous excursions to places of interest. He was always called upon to turn the pages of her music.

Sometimes he thought that perhaps he continued to go to Harewood less for his grandmother's sake than in the hope of having a private word with Judith Law. He feared that he might after all have made a dreadful mistake in maneuvering her into acting at Grandmaison. She had never been very visible at Harewood, but now she was even less so. She was never at the dinner table. Neither was the old lady. She never joined any of the excursions or outdoor activities. On the few occasions she appeared in the drawing room of an evening, she behaved more than ever like a hired companion to Mrs. Law and retired early with her.

One thing quickly became clear to Rannulf. When Tanguay invited her to partner him in a card game, Lady Effingham informed him that her mother was indisposed and needed Miss Law to help her to her room and wait on her there. When Roy-Hill invited her to join the group about the pianoforte, Miss Effingham informed him that her cousin had no interest in anything musical. When they all decided to play charades one evening and Braithwaite chose her first to be on his team, Lady Effingham told him that Miss Law had a headache and was to be excused from remaining in the drawing room any longer.

The gentlemen of the house party had clearly awoken to Judith Law's existence. And Lady Effingham was punishing her for that very fact. Yet he, Rannulf realized, was the one responsible for the unhappy situation. He had done the wrong thing. He had made her life worse, not better. And so he made no attempt to speak to her himself when her aunt or cousin might have noticed. He did not want to make matters even worse for her. He bided his time.

On the day before the ball everyone, including Lady Effingham, went into the town again since most of them needed to make some purchases for the occasion. Rannulf had declined their invitation to join them. His grandmother decided to take the opportunity to call upon Mrs. Law while she could expect to find a quiet house. Rannulf escorted her there even though she assured him that it was not necessary.

"I'll not intrude upon your visit, Grandmama," he told her. "I'll go for a walk after paying my respects to Mrs. Law."

He was hoping to be able to invite Judith Law to join him on that walk, but she was not present in the drawing room.

"She is in her room writing letters to her sisters, I believe," Mrs. Law told him when he asked after her granddaughter's health. "Though why it is necessary when she will see them very soon, I do not know."

"Miss Law's sisters are coming to Harewood?" Lady Beamish asked. "That will be very pleasant for her."

Mrs. Law sighed. "One of them will," she said. "Judith is to go home."

"I am sorry to hear that," Lady Beamish said. "You will miss her, Gertrude."

"I will," Mrs. Law admitted. "Dreadfully."

"She is an amiable young lady," Lady Beamish said. "And when she acted for us a few evenings ago, I realized too how extraordinarily lovely she is. And how very talented. She gets that from you, of course."

Rannulf excused himself and went back outside. It was a cool, cloudy day, but it was not actually raining. He made his way to the hill at the back of the house. He did not expect to see Judith Law there, but he could hardly just go up to her room and knock on the door.

She was down at the lake again, not swimming this time, but sitting in front of the willow tree, her hands clasped about her updrawn knees, staring into the water. Her head was bare, her hair braided in neat coils at the back of her head, her own bonnet—the one he had bought for her—on the grass beside her. There was no sign of a cap. She was wearing a long-sleeved pelisse over her dress.

He descended the hill slowly, not even trying to mask his progress. He did not want to startle or frighten her. She heard him when he was halfway down and looked back over her shoulder for a moment before resuming her former posture.

"It would seem," he said, "that I owe you an apology. Though my guess is that a simple apology is quite inadequate." He stood behind her and propped one shoulder against the tree trunk.

"You owe me nothing," she told him.

"You are being sent home," he said.

"That is hardly a punishment, is it?" she asked.

"And one of your sisters is to take your place here." Even in the shade of the tree and with only dull clouds overhead the hair over the crown of her head gleamed gold and red.

"Yes." She bowed her head forward until her forehead

rested on her knees, a posture he was beginning to recognize as characteristic of her.

"I ought not to have meddled," he said—an understatement if ever he had spoken one. "I knew that the most talented person in the room had not yet performed, and I could not resist enticing you to do so."

"You have nothing to feel sorry about," she said. "I am glad it happened. I had been sitting there dreaming of doing just what I *did* do when you and Lady Beamish coaxed me into contributing something of my own to the entertainment. It was the first free thing I had done since arriving here. It made me realize how very abject I had been. I have been happier during the past few days, though perhaps that has not been apparent to you the few times you have seen me. Grandmama and I have decided, you see, that it is best for me to behave as I am expected to behave when we must put in an appearance before the company, but we do that as little as we can. When we are together we talk more than ever and laugh and have fun. She . . ." She lifted her head and chuckled quietly. "She likes to brush my hair for half an hour or more at a time. She says it is good for her hands . . . and her heart. I think I help take her mind off all her imaginary illnesses. She is more animated, more cheerful than when I arrived."

He had a vivid memory of kneeling behind her on the bed at the Rum and Puncheon, brushing her hair before making love to her.

"She will miss you when you leave," he said.

"She wants to sell some of her jewels and buy a cottage somewhere so that we can live together," she said. "Though I do not know if it will really happen. Either way you must not feel guilty for having been the unwitting cause of all that is happening. I am *glad* it happened. It has brought me very much closer to my grandmother and to an understanding of my own life."

She did not offer an explanation, but he remembered suddenly something that had been said just a short while ago.

"My grandmother says that you get your talent from Mrs. Law," he said.

"Oh, so Lady Beamish *does* know?" she said. "And you too? My aunt and Julianne are so very worried that you may both discover the truth."

"Your grandmother was an actress?" he asked, pushing away from the tree and seating himself beside her on the grass.

"In London." She was smiling, he could see. "My grandfather fell in love with her when she was onstage, went to meet her in the green room of the Covent Garden Theater, and married her three months later, to the lasting horror of his family. She was a draper's daughter. She had been very successful as an actress and much sought-after by all the fashionable gentlemen. She must have been very beautiful, I think, though she had red hair like me."

It was hard to picture Mrs. Law young and beautiful and red-haired and much sought-after by the bucks and beaux of her time. But not impossible. Even now when she was old and plump and gray-haired, she possessed a certain charm, and her jewel-bedecked figure suggested a flamboyance of personality consistent with her past as an actress. She might well have been a fine-looking woman in her time.

"She kept her figure until my grandfather died," Judith said. "Then she started eating to console her grief, she told me. And then it became a habit. It is sad, is it not, that she had such a happy marriage and yet both her children—my aunt and my father—are ashamed of both her and her past? *I* am not ashamed of her."

He had possessed himself of one of her hands before he realized it.

"Why should you be," he asked her, "when she is largely

responsible for your beauty and your talent and the richness of your character?"

And yet, he thought even as he spoke, the Bedwyns would be in the forefront of those who shunned a woman of such blemished ancestry. He was surprised that his grandmother, knowing the truth about her friend, would consider Julianne Effingham an eligible bride for him even if the lineage on her father's side was impeccable. Bewcastle might have vastly different ideas on the matter.

"Tell me something," she said, her voice suddenly breathless and urgent. "And please tell me the truth. Oh, *please* be truthful. *Am* I beautiful?"

He understood suddenly—why she had been taught to see her red hair with shame and embarrassment, why she had been encouraged to think of herself as ugly. Every time he looked at her, her father, the rector, must be reminded of the mother who could yet embarrass him before his flock and his peers if the truth were ever known. His second daughter must always have seemed a heavy cross to bear.

With his free hand Rannulf cupped her chin and turned her face to his. Her cheeks were flushed with embarrassment.

"I have known many women, Judith," he said. "I have admired all the most lovely of them, worshipped a few of the unattainable from afar, pursued others with some diligence. It is what wealthy, idle, bored gentlemen of my type tend to do. I can truly say that I have never ever seen any woman whose beauty comes even close to matching yours."

Was it true, that seemingly extravagant claim? Was she really that beautiful? Or was it partly that the lovely package contained Judith Law? It did not matter. There was much truth, after all, in that old cliché that beauty is more than skin deep.

"You are beautiful," he told her, and he dipped his head and kissed her softly on the lips.

"Am I?" Her green eyes were swimming with tears when he lifted his head. "Not vulgar? I do not look vulgar?"

"How could beauty possibly be vulgar?" he asked her.

"When men look at me," she said, "and really see me, they leer."

"It is because feminine beauty is desirable to men," he said. "And where there is no restraint and no gallantry—when a man is not also a gentleman—then there is leering. The beauty is no less beautiful because some men behave badly in its presence."

"You did not leer," she said.

He felt deeply ashamed. He had set eyes on her and had wanted her and gone after her. His motive had been pure lust.

"Did I not?" he said.

She shook her head. "There was something else in your eyes," he said, "despite your words and your actions. Some . . . humor, perhaps? I do not know the exact word. You did not make me shudder. You made me . . . joyful."

God help him.

"You made me feel beautiful," she said. She smiled slowly at him. "For the first time in my life. Thank you."

He swallowed hard and awkwardly. He deserved to be horsewhipped for what he had done to her. But she was thanking him.

"We had better get back to the house," she said, looking up as he withdrew his hand from beneath her chin. "I can feel rain."

They got up and brushed themselves off, and she drew her bonnet carefully over her hair and tied the ribbons in a large bow to one side of her chin. She looked vividly pretty without a cap beneath it.

"I'll go over the hill and you can go around it to the front again," she said.

But he had had an idea, though he had neither thought it through nor wished to do so.

"Let's go together," he said. "There is no one here to see us."

He offered his arm, which she took after a moment's hesitation, and they climbed the hill together, an occasional spot of rain splashing down on them.

"I suppose," she said, "you are very bored here in the country. Yet you have not joined in many of the activities of the house party this week."

"I am learning about farming and estate management," he said, "and enjoying myself enormously."

She turned her head to look at him. "*Enjoying* yourself?" She laughed.

He chuckled too. "I have been taken by surprise," he said. "Grandmaison will be mine in time, yet I have never been interested in its running. Now I am. Picture me in years to come trudging about my land with a shaggy dog at my heel, an ill-fitting coat on my back, and nothing but crops and drainage and livestock to enliven my conversation."

"It is hard to imagine." She laughed again. "Tell me about it. What have you learned? What have you seen? Do you plan to make any changes when the property is yours?"

At first he thought the questions merely polite, but it soon became clear to him that she was genuinely interested. And so he talked all the way back to the house on topics that would have had him yawning hugely just a week or two ago.

The two elderly ladies were still in the drawing room where Rannulf had left them. Judith would have withdrawn her arm from his before they entered the house and disappeared to her own room, but he would allow neither.

"It is just my grandmother and yours," he said. "No one else has returned from town yet."

He kept her arm through his when they entered the room, and both ladies looked up.

"I found Miss Law while I was outside walking," he said, "and we have been enjoying each other's company for the last hour."

His grandmother's eyes sharpened instantly, he noticed.

"Miss Law," she said, "that is a very fetching bonnet. Why have I not seen it before? The fresh air has added a becoming flush of color to your cheeks. Come and sit beside me and tell me where you learned to act so well."

Rannulf sat down too after pulling on the bell rope at Mrs. Law's request so that she could ask for a fresh pot of tea to be brought up.

CHAPTER XV

JUDITH WAS NOT AT ALL SURE SHE WOULD ATTEND the Harewood ball even though her grandmother told her that she simply must put in an appearance, if only to keep her company.

"Though I daresay all the young gentlemen will vie with each other to dance with you," she said. "I have noticed how their attitude to you has changed during the week, my love, and so it ought. You are as much my grandchild as Julianne or Branwell."

It was a tempting prospect, Judith had to admit—to attend a ball and to have dancing partners. She had always enjoyed the village assemblies at home immensely. She had never lacked for partners. At the time she had assumed they were being kind to dance with her, but a new possibility was beginning to present itself to her mind.

I have never ever seen any woman whose beauty comes even close to matching yours.

She was tempted to go to the ball, but she was dreadfully afraid that Lord Rannulf would choose that climactic event of the house party in which to have his betrothal to Julianne announced. She would not be able to bear being there to hear it, Judith thought, or to see the look of triumph on Julianne's face and Aunt Effingham's. She would not be able to bear to see the look of mocking resignation on his—she was sure that was how he *would* look.

She had almost decided not to attend until she met Branwell on the stairs when she was going up after an early breakfast and he was coming down.

"Good morning, Jude." He set one hand on her shoulder and kissed her cheek. "Up early as usual, are you? You had better get some beauty rest this afternoon, then. All the fellows want to dance with you tonight and have been asking *me* to persuade you, as if I am the one who has been forbidding you to participate in anything for the past two weeks. I suppose it is Aunt Louisa," he said, darting a glance about him and lowering his voice. "But really, you know, it is demeaning to have my own sister treated as if she were some kind of servant just because Papa is a clergyman and Uncle George is some sort of nabob."

"I am not really interested in dancing, Bran," she lied.

"Poppycock!" he said. "All you girls have always loved the assemblies. Listen, Jude, as soon as I have paid off all these pesky and impudent tradesmen, I am going to settle to some career and make my fortune that way. And then you will be able to go back home and you and my other sisters can find yourselves respectable husbands and all will be well."

Judith had not told her brother that she *was* going back home—in disgrace—or that Hilary was going to have to come to Harewood in her place.

"But how are you going to pay your debts, Bran?" she asked unwillingly. She had been trying all week not to think about them. She had even for one ignominious moment thought of asking Grandmama . . .

His cheerful expression faltered for a moment, but then he was smiling and apparently carefree again. "Something will turn up," he said. "I have every confidence. You must not worry your head about it. Think of the ball instead. Promise me you will come, Jude?"

"Oh, very well," she said impulsively before continuing on her way upstairs. "I'll come."

"Splendid!" he called after her.

There was one more free thing she would do before returning home, then, she decided. She would go to the ball. And she would go as herself, not as the poor relation who was hidden from public view as effectively as any nun. She would dance with any gentleman who cared to ask. If she was not asked, then she would sit with her grandmother and enjoy the evening anyway. If Julianne's betrothal was announced . . . Her boldness faltered for a moment as her hand rested on the door handle of her room. If Julianne's betrothal to Lord Rannulf was announced, then she would lift her chin and smile and clothe herself in all the ladylike dignity she could muster.

Why was it, she wondered as she let herself into her room, that a brief kiss on the lips yesterday could have stirred her emotions just as powerfully as full sexual contact had done a few weeks ago at the inn by the market green? Perhaps because then it had been only sexual congress, whereas yesterday it had been . . . what? Not love. Tenderness, then? He had called her beautiful and then kissed her. But not with desire, though perhaps there had been something of that in it too, for both of them. There had been more than desire. There had been . . . yes, it must have been tenderness.

Perhaps after all, she thought, once she was back home and had blocked her mind to the image of him married to

Julianne, she would be able to recover her stolen dream and live on it through the years ahead.

"My first thought when I heard of the ball at Harewood," Lady Beamish said to her grandson, "was that it would be the perfect setting for the announcement of your betrothal to Julianne Effingham. Has the thought crossed your mind, Rannulf?"

"Yes, it has," he said quite truthfully.

"And?" She was seated opposite him in the downstairs sitting room, looking tinier and more birdlike than ever, though her back was ramrod straight, he could see, not supported by the back of her chair.

"Is it still your dearest wish?" he asked her.

She looked consideringly at him before answering. "My dearest wish?" she repeated. "No, Rannulf, that would be to see you happy. Even if the single state is what makes you happiest."

She had set him free . . . and laid on him the burden of love.

"No," he said. "I do not believe I will remain single, Grandmama. As soon as one becomes involved with the land, one understands and appreciates the eternal cycle of birth and death and renewal and reproduction. Just as you need the assurance that this land will pass to me and my descendants, so I need the assurance that it will pass to a son of mine after my passing—or perhaps to a daughter or a grandchild. I will certainly marry."

He had not even formulated the thoughts clearly for himself until this moment, but he knew they were the truth.

"Julianne Effingham?" she asked him.

He gazed back at her, but even love should not be made to encroach upon the very essence of who he was.

"Not Miss Effingham," he said gently. "I am sorry,

Grandmama. Not only do I feel no affection for her, but I also feel a definite aversion."

"I am relieved to know it," she surprised him by saying. "It was a foolish notion of mine, born of a selfish desire to see you married soon, before it is too late."

"Grandmama—"

She held up a hand.

"Do you feel an affection for Miss Law?" she asked him.

He stared at her and then cleared his throat.

"Miss Law?"

"She is many things her cousin is not," she said.

"She is poor," he said curtly, getting to his feet and walking toward the French windows, which were closed this morning against the continuation of yesterday's chilly, cloudy weather. "That ne'er-do-well of a brother of hers is likely to bring total ruin on the family soon, if my guess is correct. The father is a gentleman with a former actress for a mother, daughter of a draper. The mother is probably a lady, though equally probably she was no one of fortune or social prominence before her marriage to the Reverend Law."

"Ah," his grandmother said, "you are ashamed of her."

"Ashamed?" He glared out at the fountain, his brows drawn together in a harsh frown. "I would have to have some personal feelings for her before I could be ashamed."

"And you do not?" she asked him.

It had been his impetuous plan yesterday to make her aware of Judith Law and a possible connection between him and her. But she had said nothing during their journey home or for the rest of the day. He looked back over his shoulder at her now.

"Grandmama," he said, "I walked in the formal gardens here with her two weeks ago at your request. I encouraged her to entertain us here a week ago when almost all your other guests had done so except her. I met her outdoors at

Harewood yesterday and walked and conversed with her for an hour. Why would I have personal feelings for her?"

"It would be strange if you did not," she said. "She is an extraordinarily beautiful woman once her disguise has been penetrated, and I know you well enough to understand that you admire beautiful women. But she is more than beautiful. She has a mind. So do you when you care to use it, as you have done since coming here this time. Besides all of which, Rannulf, there was a certain look on your face when you returned from your walk yesterday."

"A certain *look?*" He frowned at her. "One of foolish infatuation, do you mean? I feel no such thing."

And yet he wanted her to argue the point, to encourage him, to persuade him that the connection would be eligible.

"No," she said. "Had it been merely a silly male look, I would have disregarded it, though I might have felt it my duty to remind you that she is a lady and the niece of Sir George Effingham and the granddaughter of my dearest friend."

He felt horribly guilty then . . . again!

"Bewcastle would never countenance such a match," he said.

"And yet," she reminded him, "Aidan has just married a coal miner's daughter, and Bewcastle not only received her but even arranged for her presentation to the queen and gave a ball for her at Bedwyn House."

"Bewcastle was presented with a fait accompli in Aidan's case," he said. "He has made the best of what he doubtless considers a disaster."

"You will give me your arm while I go up to my rooms in a moment," she said. "But I will say this first, Rannulf. If you allow pride and shame to mask more tender feelings and thus lose a chance for a marriage that would provide all your needs, including those of the heart, then it would be churlish of you to lay the blame at Bewcastle's door."

214 or Mary Balogh

"I am *not* ashamed of her," he said. "Quite the contrary. I am—" He clamped his mouth shut and hurried toward her as she got to her feet.

"I believe the correct expression may be *in love*," she said, setting her hand lightly on his sleeve. "But no self-respecting grandson of mine could admit to that foolish sentiment, could he?"

It was not true, he thought. He was, to his shame, still in lust with Judith Law. He liked her. He was drawn to her, found himself thinking about her almost constantly while he was conscious and dreaming of her when he was asleep. He found that he could talk to her as he had never been able to talk to any other woman, with the possible exception of Freyja. But even with his sister there was an attitude of bored cynicism to be maintained. He could not imagine talking with enthusiasm about farming and estate management with Freyja. With Judith Law he could relax and be himself, though he had the feeling that it was only in the past two weeks that he had begun to discover who that self was.

His grandmother had, to all intents and purposes, given her blessing to his courtship of Judith Law. Bewcastle . . . Well, Bewcastle was not his keeper.

He wondered if Judith intended to appear at the ball tonight. Of course, she had refused him once and that only two weeks ago. But perhaps he could persuade her to change her mind. He must be very careful, of course, not openly to humiliate Miss Effingham. Silly and vain as the chit was, she did not deserve that.

J UDITH WORKED DILIGENTLY WITH HER NEEDLE ALL MORNing, guessing that she might be kept busy all afternoon with preparations for the ball. She was not mistaken. Her aunt kept her running almost every minute, bearing messages and orders to the housekeeper or the butler, neither of whom was ever in the place they were supposed to be. She was given the monumental task of arranging the flowers that had been cut for the ballroom and setting them up in just the right places and in pleasing combination with potted plants. It was a job she enjoyed, but once she was in the ballroom she found that servants were forever consulting her with all their problems, however minor.

Then she was sent into the village to buy a length of ribbon for Julianne's hair, the ribbon she had bought in town the day before having been declared quite wrong in both width and color now that it had been paid for and brought home. It was a longish walk there and back. Judith would normally have welcomed the chance to be out in the fresh air, even if it was a cloudy day. But she had hoped for a chance to wash her hair and rest before it was time to dress for the evening. She hurried through the errand so that there would still be some little time for herself.

The door to Julianne's dressing room was slightly ajar when she returned. Judith lifted her hand to knock but stopped herself when she heard Horace's laugh from within. He had not openly bothered her during the past week, though he never lost the opportunity to say something nasty or sarcastic for her ears only. She avoided him whenever she could. She would wait, she decided. Or she would take the ribbon to Aunt Effingham's room and pretend she had forgotten that she was to take it directly to Julianne's.

"I simply must have him, that is all," Julianne was saying on a familiar theme, her voice petulant. "I will be mortified beyond words if he does not offer for me before everyone leaves Harewood. Everyone *knows* that he has been courting me. Everyone *knows* I have discouraged the advances of all my other admirers—even Lord Braithwaite's—because Lord Rannulf is about to offer for me."

Judith turned to leave.

"And you will have him too, you silly goose," Horace said. "Did you not hear what your mama just said? He must be *made* to offer for you. All you have to do is make sure you are found in a compromising situation with him. He will do the decent thing. I know men like Bedwyn. Being a *gentleman* means more to them than life itself."

By then Judith could not stop herself from listening.

"Horace is right, dearest," Aunt Effingham said. "And it is only proper that he should marry you after deliberately toying with your sensibilities."

"But how am I to *do* that?" Julianne asked.

"Lord," Horace said, sounding bored, "have you no imagination, Julianne? You have to tell him you are faint or warm or cold or something and lure him to a private place. Make it the library. No one ever goes there except Father, and even he will not be there tonight but will feel it his duty to remain in the ballroom. Close the door behind the two of you. Get close to him. Get him to put his arms about you and kiss you. Then I'll walk in on you there—Father and I will. Your betrothal will be announced before the ball is over."

"How are you going to persuade Papa to go to the library with you?" Julianne asked.

"If I cannot devise a way of dragging him to his favorite place in the world I'll eat my hat," Horace said. "The new beaver one."

"Mama?"

"It will do very well," Aunt Effingham said briskly. "You know, my dearest, that once you are Lady Rannulf Bedwyn you may devote yourself entirely to making Lord Rannulf realize that it was all for the best. And meanwhile you will have the fortune and the position."

"And Grandmaison after Lady Beamish dies," Julianne said, "and a house in London, I daresay. I will persuade him to buy one there. And I will be sister-in-law to the Duke of Bewcastle and will be on visiting terms at Bedwyn House. Indeed, perhaps we will live there while in town instead of buying our own house. I daresay we will spend summers in the country at Lindsey Hall. I will—"

Judith lifted her hand and knocked firmly before pushing the door open and handing the ribbon to Julianne.

"I hope this will suit you," she said. "It was the only shade of pink in the shop, but it is a lovely shade, I think, deeper and more suited to your coloring than the other."

Julianne unwound the ribbon, looked carelessly at it, and then tossed it onto the dressing table behind her.

"I believe I like the other better," she said. "You took awfully long, Judith. I think you might have hurried when the errand was for your own cousin."

"Perhaps, Cousin," Horace said, "you might wear whichever ribbon Julianne decides *not* to wear. Ah, but how tactless of me. Pink does not suit your coloring, does it? Does *anything?*"

"Judith will doubtless be more comfortable remaining in her own room this evening," Aunt Effingham said. "Let us compare these ribbons more carefully, dearest. You would not want to—"

Judith left the room and hurried to her own.

Was it true, then, that he was unlikely to propose marriage to Julianne, left to his own devices? And could Julianne and Aunt Effingham be so desperate to net him as a husband that they were prepared to use trickery, to trap him into an apparently compromising situation? Horace was right, she thought. Lord Rannulf Bedwyn *was* a gentleman and *would* offer marriage if he believed he had compromised a lady. She had had personal proof of that herself.

Her heart was pounding by the time she had closed her door behind her. That he would marry Julianne of his own

accord had been a hard enough prospect to bear. But that he
should be tricked into it . . .

J UDITH HAD HAD A QUIET DINNER WITH HER GRAND-
mother in the latter's private sitting room, both of them
being disinclined to dine with the houseguests. Then they
went their separate ways to dress for the ball.

Judith was more nervous than she cared to admit. She
had worn her cream and gold silk to a dozen assemblies at
home. It had never been in the first stare of fashion or fussily
adorned. And of course Mama and Papa had always been
strict about modesty, especially with her. But at least it had
always been an elegant garment that fit her well. She had always liked it, until Aunt Louisa's maid had let panels into
the sides of it and lined the neckline.

Judith had removed all the additions during the morning.
She had restored the dress to its former self except that it
had a new peach-colored sash of wide silk ribbon that her
grandmother had given her a few days ago because she knew
she would never use it herself and it suited Judith's coloring
so well. There was enough ribbon that the ends of it fluttered almost to the floor after it had been tied neatly at the
front of the high waist.

There was no maid to help her dress. But she had rarely
had the services of the one maid at the rectory, there being
Mama and her other three sisters all with their demands on
the girl's limited time. Judith was accustomed to dressing her
own hair, even for elegant occasions. She had had time to
both wash and dry it. It had the healthy sheen of clean hair
as she brushed it all back from her face, plaited it into two
braids, and coiled and looped them into a pleasing design at
the back of her head. She used a hand mirror to check it
while she sat in front of her dressing table mirror.

The style looked elegant, she thought. Carefully, so as

not to ruin the whole painstakingly constructed coiffure, she teased two long strands free at the sides and curled the brush about them. There was enough curl in her hair that they waved in soft tendrils over her ears. She teased out two more curls at her temples.

She did not put on a cap, not even the pretty lacy one she had always worn to assemblies or other evening gatherings.

I have never ever seen any woman whose beauty comes even close to matching yours.

She gazed at her image, standing up so that she could see herself full length. She tried to see herself through the eyes of a man who could speak those words in all honesty. She had trusted his honesty. He had meant what he said.

She was beautiful.

I am beautiful.

For the first time she could look at herself and believe that there must be some truth in the preposterous-seeming claim.

I am beautiful.

She whisked herself off to her grandmother's room before she could lose her courage. She knocked lightly on the dressing room door and let herself in.

Her grandmother was still seated at her dressing table, Tillie behind her, fixing three tall plumes into her elaborately piled gray hair. She was wearing an evening gown of a deep ruby red, but it was completely outshone by all the heavy jewelry that sparkled and glittered at her neck and bosom, on both plump wrists, on every finger of both hands except the thumbs, and at her ears. There was even a large, ornate brooch pinned to her gown beneath one shoulder. On the dressing table was a jeweled lorgnette.

Two circles of rouge had been painted high on her cheeks.

But Judith was not given more than a moment or two in which to digest her grandmother's appearance. The old lady looked at her in the mirror, swiveled about on her stool with unusual agility while Tillie stifled an exclamation and scurried around with her, clutching the plumes, and clasped her hands together with a distinct metallic clink.

"*Judith!*" she exclaimed. "Oh, my dearest love, you look . . . Tillie, what is the word I am looking for?"

"Beautiful?" Tillie suggested. "You do too, miss."

"Not nearly adequate enough," her mistress said, waving one hand dismissively. "Turn, turn, Judith, and let me have a good look at you."

Judith laughed, held her arms out to the sides in a deliberate pose of elegance, and pirouetted slowly.

"Will I do?" she asked.

"Tillie," her grandmother said, "my pearls. The long strand and the short, if you please. I never wear them, Judith, because at my age I need some glitter to distract the eye from my wrinkles and other sad attributes." She laughed heartily. "But pearls will enhance your loveliness without competing with it."

The pearls were not in the jewelry box but in a drawer. Tillie, having secured the plumes to her own satisfaction, produced them in a moment and held them up for inspection.

"They will look good on you, miss," she said.

Judith's grandmother got to her feet and gestured to the stool.

"Sit down, my love," she said, "and Tillie will arrange the longer strand in your hair without disturbing it. I do like your braids in loops like that. When I was your age, I would have had rolls and curls and ringlets bouncing all over my head and not looked half as good. But I never was famous for my good taste. Your grandfather used to tease me about it and insist that he loved me just as I was."

Ten minutes later Judith was wearing the shorter string of pearls about her neck and found that it was the perfect length for the modest scoop of her neckline. The longer strand was not very visible from the front, but Tillie showed her what the back now looked like, and when she moved her head Judith could feel the heavier swing of the pearls and hear them clinking against one another.

She smiled and then laughed.

Yes, she was. She really was. She was *beautiful*.

It did not matter that she would be the very least fashionable lady at the ball, that she would be outshone by every other guest. It simply did not matter. She was beautiful, and for the first time in her life she rejoiced in her own appearance.

Her grandmother, laughing too, picked up her lorgnette in one hand, and inclined her head, setting her plumes to nodding vigorously.

"Magnificent," she said. "That is the word I was searching for. You look magnificent, my love." She tapped Judith on the arm with the lorgnette. "Let us go down and capture the hearts of every man at the ball. I'll take the old ones and you can have the young ones."

Even Tillie laughed with them this time.

CHAPTER XVI

RANNULF HAD NEVER ATTENDED A BALL FROM personal choice. He had, nevertheless, attended his fair share, polite society having decreed that its members be forced to enjoy themselves on occasion by tripping the light fantastic. The ball at Harewood, he saw as soon as he and his grandmother had passed along the receiving line and entered the ballroom, looked as if it would be a tolerable squeeze for a country affair. A great deal of effort had been put into decorating the room pleasingly with great banks of flowers and potted plants.

He looked about and was amused and unsurprised to discover that the houseguests, all splendidly clad in their London finery, were easily distinguishable from the lowlier guests from the neighborhood in their simpler evening wear. Miss Effingham, whom he had just passed in the receiving line, was resplendent in delicate lace over pink satin, the waist fashionably high, the neckline fashionably low, her blond hair piled in elaborate curls threaded with pink ribbon twined with jewels. And he had, of course, been maneuvered into soliciting her hand for the opening set of country dances.

And then he spotted Judith Law, who was in the process of looking away from him and bending to say something to her grandmother. He inhaled slowly. She looked much as she had looked the first time he saw her in that gown—voluptuous and elegant, the simplicity of the design only emphasizing the feminine curves and the vibrant beauty of the woman wearing it. Her hair was smoothed back over her head, but she had done something intricate with the back of it, and it was prettily and delicately entwined with pearls.

He felt a surge of something that was not lust, though it certainly included desire. He had, he realized, been waiting all day for this moment and fearing that perhaps she would not put in an appearance at all.

Mrs. Law raised one glittering arm and waved her jeweled lorgnette.

"Ah, there is Gertrude," his grandmother said. "I shall go and sit with her and watch the revelries, Rannulf."

He escorted her across the room, noticing as he did so that Judith was not isolated as she had always been in the drawing room and at most other activities during the past two weeks. Roy-Hill and Braithwaite were standing close to her.

Greetings were exchanged and his grandmother seated herself beside Mrs. Law.

"You are looking remarkably lovely this evening, Miss Law," she said. "I hope you mean to dance?"

"Thank you, ma'am." Judith flushed and smiled, something he had seen her do too rarely in the past two weeks. "Yes, Lord Braithwaite has been kind enough to offer to lead me into the first set, and Sir Dudley has asked for the second."

"I would imagine, then," Lady Beamish said, "that any

gentleman wishing to dance with you this evening had better speak up soon."

"Oh." Judith laughed.

"Miss Law." Rannulf bowed. "Will you do me the honor of saving the third set for me?"

She looked fully at him then, her lovely green eyes wide, her red hair gleaming in the light from the chandeliers overhead. It was, perhaps, the moment at which he realized how very reluctant he had been over the past week or so to call a spade simply a spade. It was not lust or tenderness or affection or liking or companionship he felt for Judith Law, though all of them were included in that sentiment he had been unwilling to name.

He loved her.

"Thank you, Lord Rannulf." She made him a slight curtsy. "I would like that."

A heightened buzz of anticipation around them diverted his attention then. Lady Effingham had stepped into the ballroom and was approaching the orchestra dais. Sir George came in behind her, his daughter on his arm. It struck Rannulf that they had waited for his somewhat late arrival before beginning the ball. He stepped forward to claim his partner, who was blushing and smiling and looking very pretty indeed.

"It is said, Lord Rannulf," she said as they took their places opposite each other at the head of the lines of ladies and gentlemen, "that the rules of good *ton* do not apply to a country ball and that a gentleman may ask a lady to dance with him as many times as he wishes. But I am still afraid it may be construed as less than good manners to dance more than twice with the same partner. What do *you* think?"

"Perhaps," he suggested, "it is even better manners to choose a different partner for every set, especially when the gathering is large enough—as this one is tonight, for example—to provide more than enough choices."

He had, of course, given the wrong answer—quite deliberately.

"But sometimes," she said, tittering, "good manners can seem tiresome, can they not?"

"Exceedingly," he agreed. Braithwaite had stepped up beside him and Judith beside Miss Effingham.

"Yet even good manners, as decreed by the *ton*," Miss Effingham said, "allow for a gentleman to dance with the same partner twice without incurring censure. In all the balls I attended during the Season, I was forever being asked to dance twice with the same gentleman, and no one ever accused me of being ill-mannered when I did so, though a number of other gentlemen complained when I had no free sets to offer them."

"Can one blame them?" he asked.

She tittered again. "The fourth set is to be a waltz," she said. "I was not allowed to dance it until halfway through the Season when Lady Jersey finally gave me the nod of approval. I believe she did so because so many gentlemen had complained to her about not being able to dance with me. I suppose many people here tonight will not even know the steps, but I pleaded with Mama to include one. I suppose *you* know the steps, Lord Rannulf?"

"I have shuffled through a few waltzes without treading on my partner's toes," he admitted.

She laughed merrily. "Oh," she said, "I am sure you did not come even close to doing so but are merely funning me. I am sure you will not tread on *my* toes. Oh!" She colored prettily and set one hand over her mouth. "You *were* asking me, were you not? I shall die of embarrassment if you were not."

He pursed his lips, amused despite himself. "I cannot have you expiring in the middle of your own ball, Miss Effingham," he said. "We will show all your guests how superior your waltzing skills are."

"Oh, not just mine," she said modestly. "Yours too, Lord Rannulf. Do you waltz, Judith? But I daresay Uncle never allowed you to learn the steps, did he? It is said to be a scandalous dance, but I think it is perfectly divine. My dancing master said it must have been created just for me, dainty and light on my feet as I am. He was very foolish. I do believe he was half in love with me."

The orchestra began playing the opening bars of the country dance and prevented Judith from replying. But of course, the questions had been rhetorical anyway. Rannulf concentrated his attention on his partner, as good manners dictated, though all his awareness was on his love, moving gracefully at her cousin's side.

J UDITH WAS BREATHLESS BY THE TIME LORD BRAITHWAITE returned her to her grandmother. It had been a vigorous set and she had enjoyed it thoroughly despite the fact that she had had to endure being so close to Lord Rannulf and Julianne the whole time. But that fact had had its compensations. She had understood from the way he replied to all of Julianne's efforts to draw him into flatteries and flirtation that he really was not behaving like a man who was about to declare himself. More important, perhaps, she had overheard Julianne maneuver him into agreeing to waltz with her during the fourth set. It was the time when she, Judith, would watch most carefully, though how she would save Lord Rannulf from the proposed trap she did not know. She could not simply warn him. How foolish she would sound!

"Perhaps, Miss Law," Lord Braithwaite said, "your father *did* allow you to learn the steps of the waltz? And perhaps you will do me the honor of dancing it with me?"

He had gazed at her with open admiration thoughout the dance. It had been very flattering. He was a handsome and amiable young man.

"My father had no chance either to forbid or to approve waltzing lessons," she explained. "The dance has not even reached our neighborhood yet. I shall enjoy watching you dance it with someone else, my lord."

Her grandmother, she noticed, plumes nodding in concert with Lady Beamish's as they talked and commented upon the scene before them, was easing her earrings off her earlobes and wincing as she did so. Poor Grandmama— would she never learn that there *were* no earrings she would find comfortable?

"Grandmama." Judith leaned solicitously over her. "Shall I take them upstairs for you and put them away?"

"Oh, *will* you, my love?" her grandmother asked. "But you will miss your dance with Sir Dudley."

"No, I will not," Judith said. "It will take me only a minute."

"I would be very grateful, then," her grandmother said, putting the jewels into her hand. "Will you bring me the star-shaped ones instead, if it is not too much trouble?"

"Of course it is not."

Judith hurried from the ballroom and up the stairs to her grandmother's room, taking a candle from a wall sconce in with her. She found the large jewelry box, returned the precious earrings to the velvet bag from which most of this evening's finery had come, though there were still plenty of pieces left in it, and hunted through the section she herself had allotted for earrings. But she could not see the star-shaped ones. She rummaged around among the necklaces and bracelets with no success. She was about to choose another pair of earrings instead when she remembered that the star-shaped earrings were the ones she had taken from her grandmother's hand after the evening at Grandmaison. They must still be in the reticule she had carried that evening. She closed the box and put it away as quickly as she could, hurried to her own room, and was relieved to find the earrings just where she had thought they would be. She hastened from the room and almost collided with a chambermaid who was passing by. They both squeaked in alarm and then Judith laughed, apologized for being in such a rush, and ran back downstairs.

The sets were already forming, she could see through the ballroom doors, but as luck would have it she ran up against Horace as she hurried through them. She stopped abruptly, feeling both flushed and breathless.

"Going somewhere, Cousin, in such a hurry?" he asked her, blocking her way when she would have stepped around him. "Or should I say *coming* from somewhere in such a hurry? Some assignation, perhaps?"

"I have been to fetch some different earrings for Grandmama," she said. "Excuse me, please, Horace. I have promised this set to Sir Dudley."

To her relief he stepped aside and gestured her in with an exaggeratedly courtly sweep of one arm. She hurried to complete her errand and turned with an apology to her partner.

It was lovely to be dancing again so soon. Sir Dudley Roy-Hill engaged her in conversation as much as the figures of the dance allowed, and she met the openly admiring glances of several other gentlemen. At home she would have been somewhat disturbed, imagining that she must have done something forward to invite such leering attention. But *leering* was her father's word. Tonight, with her newfound belief in her own beauty, she could see that the looks were merely admiring. She found herself smiling more and more.

Yet all the time she was aware that the next set was to be danced with Lord Rannulf Bedwyn. He had had almost no choice, she knew. Lady Beamish's words about any gentleman having to ask her early if he wished to dance with her had quite unwittingly forced him into being gallant. But she did not really care. On two occasions—both out at the lake—he had come to spend time with her when he might easily have avoided the encounters. Let him dance with her now, then. And she did not care what Aunt Effingham had to say about it in the morning, though doubtless there would be plenty. Soon enough she would be going back home where at least she would not be expected to behave like a servant.

She could hardly wait for the next set to begin. If only it could last all night. Or forever.

I F ONLY IT COULD LAST ALL NIGHT OR EVEN FOREVER, HE thought. She danced the slow, stately steps of the old-fashioned minuet with elegance and grace. She did not look directly into his eyes except once or twice, very briefly, but there was a look on her face that spelled awareness and—surely—happiness.

His attention was focused fully on her while all about them the varied colors of gowns and coats slowly swirled in time with the music and light from the candles overhead gleamed on hair and jewels and the perfumes of colognes and hundreds of flowers mingled in the warm air.

How differently he saw her now from that time at the Rum and Puncheon. Then, though they had talked and laughed together and he had enjoyed her company, in all essentials she had been little more to him than an extraordinarily desirable body to be bedded. Now she was . . .

Well, now she was Judith.

"Are you enjoying the ball?" he asked when their joined hands brought them close to each other for a moment.

"Exceedingly well," she said, and he knew she meant it.

So was he. Enjoying a ball, which he had rarely done before, enjoying the slow minuet, which he had *never* done before.

There was something between them, he thought, like a

strong current of energy, binding them and at the same time isolating them from everyone else in the room. Surely he could not be imagining it. Surely she must feel it too. It was not just sexual desire.

"*Do* you waltz?" he asked her.

"No." She shook her head.

I will teach you one day, he thought.

She lifted her eyes to his and smiled as if she had heard the thought.

He was, he knew, the envy of every man in the room. He wondered if she realized just what a stir she was causing this evening or just what sour looks she was drawing from her aunt.

"Perhaps," he said, "if you have not promised every remaining set, you will reserve one more for me. The last?"

She looked at him again and for a few moments held his gaze.

"Thank you," she said.

That was almost the sum total of their conversation all the time they danced. But there was that feeling of being bound, of sharing hearts and emotions, of words being unnecessary.

Perhaps, he thought, by the end of the evening she would be tired of dancing and they would sit together somewhere where they were properly in view of the other guests but where they could have some private conversation. Perhaps he could ascertain if her feelings toward him and his offer had undergone any change during the past two weeks.

Perhaps he would even ask her again tonight if she would marry him, though he rather believed he would prefer to ask her tomorrow, outdoors, where they could be entirely private together. He would ask her uncle for permission, take her down to that little lake, and then declare himself.

There was something about her manner—he was sure he

was not imagining it—that encouraged him to hope that she would have him after all.

He amused himself with such thoughts and plans as he watched her dancing, that quiet glow of happiness—surely it was that—on her face.

And then the music drew to its inevitable end.

"Thank you," he said, offering his arm to escort her back to her grandmother's side.

She turned her head to smile at him.

"You dance very elegantly together," his grandmother said as they approached.

Lady Effingham was behind her mother's chair, Rannulf saw.

"Judith, dear," she said, her voice cloyingly sweet, "I hope you have thanked Lord Rannulf properly for his kind conde-scension in leading you out. Mother seems very tired. I am sure you will not mind helping her to her room and remain-ing there with her."

But Mrs. Law swelled up rather like a hot-air balloon, glittering and jangling as she did so. "I most certainly am not tired, Louisa," she said. "The very idea of my missing the rest of the ball and leaving my dear Sarah to sit here alone! Be-sides, Judith has promised the set after the waltz to Mr. Tan-guay, and it would be ill-mannered of her to disappear now."

Lady Effingham raised her eyebrows but could hardly say anything more in the presence of Rannulf and his grand-mother.

The waltz was next and he had been effectively forced into dancing it with Miss Effingham. He found her amusing, at least, he thought as he bowed and turned away to find her. Not that she would be flattered by the nature of his amuse-ment, he supposed. And he had the last set to look forward to. And tomorrow morning. Though he must not be over-confident about that. If Judith Law did not wish to marry him, she would not do so merely because of who he was or because of his money.

She would have to love him before she would accept him, he suspected.

Did she love him?

Insecurity, doubt, and anxiety were entirely new emotions to a man who had cultivated ennui and cynicism for most of his adult years.

J ULIANNE WAS LOOKING MORE FLUSHED AND BRIGHTER-eyed than she had all evening, Judith could see. But that look could be accounted for entirely by the fact that she was dancing with Lord Rannulf again. It was a reaction Judith herself could sympathize with.

More ominous was the fact that Horace was approaching Uncle George and drawing him a little apart from the group of older gentlemen with whom he had been conversing. Judith had refused an invitation to go with Mr. Warren, who did not waltz either, in search of a drink of lemonade, though she had smiled her thanks. She needed to stay in the ballroom. She watched, her heart pounding. Surely that nasty plot being hatched in Julianne's dressing room this afternoon could not have been a serious one. Whoever would want a marriage with a husband acquired in that way?

But Julianne desperately wanted to be Lady Rannulf Bedwyn, she knew.

And Aunt Effingham was just as desperate to marry her daughter to him.

Horace was probably reveling, too, in the prospect of getting some revenge for what Lord Rannulf had done to him outside the summerhouse at Grandmaison a week ago.

Judith was only partly aware of the shocking, thrilling nature of the waltz, in which ladies and gentleman danced as couples, touching each other with both hands, twirling about the dance floor in each other's arms. Under any other circumstances she might have been envious indeed of those who knew the steps and had handsome partners with whom to perform them.

She was only partly aware too of the nodding plumes of her grandmother and Lady Beamish, who sat in front of her enjoying the show and occasionally commenting upon it.

Branwell could waltz, she noticed in some surprise. He was waltzing with the elder Miss Warren, laughing with her, as if he did not have a care in the world.

But even the minor distraction of watching her brother proved almost fatal to Judith's vigilance. When she found Lord Rannulf and Julianne again with her eyes, they had stopped dancing, and he had his head bent to hear what she was saying. She was rubbing one wrist, talking fast, and looking somewhat distressed. She pointed in the direction of the door.

Horace meanwhile was still talking with his father.

Judith waited no longer. Perhaps it was all meaningless though it looked very like the beginnings of the plot she had overheard. Perhaps after she had left Julianne's dressing room they had changed the place. But she would have to take a chance on that. She slipped out of the ballroom as hastily and surreptitiously as she could, raced down the stairs, saw with relief that there was no servant to see her and wonder at her destination, and slipped into the library, which was so much her uncle's private domain that she had never been inside the room before.

It was quite dark, but fortunately she could see enough to find her way to the windows and throw back the heavy curtains. It was a moonlit, starlit night, the clouds of the day having moved off some time during the evening. There was enough light in the room that she could see what she needed to see—two walls of bookcases crowded with books from floor to ceiling. She hurried toward one that was behind both the door and a heavy sofa.

The next minute seemed endless. What if she had come to the wrong place? What if Julianne had dragged Lord Rannulf off somewhere else to be discovered kissing her or otherwise compromising her?

And then the door opened again.

"It *must* be in here." It was Julianne's voice, high-pitched and anxious. "Papa gave it to me for my come-out ball and he would be dreadfully cross with me if I were to lose it. But even if he were just to see that I am not wearing it he would be hurt and upset."

Judith could not imagine Uncle George being either cross or hurt or upset.

"If you know you left it in here," Lord Rannulf said, sounding perfectly calm, even amused, "then we will recover it and will be waltzing again within two minutes."

He strode into the room, without a candle, and Judith saw Julianne shut the door with a backward kick of one foot.

"Oh, dear," she said, "that door always swings shut." She went hurrying after Lord Rannulf and then exclaimed with triumph. "Oh, *here* it is! I *knew* I must have left it here when I came down for a little rest earlier, but of course I was terribly afraid that I was wrong and really had lost it. Lord Rannulf, how can I ever thank you for sacrificing part of our dance and slipping down with me before Papa noticed?"

"By putting it on your wrist," he said, "so that I can take you back to the ballroom before you are missed."

"Oh, this clasp," she said. "There is not enough light. Will you help me?"

He bent over her while she held up her wrist, and she slipped her free arm about his neck and leaned into him.

"I really am most terribly grateful," she said.

The door opened again as if on cue and Horace held up

his candle, muttered an oath, and tried to block his father's view of the room.

"Perhaps it was not such a good idea after all to come down here to get away from the noise," he said loudly and heartily. "Come, Father—"

But Uncle George, as he was meant to do, had smelled the proverbial rat. He moved Horace aside with one arm and came striding into the room just as Julianne shrieked, jumped back, and struggled with the bosom of her gown, which had somehow slipped down and come very close to revealing all.

It was time to begin the counterplan.

"Ah, *here* it is," Judith said, stepping forward with a large book spread open across both hands. "And here are Uncle George and Horace to help me adjudicate the winner. And that is Julianne, I am afraid, Lord Rannulf. It *was* a raven that Noah sent out first from the ark to see if the floodwaters had receded. *Then* he sent a dove. The dove was sent out three times, in fact, until it did not return and Noah knew that there must be dry land again. But still, it was the raven first."

The way all four of them turned and gaped at her would have done justice to any farce. She shut the book with a flourish.

"It was a foolish thing to argue about," she said, "and to bring the three of us downstairs in the middle of a ball to hunt for the answer. But Julianne was right, you see, Lord Rannulf."

"Well," he said with an audible sigh, "I suppose I must concede defeat, then. It is as well, though. It would have been ungentlemanly to crow over a lady if I had been right. Though I am still of the opinion that in *my* Bible it is a dove."

"What the devil—" Horace began.

"Julianne," Judith said, cutting him off as she put down

the book, "are you *still* struggling with the catch of that bracelet? Can you not do it, Lord Rannulf? Let me try."

"Hmph," Uncle George said. "I came down for a moment's peace and find that my library has been invaded. Does your mother know you are wearing her bracelet, Julianne? I daresay she does, though. A word of advice, Bedwyn. Never argue with a lady. She is always right."

If she could have painted thunder in visible form, Judith thought, it would surely bear a remarkable resemblance to Horace's face. She locked glances with him for a moment and saw murder in his eyes.

"I'll bear it in mind, sir," Lord Rannulf said. "That is definitely the last time I argue about ravens and doves."

Julianne, tight-lipped and white-faced, pulled her arm away from Judith, fumbled with the catch of the bracelet, failed to do it up, snatched it off, and slammed it back onto the table where she had found it.

"Horace," she said, "take me to Mama. I am feeling faint."

"I suppose I had better return to my duty," Uncle George said with a sigh.

A moment later all three of them had left, taking the candle with them and leaving the door ajar.

"What book *was* that?" Lord Rannulf asked after a few moments of silence.

"I have no idea," Judith said. "It was too dark in the room for me to distinguish one title from another."

"Are you *quite* sure," he asked, "that the first bird out of the ark was a raven? I'll wager it was a dove."

"You will lose," she said. "I am a clergyman's daughter."

"I suppose," he said, "it was a plot to have Sir George Effingham believe I had seriously compromised his daughter."

"Yes."

"Careless of me," he said. "It almost worked. I thought the chit silly and tedious but essentially harmless."

"But Horace is not," she said. "Neither is Aunt Louisa."

"Judith." He was coming toward her. "You have saved me from a miserable life sentence. How am I ever to thank you?"

"We are even," she said. "You saved me last week in the summerhouse. I saved you this week."

"Yes." His hands were on her shoulders, warm, solid, familiar. "Judith."

When had he started calling her by her given name? Had he done it before tonight? She fixed her gaze on his elaborately tied neckcloth, but only for a moment. His face got in the way, and then his mouth was on hers.

It was a deep kiss even though his hands did not move from her shoulders and hers did no more than grip the lapels of his evening coat. He teased her lips apart with his own and she opened her mouth to his. His tongue came into her mouth, filling her, possessing her, and she sucked on it, drawing it deeper.

She felt like someone who had been starved and then presented with a feast. She could not get enough of him. She would never be able to have enough of him. She could smell the familiar scent of his cologne.

And then his mouth was gone from hers and he was gazing at her in the moonlit room.

"We are going back upstairs," he said, "before someone can make an issue of your absence. Thank you, Judith. The time between now and the last dance is going to seem tedious indeed."

She tried not to refine too much on his words. He was relieved at his near escape. He was grateful to her. He remembered their time together when he had thought she was Claire Campbell, actress and experienced courtesan. That was all.

CHAPTER XVII

JUDITH HAD VERY LITTLE TIME IN WHICH TO GATHER her scattered thoughts and emotions. Perhaps very few people noticed her return to the ballroom on Lord Rannulf's arm, but Aunt Effingham certainly did, and the look on her face did not bode well for her niece later. Julianne had somehow surrounded herself with gentlemen, the waltz having just finished, and was laughing and fluttering in their midst. Uncle George was back with his group of older gentlemen, engrossed in conversation with them. Of Horace there was no sign.

"But where did you go, Rannulf?" Lady Beamish asked when he escorted Judith to her grandmother's side. "One moment you were waltzing and the next moment you were gone."

"Miss Effingham suddenly missed her bracelet," he explained, "and Miss Law was kind enough to help us search for it. Fortunately it was discovered in just the place Miss Effingham thought she might have left it."

Judith's grandmother smiled placidly, but Lady Beamish looked from one to the other of them with sharp eyes. Of course, Judith thought, she had been the one eager to promote the match between her grandson and Julianne. She must be disappointed that the courtship was not proceeding faster.

And then Lord Rannulf strolled away to ask a young lady to dance who to Judith's knowledge had danced only once before during the evening, and Mr. Tanguay arrived to claim his set.

Judith smiled and gave him her attention, but it was very difficult to do when her heart was still pounding from the tensions of the past fifteen minutes.

She was laughing by the time the set ended. It had been a vigorous dance with intricate steps and patterns. But Mr. Tanguay did not have the opportunity to escort her back to her grandmother. Branwell appeared in front of them instead and took her arm.

"Excuse us if you will, Tanguay," he said. "I need to talk to my sister for a minute."

She looked at him in surprise. Though he had exchanged glances and smiles with her and even one wink in the course of the evening, he had been too busy enjoying himself with other young ladies to hunt out a mere sister for conversation. He was still smiling, though there was something stiff about the set of his lips. He was unusually pale. His fingers were digging rather painfully into her arm.

"Jude," he said when they were on the landing outside the ballroom and he had looked about to ascertain that they could not be overheard, "I just wanted to let you know that I am leaving. Now. Tonight."

"The ball?" She looked at him with incomprehension.

"Harewood." He smiled and nodded at Beatrice Hardinge, who was passing on the arm of an unknown young man.

"Harewood?" She was further mystified. "Tonight?"

"Effingham just had a word with me," he said. "It seems

someone else came here a couple of days ago demanding payment of me for some trifling bill. Effingham paid him without even informing me. Now he wants the money back as well as the thirty pounds I owe him for the journey here." He raked the fingers of one hand through his hair. "Of course I mean to pay him back, but I cannot do it just now. He cut up rather nasty about the whole thing and said some pretty offensive things, not just about me but about you too. I would have popped him a good one to the nose or even challenged him, but how could I, Jude? I am at Uncle George's as a guest, and we are surrounded by other guests. It would be in the depths of bad taste. I am going to have to go, that is all."

"But tonight, Bran?" She grasped his hand in both her own. Oh, she knew very well what this was all about. How dare Horace take out his anger and frustration on her brother in this way? "Why not wait at least until the morning?"

"I cannot," he said. "I have to go now. As soon as I have changed my clothes. There is a reason."

"But in the middle of the night? Oh, Bran," she said, "whatever are you going to do?"

"You must not worry about me," he said, reclaiming his hand and looking considerably agitated. "I have a—a lead on something. I'll have my fortune made in no time at all, I promise you." He flashed her a ghost of his old grin. "And then I'll pay Papa back everything extra he has spent on me lately and you girls will be secure again. I have to go, Jude. I must not delay any longer."

"Let me at least come upstairs with you," she said, "and then see you on your way after you have changed."

"No, no." He looked around him again, obviously anxious to be gone. "You stay here, Jude. I want to slip away unnoticed. I'll pay Effingham first as soon as I can, and then I'll pay him back in a different way for what he said about my sister." He bent his head and pecked her on the cheek.

She watched him go in some dismay and with a strong sense of foreboding. He obviously owed a great deal of money to a great many people, and now their number included Horace—obviously for a far larger sum than thirty pounds. Yet he was dashing off furtively in the middle of the night, convinced that at last he had found a way to make his fortune quickly and rid himself of debt. He was surely only going to dig himself a deeper grave.

And in the process completely ruin his family.

It was with a heavy heart that she returned to the ballroom. Even the prospect of dancing the last set with Lord Rannulf Bedwyn failed to cheer her.

She was to be further disappointed within a few minutes.

"Judith," her grandmother said, taking her hand and squeezing it, "my dear Sarah is not feeling at all the thing. It is too drafty in here with the doors and windows open, I daresay, and too noisy. Perhaps you would fetch Lord Rannulf."

"There really is no need to fuss, Gertrude," Lady Beamish said. "I feel better already since you fanned my face."

But looking at her, Judith could see that the old lady's always-pale complexion had a gray tinge and her always-correct posture was drooping somewhat.

"You are weary, ma'am," she said, "and it is no wonder. It is after midnight already. I shall certainly fetch Lord Rannulf."

It proved unnecessary. He came even as Judith started to look around for him in the milling crowd between sets. He bent over his grandmother's chair and took one of her hands in his.

"You are tired, Grandmama?" he asked, such gentleness in his face and voice that it felt to Judith that her heart turned over. "So am I, I must confess. I shall have the carriage brought around immediately."

"Nonsense!" she said. "I have never left a ball early in my life. Besides, there are two sets left and two young ladies to whom you have committed your time."

"I have not engaged anyone for the next set," he said, "and Miss Law was to be my partner for the last one. I am sure she will excuse me."

"Indeed I will," Judith assured them both.

Lady Beamish looked at her, her eyes still sharp despite her obvious weariness.

"Thank you, Miss Law," she said. "You are both gracious and kind. Very well, then, Rannulf, you may call the carriage. Gertrude, my dear, I am going to have to abandon you."

Judith's grandmother chuckled. "I have scarcely known how to keep my own eyes open for the last half hour," she said. "After the next set is over, I will have Judith help me to my room, if she will be so good. Then she can return for the last set if she wishes. It has been a thoroughly pleasant evening, has it not?"

"Miss Law," Lord Rannulf said, "would you care to help me find a servant to take a message to the stables?"

Someone of his rank and demeanor had no difficulty in finding and attracting the attention of a servant, of course. The message was sent in no time at all. Judith used the opportunity to ask the same servant to send Tillie up to her grandmother's room. But Lord Rannulf had wished to speak with her privately. They stood outside the ballroom, on almost the exact spot where she had stood with Branwell just a short while earlier. He clasped his hands at his back and leaned a little toward her.

"I am sorrier than I can say," he said, "about the last set."

"But we are not children," she said, smiling, "to have a tantrum whenever we are deprived of an expected treat."

"Perhaps you are a saint, Judith," he said, his eyes narrowing with the old mockery. "I am not. I could throw a tantrum in the middle of the ballroom right now, lying on my back, drumming my heels on the wooden floor, punching my fists in the air, and cursing most foully."

She burst into delighted laughter, and he tipped his head to one side and pursed his lips.

"You were created for laughter and happiness," he said. "May I call on you tomorrow morning?"

Whatever for?

"I am sure everyone would be delighted," she said.

He regarded her with steady eyes, mockery still lurking in their depths.

"You are being deliberately obtuse," he said. "I asked if I might call upon *you,* Judith."

He could mean only one thing, surely. But he had asked before—in a manner she had found offensive—and she had answered quite firmly in the negative. But that had been two weeks ago. Much had happened since. Much had changed, though perhaps nothing more than her own opinion of him. His of her could not have changed much, could it? She was still the impoverished daughter of a never wealthy but now impoverished country clergyman, while he was still the son of a duke and second in line to the title.

"If you wish." She found that she was whispering, but he heard her.

He made her a deep bow, and they returned together to the ballroom, where he helped his grandmother to her feet, tucked her arm protectively through his, led her toward Aunt Effingham, whose tall hair plumes nodded with stiff graciousness, and then out of the ballroom.

Judith sat down in the chair Lady Beamish had just vacated and wondered if the rest of the night would be long enough in which to digest all that had happened this evening.

"Do not worry, Judith, my love," her grandmother said, setting one plump hand over both hers in her lap and patting them. "I have no intention of leaving the ballroom before the last bar of music has died away. But I did not want Sarah to feel that she was abandoning me. I fear she is quite ill and has been for some time past, though she will never talk of her health."

And so after all Judith danced the final set—with Lord Braithwaite again—though she would have far preferred to retire to her own room. Upsetting thoughts of Branwell churned about in her head with anxious, euphoric ones about tomorrow morning's visit, while at the same time she had to smile and respond to Lord Braithwaite's mildly flirtatious conversation.

A FULL-BLOWN BALL THAT DID NOT FINISH UNTIL AFTER one o'clock in the morning was rare in the country. Many of the outside guests left even before the final set ended. None of them lingered long afterward. Neither did the orchestra. Only the family, the houseguests, and a few servants were left in the ballroom when a small commotion was heard outside the doors.

Tillie's voice could be heard raised above the softer, haughtier tones of the butler.

"But I have to talk to her *now*," Tillie was saying, obviously agitated over something. "I have waited long enough. Perhaps too long."

The butler argued, but Judith's grandmother, who had just got to her feet and was leaning on Judith's arm, looked toward the doors in some surprise.

"Tillie?" she called. "Whatever is the matter? Come in here, do."

Everyone stopped to watch and listen as Tillie hurried into the ballroom, wringing her hands, her face distraught.

"It is your jewels, ma'am," she cried.

"What about them?" Uncle George asked, exerting himself.

"Gone!" Tillie announced in tones a tragic heroine might have envied. "All gone. The box was open and upside down on the floor in your dressing room, ma'am, when I got there, and there is not a sign of a single piece except what you are wearing on your person."

"Nonsense, Tillie," Horace said, stepping up beside his father. "I daresay they were spilled earlier in Stepgrandmama's hurry to be ready in time for the ball and you piled them into a drawer to be put away properly later. You have simply forgotten."

Tillie gathered together her dignity. "I would not have done any such thing, sir," she said. "I would not have spilled the box, and if I *had*, I would have stayed until every piece was picked up and put back where it belonged."

Her mistress meanwhile was gripping Judith's hand so tightly that all her rings were digging painfully into her granddaughter's hand.

"They are gone, Tillie?" she asked. "*Stolen?*"

It was as if everyone else had been waiting only for that word to be spoken. There was a buzzing of sound and a crescendo of excitement.

"There are no thieves in this house," Aunt Effingham said sharply. "The very idea! You must look harder, Tillie. They must be *somewhere*."

"I hunted everywhere, ma'am," Tillie said. "*Three times.*"

"There have been a number of outsiders here tonight," Mrs. Hardinge pointed out, "and some of their servants."

"*We* are all outsiders too," Mr. Webster reminded her.

"We cannot possibly suspect any of our guests," Uncle George said.

"*Someone* has stolen Mother's jewels," Aunt Louisa told him. "They obviously did not disappear on their own."

"But whoever would have had a motive?" her mother asked.

Branwell, Judith thought and felt instantly ashamed. Bran would never steal. Would he? From his own grandmother? But would he for that very reason have justified his act as one of borrowing rather than stealing? Who else could have done it? Bran had been backed farther into a corner this evening. He had left Harewood in the middle of the ball, in the middle of the night. He had been very agitated. He had not wanted her to go upstairs with him or see him on his way. Branwell. It was Bran. And soon everyone else would realize it too. She felt dizzy and had to concentrate hard upon not fainting.

"Who is short of money?" Horace asked.

His words hung in the air rather like an obscenity. No one answered.

"And who had the opportunity?" he asked. "Who knew where Stepgrandmama keeps her jewels and would be bold enough to go into her room to get them?"

Branwell. It seemed to Judith that the name fairly screamed itself into the silence.

"It could not have been an outsider," Horace continued. "Not unless he was a very bold man indeed or had an accomplice in the house. How would anyone know the right room? How would he accomplish the task without being detected? Or missed from the ballroom? *Was* anyone missing from the ballroom for any length of time?"

Branwell.

Everyone seemed to speak at once after that. Everyone had an opinion, a suggestion, or a shocked comment on the theft. Judith bent her head to her grandmother's.

"Will you sit down, Grandmama?" she asked. "You are trembling."

They both sat, and Judith chafed the old lady's hands.

"They will be found," she said. "Don't worry."

But how far had Branwell ridden by now? And where was he going? What would he do with the jewels? Pawn them? Sell them? Surely he would not do that. Surely there were some remnants of honor left in his conscience. He must see that the jewels would have to be retrievable. But how would they ever be redeemed?

"It is not so much the value of the jewels," her grandmother said, "as the fact that your grandpapa gave them to me. Who could hate me this much, Judith? There was a thief *in my own room*. How can I ever go into it again?"

Her voice was shaking and breathless. She sounded old and defeated.

Uncle George and Horace finally took charge again. They sent the butler to fetch all the servants so that all could be questioned. Judith wanted to take her grandmother upstairs, even if only to her own room, where she could be quiet and Tillie could perhaps bring her a cup of tea and her night things to change into. But her grandmother would not move.

It was a long, tedious process, which was clearly going to lead nowhere, Judith thought over the next half an hour. What amazed her more than anything else was that no one had missed Branwell yet. Uncle George asked if any servant had been upstairs to the bedchamber floor since the ball began. Three of them had, including the chambermaid Judith had bumped into on the way out of her room. All of them had had a good reason to be up there and all of them had worked at Harewood long enough to be judged trustworthy.

"And no one else went up there?" Uncle George added with a sigh.

"If you please, sir," the maid said. "Miss Law did."

All eyes turned Judith's way, and she felt herself flushing.

"I went up to exchange Grandmama's earrings," she said. "The others were pinching her. But the jewel box was in its accustomed place at that time and all the jewelry was in it. I made the exchange and came back down. The theft must have happened since that time. It was . . . let me see. It was between the first and second sets."

"But you was coming out of *your* room, miss," the chambermaid said. "You was flying and we ran right into each other. Remember?"

"That is right," Judith said. "The earrings Grandmama wanted were in my reticule, where they had been since the evening we were all at Grandmaison."

"It must have been when you were returning to the ballroom that you almost ran into me, Cousin," Horace said. "You were quite breathless. You looked to be almost in a panic. But yes, I can confirm that that was between the first and second sets."

"Judith, my love." Her grandmother was very close to tears. "I sent you up there and might have been sending you to your death. What if you had walked in on the thief? You might have been struck over the head."

"It did not happen, Grandmama," she said soothingly. She wished she *had* walked in on Bran. She could have prevented this whole nightmare.

"Well," Horace said briskly, "we are going to have to start searching, that is all."

"Distasteful," Uncle George said. "We cannot search people's rooms, and the thief would hardly have hidden the jewels in any of the public rooms."

"Well, I for one do not object to having *my* room searched," Horace said. "In fact, Father, I insist that it be the first to be searched."

"If I may make so bold, Sir George," the butler said, stepping forward, "I will volunteer my own room to be searched and those of the other servants too unless anyone has an objection. If anyone does, speak up now."

The servants all held their peace. Which of them, after

all, would voice an objection when doing so must throw in-
stant suspicion on them?

Lord Braithwaite cleared his throat. "You may search my
room too, sir," he said.

There was a murmuring of assent from all the other
guests, though Judith guessed it was grudging in many cases.
It would feel like violation to have one's room searched, to
feel even if only for a few minutes that one was being suspected of theft. But she kept her mouth shut.

"Would you like to go to your room, Grandmama?" she
asked again after Uncle George, Horace, the butler, and
Tillie had left the ballroom. "Or to mine if you would
prefer?"

"No." Her grandmother was looking more dejected than
Judith had ever seen her. "I will stay here. I hope they do *not*
find the jewels. Is that not foolish? I would rather never see
them again than know that someone in this house has
stolen them. Why did whoever it is not *ask* me? I have
plenty. I would give to any relative or friend or servant
in need. But I suppose people are too proud to ask, are
they not?"

Julianne was sobbing in her mother's arms, and looking
remarkably pretty in the process.

"This has turned out to be a perfectly *horrid* evening," she
wailed. "I have hated every moment of it, and I am sure
everyone else will pronounce it a disaster and never accept
another invitation from us all their lives."

The servants stood in silence. The guests huddled in
small, self-conscious groups, talking in lowered voices.

Another half hour passed before the search party returned, looking grave.

"This has been found," Uncle George said into the hush
that had fallen over the ballroom. "Tillie recognized it. It is
from Mother-in-law's jewelry box." He held aloft the wine-
colored velvet bag that usually contained her most valuable

jewels. It was very obviously empty. "And this, also from the box." He held up a single diamond earring between the thumb and forefinger of his other hand.

The small swell of sound instantly died away again.

"Does anyone wish to say anything about these items?" Uncle George asked. "They were found in the same room."

Branwell's. Judith felt sick to her stomach.

No one wished to say anything, it seemed.

"Judith," Uncle George said, his voice low and devoid of all expression, "the bag was at the bottom of one of your dressing table drawers. The earring was on the floor, almost out of sight behind the door."

Judith suddenly felt as if she were looking at him down a long, dark tunnel. She felt as if her mind were still grappling to decode the sounds he had just spoken, to make sensible words out of them.

"Where have you hidden everything else, Judith?" he asked her, still in that flat voice. "It is not in your room."

"What?" She was not sure any sound had come out of her mouth. She was not even sure her lips had formed the word.

"There is no point in even pretending that there must be some misunderstanding," Uncle George said. "You have stolen costly jewels, Judith, from your own grandmother."

"Oh, you ungrateful, wicked girl!" Aunt Effingham cried shrilly. "After all that I have done for you and your worthless family. You will be punished for this, believe me. Criminals hang for less."

"We should send for the constable, Father," Horace said. "I do apologize to everyone else that we must be seen airing our dirty family linen thus publicly. If only we had known it was Judith, we would have hushed all up and waited until everyone had gone to bed before investigating. But how were we to know?"

Judith was on her feet without any memory of having stood up.

"I have not taken anything," she said.

"Of course you have not. Of course she has not," her grandmother said, grabbing her hand again. "There is certainly some misunderstanding, George. Judith is the very last person who would steal from me."

"And yet," Julianne said scornfully, "she does not have a penny to her name, Grandmama. Do you, Judith?"

"And her brother is deep in debt," Horace said. "I must confess that I suspected *him* when Tillie first came here with her discovery. Did anyone else notice that he disappeared in the middle of the ball? It was, I fear, because I reminded him of a trifling debt he owed me. I really thought he had done something foolish, though I hated to say it aloud. But it appears that it was Judith."

"Or Judith in league with Branwell," Aunt Effingham said. "That is it, is it, you evil girl? That is why the jewels are not in your room? Your brother has made off with them?"

"No, no, no!" Grandmama cried. "Judith has done nothing wrong. That bag . . . I-I gave it to Judith to keep some of her own things in. And that earring. Judith often takes them from me when they pinch my ears, just as she did these I am wearing now. She must have dropped one when she brought them back to me and we did not notice."

"That is not even a very good try, Mother-in-law," Uncle George said in the same flat voice. "I believe we should all go to bed now and try to sleep. Judith will be dealt with in the morning. No one will have to face the embarrassment of having to see her again. She will be sent home, I daresay, for her father to deal with. In the meanwhile we will have to have Branwell pursued."

"Father," Horace said, "I still believe a constable would—"

"We will not have Judith thrown into a cell and create a sordid sensation for the whole countryside to gossip over," Uncle George said firmly.

Judith raised both hands to her mouth. This was all too

horrifying even to be a nightmare from which she might hope to awake.

"I fervently hope my brother will take a whip to you, Judith," Aunt Effingham said, "as he ought to have done years ago. I shall write making that very suggestion. And I hope you intend to lock her into her room tonight, Effingham, so that she cannot rob us all in our sleep."

"We will not be melodramatic," Uncle George said, "though this scene bears an uncomfortable resemblance to the worst of melodrama. Judith, go to your room now and remain there until you are fetched in the morning."

"Grandmama." Judith turned to her and stretched out both hands. But her grandmother had her own hands clasped tightly in her lap and did not look up.

"Branwell is in debt," she said so quietly that no one but Judith could hear, "and you did not tell me. I would have *given* him some of my jewels if he had asked or if you had asked. Did you not know that?"

Grandmama believed it, then. She believed that Judith had conspired with Bran to rob her. It was the worst moment of all.

"I did not do it, Grandmama," Judith whispered as she saw a tear plop onto the old lady's hands.

She never afterward knew how she got herself out of the ballroom and up to her room. But she stood against the closed door after she arrived there for a long, long time, her hands with a death grip on the handle behind her back, as if the weight of her body was all that stood between herself and the universe crashing in on top of her.

CHAPTER XVIII

IT WAS REALLY FAR TOO EARLY IN THE DAY TO BE making a social call, Rannulf thought as he rode up the long driveway toward Harewood Grange, especially the morning after a ball. But he had paced his room rather like a bear in a cage from dawn onward and had not been able to settle to anything even after going downstairs, though there were letters to answer and another account ledger he needed to study.

And so he had come early in the hope of finding at least Sir George Effingham up and about and in the confident belief that Judith would not still be in her bed. Had she found sleep last night as difficult as he had? She surely could not have mistaken his meaning last evening. How did she feel about him? What answer did she plan to give him?

If it was no again, then he would have to accept it.

It was a gloomy thought, but he clung to the hope that he had not imagined that magnetic sort of pull between them last night. He *surely* could not have. But his heart pounded with unaccustomed anxiety as he rode into the stable yard, turned Bucephalus over to the care of a groom, and strode toward the house.

"Ask Sir George if I may have a private word with him," he said to the servant who opened the door.

A minute later he was being ushered into the library, where he had very nearly met his doom last night. Sir George was seated at a large oak desk looking glum. But then he rarely looked any different, Rannulf reflected. He was the picture of a man discontented with his family circle yet not quite content with his own company either.

"Good morning, sir," Rannulf said. "I trust everyone has slept well after last evening's revelries?"

Sir George grunted. "You are out early, Bedwyn," he said. "I am not sure Julianne or the others are up yet. But your business is with me, is it?"

"Only briefly, sir," Rannulf said. "I would like your permission to have a private word with your niece."

"With Judith?" Sir George frowned, and his hand reached for a quill pen and fidgeted with it.

"I thought I might take her walking outside," Rannulf said. "With your permission, that is, and if she is willing."

Sir George put the pen down. "You are too late," he said. "She has gone."

"*Gone?*" He knew she was to be sent home, but so abruptly, so soon, the morning after a late ball? Because of the way she had thwarted her cousin's marriage scheme, perhaps?

Sir George sighed deeply, sat back in his chair, and indicated that his guest should take the one across from him. "I suppose there will be no keeping it entirely from you or Lady Beamish," he said, "though I was hoping and still hope to keep the sordid details from the rest of our neighbors. There was some unpleasantness here last night, Bedwyn. My mother-in-law's jewels were stolen sometime in the course of the evening and a search turned up quite unmistakable and damning evidence in Judith's room. She was also seen hurrying out of her room at a time during the ball when she had no clear reason for being there, and soon after that, Branwell Law disappeared. He left Harewood in the middle of the ball without a word to anyone."

Rannulf sat very still.

"Judith was confined to her room overnight," Sir George continued, "though I refused to have her either locked in or guarded. It seemed somehow demeaning to my whole family to treat her like a prisoner. My intention was to send her home under escort this morning in my own carriage with a letter to her father. *This* letter." He tapped a folded, sealed paper on the desk. "But when I went up very early, with a maid, and knocked on her door, there was no answer. The room was empty. Most, if not all, of her belongings are still there, but she most certainly is not. She has flown."

"You think she has gone home?" Rannulf asked, breaking a heavy silence.

"I doubt it," Sir George said. "My brother-in-law is a stern man. He is not the sort to whom a woman in her predicament would run voluntarily. And her brother would certainly not go there, would he? I suppose they have a plan to meet somewhere and divide the spoils. Those jewels must be worth a very sizable fortune, yet my mother-in-law would never allow me to put the most valuable of them in a safe place."

"What do you plan to do now?" Rannulf asked.

"I wish I could simply do nothing," Sir George told him quite frankly. "They are Lady Effingham's own niece and nephew and my mother-in-law's grandchildren. But the jewels at least must be recovered. I suppose now they have fled and must be pursued it is too late to treat the matter with quiet discretion. I suppose they will have to be brought to justice and made to serve time in jail. It is not a pleasing prospect."

"There will be pursuit, then?" Rannulf asked.

Sir George sighed again. "We will keep the matter quiet as long as we are able," he said, "though with a houseful of servants and guests I daresay I might as easily attempt to muzzle the wind. My son will go after them tomorrow morning after seeing our houseguests on their way. He believes— and I must concur with him—that their only sensible destination is London since they carry jewels, not money, and jewels are not easily disposed of. He will pursue them there and apprehend them himself if he is fortunate—if we are *all* fortunate. It is more likely that he will be compelled to engage the services of the Bow Street Runners."

They sat for a short while in silence and then Rannulf got abruptly to his feet.

"I will intrude upon you no longer, sir," he said. "You may rest assured that no one else except my grandmother will hear anything of this through me."

"That is decent of you." Sir George too got to his feet. "It is a nasty business."

Rannulf rode down the driveway somewhat faster than he had ridden up it just a short while earlier. He might have guessed that something like this would happen. He himself had come very close to being trapped into marrying Miss Effingham, yet he was probably not even the primary enemy as far as Horace Effingham was concerned. It was by Judith he would have felt most humiliated. She was the one he must be most intent upon punishing.

It was a nasty punishment he had chosen and was likely to get nastier.

His grandmother was in her private sitting room, writing a letter. She smiled at him and set her pen down when he answered her summons to enter.

"How delightful it is," she said, "to see the sun shining again. It lifts one's spirits, does it not?"

"Grandmama." He strode across the room toward her and

took one of her hands in his. "I must leave you for a few days. Perhaps even longer."

"Ah." She continued to smile, but something had turned flat behind her eyes. "Yes, of course, you have grown restless. I understand."

He raised her hand to his lips.

"Someone stole Mrs. Law's jewels last night during the ball," he said, "and the blame fell squarely upon Judith Law. Evidence was found in her room."

"Oh, no, Rannulf," she said, "that cannot be."

"She fled sometime during the night," he said, "making herself, I suppose, look even more guilty."

She stared at him. "I would never believe it of Miss Law," she said. "But poor Gertrude. Those jewels have great sentimental value to her."

"I do not believe it of Judith either," he said. "I am going after her."

"Judith," she said. "She is Judith to you, then, Rannulf?"

"I rode over to Harewood this morning to propose marriage to her," he said.

"Well." The usual briskness was back in her voice. "You had better not delay any longer."

Fifteen minutes later she stood out on the terrace, straight-backed and unsupported, to wave him on his way when he rode out of the stable yard.

J UDITH WOULD DOUBTLESS HAVE BEEN FEELING VERY frightened indeed if she had allowed her mind to dwell upon the nature of her predicament. She was alone with only a small bag of essential possessions in her hand. She was on her way to London, which she might hope to reach after walking for a week or perhaps two. She really had no idea how long it would take. She had no money with which to buy a coach ticket or a night's lodging or food. Even when—or if—she reached London, she did not know how she would find Branwell or whether it would be too late to recover the jewels and take them back to their grandmother.

Meanwhile there was bound to be pursuit. Uncle George or a constable or—worst of all—Horace might come galloping up behind her at any moment and drag her off to jail. Having escaped from Harewood, she would probably no longer be given the option of returning home. She was not sure that would not be worse than going to prison anyway. How would she face Papa when it was so impossible to prove her innocence and when no one could prove Branwell's?

No, it was the very thought of facing the dreadful disgrace of going home and of seeing Bran crash down off the pedestal he had always occupied that had finally convinced her just before first light to flee alone and on foot while she still had the chance. She had been surprised at how easy it was. She had fully expected to find guards outside her door or at least in the hall below.

She refused to give in to fear now. What was the point, after all? She trudged along the road on an afternoon that was growing hotter by the minute, concentrating upon setting one foot in front of the other and living one moment at a time. It was more easily said than done, of course. She had had a ride for a mile or two early in the morning in a farmer's cart, and he had been good enough to share a piece of his coarse, dry bread with her. Since then she had drunk water at a small stream. But even so her stomach was beginning to growl with emptiness, and she was feeling slightly light-headed. Her feet were sore and probably acquiring blisters. Her bag was feeling as if it weighed a ton.

It was difficult not to give in to self-pity at the very least. And ravening fear at the worst.

The fear crawled along her back at the sound of clopping hooves behind her. It was a single horse, she thought, not a carriage. It had happened a number of times during the day, but she had stopped ducking into the hedgerow to hide until the road was clear again. She waited for the relief of seeing a strange horse and a strange rider go past.

But this horse did not pass her. Its pace slowed as it came up to her—she prayed that she was imagining it—and it clopped along for a while just behind her right shoulder. She would not look, though she braced herself for she knew not what. A whip? Chains? A flying human body to knock her over and pin her to the ground? She could hear her heartbeat thudding in her ears.

"Is this an afternoon stroll?" a familiar voice asked. "Or a serious walk?"

She whirled around and gazed up at Lord Rannulf Bedwyn, huge and faintly menacing on horseback. He had stopped his horse and was looking gravely down at her despite the mockery of his words.

"It is no business of yours, Lord Rannulf," she said. "You may ride on." But where was he going? Home again?

"You failed to keep our appointment this morning," he said, "and so I was forced to ride after you."

Their appointment. She had completely forgotten about it.

"Don't tell me you forgot about it," he said as if he had read her mind. "That would be very lowering, you know."

"Perhaps they did not tell you—" she began.

"They did."

"Well, then," she said when it appeared that he would say no more, "you may ride on or ride back, Lord Rannulf, whichever you choose. You would not wish to associate with a thief."

"Is that what you are?" he asked her.

It was incredibly painful to hear him ask the question.

"The evidence was overwhelming," she told him.

"Yes, I know," he said. "You are a particularly inept thief, though, Judith, to have left evidence lying about your room when you must have guessed that sooner or later it would be searched."

She still could not understand why Bran had put the bag in her room. The earring she *could* understand. Panicky in his haste, he must have dropped it without even realizing it. The floor was carpeted. There would have been no loud clatter as it landed. But the bag . . . The only explanation she had been able to devise was that he had known he would be suspected from the first moment but had *not* expected that her room would be searched. He had hidden the bag in her drawer, she guessed, as a sort of private acknowledgment of his guilt to her and a pledge that he would return the contents as soon as he was able. It was not a very satisfactory explanation, but she could think of no other.

"I am not a thief," she said. "I did not steal anything."

"I know."

Did he? Did he trust her? No one else did or probably ever would.

"Where are you going?" he asked her.

She pressed her lips together and stared up at him.

"To London, I suppose," he said. "It is a pleasant stroll, I believe."

"It is not your business," she said. "Go back to Grandmaison, Lord Rannulf."

But he leaned down from the saddle and held out one hand to her. She was powerfully reminded of the last occasion on which this had happened and of her first impression of him then—broad, rugged, dark-complexioned, blue-eyed and big-nosed, his fair hair too long, not handsome but disturbingly attractive. Now he was simply Rannulf, and for the first time today she wanted to cry.

"Set your hand in mine and your foot on my boot," he said.

She shook her head.

"Do you know how long it will take you to walk to London?" he asked her.

"I will not be walking all the way," she said. "And how do you know that London is my destination?"

"Do you have any money?"

She compressed her lips again.

"I will take you to London, Judith," he said. "And I will help you find your brother."

"How do you know—"

"Give me your hand," he said.

She felt bowed down by defeat then and at the same time strangely comforted by his large presence, by his knowledge of what had happened, and by his insistence that she ride up with him. She did as he had directed her and within moments was up before his saddle again, bracketed safely by his arms and legs.

How she wished time could be wound backward, that that adventure of three weeks ago could be lived all over again and what had followed it could be changed.

"What are you going to do when we find him?" she asked. "Turn him over to the authorities? Have him sent to jail? Could it be even worse than that for him? Could he be . . ." She could not complete the appalling possibility.

"Is he guilty, then?" he asked.

"He is very deep in debt," she said, "and his creditors have followed him even to Harewood and pressed him to pay."

"All men in debt steal their grandmothers' jewels, then?" he asked.

"He knew about them," she said. "He had even seen the box. He joked about how they could get him out of his difficulties. At least, I thought it was a joke. And then last night he came to me in the middle of the ball to tell me that he was leaving, that he thought he would be out of debt and would make his fortune very soon. He was very agitated. He kept looking around him as if he expected someone to pounce on him and stop him. He would not let me see him on his way."

"The evidence seems overwhelming," he said.

"Yes."

"As it seems in your case too."

She turned her head sharply to look into his face. "You *do* believe I am guilty," she cried. "Please set me down. *Set me down.*"

"My point being," he said, "that evidence can sometimes lie. As it obviously does in your case."

She gazed at him. "You think it is possible that Branwell is *innocent*, then?" she asked him.

"Who else might have taken the jewelry?" he asked her. "Who else but the two of you had a motive?"

"No one," she said, frowning at him. "Or perhaps a large number of people to whom the prospect of riches is enticing."

"Precisely," he said. "We could easily narrow down the number of possibilities to nine-tenths of the population of England. Who might have had a motive to ruin you and your brother?"

"No one." Her frown deepened. "Everyone loves Bran's charm and sunny nature. And as for me, no one . . ."

"It is at least a possibility, is it not?" he said when her eyes widened.

"*Horace?*" The idea was an overwhelmingly attractive one, deflecting as it would the guilt from Branwell.

"He certainly had a vicious plan for me," he reminded her.

But she could not accept a theory merely because she wanted to believe it. Except that the velvet bag in her drawer and the earring on the floor would make far more sense if Horace were the culprit.

"I must find Bran anyway," she said, "even if only to warn him. I need to find out the truth."

"Yes," he said, "you do. When did you last eat?"

"This morning," she said. "I am not hungry."

"Liar," he said. "Claire Campbell tried that one on me too. You could well starve on pride, you know. Did you sleep last night?"

She shook her head.

"It shows," he told her. "If I were meeting you now for the first time, I might mistake you for only a marginally lovely woman."

She laughed despite herself and then had to clap the back of her hand over her mouth and swallow several times in order to prevent herself from bawling.

One of his hands pulled loose the ribbons of her bonnet from beneath her chin. He took the bonnet off—it was the one he had bought her—tied the ribbons inexpertly again, and looped them over his saddle. Then he drew her sideways against him and pressed her head to his shoulder.

"I do not want to hear another word from you until I can find a respectable-looking inn at which to feed you," he said.

She ought not to have been comfortable. Perhaps she was not. She was suddenly too tired to know. But she could feel the strong, firm muscles of his shoulder and chest, and she could smell his cologne or whatever it was about him that made him unique, and his head and hat were shading her from the rays of the sun. She drifted into a pleasant state between sleeping and waking and imagined lying safe on the bottom of a Viking boat while he stood massive and protective at the prow. Or standing beside him on a cliff top while his Saxon locks and his Saxon tunic fluttered in the breeze and she knew that he would take on every fierce warrior who dared invade his shores and vanquish them single-handed. She would have thought she was asleep and dreaming except that she was aware that she dreamed and seemed to have the ability to direct the dream in whichever direction she wanted.

She wanted to believe in him as the eternal hero of mythology.

CHAPTER XIX

H E LET ONE INN GO BY SINCE SHE WAS DOZING
on his shoulder and he guessed that she needed
sleep at least equally as much as she needed food.
He stopped at the next decent inn and insisted that she eat
every mouthful of the meal that was set before her even
though after the first few bites she told him that she did not
think she could eat any more.

It was already late afternoon. They would not make it to
London tonight. He thought briefly of hiring a carriage and
going as far as Ringwood Manor in Oxfordshire. Aidan had
told him fondly in London, while waiting impatiently for all
the business of selling his commission to be completed so
that he could return to his wife, that Eve had a strong tendency to reach out to all sorts of lame ducks, most of whom
ended up in her employment. She would take Judith in even
if Aidan pokered up and looked askance at her. She would
perhaps be able to offer Judith some of the comfort she
needed.

There would be no real comfort, though, until she found
her brother, until she was convinced beyond all doubt that

he had had no hand in the robbery of their grandmother's jewelry. And no comfort, he supposed, until the jewels and the thief had been found and she and her brother were totally exonerated.

"We had better go," she said, setting down her knife and fork on her empty plate. "What time will we reach London? Will Bran be at his lodgings, do you suppose?"

"Judith," he said, "you are almost dropping with fatigue."

"I must find him," she said. "And it must be before he disposes of the jewelry if he has it."

"We will not get there tonight," he told her.

She gazed at him blankly.

"And even if we did," he said, "you would be fit for nothing. You would be dead on your feet. You almost are even now."

"I keep thinking," she said, "that I will wake up and find that all this is a bad dream. *All* of it—Bran's extravagances, my aunt's letter inviting one of us to go to live at Harewood, everything that has happened since."

Including what had happened on her journey? He stared at her silently for a few moments. Could it possibly have been just last night that he had felt a strong bond with her and had been convinced she would gladly accept his marriage offer this morning?

"We had better stay here for the night," he said. "You can have a good rest and be ready to make an early start in the morning."

She set both hands over her face briefly and shook her head, but when she looked up at him it was with weary eyes and a look of resignation.

"Why did you come after me?" she asked.

He pursed his lips. "Perhaps after last night's near disaster with Miss Effingham," he said, "I was glad of some excuse to avoid further visits to Harewood Grange. Perhaps I was tired of being incarcerated in the country. Perhaps I was not fond of the idea that Horace Effingham would be your only pursuer."

"*Horace* is pursuing me?"

"You are safe with me," he said. "But I would prefer to have you in the same room with me tonight. I repeat—you are *safe* with me. I will not force myself on you."

"You never did." She looked wearily at him. "I am too tired to move from this chair. Perhaps I will just stay here all night." She smiled wanly.

He got to his feet and went in search of the landlord. He took a room in the name of Mr. and Mrs. Bedard and went back to the dining room, where Judith was still sitting, her elbows on the table, her chin cupped in her hands.

"Come," he said, setting a hand between her shoulders, feeling the tense muscles there. He picked up her bag with the other hand.

She got to her feet without a word and preceded him from the room and up the stairs to the bedchamber he indicated.

"Hot water is being brought up," he said. "Do you have everything else you need?"

She nodded.

"Sleep," he instructed her. "I'll go back downstairs for the evening so as not to disturb you. I'll sleep on the floor when I return."

She looked at the bare boards beneath her feet, as did he.

"There is no need," she said.

He thought there was probably every need. He had never forced himself on any woman. His sexual appetites, though healthy, had never been unbridled. But there were limits to any man's control. Even tired and dusty and disheveled she was a feast to the eyes.

"Sleep," he told her, "and do not worry about anything."

That was, of course, more easily said than done, he admitted as he left the room and went down to the taproom, positioning himself so that he could see the entrance from the stable yard. Even if they could find her brother and he protested his innocence—as Rannulf fully expected he would—and even if she believed him, there was still the whole problem of proving their innocence to the rest of the world. And even if *that* was accomplished, the brother was still a spendthrift who was doubtless deeply enough in debt to ruin his family.

Rannulf wondered if *he* would have been as idle and expensive as he had been if he had not had a personal fortune to finance his bad habits. He was not at all sure of the answer.

J UDITH WASHED HERSELF FROM HEAD TO TOE WITH HOT water and soap and pulled on the nightgown she had brought with her together with one clean dress and a few essential undergarments. She lay down on the bed, almost dizzy with fatigue, fully expecting that she would be asleep as soon as her head rested on the pillow.

It did not happen.

A thousand thoughts and images, all of them infinitely depressing, whirled around and around in her head. For two hours she tossed and turned on the bed, keeping her eyes determinedly closed to the daylight and her ears closed to the sounds from both outside and indoors of a bustling posting inn. She was almost crying from tiredness and the need to find some momentary oblivion when she finally threw the covers aside and stood up. She pushed her hair back from her face and went to stand at the window, her hands braced on the sill. It was getting dark. If they had continued on their way, they would have been two hours closer to London by now.

Bran, she thought, *Bran, where are you?*

Had he taken the jewels? Was he now a thief in addition

to everything else? Would she be able somehow to save him? Or was this pursuit simply futile?

But if it *was* Branwell, why had he put that velvet bag in her drawer? It really made far more sense for Horace to have done it. But how would she ever be able to prove it?

And then she had a cheering thought that had not occurred to her before. If Bran *had* decided to solve his debt problems by robbing Grandmama, he surely would not have taken all the jewels. He would have taken just enough to cover his expenses. He would have taken a few pieces, hoping they would never be missed or at least that they would not be missed for so long that suspicion would not fall on him. He would not have done something as openly incriminating as running away in the middle of the ball if he had taken everything, surely?

But guilt could have set him to fleeing instead of thinking rationally as a deliberate, coldhearted thief would.

She set her forehead against the window glass and sighed just as the door opened quietly behind her. She whirled around in some alarm, but it was only Rannulf who stood there, frowning at her.

"I cannot sleep," she told him apologetically. He had gone to the expense of taking a room so that she could have a good night's rest, and she was not even lying down on the bed.

He shut the door firmly behind him and came across the small room toward her.

"You are overtired," he said, "and overanxious. All will be well, you know. I promise you."

"How can you do that?" she asked him.

"Because I have decided that all will be well," he said, grinning at her. "And I always get my way."

"Always?" She smiled despite herself.

"Always. Come here."

He took her by the shoulders and drew her against him.

She turned her head to rest her cheek on his shoulder and sighed aloud. She wrapped her arms about his waist and abandoned herself to the exquisite pleasure of feeling his hands rubbing hard up and down her back, his fingers digging into tense muscles and coaxing them into relaxation.

All will be well . . .

Because I have decided . . .

. . . I always get my way.

She came half awake when she realized she was being carried over to the bed and deposited on it.

"Mmm." She looked sleepily up at him.

He was grinning again. "Under other circumstances," he said, "I might be mortally offended at a woman's falling asleep as soon as I put my arms about her." He leaned over her to pick up the other pillow.

"Don't sleep on the floor," she said. "Please don't."

She was half aware a minute or two later of an extra weight depressing the other half of the mattress and of a cozy heat against her back. Blankets came up about her shoulders, making her aware that yes, indeed, she had been chilly. The arm that had lifted them settled reassuringly about her waist and drew her back against the body that had provided the heat. Then she slid down into a deliciously deep and dreamless sleep.

R ANNULF CAME AWAKE WHEN DAWN WAS GRAYING THE room. In her sleep she had just turned over to face him, rubbing herself against his length as she did so. Her hair, he could see, was in wild disarray all about her face and shoulders.

Good Lord, who was putting him to this excruciatingly painful test? Did whoever it was not know he was *human*?

It was too early to get up and prepare to ride on. She must

have had a good five or six hours of sleep, by his calculation, but she needed more.

He could feel her breasts against his bare chest, her thighs against his. She was warm and relaxed. But he no longer had the luxury of seeing her as Claire Campbell, actress and woman of experience in sexual matters. She was Judith Law. She also happened to be his love.

He tried determinedly to list her defects. Carrots. Her hair was carroty, by her mother's description. She had freckles. If there were only a little more light coming into the room, he would be able to see them. And a dimple beside her mouth on the right side . . . no, big mistake. A dimple was not a defect. What else? God help him, there *was* nothing else.

And then her eyes came open, sleepy and long-lashed. No defect there either.

"I thought I was dreaming," she said in the throaty voice Claire Campbell had used.

"No."

They stared at each other in the morning twilight, she with sleepy eyes, he feeling like a drowning man who is trying to convince himself that he is immersed in a mere teacup of water. He desperately wished there was a little more space between them. She was going to become physically aware of his perfidy any moment despite the presence of his breeches, which he had kept on for decency's sake.

And then she lifted one warm hand and feathered her fingers over his lips.

"You are an amazingly kind man," she said. "You promised me last night that all would be well, and you meant it, did you not?"

He had also promised that she was safe from him. He was not at all sure he was going to be able to keep either promise.

"I meant it," he said.

She moved her hand and replaced it with her lips.

"Thank you," she said. "A night's sleep has made all the difference. I feel very safe now."

"If you only knew your peril," he said, "you would start running down the road in your nightgown."

And then she smiled at him—showing her dimple. "I did not mean that sort of safety," she said and touched her lips to his again.

"Judith," he said, "I am not made of stone."

"Neither am I," she said. "You cannot know how much I have needed to be held and . . . well, held."

He was not sure even now that this was not an ungallant thing to do, that he was not merely taking advantage of her vulnerability. But he was not some sort of fleshless, bloodless superhero. God help him, he was a man.

He closed his arms more tightly about her and opened his mouth over hers, pressing his tongue deep into the heat within. She made a sound of appreciation deep in her throat, one of her arms came about him, and he was finally lost.

He turned her onto her back, tore at the buttons of his breeches, released himself without stopping to remove the garment, and pushed up her nightgown to the waist.

"Judith," he whispered to her as he came down on top of her, "are you sure you want this? Stop me if you do not. Stop me."

"Rannulf," she whispered back. "Oh, Rannulf."

It was not an occasion for foreplay. She was obviously as ready as he was. He slid his hands beneath her, half lifted her from the mattress, and pressed deep into her.

It felt curiously like a homecoming. He slid his hands free, lifted himself on his forearms, and looked down at her. She gazed back, her lips parted, her eyes heavy with sleep and desire, her hair spread all about her on the pillow and sheet.

"I tried very hard not to let this happen," he told her.

"I know." She smiled again. "I'll never blame you. Not for anything."

He took her hands then, raised them and crossed them above her head, laced his fingers with hers, and lowered all his weight onto her. Her legs, he realized, were twined about his. He worked in her with deep, rhythmic strokes, reveling in her soft, wet heat encasing him, thankful for her initial relaxation, even more thankful for the way she took up his rhythm after a while, pulsing about him with inner muscles, drawing him toward what would be a powerful and powerfully satisfying climax.

He moved his head and kissed her.

"Come with me," he said.

"Yes."

It was the only time it had happened in his life, he realized, he and his woman cresting the tide of passion together, crying out together, descending into satiety and peace together. He felt blessed beyond words.

He lifted himself off her, took her hand in his, and drifted off to sleep for a few minutes. When he opened his eyes again, it was to find that her head was turned toward him. She was looking at him with a half-smile. She looked flushed, contented, and utterly beautiful.

"Well, that settles something," he said, squeezing her hand. "After this business is all over and settled, we are getting married."

"No," she said. "That was not entrapment, Rannulf."

His eyebrows snapped together in a frown.

"What *was* it exactly?" he asked.

"I am not sure," she said. "There has been some . . . madness between us in the last few days. I cannot presume to know why you wished to call on me yesterday morning, but I can guess. It would have been a dreadful mistake. I might have said yes, you see."

What the devil?

"Saying yes would have been a mistake?"

"Yes." She nodded. "Look at us, Rannulf. We are so far apart on the social scale that even in the best of circumstances a match between us would be considerably frowned upon. But these are not the best of circumstances. Even if Branwell did not steal all that jewelry and even if he and I can be cleared of all blame, he is still in disgrace, and we are still poor. I grew up in a country rectory, you in a duke's mansion. I could never fit into your world, and you could never stoop to mine."

"Do you not believe in love as the great equalizer?" he asked. He could hardly believe that he, Rannulf Bedwyn, was actually asking such a question.

"No." She shook her head. "Besides, there is no real love. Only some liking, I believe, and some . . . some lust." Her eyes held his.

"That was why this just happened?" he asked her. "It was just lust?"

For the merest moment her glance wavered.

"And liking," she said. "We *do* like each other, do we not?"

He sat up on the edge of the bed and buttoned up the flap of his breeches. "I do not usually bed women simply because I like them," he said.

"But there is also the lust," she said. "The mutual lust. You found it hard to lie in bed with me, Rannulf, without touching me. I found it hard too. Lust is not something only men feel."

He did not know whether to be furiously angry or to laugh. If he could ever have predicted this conversation, it would have been with their roles reversed. *He* would have been the one carefully deflecting any suggestion that it had been a love encounter and not simply sex.

"I take it we are done sleeping," he said, getting to his

feet. "Get dressed, Judith, while I see about hiring a carriage for the rest of our journey. And do *not* run away this time."

"I won't," she promised.

I T WAS LATE AFTERNOON BY THE TIME THEY REACHED LONdon. They had exchanged no more than a dozen sentences all day. Judith had had one more bleakness to add to all her other worries.

She could not marry him. She had almost been seduced by madness a couple of days ago. It had seemed almost possible. But no longer. No, she could never marry him. Nevertheless she was glad the events of the past week had at least enabled her to like him and to admire his nobler qualities— and they were many. She was glad of this morning. She was glad she loved him. Her stolen dream had been restored to her and would surely sustain her for a lifetime once the pain was over. There was going to be pain, she knew.

She had never been to London before. She knew it was large, but she had never dreamed that any urban area could be this large. It seemed to go on forever and ever. The streets were all lined with buildings and crowded with people and vehicles and the noises of wheels and horses and people shouting. Any wonder she might have felt was quickly submerged beneath terror.

However was she going to find Branwell?

She had, she supposed, expected that she would simply stop at some inn or other public building, ask for directions to his lodgings, and follow them without any trouble at all— and all within a few minutes of her arrival in London.

"Does it ever end?" she asked foolishly.

"London?" he said. "It is not my favorite place in the world. Unfortunately one sees the worst of it first. You will find Mayfair quieter and cleaner and more spacious than this."

"Is that the area where Branwell lives?" she asked. "Will we find him at home, do you suppose?"

"Probably not," he said. "Gentlemen do not usually spend much of their time in their rooms."

"I hope he comes home sometime this evening," she said, all of yesterday's anxiety returning in full force again. "Whatever will I do if he does not? Will his landlord allow me to wait in his rooms, do you think?"

"He would probably have an apoplexy if you were even to suggest it," he said. "It is not the thing for young ladies to call upon young gentlemen, accompanied only by another gentleman, you know."

"But I am his sister." She looked at him in amazement.

"I daresay," he said, "landlords meet any number of *sisters*."

She stared at him, speechless for a minute.

"What will I do if I cannot see him today?" she asked. "I cannot ask you to sit outside his rooms all night in the carriage. I—"

"I am not taking you to his rooms," he said. "I'll go there alone some other time."

"What?" She looked at him in incomprehension.

"I am taking you to my brother's," he said. "To Bedwyn House."

"*To the Duke of Bewcastle's?*" She stared at him in horror.

"Bewcastle and Alleyne may be the only ones in residence," he said, "in which case I'll have to think of somewhere else to take you—my Aunt Rochester's probably, though she is something of a dragon and would have your head for breakfast if you did not stand up to her."

"I am not going to the Duke of Bewcastle's," she said, aghast. "I came here to find Branwell."

"And find him we will," he said, "if indeed he came to London. But you are *in London* now, Judith. This is the height of impropriety, our riding alone together in a carriage without any maid or chaperon. But it will be the last such impropriety while you are here. I have my reputation to think about, you know."

"How absurd," she said. "How absolutely absurd. If you will not take me to Bran, then set me down and I will find my own way there."

He looked maddeningly cool. He was slightly slouched down in the seat, one booted foot propped against the seat opposite. And he had the gall to grin at her.

"You are afraid," he said. "Afraid of facing Bewcastle."

"I am *not*." She was mortally afraid.

"Liar."

The carriage lurched to a halt as she was drawing breath to make a sharp retort. She glanced beyond the window and realized that they were indeed in a quieter, grander part of London. There were tall, stately buildings on her side of the carriage, a small park on the other, more buildings beyond it. It must be one of London's squares! The door opened and the coachman busied himself setting down the steps.

"This is *Bedwyn House?*" she asked.

He merely grinned at her again, vaulted out of the carriage, and reached up a hand to help her out.

She was wearing a shapeless cotton dress that had been folded inside her bag all day yesterday and worn inside a carriage all day today. She had not brushed or replaited her hair since this morning. It had been squashed beneath her bonnet all day. She must look an absolute fright. Besides all of which she was Judith Law from the rectory at Beaconsfield, fugitive and suspected thief, on her way to meet a duke.

The door was open by the time she alighted from the carriage. A moment later a very stately looking butler was informing Lord Rannulf that his grace was indeed at home and was in the drawing room. He led the way up a grand staircase. Judith thought her knees might well have buckled under her if she had not just been called a liar when she had claimed not to be afraid and if Rannulf's hand had not been beneath one of her elbows.

A footman opened a set of huge double doors as they appeared at the top of the staircase, and the butler stepped between them.

"Lord Rannulf Bedwyn, your grace," he announced. His eyes had alit on Judith downstairs for one brief moment but had not drifted her way since.

Horror of horrors, Judith saw as she was led through the doors, the room had more than one occupant. There were four to be exact, two men and two women.

"Ralf, old fellow," one of the men said, jumping immediately to his feet, "are you back already? Did you escape Grandmama's clutches intact yet again?" He stopped abruptly when he saw Judith.

He was a tall, slender, dark, remarkably handsome young man, only his prominent nose identifying him as Rannulf's brother. One of the ladies, a very young, very beautiful one, looked very much like him. The other lady was fair, like Rannulf, with long, curly hair worn loose. Like him she was dark-complexioned and dark-browed and big-nosed.

They were fleeting impressions. Judith studiously kept her eyes from the other man, who was just then rising to his feet. Even without looking at him she could sense that he was the duke.

"Rannulf?" he said with soft hauteur, sending shivers of apprehension along Judith's spine.

She looked at him to find that he was looking directly back at her, his eyebrows raised, a quizzing glass in one long-fingered hand and half raised to his eye. He was dark and slender like the younger brother, with the family nose and eyes of such a pale gray that it might be more accurate to describe them as silver. His face was cold and haughty, apparently without any humanity. He looked, in fact, much as

Judith had expected him to look. He was, after all, the Duke of Bewcastle.

"I have the honor of presenting Miss Judith Law," Rannulf said, his hand tightening about her elbow. "My sisters, Miss Law—Freyja and Morgan. And my brothers, Bewcastle and Alleyne."

The ladies looked at her with haughty disdain, Judith thought as she curtsied. The younger brother was looking her over slowly with pursed lips, obvious appreciation in his eyes.

"Miss Law," he said. "This is a pleasure."

"Ma'am," the duke said more distantly. His eyes had moved to his brother. "Doubtless you left Miss Law's maid downstairs, Rannulf?"

"There is no such person," Rannulf said, releasing her arm. "Miss Law ran away from Harewood Grange near Grandmaison after being accused of robbing her own grandmother, and I rode after her. We have to find her brother, who may have the jewels but probably does not. In the meantime she must stay here. I am delighted to find that Freyja and Morgan have come up from Lindsey Hall so that I don't have to take her to Aunt Rochester's."

"Oh, I say," Lord Alleyne said. "Cloak and dagger stuff, Ralf? How splendid!"

"Miss Law," the Duke of Bewcastle said, his voice so soft and cold that she was surprised the air did not freeze into icicles about his head, "welcome to Bedwyn House."

CHAPTER XX

D OUBTLESS," WULFRIC, DUKE OF BEWCASTLE
said, one hand spread elegantly about the bowl of
his brandy glass, the other loosely holding the
handle of his quizzing glass, "you are about to explain, Rannulf, why I am playing host to a suspected jewel thief, who
also happens to be young, female, and unchaperoned?"

"And also well above the ordinary in the looks depart-
ment," Alleyne added, grinning. "There you probably have
explanation enough, Wulf."

Bewcastle had invited Rannulf to follow him to the library after the housekeeper had been summoned to show
Judith to a guest room. Such invitations were rarely issued
for purely social purposes. Alleyne had come along too, uninvited. His eldest brother ignored him now and focused his
languid attention on Rannulf—though the pose was decep-
tive. He was, as usual, keen-eyed.

"She is Judith Law, niece of Sir George Effingham,
Grandmama's neighbor," Rannulf explained. "She was liv-
ing there at Harewood Grange as a sort of companion to
Lady Effingham's mother, her own grandmother. There has

been a house party there for the past two weeks. Miss Law's brother was a guest—a young jackanapes who lives a life of expensive idleness, well beyond the means provided him by his father, a country rector. My guess is that the family is very close to being ruined."

"Miss Law, then," Wulfric said after sipping his brandy, "was a poor relation at Harewood. Her brother is up to his neck in debt. And their grandmother owns—or owned—expensive jewels."

"They disappeared during a ball," Rannulf said. "So did Branwell Law. And one piece of jewelry as well as an empty velvet bag that usually held the most expensive jewels were found in Miss Law's room."

"Incriminating indeed," Wulfric said softly, raising his eyebrows.

"Too incriminating," Rannulf said. "Even the rawest of amateurs could have done better."

"Oh, I say," Alleyne said cheerfully, "someone set them up for a fall. Some dastardly villain. Do you have any idea who, Ralf?"

The duke turned toward him, his glass halfway to his eye. "We will not turn this into a farcical melodrama if you please, Alleyne," he said.

"But he is almost right," Rannulf told him. "Horace Effingham, Sir George's son, tried to force himself on Miss Law during a garden party at Grandmaison a week or so ago. He would have succeeded too if I had not happened along just in time and given him a bit of a thrashing. On the night of the ball he attempted revenge by almost trapping me into compromising his sister and being forced to offer for her—Miss Law saved me from that fate. It was during the same ball that young Law abruptly left Harewood and Mrs. Law's jewels disappeared."

"Splendid stuff," Alleyne said. "And while all that excitement was going on in Leicestershire, I have been stuck here shepherding Morgan about to see all the famous sights."

Wulfric had released his hold on his quizzing glass. He was pinching the bridge of his nose with his thumb and middle finger, his eyes closed.

"And so Miss Law ran away and you followed after," he said. "When was that, Rannulf?"

"Yesterday," his brother said.

"Ah." Wulfric removed his hand and opened his eyes. "And dare one ask where you stayed last night?"

"At a posting inn." Rannulf's eyes narrowed. "Look, Wulf, if this is an interrogation into my—"

His brother held up his hand and Rannulf fell silent. One tended to do that with Wulf, he thought, irritated with himself. A single gesture—even the simple raising of an eyebrow would do it—and Bewcastle commanded his world.

"You have not considered," Wulfric asked, "the possibility of a clever trap, Rannulf? That perhaps the lady is poor, greedy, *and* ambitious?"

"If you have any other observations of that nature," Rannulf said, sitting forward in his chair, his hands on the arms, "you had better keep them to yourself, Wulf, if you do not want to be looking for your teeth a moment after."

"Oh, bravo!" Alleyne exclaimed admiringly.

Wulfric merely curled his fingers lightly about the handle of his quizzing glass and raised his eyebrows.

"I take it," he said, "that you are enamored of the lady? The daughter of an impoverished, soon to be ruined, country clergyman? Red hair and certain, ah, generous endowments have turned your head? Infatuation does tend to have a blinding effect on the rational mind, Rannulf. Can you be quite sure you have not been so blinded?"

"Horace Effingham volunteered to pursue the Laws to London," Rannulf said. "My guess is that apprehending them will not be good enough for him. He will want to find evidence that will prove beyond all doubt that they are the thieves."

"If he intends to plant it, we will thwart him," Alleyne said. "I know him by sight, Ralf—a toothy, oily individual, right? I am delighted to discover that he is a villainous cur. I say, life has brightened considerably since this morning."

Wulfric was pinching the bridge of his nose again.

"What I need to do," Rannulf said, "is find Branwell Law. I doubt he is in his rooms at this time of day. He is more likely out somewhere trying to make his fortune on the turn of a card. But I'll go around there anyway to see."

"That is what servants are for," Wulfric said. "It is almost dinnertime, Rannulf. Miss Law will doubtless feel even more uncomfortable than she did earlier if you are absent from the table. I will have a servant sent around, and if he is at home, you may go there in person later."

"She is determined to go there herself," Rannulf said.

"Then she must be dissuaded from doing so," Wulfric said. "How is our grandmother?"

Rannulf sat back in his chair. "Dying," he said.

Both his brothers gave him their full attention.

"She will not talk about it," he said. "She is as elegant, as independent, as active as ever. But she is clearly very ill indeed. Dying, in fact."

"You did not speak with her physician?" Wulfric asked.

Rannulf shook his head. "It would have been an invasion of her privacy."

"Poor Grandmama," Alleyne said. "She has always seemed immortal."

"This business with Miss Law, then," Wulfric said, "must be cleared up without delay. Our grandmother will need you back there at Grandmaison, Rannulf. And I will want to see her once more. The bride she has chosen for you is perhaps the Miss Effingham you referred to? The family is of respectable, though not brilliant, lineage."

"She has changed her mind," Rannulf said. "Grand-mama, I mean. And she knew I was coming after Judith."

"*Judith?*" his brother said softly, his eyebrows rising again. "Our grandmother approves of her? Normally I have great respect for her judgment."

But not for his brother's? Rannulf thought ruefully. He got to his feet.

"I'll send a servant," he said.

J UDITH WAS UP EARLY THE FOLLOWING MORNING, THOUGH she had slept surprisingly well all night. The guest room assigned to her was one of opulent splendor. It even had a spacious dressing room attached to it. The large four-poster bed was soft and comfortable and smelled faintly of laven-der. Even so, she had not expected to sleep.

Being at Bedwyn House was surely the most embarrassing experience of her life. Lord Rannulf's brothers and sisters had all been perfectly well mannered during dinner and the hour in the drawing room that had followed it. But she had felt very far out of her depth. The thought of leaving her room this morning was daunting indeed.

Branwell had not been found. A servant had been sent around to his rooms last night, but he had not been there. When she had said that she would go in person this morn-ing, the Duke of Bewcastle had raised his quizzing glass to his eye, Lord Rannulf had told her it would not be at all the thing, and Lord Alleyne had smiled at her and advised her to leave all to Rannulf. It was not what she had come here to do. But if the thought of leaving her room was daunting, the thought of leaving Bedwyn House was doubly so.

Fifteen minutes after getting out of bed, Judith was on her way downstairs to the breakfast room, wearing a dress that one of the servants must have ironed during the night. She braced herself to meet the whole family again, but the room was empty, she discovered with great relief, except for the butler, who bowed to her from beside the sideboard and then suggested what she might like to eat from a dizzying array of warming dishes. He poured her a cup of coffee after she had sat down.

It was a relief to be alone, but she was going to have to go in search of Lord Rannulf after breakfast. She needed him to direct her to Branwell's lodgings. She hoped he would accompany her there too.

She was not to remain alone for long. Before she had taken more than a few bites, the door opened to admit Lady Freyja and Lady Morgan, both dressed in elegant riding habits. Judith was terrified of both of them—and thoroughly despised herself for being awed by aristocratic arrogance.

"Good morning," she said.

They returned her greeting and busied themselves at the sideboard.

"You have been out riding?" Judith asked politely when they seated themselves.

"In Hyde Park," Lady Freyja said. "It is insipid exercise after having the whole of the park at Lindsey Hall to gallop about until a few days ago as well as the countryside beyond it."

"You were the one who insisted that I wanted to come to town, Free," Lady Morgan said, "even though I protested."

"Because I wanted you to see some of the sights," Lady Freyja said, "and rescue you from the schoolroom and Miss Cowper's clutches for a week or two."

"Nonsense!" her sister said. "We both know *that* was not the reason. Miss Law, I *do* wish I had your color hair. You must be the envy of all your acquaintance."

"Thank you," Judith said, surprised. She had been feeling embarrassed that she had no cap to wear. "Did Lord Rannulf ride with you? I am waiting for him to escort me to my brother's lodgings this morning. I hope to be able to begin my journey home this afternoon." Though how she was going to get there she did not know. She would have to beg the stagecoach fare from Rannulf, she supposed.

"Ah, yes," Lady Freyja said. "I was to tell you when I returned that you are not to worry your head about a thing, that Ralf will take care of it all for you."

Judith jumped to her feet, scraping back her chair with her knees. "But Branwell is *my* brother," she said. "Finding him is *my* concern, not Lord Rannulf's. I will *not* stay here like a good little girl, not worrying my empty little woman's head, letting a *man* take care of my business for me. I am going to find Bran whether there is someone here to direct me to his lodgings or not. And I do not *care* that it is not the thing for a lady to call upon a gentleman alone in London. How absurd when the gentleman is her own brother. Excuse me, please."

She was not given to displays of temper, but the sense of helplessness that had dogged her ever since she arrived at Harewood almost three weeks ago was finally too, too much.

"Oh, splendid!" Lady Freyja exclaimed, looking at her with rather surprised approval. "I have done you an injustice, Miss Law—at least, I sincerely hope I have. I took you for an abject clinging vine. But you are a woman after my own heart, I see. Men can be the most ridiculous creatures, especially *gentlemen* with their archaic notions of gallantry to ladies. I'll come with you."

"So will I," Lady Morgan said eagerly.

Her sister frowned at her. "You had better not, Morgan," she said. "Wulf would have my head. It was bad enough that I brought you to London without consulting him first. His voice was so quiet when I went to the library on his summons that it was almost a whisper. I *hate* it when he does that, especially when I cannot restrain myself from yelling back at him. It puts one at *such* a disadvantage—as he well knows. No, you really must stay at home."

"There is no need for either of you to accompany me," Judith said hastily. "I do not need a chaperon."

"Oh, but I could not possibly deprive myself of the fun of calling at a gentleman's lodging," Lady Freyja assured her, setting her napkin beside her half-empty plate and getting to her feet. "Especially when there are stolen jewels and avengers in hot pursuit to add to the excitement."

"Wulf will have your head anyway, Free," Lady Morgan predicted.

Judith and Lady Freyja set out from Bedwyn House a short while later. They walked until they were well away from the square, and then Lady Freyja hailed a hackney cab and gave the driver Branwell's address.

Judith found herself intrigued by her companion. Lady Freyja Bedwyn was dressed now in a smart green walking dress, her fair hair piled up beneath a fetching hat that Judith guessed must be in the very newest fashion. She was a small woman, and should have been ugly with her incongruously dark eyebrows, dark complexion, and prominent nose. But there was something that rescued her face from ugliness—an unconscious arrogance, a certain strength of character. She might almost be called handsome.

Judith's spirits rose, knowing that finally she was going to see Bran, that she would be able to hear his story from his own lips. She fervently hoped he would be able to deny all knowledge of the theft of Grandmama's jewels, but even if he could not then perhaps she would be in time to salvage something from the situation. Perhaps she could persuade him to restore the jewels and beg Grandmama's pardon, inadequate as the gesture would be. Time was of the essence, though, she knew. She was very thankful that Rannulf had come after her and brought her to London so quickly.

Why had Horace decided to wait a whole day before pursuing her? she wondered. If he had hoped to catch Bran redhanded before he could dispose of the jewels, would he not have wanted to set out that very day? Had he waited perhaps because he knew there was no hurry? Because he knew there were no jewels for Bran to get rid of?

So much pointless speculation was sending her brain into a spin again.

The journey proved to be a wasted one. Branwell was not at home and his landlord did not know when to expect him.

"Though the 'ole world 'as been arsking for 'im last night and this morning," he said, "And now two females. If *that* don't beat all."

"Mr. Law is my brother," Judith explained. "I need him urgently on . . . on family business."

"Ah," the man said, leering at them and revealing a wide array of half-rotten teeth, "I figured one of you was prob'ly 'is sister."

"Did you indeed, my man?" Lady Freyja said, looking at him along the length of her nose. "And did you also figure to amuse us with your impudent observation? Who else has been asking for Mr. Law?"

The man lost his leer and looked instantly more respectful. "Now that, begging your pardon, ma'am," he said, "is confidential."

"Of course it is," Lady Freyja said briskly, opening her reticule. "And you are, of course, the soul of integrity. *Who?*"

Judith's eyes widened when she saw that her companion had drawn a bill worth five pounds from her reticule and was holding it folded between the middle and forefingers of one hand.

The landlord licked his lips and half reached out one hand. "There was someone come last night," he said. " 'e was some nob's servant, wearing blue and silver livery. Two gents come this morning and a tradesman right on their 'eels. I know 'im—Mr. Cooke. I s'pose Mr. Branwell owes 'is bootmaker some money again. I din't know them gents from Adam, and I din't arsk, though they was both real nobs.

Then another gent come 'ere just before you. I didn't arsk 'o 'e were neither. And I ain't arsking 'o you are."

Lady Freyja handed over the bribe though she had got precious little information for such a vast fortune. Judith looked on aghast. Bran's creditors were still after him, then. Who were the three gentlemen? Lord Rannulf and two others? Or Lord Rannulf and one of his brothers and *one* other? *Horace?*

Where on earth was Bran? Was he just out for the morning? Selling or pawning some jewels perhaps? Or had he left London again?

She felt sick to her stomach.

"Come along," Lady Freyja said to her. "We will get no more information here, I believe." She gave directions to the hackney cab driver. "Take us to Gunter's."

"I am so sorry," Judith said. "I have no money with which to reimburse you. I—I left Leicestershire in such a hurry that I forgot to bring some. I will have to repay you some other time." *But when?*

"Oh, pooh," Lady Freyja said with a dismissive wave of one hand. "That is nothing. But I wish we might have been more royally entertained. You do not really believe your brother is the thief, do you? I far prefer the idea of its being Mr. Effingham. I have set eyes on him once or twice. He gives me the shudders though he presents all the appearance of believing himself to be the consummate ladies' man."

"I do *hope*," Judith said fervently, "that he is the guilty one. But however am I to prove it?"

Gunter's, she discovered, sold ices. What an indescribable luxury! And in the morning too. She and Lady Freyja sat at one of the tables, and Judith took small mouthfuls from her spoon and savored every one, letting the ice melt on her tongue before swallowing. It seemed strange to indulge her senses this way when disaster hovered about every corner.

Whatever was she going to do next? She could not keep on staying at Bedwyn House or keep on relying on Rannulf to fight her battles. Yet there was no hope that she could move into Branwell's rooms and await his return.

What was she going to *do*?

T HE DUKE OF BEWCASTLE, HAVING RETURNED AT DAWN from a night spent with his mistress, had gone out for his usual early morning ride with his brothers and sisters. He had gone to White's for breakfast afterward, but did not then proceed to the House of Lords, the spring session having finally ended two days before. In fact, had his sisters not arrived unexpectedly from the country just two days before that, he would probably have been at home in Lindsey Park by this time to spend the rest of the summer.

He returned home from White's and withdrew to his library for the rest of the morning to deal with some correspondence. He looked up with a frown not half an hour later when his butler tapped on the door and opened it.

"There is a Mr. Effingham waiting in the hall to see you, your grace," he said. "Shall I tell him you are from home?"

"Effingham?" The duke frowned. The whole melodrama surrounding Rannulf's return to London the day before was something he would prefer to ignore. But the matter needed to be cleared up. He must go to Grandmaison before it was too late to see his grandmother. "No, show him in, Fleming."

Horace Effingham was unknown to the Duke of Bewcastle. But he came striding into the library, smiling and confident, as if the two of them were blood brothers. The duke did not rise. Effingham strode across to his desk and half leaned across it, his right arm outstretched.

"It is good of you to see me, Bewcastle," he said.

His grace availed himself of his quizzing glass, through

which he looked briefly at the offered hand before letting the glass fall on its ribbon against his chest.

"Effingham?" he said. "What may I do for you?"

The other man smiled even more broadly as he withdrew his hand. He looked about as if for a chair, did not see one close by, and so continued to stand.

"I understand that your brother is in residence here again," he said.

"Do you?" his grace said. "I trust that my butler has seen fit to inform my cook. I do, of course, have three brothers."

Effingham laughed. "I referred to Lord Rannulf Bedwyn," he said.

"Ah, quite so," the duke said.

There was a short silence during which Effingham appeared disconcerted for a moment.

"I must ask your grace," he said, "if he brought a lady here with him. A Miss Judith Law?"

"You *must* ask?" The duke's eyebrows rose.

Effingham set both hands flat on the desk and leaned slightly across it. "Perhaps you do not know," he said, "that if she *is* here, you are harboring a criminal and a fugitive. It is a crime in itself, your grace, though I am certain you would not continue to harbor her once you knew the truth."

"It is a relief," his grace said, repossessing himself of his quizzing glass, "to know that I hold such a high place in your esteem."

Effingham laughed heartily. "*Is* Miss Law here, Bewcastle?" he asked.

"It is my understanding," the duke said, half raising the glass, "that rape is also a felony. When the charge is merely *attempted* rape, of course, a conviction might be less assured. But the word of two persons against one might carry some weight with a judge and jury, especially when one of those persons is the brother of a duke. Can you find your own way out, or shall I summon my butler?"

Effingham straightened up, all pretense of affability gone.

"I am on my way to hire a Bow Street Runner," he said. "I plan to run them to earth, you know, Judith and Branwell Law. And I mean to recover my stepgrandmother's jewels. There will be a nice little scandal surrounding the trial and sentencing, I daresay. If I were you, your grace, I would distance myself from it and advise your brother to do the same."

"I am infinitely grateful," the Duke of Bewcastle said, raising his glass all the way to his eye, "that you esteem me sufficiently to come all the way to Bedwyn House to advise me. You will close the door quietly on your way out?"

Effingham was slightly white about the mouth. He nodded slowly before turning on his heel and striding out. He banged the door shut.

His grace looked after him thoughtfully.

CHAPTER XXI

R ANNULF LOOKED AT JUDITH IN SOME EXASPERATION.
She looked vivid and gorgeous with her red hair
uncovered, nothing like the almost invisible
shadow she had been at Harewood. She had also been out
this morning, venturing into an area of London where respectable ladies did not go, dragging Freyja with her. No,
that at least was unfair. Freyja would have needed no
dragging.

It had been entirely unnecessary for her to go. She knew
that he was going himself to see if her brother was at home.
Branwell Law had not been there, of course, and all the in-
quiries he and Alleyne had made at various likely places had
turned up nothing useful. Several men knew Law. None of
them knew where he might be.

But Bewcastle came into the room before Rannulf could
rip into Freyja—since he had no real right to rip into Judith.
Perhaps it was just as well. Judith would surely have witnessed a family brawl. Wulf had come to suggest in that soft,
deceptively languid way of his that it might be in the inter-

ests of all concerned if the effort to find Branwell Law were redoubled.

"I have just had a fascinating visit from Mr. Effingham," he said. "He was under the strange illusion that I harbor felonious fugitives at Bedwyn House. Since he received no satisfaction here, he will no doubt seek it elsewhere from another perceived fugitive, who has presumably not found a safe sanctuary and perhaps is even unaware that he needs to. You did not, I suppose, find Mr. Law at home this morning, Rannulf?"

Rannulf shook his head.

"Someone else is looking for him, though," Freyja said and won for herself a long, silent stare from Wulf's silver eyes. But Freyja was made of stern stuff. She merely stared right back and told Wulf what she and Judith had already told Rannulf and Alleyne. She added that she had bribed the information about the other visitors out of the landlord.

Wulf's eyes, still regarding their sister, narrowed. But instead of the blistering setdown Rannulf had fully expected, Bewcastle's next words were directed at him.

"You had better go back there, Rannulf," he said. "I smell a proverbial rat. I'll go with you."

"I am coming too," Judith said.

"Judith—"

"I am coming too."

She gazed with stormy determination into Rannulf's eyes, and for the first time he wondered if there were not perhaps some truth to the old cliché about redheads and tempers. All he wanted to do was sort out this mess for her so that she could be at peace, so that he could get back to the business of wooing her. And *this* time he would do it properly. He would make her his lady . . .

"In that case," Bewcastle said with a sigh, "Freyja had better come too. It will be a veritable family outing."

They went in one of Bewcastle's private carriages—a

plain one that he used when he did not wish to draw atten-
tion to himself. Soon they were back at Law's lodging house.
Rannulf could see no particular point in returning there, but
Wulf was in one of his incommunicable moods.

The landlord tossed his glance skyward when he opened
the door to the coachman's knock and saw them all arrayed
on his doorstep.

"Lord love us," he said. " 'ere we go again."

"Quite so," Bewcastle said, quelling the man's impudence
with a single cold glance and causing him to bob his head
respectfully instead and pull at his forelock. How did Wulf
do that, even to strangers? "I understand that Mr. Branwell
Law is a popular young man this morning."

"That 'e is, sir," the man said. "First a servant last night,
then that gen'leman there with another this morning, then
a different gent, then them two ladies back there. Quite a
morning it 'as been."

"And you could give none of them any information
about Mr. Law?" Bewcastle asked. "About whether he has
been here during the last few days? About when you last saw
him?"

"I could not, sir." The man drew himself up to his full
height. "I do not give out personal hinformation about my
tenants."

"You are to be commended," Bewcastle said. "Some men
in your position might try to make some extra money on the
side by taking bribes in exchange for information."

The landlord's eyes slid uneasily toward Freyja and away
again.

"When did you last see Branwell Law?" Bewcastle asked.

The man licked his lips. "Last night, sir," he said, "after
that servant come 'ere. And this morning."

"*What?*" Judith cried. "You said nothing about this to me
this morning."

" 'e come after you left, miss," the man said.

"But you could have told me he was here *last night*," she said. "I told you he was my brother. I told you there was a family emergency."

Bewcastle held up his hand in a slight staying gesture, and Rannulf drew Judith's hand through his arm and settled his hand over hers. She was trembling—with rage, at a guess.

"The gentleman who called alone this morning," Bewcastle said. "Describe him, if you will."

"Blond hair, blue eyes," the landlord said. His eyes had become shifty, Rannulf noted. "Short. With a limp."

"Ah," Wulf said. "Yes, quite so."

It had not been Effingham, then, Rannulf thought with some disappointment. But surely he would be here soon. He was in London—he had already called at Bedwyn House.

"That is all I can tell you, sir," the landlord said, making to close the door. Bewcastle set his cane against it.

"I suppose," he said, "you did not admit this blond-haired, blue-eyed, short gentleman with a limp to Mr. Law's rooms?"

The man recoiled in shock. "Let 'im in, sir?" he said. "When Mr. Law was from 'ome? Not me. No, indeed not."

"I wonder," Bewcastle said, "how much he paid you."

The man's eyes widened. "I do not take—"

"Ah, but you do," Bewcastle said gently. "I will not pay you one penny. I do not deal in bribes. But I will warn you that if a felony has been committed in Branwell Law's rooms this morning and if you took money from the felon to let him into those rooms, you are an accessory to a crime and will doubtless pay the price in one of London's notorious jails."

The landlord gaped at him, his eyes as round as saucers, his color suddenly pasty. "A felon?" he said. "A felony? 'e was a *friend* of Mr. Law's. I seen 'im 'ere before with Mr. Law.

'e just needed to go in for a minute to get something 'e forgot last time 'e was 'ere."

"Then it was magnanimous of you to allow him in," Bewcastle said while Judith's hand tightened about Rannulf's arm. "Unescorted, I presume? This *dark*-haired man?"

The landlord licked his lips and turned shifty-eyed again.

"I daresay," Bewcastle said, "he paid you very well indeed to describe him as you did if questioned, to allow him in unescorted, and to claim that Mr. Law was here both last night and this morning?"

"Not very much," the man mumbled after a lengthy pause.

"Then the more fool you," Bewcastle said, sounding bored.

"You villain!" Rannulf dropped Judith's arm and stepped forward. "I should throttle you within an inch of your life. What did he take from the rooms? Or, more important, what did he leave there?"

The landlord took one terrified step back and held up both hands.

"I din't know 'e were up to no good," he said. "I swear I din't."

"Save the pathetic pleas for a judge," Rannulf said. "Take us to Law's rooms immediately."

"I believe it might be preferable," Wulf said, still sounding damnably unruffled, "to proceed more calmly, Rannulf. I am sure this good man has a tolerably comfortable room in which we can wait. I believe too that from this moment on he will be scrupulous in telling the exact truth to whoever asks it of him. It might save him his neck or at least years of his liberty."

"Wait?" Rannulf's eyebrows snapped together in a frown. *Wait?* When Effingham was out there somewhere and so was Branwell Law? When Judith's good name and liberty were still in peril? When there was probably planted evidence in Law's rooms?

"If I am not much mistaken," Bewcastle said, "this house will be receiving yet another visit soon." He looked at the landlord again. "I believe you also agreed to show no recognition when the same *dark*-haired gentleman returns with a Bow Street Runner?"

The man's Adam's apple bobbed as he swallowed and looked from Bewcastle to Rannulf.

"Show us to a room within earshot of the door," Bewcastle said.

It was a small, dingy room with dark, faded furniture. The four of them were ushered inside and left alone there, the door ajar.

Freyja laughed softly. "Sometimes, Wulf," she said, "I cannot help but admire you. How did you guess?"

"I believe it was at our mother's knee," he said, "that I learned that two and two invariably add up to four, Freyja."

"But what if they do not on this occasion?" Judith asked. "What if there is nothing in Bran's room? Why will you not let us look, your grace?"

"The landlord will tell the truth now," he said. "It is best, Miss Law, if he can say with all honesty that no one has been into your brother's rooms since Effingham left them this morning."

"Bran was not here last night or this morning, then, was he?" she said. "Where is he?"

They were rhetorical questions. She was not looking for answers to any of them. Rannulf took both her hands in his, squeezed them tightly, and then held them flat against his chest. He did not care what Wulf or Freyja might think.

"We will find him," he told her. "And if Wulf's guess is correct, as I would wager it is, his name will have been cleared by the time we do. Stop worrying."

Though, of course, the brother was probably in serious

trouble even apart from all this business of stolen property. If he had been desperate enough to leave Harewood in the middle of the night because so many creditors were hounding him, he would be desperate enough to do some pretty heavy gambling to recoup his fortunes.

"Don't worry," he said again, raising one of her hands to his lips and holding it there for a few moments until she looked into his eyes and half smiled.

Freyja, he saw, had taken a seat and was looking at them with an unreadable expression in her eyes. Bewcastle was standing slightly to one side of the window, looking out at the street.

"Ah," he said, "not a moment too soon."

JUDITH WAS TERRIBLY AFRAID. AFRAID OF WHAT WAS about to happen, afraid of what would be discovered in Branwell's rooms, afraid of what might *not* be discovered. She was afraid for Bran even apart from all this, afraid for her family and for herself. And she was afraid of this proud, haughty, powerful family which was fighting her battles for her.

Most of all perhaps she feared the look in Rannulf's eyes, the firm kindness of his hands, the warm gentleness of his kiss on one of them. Did he not *understand*?

She could hear the landlord open the door again—they were all very still, listening. She recognized Horace's voice and another, deeper, gruffer voice.

"I am with the Bow Street Runners," that other voice was saying, "and investigating a large jewel theft. I must insist upon your letting us into Mr. Branwell Law's rooms, where I expect to find evidence."

"I s'pose it is all right, then," the landlord said.

"I am *hoping*," Horace said, sounding both grave and pompous, "that we will find nothing, Witley, though I fear the worst. Branwell Law *is* my stepcousin, after all. But I do not know who else would have stolen his grandmother's jewels but him and his sister. They both fled during that same night. I pray this will be a wild-goose chase and they have already discovered back at Harewood that some vagrant broke into the house during the ball."

"It is unlikely, sir," the Bow Street Runner said.

There was the sound of boots on the stairs going up and then the jingle of keys and the squeak of a door opening upstairs.

"Wulf and I will go up," Rannulf said. "Judith, stay here with Freyja."

Freyja snorted.

"I am coming up too," Judith said. "This concerns me as well as Bran."

There was an open door at the top of the first flight of stairs, presumably opening into Branwell's rooms. Judith could see the landlord standing just inside. He turned a worried face toward them as they stepped onto the landing. Horace was standing in the middle of the room, his back to the door, his arms crossed over his chest. The Bow Street Runner, a short, rotund, bald man, was coming out of an inner room, perhaps the bedchamber, clutching a glittering pile of what must be Grandmama's jewelry.

"He did not even hide it very carefully," he said with some contempt.

"And *that*, if I am not much mistaken," Horace said, pointing to a chair that was just in Judith's line of vision, "is one of Judith Law's caps. Oh, my poor Judith, how careless of you. I was hoping you might be left out of this."

"She more or less had to be an accomplice, though, did she not, sir?" the Runner said, setting down the jewels with a clatter on a small table and picking up the bonnet cap Judith had so detested.

She did not know what everyone else was waiting for.

"You are a liar and a villain, Horace!" she cried, striding into the room and drawing to herself the astonished attention of both men. "You planted the evidence in my room at Harewood, and you planted the evidence here. It is a wicked, dastardly form of revenge, especially against Branwell, who has done nothing to offend you."

"Well, my dear cousin herself," Horace said. "You have one thief to arrest without any further searching, Witley." And then his eyes moved beyond Judith and the smirk on his face froze there.

"You might well lose that cocky air," Rannulf said quietly.

"These are the Bedwyns, Witley," Horace said, not taking his eyes off Rannulf. "With the Duke of Bewcastle himself. A powerful family, as you doubtless know. But I would expect your integrity to be above fear of such power. Lord Rannulf Bedwyn fancies Judith."

"The game is up, Effingham," Rannulf said. "The landlord who just let you into these rooms will swear that Branwell Law has not been home here for longer than two weeks—before the theft, that is. He will also swear that this morning you paid him a hefty bribe to let you in here unescorted and to tell certain lies if he was questioned, including one about Law's having been here yesterday and today. I will swear to the fact that I last saw that cap at Harewood last week, that I have not seen it since though I escorted Miss Law to London. She has also not been out of the company of one or another of my family since we arrived here yesterday afternoon. If that is *all* the jewelry that can be found in these rooms, I would guess that there is far more elsewhere. Judith, you would know better than I. Should there be more?"

"Much more," she said.

"I wonder," Rannulf said, "if you have been cocky enough

to keep them in *your* lodgings, Effingham, on the assumption that no one would dream of searching for them there."

The Bow Street Runner cleared his throat. "These are serious charges you are making, my lord," he said.

"They are indeed," Rannulf agreed. "Perhaps since we are on a treasure hunt, we should all invite ourselves to Effingham's lodgings and have a look around."

It was the moment at which Judith, watching Horace closely, knew that he was finally beaten. He *had* been foolish enough to keep the jewels in his rooms. And now he was further incriminating himself by turning red in the face and blustering. He was as cowardly now as he had been outside the summerhouse at Grandmaison.

She set her hands over her face briefly and stopped listening. This had all happened—all of it—because she had worn one of her unaltered dresses at Harewood the day of Horace's arrival there and had *not* worn a cap. He had looked at her and leered at her, as men had been doing since she grew out of her girlhood, and everything had developed from that moment. It was all her fault.

Freyja, she could see, was seated on one of the chairs in the room, her legs crossed, one foot swinging. She looked as if she was actually enjoying herself. The duke was still out on the landing, his back to the room, his hands clasped at his back, not participating in the proceedings at all.

"I-I *was* here earlier," Horace was saying when she returned her attention to what was going on, "and found everything—*all* the missing jewels. I took most of them with me for safekeeping and left the rest so that I could bring you here with me, Witley, as a witness."

"I believe, sir," the Bow Street Runner said, "we had better go to your lodgings and get the rest of the jewels. And then I believe I am going to have to arrest you."

Judith spread one hand over her mouth and closed her eyes. Arrests led to trials and witnesses and publicity and

terrible pain for the families involved. They led to punishment, often very harsh indeed. She heard herself moan and
Rannulf's arms came about her from behind to clasp her
elbows.

"Since you have been hired by Mr. Effingham," the duke
said, finally stepping into the room and strolling across the
floor to glance down at the jewels and the cap with apparent
distaste, "it would perhaps be unsporting of you to arrest
him . . . Witley, is it? You may wish to leave me and Lord
Rannulf Bedwyn to deal with the matter ourselves?"

The Bow Street Runner looked dubious, and Horace
gazed about him in some dismay—wondering perhaps
whether the devil or the deep blue sea was the worse fate.

"I am not sure about that, your grace," the Runner said.
"It goes against the grain to allow a man to escape his just
and lawful punishment just because he is a gentleman."

"Oh, I can assure you," the duke said, his voice so coldly
quiet that Judith found herself shivering, "there will be punishment."

"Miss Law," Lady Freyja said, getting to her feet, "I believe this is the point at which we are to be ordered from the
room. Shall we go voluntarily?"

The day was already feeling quite surreal to Judith. It suddenly became more so. As she and Lady Freyja turned
toward the open doorway, someone else stepped into it.

"I say," a familiar voice said, "what the deuce is going on
in here?"

"*Bran!*" Judith hurled herself into his arms.

"Jude?" he said. "Effingham? Bedwyn? What the devil?"

"You did not take the jewels, did you?" she said, raising
her head and gazing into his pale, frowning face. "I am sorry
I ever suspected you, Bran. It was dreadful of me, and I do
beg your forgiveness."

"*What* jewels?" he asked, his brows knitted together in a
deep frown. "Has the world gone mad?"

"Grandmama's," Judith told him. "They all disappeared just after you left in the middle of the ball, and the empty velvet bag and one earring were found in my room. Horace planted the jewels on the table over there in your rooms this morning together with the bonnet cap Aunt Effingham made me wear at Harewood and then he brought a Bow Street Runner here to find them. But the Duke of Bewcastle guessed it all and we arrived in time to catch Horace at it and now Lady Freyja and I have to leave the room because I think Lord Rannulf is going to f-fight Horace."

She buried her face against his shoulder and burst into tears.

"Well, if that don't beat all," she heard Branwell say as she tried to control herself—she was dreadfully embarrassed. "Is *that* why you came on so nasty during the ball, Effingham, and then suggested that I go to Darnley's weeklong gaming party to win enough money to pay you back?"

"How much *did* you win, Law?" Even now Horace had the gall to sneer.

"Thirty pounds actually," Branwell said. "I say, thank you, Bedwyn."

He took something from Rannulf's hand and gave it to Judith—a large handkerchief. She stepped out onto the landing, dried her eyes with it, and blew her nose.

"I was about to bet it when I came to my senses," Branwell said. "I would certainly have lost it all and then more on top of it. But with the thirty pounds I could pay you back for my traveling expenses, I thought, and then all those other debts when I could. And I will too. I left the party a day early and came back to town. Here!" Judith could hear him striding across the room. "Thirty pounds. And now I have some fighting of my own to do."

Judith felt a hand on her shoulder. "Ladies always have to

miss the greatest fun," Freyja said with a sigh. "Come on, we will go home in Wulf's carriage."

"*Fun!*" Judith looked up at her with some indignation. Everything in her world had fallen apart and Lady Freyja thought it was *fun?*

But she did not resist the pressure of the other's hand. Truth to tell, she could not get away fast enough. She felt deeply, horribly embarrassed even if she ignored all the more personal pain. That Lord Rannulf's family should be witnesses to such sordid dealings involving *her* family! That they should know all about Bran and his foolish extravagances and Papa's impoverishment! That they should know the villainy of her own stepcousin! That they should have witnessed her breaking down and weeping as if her heart would break! And to think that just a few days ago—was it really only three?—she had danced with Lord Rannulf and thought it might just be possible to listen to his marriage proposal and accept it.

How thankful she ought to be that something had happened to bring her to her senses.

Appropriately for the mood of the day it was wet outside. The rain was drizzling down, and they had to make a dash for the carriage.

"Ugh!" Lady Freyja said, shaking out her dress when they were seated within and the vehicle lurched into motion. "I will be glad to get home even though I would have far preferred to stay and watch."

Home. It was the only word Judith heard.

"Lady Freyja," she said, "may I beg a great, great favor of you?"

Lady Freyja turned a look of inquiry on her.

"Will you lend . . . No." Judith stopped herself. "I cannot ask for a loan. I doubt if I will ever be able to repay it though I promise to try. Will you *give* me the fare of a stagecoach ride to my home in Wiltshire? Please? I know this is dreadful presumption."

"Why?" Lady Freyja asked.

"I have no reason to stay here any longer," Judith said, "and I cannot presume on the Duke of Bewcastle's hospitality anymore. I want to go home."

"Without saying good-bye to Ralf?" Lady Freyja asked.

Judith closed her eyes briefly.

There was silence within the carriage for several moments.

"There are those," Lady Freyja said quietly, "who would give a great deal to be looked at as Ralf looked at you back there in the room where we waited."

Judith swallowed. "You cannot pretend," she said, "that you did not see the ineligibility of such a connection the moment you set eyes upon me yesterday, that your brothers and your sister did not. Today you must have become even more aware of it. I am leaving as soon as I have fetched my bag from Bedwyn House, with or without your assistance. I would have thought you would be glad to part with the price of my fare just to have me out of Lord Rannulf's life."

"You know little about us Bedwyns," Lady Freyja said.

"You will not help me, then?"

"Oh, I will," Lady Freyja said.

Illogically, Judith's spirts sank even lower if that were possible.

She had stood on the landing blowing her nose and not even looking around once, she thought. She had not turned to have a final look at him. All she had to remember him by was the handkerchief still balled up in one of her hands— and her straw bonnet.

"Thank you," she said.

CHAPTER XXII

A FEW HOURS PASSED BEFORE HORACE EFFING-
ham was led away from Branwell Law's rooms under the escort of two burly men Bewcastle had
conjured up from somewhere without ever leaving the room
himself. Effingham was to spend the night in his own lodgings, under guard, and was then to be escorted back to Harewood Grange for his father to deal with, presumably in
consultation with Mrs. Law, who was the injured party.

Effingham left with a red, bulbous nose and an eye that
would be closed and black by the morning—both courtesy
of Branwell Law within two minutes of the ladies' departure.
The Bow Street Runner had left a few minutes after that.

Rannulf had not laid a violent hand upon Effingham except to grab him by the scruff of the neck and hoist him up
onto his toes a couple of times when he attempted obstinacy
and insolence. Rannulf would have liked nothing better
than to pound the villain to a bloody pulp, but Bewcastle's
cold, silent presence had a calming effect on him. What did
violence prove, after all, but that one was physically
stronger than the other? A physical show of force had been

altogether appropriate outside his grandmother's summer-house. Here it would have been mere self-indulgence.

Law produced pen, ink, and paper when asked to do so and Effingham was instructed to sit at the table and write his letters of confession and apology—one to Mrs. Law, one to Sir George Effingham, one to the Reverend Jeremiah Law. The task took almost two hours, principally because Rannulf did not like most of the letters. Before there were three that were acceptable to both him and Branwell Law—Bewcastle did not involve himself—they were both wading in crumpled-up sheets of paper that had been tossed to the floor.

The letters were sent on their way, franked by Bewcastle, before Effingham was led away. Detailed, abject, and groveling, they would arrive in the hands of Mrs. Law and Sir George before the culprit himself appeared. It would be a severe enough punishment, Rannulf decided, even though in some ways it seemed less satisfying than a thorough drubbing would have been. Public humiliation was a terrible thing for any man. Effingham's face when he left, sullen and ugly with hatred and frustration, was testament to that. It would not be easy for him to return to Harewood, to face his father and his stepgrandmother.

The jewels, the rest of which had been fetched from Effingham's lodgings, again at Bewcastle's command, were to be returned to Harewood by special messenger.

"So," Branwell Law said, sinking into a chair when Effingham and his escorts had finally left, tipping back his head against the rest and placing the back of one hand over his eyes, "that is that. What a ghastly to-do. And to think that I once considered him my friend. I even admired him." He seemed to remember suddenly in whose company he was and sat up straighter. "I do not know what we would have done without your assistance, Your Grace, and yours,

Bedwyn. I cannot thank you enough. Really. On behalf of Jude too. She did not deserve this."

"No," Rannulf agreed, "she did not."

Law smiled uncertainly and looked from one to the other of them, clearly embarrassed now that he was alone with a duke and the duke's brother.

"I want to know the extent of your debts," Rannulf said, remaining on his feet and clasping his hands at his back.

"Oh, I say." Law flushed. "They are trifling. Nothing I cannot handle."

Rannulf took one step closer to him. "I want to know the full extent of them," he said, "down to the last penny." He indicated the table, still strewn with paper, ink, and one un-used quill pen. "Write it all down, every last trifling amount."

"Oh, I say," Law said again. "I most certainly will not do that, Bedwyn. You have no business—"

Rannulf reached down, took hold of the young man's neckcloth, and lifted him to his feet. "I am making it my business," he said. "I want to know everything you owe— *everything*, do you understand me? I am going to pay your debts for you."

"Oh, I say," Law said for the third time, indignant now. "I cannot let you do that for me. I will come about—"

"I will not be doing it for *you*," Rannulf told him.

Law drew breath again and then closed his mouth. He frowned. "For Jude?"

"You have all but beggared your family," Rannulf said, "and are clearly about to complete the process. Miss Judith Law has already been farmed out to wealthier relatives, who treated her like a glorified servant. One of your other sisters is about to suffer the same fate. And there are two more as well as your mother at home. A young puppy is entitled to sow a few wild oats, tiresome as he may become to all who know him. He is *not* entitled to bring ruin and misery on his whole family. *You* are not entitled to bring unhappiness to Miss Judith Law. Start writing. Take your time and make sure you forget nothing. Your debts will be paid, you will be given enough ready cash to pay your rent and the barest of your expenses for the next month, and then you will support yourself on your own earnings or starve. One thing I will have your gentleman's word on. You will never again apply to your father for even as much as a single penny."

Law was white-faced. "You would do all this for *Judith?*" he asked.

Rannulf merely narrowed his eyes and pointed to the table again. Law sat, picked up the pen, and dipped it in the inkwell.

Rannulf glanced at Bewcastle, who was seated at the other side of the room, one leg crossed elegantly over the other, his elbows on the armrests, his fingers steepled. He raised his eyebrows when he met his brother's eyes but offered no comment.

The following half hour passed in silence except for the scraping of Law's pen and a few whispers as he added up columns of figures. Twice he got up and disappeared into the bedchamber to reappear with a bill.

"There," he said at last, blotting the sheet and turning to hand it to Rannulf. "That is everything. It is a considerable amount, I'm afraid." His cheeks were flushed with embarrassment.

It did not seem a particularly enormous sum to Rannulf, but to a man who did not have the means with which to pay even the first pound of the debt, it must seem astronomical indeed.

"One word of advice," Rannulf said. "Gaming can be a pleasurable activity if one has money to lose and if one sets strict limits on the amount one is prepared to bet. It is a miserable, hellish way to try to recoup nonexistent fortunes."

"Don't I just know it," Law said fervently. "I will never make another wager in my life."

Rannulf raised his eyebrows.

"Now, Mr. Law," Bewcastle said, breaking a long silence, "you will tell me what sort of career you think yourself best fitted for."

They both turned to stare at him.

"The diplomatic service?" Bewcastle suggested. "The law? The military? The church?"

"Not the church," Law said. "I cannot imagine anything more tedious. And not the military. Or the law."

"The diplomatic service, then?"

"I have always thought I would enjoy something in commerce or trade," Law said. "The East India Company or something like that. I would like to go to India or somewhere overseas. But my father always said it would be beneath the dignity of a gentleman."

"Certain positions are not," Bewcastle said, "though of course a novice could not expect to occupy one of the hallowed positions in any company before working hard at lowlier tasks and proving himself."

"I am ready to work hard," Law said. "To tell the truth, I am rather sick of the life I have been living. There is no enjoyment in it when one does not have the money one's companions have."

"Quite so," Bewcastle agreed. "You may call on me tomorrow morning, Mr. Law, at ten o'clock. I will see what I can do for you by then."

"You would help me start a *career*?" Law asked. "You would do that for me, Your Grace?"

Bewcastle did not deign to reply. He got to his feet and picked up his hat and cane. He nodded curtly to Branwell Law by way of farewell.

"I trust Freyja had the carriage returned for our use, Rannulf," he said.

She had. And it was a good thing too—it was raining. Rannulf left the seat facing the horses for Bewcastle and settled into the other with a sigh. He felt exhausted. All he wanted was to get back home to see Judith, to take her in his arms—he would not care if all his brothers and sisters were lined up to see him do it—and assure her that her ordeal was over, that all was well, that there was nothing left for them to do but waltz off into their happily ever after together.

"That was decent of you, Wulf," he said when the door had been closed and the carriage was in motion. "The only chance he has to reform his life is to settle into a steady career. Yet without influence his choices would be severely limited."

"You are planning to marry Miss Law?" his brother asked.

"I am." Rannulf looked at him warily.

"She is," Wulfric said, "despite the plainness of her dress and the severity of the style of her hair, quite extraordinarily beautiful. You have always had an eye for such women."

"There is no one to compare to Judith Law," Rannulf said. "But if you think I see nothing but her physical beauty, Wulf, you are wrong."

"She has been something of a damsel in distress," Wulfric said, "in more ways than one. The gallant urge to ride to the rescue can sometimes be mistaken for love, I believe."

"She has never behaved like a victim," Rannulf assured him. "And I am not mistaken. If you are about to recite all the ways in which she is *not* an eligible bride for me, Wulf, you may save your breath. I know them all and they make no difference whatsoever to my feelings for her. I have position, money, and prospects enough that I do not need a wealthy bride."

His brother did not comment.

"I take it, then," Rannulf said after some moments of silence, "that I will not have your blessing, Wulf?"

"Is it important to you?"

Rannulf thought for a moment. "Yes," he said at last, "It is. You frequently infuriate me, Wulf, and I will never allow myself to be dominated by you, but I respect you perhaps more than I respect anyone else I know. You have always done your duty, and sometimes you go the extra mile for one of us even when it must be distasteful or tedious for you to do it. Like the time a month or two ago when you went into Oxfordshire to help Eve and Aidan regain custody of her foster children—the orphans of a lowly shopkeeper. And like what you have done for me today. Yes, your blessing is important to me. But I will marry Judith with or without it."

"You have it," Wulf said softly. "I would not be doing my duty if I did not point out to you all the possible sources of future dissatisfaction, once the bloom of romance has faded. Marriage is a lifetime commitment, and we Bedwyns have always been faithful to our spouses. But your choice of bride is yours to make, Rannulf. You are of age, and it is you who must live with her for the rest of your life."

Was that why Bewcastle had never married? Rannulf wondered. In his cold, calculated way, had he always considered the possible sources of future dissatisfaction? But as far as Rannulf knew, his eldest brother had never shown even the slightest interest in any lady despite the fact that for years he had been one of England's most eligible bachelors. He had kept the same mistress for years, but no romance that might have led to matrimony.

"I am not expecting happily ever after, Wulf," Rannulf said. "But I *am* expecting to be happy even after the bloom has faded from the rose. As you just said, marriage is a lifetime commitment."

They did not talk anymore, and as soon as the carriage drew up before the doors of Bedwyn House Rannulf vaulted out and hurried inside and up the stairs to the drawing room. Alleyne, Freyja, and Morgan were there but not Judith.

"Ah, at last," Alleyne said. "Come and tell us the rest of

the story, Ralf. Apparently Free and Miss Law were banished at the most interesting moment. Let me see your knuckles."

"Where is Judith?" Rannulf asked.

"In her room, I suppose," Alleyne said. "Overcome by all the excitement, no doubt. Did Effingham put up a fight? If he did, he missed your face, even the large target of the Bedwyn nose." He grinned.

"She is not," Morgan said. "That is all *you* know, Alleyne. She is not in her room. She has gone."

Rannulf looked sharply at her and then at Freyja, who was sitting unnaturally still and had not clamored immediately for a report on what had happened after she left Law's rooms.

"She has gone home," she said, "by stagecoach."

"Home?" Rannulf stared blankly at her.

"To Beaconsfield in Wiltshire," she explained. "To the rectory. Home, Ralf, where she feels she belongs."

He stared at her, aghast.

"Bloody hell," he said.

It spoke volumes of the Bedwyns that neither lady displayed even the slightest evidence of shock.

I T RAINED THROUGH MOST OF THE NIGHT, SLOWING THE progress of the stagecoach and a couple of times causing Judith's stomach to clench in terror as the coach slithered on particularly bad stretches of mud. But by morning the sky had cleared and the sun was shining again, and there were familiar faces to smile at her and call greetings to her when she was set down outside the inn in Beaconsfield.

They were hardly reassuring. As she trudged along the street toward the rectory at the other end of the village, she felt as if she trod on her heart every step of the way. She had not even taken a final look at him, and foolishly she had kept on panicking throughout the seemingly interminable journey, not being able to bring his face into focus in her mind.

Her story had had a happy ending. She kept telling herself that. Both she and Bran had been cleared of the robbery charges against them and the true culprit caught. Grandmama's jewels had been recovered—at least she assumed they would all be recovered since Horace had not denied having the rest of them at his lodgings. She was going home—Aunt Effingham would certainly not want her back at Harewood now. It was unlikely that she would want any of them there, and so even Hilary might be safe from the misery of going there to live.

But it did not feel like a happy ending. Her heart was crushed and she thought it might take longer than forever to heal.

Besides, it was not a completely happy ending even if she ignored the state of her heart. Nothing had been solved for her family. Quite the contrary. Bran was hopelessly in debt, and it seemed as if the only ways he could think of to get himself out of debt were to gamble and to beg Papa for help. He would be forced to take that latter course soon, and then they would all descend into poverty indeed. It seemed altogether possible that Bran's ultimate destination was going to be debtors' prison. Perhaps Papa's too.

No, it was a miserable morning in every way it was possible to be miserable. But even as she thought it, the door of the rectory opened and Pamela and Hilary came dashing outside, Hilary shrieking.

"Jude!" she cried. "Jude, you have come home."

Judith set down her bag in the roadway by the garden gate and laughed with happiness despite herself as first one sister and then the other flung themselves into her arms and hugged all the breath out of her. Cassandra came more slowly behind them smiling warmly and holding out both arms as she came.

"Judith," she said, hugging her too. "Oh, Jude, we have been so afraid that you would not come home and we would never see you again." Tears were welling from her eyes. "I *know* there must be an explanation. I just know it. Where is Bran?"

But before Judith could reply, she became aware of her father's stern, silent figure in the doorway. Invisible fingers of doom reached out to envelop her.

"Judith," he said without raising his voice—it was his pulpit voice, "you will come into my study, if you please."

Obviously they had heard something from Harewood.

"I have just come from London, Papa," she said. "Grandmama's jewels have all been recovered. It was Horace Effingham who stole them with the sole purpose of incriminating Branwell and me. But he has been caught and has confessed. There were more witnesses than just Bran and me, the Duke of Bewcastle among them. I daresay all will be explained to Grandmama and Uncle George within the next few days."

"Oh, Jude." Cassandra was weeping in earnest now. "I knew it. I did, I did. I never doubted you for a moment."

Mama came elbowing past Papa then and rushed down the path to catch Judith up in a mighty hug. "I was in the kitchen," she cried. "Girls, why did you not call me? Judith, my love. And Branwell has been cleared too? That boy is a trouble to poor Papa, but he could never be a thief any more than you could. You came on the coach?" She smoothed back a lock of hair that had fallen from beneath Judith's bonnet. "You look dead on your feet, child. Come and have some breakfast and I will tuck you into your bed."

For once Papa was overpowered by his women. He stood frowning and troubled, but he made no other attempt to take Judith aside to chastise her in any way for what he had heard from Harewood. And no one, Judith realized, commented on her mention of the Duke of Bewcastle. After she had been led off to the kitchen, she did not see her father again until after noon. She had not lain down as she had been pressed to do but had spent the morning with her mother and sisters in the sitting room. While they had all been busy sewing, she had written two letters—one to the Duke of Bewcastle and one to Lord Rannulf. She owed them both a deep debt of gratitude, yet she had rushed away from Bedwyn House without a word to either of them. She had just finished the long and difficult task when her father came into the room, the habitual frown on his face, an open letter in his hand.

"I have just received this from Horace Effingham," he said. "It bears out what you told me this morning, Judith. It is a complete confession, not only of the theft and the attempt to incriminate you and Branwell, but also of his motive. He tried to force his attentions on you at Harewood, Judith, and you very properly repelled them. His scheme was an attempt to avenge himself on you. According to his letter, he has also written to my mother and to Sir George."

Judith closed her eyes. She knew they had all believed her this morning—even Papa. But what a relief it was to be fully exonerated. Horace would never have written such a letter of his own volition, of course, especially the humiliating part about her rejecting his advances and his wanting revenge. He had been forced into writing it—by Lord Rannulf. Had it really all happened just yesterday? It seemed an age ago.

Rannulf had done it all for her sake.

"Your name is cleared, Judith," Papa said. "But why would Horace Effingham have believed that you might welcome his improper advances? And where is your cap today?"

It was the old story. Men looked on her with lust, and Papa blamed her. The only difference was that she now knew she was not ugly.

I can truly say that I have never ever seen any woman whose beauty comes even close to matching yours.

318 ᴄ Mary Balogh

She tried to bring back the sound of his voice as he spoke the words to her out at the pool behind Harewood.

"I do not want to wear one any longer, Papa," she said.

Surprisingly he did not reprimand her or order her to her room to put one on. Instead he held up another letter, still sealed.

"This came for you yesterday," he said. "It is from your grandmother."

Her stomach churned. She did not want to read it. Grandmama had believed she was the thief. She would still have believed it when she wrote the letter. Judith got to her feet anyway and took it from her father's hand. But suddenly she could not bear to be indoors, surrounded by all the comfortable normality of family life. Nothing was normal. Nothing ever would be again.

"I'll read it in the garden," she said.

She did not stop to fetch her bonnet. She went out through the back door and saw that all her mother's summer flowers were blooming in a riot of color. But she could not enjoy the beauty. Soon Branwell was going to have to apply to Papa again to help him out of his difficulties. And even if she could blank her mind to that, Judith could think of very little to buoy her spirits.

She had not even turned to take a final look at him.

The garden was too suffocatingly close to the house. She looked longingly at the rolling hills beyond the back fence, long her refuge when she had wanted to be alone. The hills, where she had roamed and sat and read during her girlhood, and where she had acted, proclaiming other identities aloud to the listening hills. She opened the gate and strode upward, stopping only when she came to a familiar large, flat stone two-thirds the way to the top of the closest hill. From it she could see the valley and the village below and the hedgerows of the surrounding farms. She sat there for perhaps half an hour before pulling her grandmother's letter out of her pocket.

It was a tearful one even though there was no physical sign of the tears. For one weak hour, she had written to Judith, she had believed the damning evidence. She had grown to love her granddaughter during two weeks more dearly than she had loved anyone since Judith's grandpapa died, and she would have forgiven her, but she *had* believed. But only for one hour. She had lived through a wretched night of remorse and had gone as soon as she felt she decently could to Judith's room to beg her pardon—on her old knees if necessary. But Judith had gone. She was not sure she would ever be able to forgive herself for doubting even for that hour. Could Judith forgive her?

Judith could not. She crumpled the letter in one hand and stared away from the valley with tear-filled eyes. She could not.

But then she remembered how she had suspected Branwell—for a great deal longer than an hour. Indeed, she had not been quite certain of his innocence until the proof was finally offered to her. In what way was she different from Grandmama, who had not even had proof of her innocence when she wrote this letter?

Would she allow Horace that final victory of having caused lasting bitterness between Judith and the old lady who had become as dear to her in two weeks as any of her family members in the rectory below?

"Grandmama," she whispered, holding the letter against her lips. "Oh, Grandmama."

She sat there for a long while after smoothing out the letter, folding it carefully, and putting it back in the pocket of her dress, her knees drawn up, her arms clasped about them, gazing across the hills rather than down, basking in the heat of the sun and the coolness of the breeze, turning her unhappiness inside out and looking squarely at it.

She had a family who loved her. Soon life was going to become more and more difficult for them. But they *were* a family, and Papa would still have his living. They would surely not be quite, quite destitute. How selfish of her to be afraid of being poor. Thousands of poor people survived and lived lives of dignity and worth. She had a grandmother who loved her perhaps more than she loved anyone else in this world. How blessed to be so loved! She could not have the *man* she loved, it was true, but thousands could not. Heartache was not a death sentence. She was twenty-two years old. She was still young. She would never marry—she *could* not now even if some decent man was ever willing to take her without any dowry. But life without marriage did not mean life without all meaning or life without all happiness.

She would make her own happiness. She *would*. She would not have unreasonable expectations of herself. She would allow some time for grieving, but she would not wallow in her own misery. She would not become mired in self-pity.

She would do more than exist through the years that remained to her. She would *live*!

"I was beginning to think," a familiar voice said, "that I would have to climb all the way to the top before finding you."

She spun around, shading her eyes against the sun as she did so.

She had forgotten, she thought with utter foolishness, just how very attractive he was.

CHAPTER XXIII

S HE WAS SITTING ON A LARGE FLAT ROCK IN A blaze of sunlit beauty that felt as if it contracted his chest muscles and pressed on his heart. She was wearing neither bonnet nor cap. She looked like someone who had climbed to freedom, away from all those who would have imposed their standards of beauty and propriety on her.

"What are you doing here?" she asked him.

"Gazing at you," he said. "It seems more like a week since I saw you last than just twenty-five or -six hours. You have a habit of running away from me."

"Lord Rannulf," she said, removing her hand from above her eyes and clasping her knees again in a tight, protective gesture, "why have you come here? Is it because I left without a word or without even writing to you? I *have* written, you know, to both you and the Duke of Bewcastle. The letters are ready to send."

"This one is mine?" He held up the sealed sheet addressed to him in her neat hand.

"You have been to the house?" Her eyes widened.

"Of course I have been to the rectory," he said. "Your housekeeper admitted me to the sitting room, where I met your mother and your three sisters. They were all charming. I could easily distinguish the one you described as the beauty of the family. But you were wrong, you know. Her beauty does not come close to matching yours."

She merely hugged her knees more tightly.

"Your mother gave me this," he said, indicating the letter. With his thumb he broke the seal. She half reached out a hand to stop him, but then pulled it back again. She dipped her head to rest her forehead on her knees.

" 'Dear Lord Rannulf,' " he read aloud, "I cannot even begin to thank you for all the kindness you showed me from the time I left Harewood Grange until yesterday." He looked at her bent head. "*Kindness*, Judith?"

"You *were* kind," she said. "Exceedingly kind."

He glanced through the rest of the short letter, which continued in the same vein as it had begun. " 'Respectfully yours,' " he read aloud when he came to the end. "And this is all you had to say to me?"

"Yes." She looked up at him then, and he folded the letter and put it away in his coat pocket. "I am sorry I did not stay to say it in person, but you should know by now that I am a coward when it comes to saying good-bye."

"Why did you feel you had to say good-bye?" he asked her. He sat down on the stone beside her. It was warm from the heat of the sun.

She sighed. "Is it not obvious?"

As obvious as the nose on his face—and that was obvious enough. She was a proud, stubborn woman, and yet paradoxically she had very little confidence in herself. It had been squashed out of her by repressive parents, who doubtless meant well, but who had done untold harm to the daughter who was a swan among their other ducklings.

"The Duke of Bewcastle is my brother," he said, "and he

is a haughty aristocrat, as high in the instep as any monarch. He wields power with the mere lifting of a finger. Freyja and Morgan and Alleyne are my sisters and brother, and they dress grandly and bear themselves proudly and behave as if they are a cut or two above ordinary mortals. Bedwyn House is one of my family's homes, and it is a rich and splendid mansion. Only Bewcastle and Aidan stand between me and the dukedom and fabulous riches and properties and estates stretching over vast areas of England and Wales. Have I come close to describing half of what is obvious?"

"Yes." She did not look at him but gazed off down the hill.

"The Reverend Jeremiah Law is your father," he continued. "He is a gentleman of moderate means and rector of a less-than-prominent living. He has four daughters to provide for on a competence that has been severely depleted by the extravagances of a son who has not yet settled to earning his own living. He has moreover the embarrassment of being the grandson on his mother's side of a draper and the son of an actress. Have I described the other half of what is obvious?"

"Yes." But she was no longer gazing down the hill. She was looking at him, and he saw with some satisfaction that she was angry. He would take her anger over her passivity any day of the week. "Yes, that is it exactly, Lord Rannulf. But I am not ashamed of Grandmama. I am *not*. I love her dearly."

"I would think so too," he said. "She thinks the world of you, Judith."

"I'll not be your mistress," she said.

"Good Lord!" He looked at her, aghast. "Is *that* what you have thought I am offering?"

"There could never be anything else between us," she said. "Can you not see? *Did* you not see? Even the servants at Bedwyn House were grander than I. Everyone was very courteous to me and Lady Freyja and the Duke of Bewcastle were marvelously kind in their efforts to help me. But they must have been aghast at my appearing among them."

"It would take a great deal more than that to shock any of the Bedwyns," he said. "Besides all of which, Judith, you are not being asked to live at Bedwyn House or with any of my brothers and sisters. You are being asked to live with *me*, probably at Grandmaison, as my wife. I do not believe my grandmother would allow me to take you there as my mistress. She is a stickler about such matters."

She jumped to her feet then, though she did not immediately move away.

"You cannot wish to marry me," she said.

"Can't I?" he asked her. "Why not?"

"It would not work," she said. "It *could* not work."

"Why not?" he asked again.

She turned then and strode away, choosing to go upward rather than down. Rannulf got to his feet and went after her through short, springy grass that was very green from the recent rain.

"Is it because I may be with child?" she asked him.

"I almost hope you are," he said. "Not because I want to trap you into marriage against your will, but because I would like to fulfill my grandmother's last dream while she still lives. She is dying, you know. It is her final wish that I marry before she does and it is her dream that my wife and I will present her with a grandchild while she still lives."

She had stopped walking. "*This* is why you wish to marry me?"

He lifted one hand and set his forefinger beneath her chin. "That question hardly dignifies an answer," he said. "Do you not know me better, Judith?"

"No, I do not." She pushed his hand away and resumed her climb. The slope was getting steeper, but her pace was relentless. Rannulf took off his hat and carried it at his side.

"You told me yourself that marriage was for wealth and position only, that all your true pleasure would be taken outside of marriage."

"Good Lord, did I say that?" But he had, he knew. He could remember saying it or something similar. Even at the time he had not meant it but had merely meant to shock her. "Did you not know that Bedwyns are not allowed to carry on extracurricular activities outside their marriage beds? There is some rule in the family archives, I believe. Anyone who transgresses is banished to outer darkness for the rest of eternity."

If anything her pace became faster.

"Once I am married, Judith," he said, realizing that she was not in the mood to be teased, "my wife will be entitled to my undivided devotion, in and out of the marriage bed. That would be true even if for some reason I were ever persuaded to marry a woman not of my own choosing—as I almost was during the past few weeks. You are the bride of my choosing, the love of my heart, for all the rest of my life."

He heard his own words almost as if there were a spectator in him uninvolved in his emotions, in his fear that there was going to be no way of persuading her. The spectator was very aware that he would have found the extravagance of his own words excruciatingly embarrassing even just a few weeks ago. . . . *the bride of my choosing, the love of my heart . . .*

Her head was down. She was crying, he realized. He did not comment on the fact or say any more. He merely kept pace with her. They were almost at the summit of this particular hill.

"You cannot marry me," she said eventually. "We are soon going to be quite ruined. That was no happily ever after at Bran's rooms yesterday. He is still dreadfully in debt. He is either going to end up in debtors' prison, or he is going to beggar Papa—or both. You *cannot* ally yourself with such a family."

She stopped suddenly. There was nowhere else to go except down the other side of the hill to a sort of no-man's-land before the next hill began.

"Your brother is no longer in debt," he told her, "and I am hopeful that he never will be again."

She looked at him, her eyes widening.

"The Duke of Bewcastle did not . . ." She did not complete the thought.

"No, Judith," he said. "Not Wulf."

"You?" One of her hands crept up to her throat. "*You* have paid his debts? How are we ever going to repay you?"

He took her hand in his and drew it away from her throat. "Judith," he said, "it is a family matter. Branwell Law is going to be a part of my family, I fervently hope. There is no question of repayment. I will always do all in my power to keep you from harm or misery." He tried to smile and was not at all sure he had succeeded. "Even if that means removing myself from your life and never seeing you again."

"Rannulf," she said, "you paid his debts? For my sake? But Papa will never allow it."

It had not been easy. The Reverend Jeremiah Law was a severe, proud man who did not unbend easily into affability. He was also an upright and honest man who loved his children, even Judith, whose spirit he had so unwittingly crushed over the years.

"Your father has accepted the fact that it is quite unexceptionable for his future son-in-law to give some assistance to his son," he said. "I am up here with his permission, Judith."

Her eyes widened again.

"*Your* future brother-in-law helped too," he said. "He used his influence and has found your brother a junior post with the East India Company. With hard work he will be able to improve his position considerably. The sky, one might say, is the limit for him."

"The Duke of Bewcastle? Oh." She bit her lip. "Why has he done so much for us when he must despise us heartily?"

"I am here with his blessing too, Judith," he said, raising her hand to his lips.

"Oh," she said again.

"You seem to be in a minority of one in considering a marriage with me ineligible," he said.

"Rannulf." Tears welled into her eyes again, making them look greener than ever.

The spectator in him looked on appalled as he risked murder to one leg of his pantaloons by dropping to one knee on the grass in front of her, possessing himself of her other hand too as he did so.

"Judith," he said, looking up into her startled, arrested face, "will you do me the great honor of marrying me? I ask for one reason and one reason only. Because I adore you, my love, and can imagine no greater happiness than to spend the rest of my life making *you* happy and sharing companionship and love and passion with you. *Will* you marry me?"

He had never in his life felt so helpless or so anxious. He gripped her hands, fixed his gaze on the grass, and tried to ignore the fact that the course of all the rest of his life hung on the answer she would give him.

It seemed to him that it took forever for her to answer. When she drew her hands free of his, he thought his heart had surely slipped all the way to the soles of his boots. And then he felt her hands very light against the top of his head and then gently twining in his hair. He was aware of her leaning over him, and then she kissed his head between her hands.

"Rannulf," she said softly. "Oh, Rannulf, my dearest love."

He was on his feet then and catching her about the waist and lifting her off her feet and twirling her twice about while she threw back her head and laughed.

"Look what you have done," she said, still laughing, when he set her down.

Her hair on one side had come tumbling down, and the braid was fast unraveling. She lifted her arms, took down the other side too, and stuffed the hairpins in her pocket. She shook her head, but he closed the small distance between them.

"Allow me," he said.

He combed his fingers through her hair, untangling the last of the braiding until her hair was loose and falling in shining ripples about her shoulders and down her back. He gazed into her bright, happy eyes, smiled at her, and kissed her. She wound her arms about his neck and leaned into him while he wrapped his own about her waist and drew her to him as if they could have melded into one right there on the hilltop.

They smiled at each other when he finally lifted his head, words unnecessary, unwilling to let each other go. And then he stood back, holding her hands out to the sides with his own, and looked at her—his prize, his own, his love.

There was a noticeable breeze on the hilltop. It sent her dress fluttering behind her and flattened it against her at the front. It lifted her hair in a red-gold cloud behind her back. Just a few weeks ago, he knew, she would have been deeply embarrassed to be seen thus in all her vivid, voluptuous glory. But today she gazed back at him, her head tipped proudly back, a soft smile on her lips, her cheeks flushed.

She was all beautiful, breathtaking goddess and woman, and now at last she had accepted herself as she was.

"May I assume that your answer is yes?" he asked.

"Yes, of course," she said, laughing. "Did I not say so? Oh, *yes*, Rannulf."

They both laughed then and he scooped her up in his arms again and twirled her about and about until they were both dizzy.

CHAPTER XXIV

J UDITH'S SMALL DRESSING ROOM WAS SO CROWDED
with people that Tillie could scarcely bend her elbows to
place her bonnet carefully on her head so as not to disturb the soft, shiny curls of her coiffure.

"You look *beautiful*, Jude," Pamela said, tears shining in
her eyes. "I always did say you were the loveliest of us all."

"Lord Rannulf is going to be *ecstatic*," Hilary said, clasping her hands to her bosom.

"Judith," Cassandra said, gazing at her. But she had always been Judith's closest friend. Words failed her. "Oh,
Judith."

Their mother did more than gaze. She reached up for the
lace over the brim of the bonnet, pulled it down, and
arranged it over her daughter's face.

"It seems I have waited forever to see one of my daughters
happily married," she said. "Promise me you will be happy,
Judith." Although her manner was brisk, it was very obvious
that she was on the verge of tears.

"I promise, Mama," Judith said.

Her grandmother, dressed in bright fuchsia and decked

out in surely every jewel from the velvet bag, glittered and clinked as she clasped and unclasped her hands and beamed at her favorite granddaughter. She had complained of no ailments today. Nor had she eaten any breakfast beyond her usual morning cup of chocolate. She was too excited, she had said.

"Judith, my love," she said now, "I wish . . . oh, *how* I wish your grandpapa were here to share my pride and joy. But he is not and so I will have to be doubly proud and doubly joyful."

And then there was a tap on the door and yet another body squeezed inside.

"Oh, I say!" Branwell exclaimed. "You look as fine as fivepence, Jude. Uncle George sent me to announce that the carriages are ready outside the door to take everyone to church except Jude and Papa."

There was a swell of sound and many tearful final greetings and words of wisdom before the room emptied, leaving Judith alone with Tillie.

She was in a new room—a larger one than before—at Harewood Grange. It was her wedding day. There had been much discussion about the most suitable place for the wedding. Papa had wanted it at home in Beaconsfield, and Rannulf had been quite willing to oblige. But there were a few problems. Where would all his family members stay? Would it be too far for the two grandmothers to come, especially Lady Beamish, who was in ill health? London was suggested and rejected as equally far for the elderly ladies to travel. Leicestershire was perhaps the best possibility since both Judith and Rannulf had relatives there with large enough homes to accommodate the two families. And yet at first it had seemed an impossibility. How could Judith and her family invite themselves to Harewood Grange after recent events?

The problem had been solved with the arrival at the

rectory of a very civil letter from Sir George Effingham, who had just been informed of the betrothal by his mother-in-law. His brother-in-law was very welcome to bring his family to Harewood, he had written, if the nuptials were to be held close by. In the same letter he mentioned the fact that his son had recently sailed for America and that his wife and daughter were making a protracted visit at the parental home of Mr. Peter Webster, Julianne's intended husband.

Rannulf had been at Grandmaison for the past month while the banns were being read. His brothers and sisters had been there for most of that time too, brought there by the news of Lady Beamish's failing health as well as by the wedding. Judith herself had not arrived until yesterday and had had only one brief meeting with Rannulf, who had ridden over from Grandmaison after dinner with Lord Alleyne. All her family had been present, and he had stayed for only half an hour.

But at last—oh, at last, six weeks after the wonder of his appearance on the hill above the rectory—it was their wedding day.

"You look as pretty as any picture, miss," Tillie said.

"Thank you." Judith turned to look in the pier glass, which had been hidden behind the press of bodies until a minute ago. She had decided upon simplicity though Papa had insisted that no expense be spared. Her ivory silk dress was moderately low at the bosom and fashionably high-waisted, its short sleeves and hemline scalloped and trimmed with gold embroidery. Its chief distinguishing feature was that it hugged the contours of her upper body quite unashamedly before falling in soft folds about her hips and long legs. Her bonnet, like her long gloves, matched the dress exactly in color, though its one curling plume was gold. So were her slippers. About her neck she wore a delicate double chain of gold, a wedding gift Rannulf had brought with him last evening.

Yes, Judith thought, she looked as she had wanted to look. But the butterflies that had danced in her stomach from the moment she arose early until all the excitement of dressing had begun were back in full force. She had not fully believed in the reality of this day until now. And even now . . .

"Your papa will be waiting for you, miss," Tillie said.

"Yes." Judith turned resolutely from the mirror and stepped out of the dressing room, whose door a smiling, curt-sying Tillie was holding open for her.

Her father was waiting for her at the bottom of the stairs, stern and formal in his best black coat and breeches. His eyes took in her full appearance as she descended, the verti-cal frown line between his eyebrows prominently displayed. Judith braced herself for his critical comment, determined not to allow it to dampen her spirits.

"Well, Judith," he said, "for years past I have been very afraid that all that beauty was going to be snatched up by a man who could see no deeper than surfaces. But I believe you have avoided that fate so common to extraordinarily beautiful women. You are lovely indeed today."

She could hardly believe the evidence of her own ears. He had always thought her beautiful? Why had he not said so at least once during her life before now? Why had he not explained . . . But parents, she supposed, were not the pin-nacles of perfection their children thought and expected them to be. They were humans who usually did the best they could but often made the wrong choices.

"Thank you, Papa." She smiled at him. "Thank you."

He offered his arm to lead her outside to the waiting carriage.

THE VILLAGE CHURCH AT KENNON, WITH ITS ANCIENT stone walls and stained-glass windows, was picturesque but small. That latter fact did not matter greatly since the guest list for the marriage of Miss Judith Law to Lord Rannulf Bedwyn was confined to their two families.

Rannulf felt as nervous as if this were a grand show of a *ton* wedding at fashionable St. George's on Hanover Square in London. He almost wished they could have done what Aidan had done—he had taken Eve to London, married her privately by special license with only her great-aunt and his batman for witnesses, and then taken her home to Oxfordshire without informing even Bewcastle of the event.

Rannulf waited at the front of the church with Alleyne, his best man. Bewcastle sat in the second pew, their grandmother next to him, Freyja and Morgan beside her. Aidan sat in the next pew with Eve and their two foster children—though they never referred to the children in any other way than as their own. Behind them were the Marquess and Marchioness of Rochester, Rannulf's uncle and aunt. Judith's mother sat in the second pew on the other side of the aisle, between her son and her mother-in-law. The three sisters sat behind them with Sir George Effingham. Some servants from Grandmaison and Harewood sat farther back in the church.

The past month had seemed interminable even though he had had all his brothers and sisters with him except Aidan, who had come just a week ago. Every day he had expected a letter from Judith terminating their engagement for some flimsy reason or other. Her confidence in herself, he feared, was still a fragile thing. But the letter had not come, and when he had ridden over to Harewood last evening, it was to the happy discovery that she had indeed arrived, just as planned.

He still did not quite believe even this morning.

But then in the hush of the church interior he was aware of the church door opening and closing again, and Alleyne touched his elbow to remind him that it was time to stand.

The vicar, robed and smiling, was signaling the organist and the music began.

Rannulf turned his head and then his whole body.

Lord, but she was breathtakingly beautiful—not just because of the luscious body, displayed to full advantage in her wedding dress, or the glorious hair, half hidden beneath her bonnet, or the lovely face shadowed by her veil. Not just because of her looks and figure, but because she was Judith.

His Judith. *Almost* his.

She was not smiling, he saw when she came closer on her father's arm. Her green eyes were huge. She looked terrified. But then her glance focused on him and she looked suddenly transformed by joy.

He smiled at her.

And believed.

"Dearly beloved," the vicar began a few moments later.

IT FELT STRANGELY AS IF TIME HAD SLOWED—QUITE THE opposite of what she had feared would happen. She listened to and savored every word of the service that joined her in holy matrimony to Rannulf for the rest of their lives. She heard her father give her hand in marriage and turned to flash him a smile. She noticed the unusual brightness of his eyes and realized that he was affected by the moment. She saw Lord Alleyne, handsome and elegant and smiling. She heard the rustle of the people behind her and heard her grandmother sniff and someone shush a child who asked in a loud whisper if that was her new aunt. She could smell the roses, which were displayed in two large vases on either side of the altar.

And with every fiber of her being she was aware of Rannulf, of the fact that she had missed him dreadfully during the past month, of the fact that after today they would be together for as long as they both lived. He had had his hair cut though he still looked like a Saxon warrior. He looked achingly attractive in a brown, form-fitting coat with gold waistcoat, cream knee-breeches, white stockings and linen and lace, and black shoes. His hand was large and firm and warm as it held hers, and his fingers were steady as they slid her wedding ring onto her hand. His blue eyes smiled into hers from the moment she first saw him until after the vicar spoke his final words.

"I pronounce that they be man and wife together, in the name of the Father, and of the Son, and of the Holy Ghost. Amen."

She wondered how it was possible for happiness to be so intense that it was almost painful.

"My wife," Rannulf whispered for her ears only, and he lifted the veil from her face, arranged it over the brim of her bonnet, and looked at her with bright, intense eyes. For a startled moment she thought he was going to kiss her right there at the front of the church with the vicar and both their families looking on.

They signed the register to make their marriage finally official, and then walked out of the church together as man and wife. It was September. The heat of summer was gone but autumn had not yet arrived. The sun shone from a clear sky.

"My love," Rannulf said as soon as they stepped out onto the church steps, circling her waist with one arm and dipping his head to kiss her.

There was cheering and applause, and Judith looked up and saw a large crowd of people gathered about the lychgate at the end of the stone path that curved through the churchyard. All the villagers must have come out to see them.

She laughed and looked up at Rannulf, who was laughing back.

"Shall we make a dash for it?" he asked.

The open barouche drawn up beyond the gate was decorated with large white bows, she could see. It was also surrounded by people.

"Yes." She clasped his hand, lifted the front of her dress with her free hand, and ran with him to the carriage. For the final few yards they were pelted with flower petals and surrounded by laughter and shouted greetings.

They drove off after Rannulf had taken a fat pouch from one corner of the seat and hurled handfuls of coins into the crowd. He sat down beside her, laughing, though his smile faded from all but his eyes as he took her hand in one of his again and laid the other on top of it.

"Judith," he said. "My love. Are you happy?"

"Almost too happy," she told him. "Happiness wants to burst out of me and cannot find a way."

"We will find a way," he said, dipping his head to kiss her again. "Tonight. I promise."

"Yes," she said, "but first the wedding breakfast."

"First the wedding breakfast," he agreed.

"I am so glad both our families are here to celebrate with us," she said. "I think it is only today that I have realized fully how very precious families are."

He squeezed her hand with both his own.

FAMILY WAS INDEED A PRICELESS COMMODITY. AND THE two families—the Bedwyns and the Laws—were not as awkward with each other as Rannulf had feared. Bewcastle unbent sufficiently to make himself agreeable to each of the Laws as he was presented to them and engaged the Reverend Jeremiah Law in a conversation during breakfast that sounded as if it were about theology. The Marquess of Rochester spoke at length with Sir George Effingham about politics. Aunt Rochester, that haughtiest of aristocrats, allowed herself to be drawn into conversation with Judith's mother and grandmother as well as Rannulf's grandmother. Alleyne maneuvered matters so that he was seated between Hilary and Pamela Law at table. Morgan, seated opposite them, conversed with Branwell Law. Eve, smiling and charming, spoke with everyone, her children at her side except when the little girl finally tired from all the excitement of the day and Aidan scooped her up on one arm.

Rannulf's Uncle and Aunt Rochester were gracious to Judith when he presented her to them.

"If you have captured Rannulf's heart you must be something out of the ordinary," his aunt said in her usual forthright manner, her lorgnette poised for use in one hand, "even apart from your good looks. Bewcastle informed me that you are a beauty."

"Thank you, ma'am." Judith smiled and curtsied.

Morgan and Freyja had kissed her on the cheek when they arrived from the church. Eve, whom she had never met before, hugged her tight.

"Rannulf came to Grandmaison a couple of months ago determined to resist all attempts to marry him off," she said with a twinkle in her eye and a swift, mischievous glance at Rannulf. "I am so glad you thwarted him, Judith."

Aidan—tall, dark, dour Aidan—made his bow to Judith, probably forcing her to the conclusion that he was even stiffer and colder than Bewcastle. But then he took her by the shoulders, bent his head to kiss her on the cheek, and smiled at her.

"Welcome to our family, Judith," he said. "We are a ramshackle lot. It takes a brave woman to take one of us on."

Eve laughed and reached down to set a hand lightly on the young boy's head. "I can tell," she said, "that Judith is as intrepid as I."

Freyja moved from group to group, making herself perfectly civil. Yet she seemed the one most out of place in the cheerful scene of celebration, Rannulf thought. He drew her to one side while Judith was with her grandmother, who had just declared in his hearing that she had already soaked three handkerchiefs but still had three more dry ones in her reticule.

"Feeling maudlin, Free?" he asked.

"Of course not," she said briskly. "I am happy for you, Ralf. I was somewhat appalled when you first arrived at Bedwyn House with Judith, I must confess, but she is not a milk-and-water miss or a gold digger, is she? I daresay you will be happy."

"Yes, I daresay I will." He tipped his head to one side and regarded her more closely. "You will be going home to Lindsey Hall with Wulf and the others tomorrow?"

"No!" she said sharply. "No, I am going to go to Bath. Charlotte Holt-Barron is there with her mother and has invited me to join them."

"Bath, Free?" He frowned. "It is not a place where you are likely to find a great deal of young company or agreeable entertainment, is it?"

"It will suit me," she said.

"This does not have anything to do with Kit, does it?" he asked. "And the fact that his wife is expecting to be confined soon?"

Kit Butler, Viscount Ravensberg, Freyja's former beau and her expected husband just last summer, lived unfortunately close to Lindsey Hall. And Lady Ravensberg was soon to give birth.

"Of course not!" she said altogether too vehemently. "How foolish you are, Ralf."

The imminent event and the wedding of a brother must be painful for Freyja.

"I *am* sorry, Free," he said. "But there will be someone else, you know, and then you will be glad you waited."

"Drop this ridiculous subject," she commanded him, "if you do not want to be punched in the nose, Ralf."

He grinned at her and kissed her cheek—something he rarely did.

"Enjoy Bath," he said.

"I intend to," she told him. She looked beyond his shoulder. "Grandmama, how are you feeling?"

Rannulf turned and wrapped his arms gently about the old lady. "Grandmama," he said.

"You have made me very, very happy today, Rannulf," she said.

He grinned at her. Having her grandchildren about her during the past month appeared to have done her health some good. Though one never quite knew with her, of course. Her health was one topic she would never discuss.

"I am happy too," he said.

"I know." She tapped him on the arm. "That is *why* I am happy."

F INALLY THE OPPORTUNITY CAME TO HAVE A PRIVATE MO-
ment with Judith. They would spend their wedding night at the dower house, which had been opened up, cleaned, and prepared for the occasion. But most of the rest of the day would be spent at Grandmaison with their families. It was a stolen moment, then, in the middle of the afternoon, when they slipped outside together and strolled to the rose arbor. It was not as laden with blooms as it had been earlier in the summer, but even now it was a secluded and lovely area, its terraces bathed in late-afternoon sunshine, the stream gurgling over the stones in its bed.

They sat down together on the very bench where Judith had sat that first time she came to Grandmaison, the day when he first offered her marriage. He laced his fingers with hers.

"At the risk of sounding callous," he said, "I am glad it rained that day and that neither your coachman nor I heeded the warnings not to travel onward. I am glad the coach overturned in the ditch. How different our lives would be today if those things had not happened."

"And if I had said no when you offered me a ride," she said. "It was on the tip of my tongue to say so. I had never done anything nearly so improper before. But I decided to steal a little dream for myself and it has turned into the dream of the rest of my life. Rannulf, I love you so very, very dearly. I wish there were words adequate for the feeling."

"There are not," he said, lifting their hands and kissing the back of hers. "Even when we make love tonight, it will not adequately express love itself, will it? That has been the great surprise of the last couple of months—that love is not entirely physical or mental or even emotional. It is larger than any of those things. It is the very essence of life itself, is it not? That great inexpressible mystery that we can best grasp through the discovery of a beloved. Rescue me here, Judith. Am I spouting nonsense?"

"No." She laughed. "I understand you perfectly."

Her head tipped down then and the fingers of her free hand played along the back of his.

"Rannulf? Do you remember when we were up in the hills at home six weeks ago and you said that you *almost* wished it were true?"

"About . . ." He gazed at the shining curls at the back of her head, his mouth turning dry.

"It *is* true," she said softly, and lifted her head to look into his eyes. "I am with child. At least, I am almost certain I must be."

He stared at her, transfixed.

"Do you mind dreadfully?" she asked him.

He bent to her then, releasing her hand so that he could place his arm about her shoulders, sliding the other beneath her knees and swinging her up into his arms as he stood. He twirled her once about.

"I am going to be a *father*," he told the blue sky above them, tipping back his head. "We are going to have a *child*."

He whooped loudly and then bent his face to hers. She was bright-eyed and laughing.

"I think," she said, "you do not mind dreadfully."

"Judith," he said, his lips touching hers. "My wife, my love, my heart. Am I spouting nonsense again?"

"Probably," she said, still laughing and twining both arms about his neck. "But there is only me to hear. Spout more of it."

But how could he? She was kissing him hard.

Can't wait to read the next
romantic adventure about the charming
Bedwyn siblings? You don't have to!
Look for the stories of the dashing
Aidan and the headstrong Freyja in . . .

SLIGHTLY MARRIED

and

SLIGHTLY SCANDALOUS

Read on for a preview of these tantalizing
romances from Mary Balogh. . . .

SLIGHTLY MARRIED

Toulouse, France
April 10, 1814

T HE SCENE WAS ALL TOO FAMILIAR TO THE MAN
surveying it. There was not a great deal of difference
between one battlefield and another, he had discovered through long experience—not, at least, when the battle was over.

The smoke of the heavy artillery and of the myriad mus-
kets and rifles of two armies was beginning to clear sufficiently
to reveal the victorious British and Allied troops establishing
their newly won positions along the Calvinet Ridge to the
east of the city and turning the big guns on Toulouse itself,
into which the French forces under Soult's command had recently retreated. But the acrid smell lingered and mingled
with the odors of dust and mud and horse and blood. Despite
an ever-present noise—voices bellowing out commands,
horses whinnying, swords clanging, wheels rumbling—there
was the usual impression of an unnatural, fuzzy-eared silence
now that the thunderous pounding of the guns had ceased.
The ground was carpeted with the dead and wounded.

It was a sight against which the sensibilities of Col. Lord Aidan Bedwyn never became totally hardened. Tall and solidly built, dark-complexioned, hook-nosed, and granite-faced, the colonel was feared by many. But he always took the time after battle to roam the battlefield, gazing at the dead of his own battalion, offering comfort to the wounded wherever he could.

He gazed downward with dark, inscrutable eyes and grimly set lips at one particular bundle of scarlet, his hands clasped behind him, his great cavalry sword, unsheathed and uncleaned after battle, swinging at his side.

"An officer," he said, indicating the red sash with a curt nod. The man who wore it lay facedown on the ground, spread-eagled and twisted from his fall off his horse. "Who is he?"

His aide-de-camp stooped down and turned the dead officer over onto his back.

The dead man opened his eyes.

"Captain Morris," Colonel Bedwyn said, "you have taken a hit. Call for a stretcher, Rawlings. Without delay."

"No," the captain said faintly. "I am done for, sir."

His commanding officer did not argue the point. He made a slight staying gesture to his aide and continued to gaze down at the dying man, whose red coat was soaked with a deeper red. There could be no more than a few minutes of life remaining to him.

"What may I do for you?" the colonel asked. "Bring you a drink of water?"

"A favor. A promise." Captain Morris closed parchment-pale eyelids over fading eyes, and for a moment the colonel thought he was already gone. He sank down onto one knee beside him, pushing his sword out of the way as he did so. But the eyelids fluttered and half lifted again. "The debt, sir. I said I would never call it in." His voice was very faint now, his eyes unfocused.

"But I swore I would repay it nonetheless." Colonel Bedwyn leaned over him, the better to hear. "Tell me what I can do."

Captain Morris, then a lieutenant, had saved his life two years before at the Battle of Salamanca, when the colonel's horse had been shot out from under him and he had been about to be cut down from behind while engaging a mounted opponent in a ferocious frontal fight. The lieutenant had killed the second assailant and had then dismounted and insisted that his superior officer take his horse. He had been severely wounded in the ensuing fight. But he had been awarded his captaincy as a result, a promotion he could not afford to purchase. He had insisted at the time that Colonel Bedwyn owed him nothing, that in a battle it was a soldier's duty to watch the backs of his comrades, particularly those of his superior officers. He was right, of course, but his colonel had never forgotten the obligation.

"My sister," the captain said now, his eyes closed again. "Take the news to her."

"I'll do it in person," the colonel assured him. "I'll inform her that your last thoughts were of her."

"Don't let her mourn." The man's breath was being drawn in on slow, audible heaves. "She has had too much of that. Tell her she must not wear black. My dying wish."

"I'll tell her."

"Promise me . . ." The voice trailed away. But death had still not quite claimed him. Suddenly he opened his eyes wide, somehow found the strength to move one arm until he could touch the colonel's hand with limp, deathly cold fingers, and spoke with an urgency that only imminent death could provoke.

"Promise me you will protect her," he said. His fingers plucked feebly at the colonel's hand. "Promise me! No matter what!"

"I promise." The colonel bent his head closer in the hope

that his eyes and his voice would penetrate the fog of death engulfing the agitated man. "I give you my solemn vow."

The last breath sighed out of the captain's lungs even as the words were being spoken. The colonel reached out a hand to close Morris's eyes and remained on one knee for a minute or two longer as if in prayer, though in reality he was considering the promise he had made Captain Morris. He had promised to take the news of her brother's death to Miss Morris in person though he did not even know who she was or where she lived. He had promised to inform her of Morris's dying wish that she not wear mourning for him.

And he had sworn on his most sacred honor to protect her. From what—or from whom—he had no idea.

No matter what!

The echo of those last three words of the dying man rang in his ears. What could they possibly mean? What exactly had he sworn to?

No matter what!

England, 1814

Eve Morris was knee-deep in bluebells. She had decided that it was too glorious a morning to be spent in any of the usual activities about the house and farm or in the village. The bluebells were in bloom for such a short time, and picking them for the house had always been one of her favorite springtime activities. She was not alone. She had persuaded Thelma Rice, the governess, to cancel classes for a few hours and bring her two pupils and her infant son out flower picking. Even Aunt Mari had come despite her arthritic knees and frequent shortness of breath. Indeed, it had been her idea to turn the occasion into an impromptu picnic. She was sitting now on the sturdy chair Charlie had carried down for her, her knitting needles clicking steadily, a large basket of food and drink at her side.

Eve straightened up to stretch her back and savored a conscious feeling of well-being. All of the summer stretched ahead, a summer unmarred by anxiety for the first time in many years. Well, *almost* unmarred. There was, of course, the continuing question of what was keeping John away. He had expected to be home by March, or April at the latest. But he would come as soon as he was able. Of that she was certain. In the meantime, she viewed her surroundings and her companions with placid contentment.

Seven-year-old Davy was picking earnestly, a frown on his thin face, as if he had been set a task of grave importance. Close behind him, as usual, five-year-old Becky, his sister, picked with more obvious enjoyment and less concentration, humming tunelessly as she did so.

Young Benjamin Rice toddled up to his mother, a cluster of azalea and bluebell heads clutched tightly in one outstretched fist. Thelma bent to take them in her cupped hands as if they were some rare and precious treasure—as of course they were.

Eve felt a moment's envy of that mother love, but she shook it off as unworthy of her. She was one of the most fortunate of mortals. She lived in this idyllic place, and she was surrounded by people with whom she shared a reciprocal love, the loneliness of her girlhood a thing of the distant past. Soon—any day now—John would be back, and she could admit to the world at long last that she was in love, love, love. She could have twirled about at the thought, like an exuberant girl, but she contented herself with a smile instead.

And then there was the other prospect to complete her happiness. Percy would be coming home. He had written in his last letter that he would take leave as soon as he was able, and now surely he must be able. A little over a week ago she had heard the glorious news that Napoléon Bonaparte had surrendered to the Allied forces in France and that the long wars were over at last. James Robson, Eve's neighbor, had come in person to Ringwood as soon as he heard himself, knowing what the news would mean to her— the end to years of anxiety for Percy's safety.

Eve stooped to pick more bluebells. She wanted to be able to set a filled vase in every room of the house. They would all celebrate springtime and victory and security and an end to mourning with color and fragrance. If *only* John would come.

"I suppose," Aunt Mari said, "we'd better pack up and take all these flowers back to the house before they wilt. If someone would just hand me my cane as soon as I have my wool and needles in this bag, I could haul these old bones upright."

"Oh, must we?" Eve asked with a sigh as Davy scrambled to offer the cane.

But at that moment someone called her name.

"Miss Morris," the voice called with breathless urgency. "Miss Morris."

"We are still here, Charlie." She swiveled around to watch a large, fresh-faced young man come lumbering over the top of the bank from the direction of the house and crash downward toward them in his usual ungainly manner. "Take your time or you will slip and hurt yourself."

"Miss Morris." He was gasping and ruddy-cheeked by the time he came close enough to deliver his message. "I am sent. By Mrs. Fuller. To fetch you back to the house." He fought for air between each short sentence.

"Did she say why, Charlie?" Eve got unhurriedly to her feet and shook out her skirt. "We are all on our way home anyway."

"Someone's come," Charlie said. He stood very still then, his large feet planted wide, his brow creased in deep furrows of concentration, and tried to bring something else to mind. "I can't remember his name."

Eve felt a lurching of excitement in the pit of her stomach. *John?* But she had been disappointed so many times in the last two months that it was best not to consider the possibility. Indeed, she was even beginning to wonder if he was coming at all, if he had ever intended to come. But she was not yet prepared to draw such a drastic conclusion—she pushed it firmly away.

"Well, never mind," she said cheerfully. "I daresay I will find it out soon enough. Thank you for bringing the message so promptly, Charlie."

"He is a military feller," he said. "I seen him before Mrs. Fuller sent me to fetch you and he was wearing one of them red uniform things."

A military man.

"Oh, Eve, my love," Aunt Mari said, but Eve did not even hear her.

"*Percy!*" she cried in a burst of exuberance. Basket and flowers and companions were forgotten. She gathered up her skirts with both hands and began to run up the bank, leaving her aunt and Thelma and Charlie to gather up the children and the bluebells.

It was not a long way back to the house, but most of the distance was uphill. Eve scarcely noticed. By the time she burst into the entrance hall, she was flushed and panting and probably looking alarmingly disheveled, even grubby. She did not care one iota. Percy would not care.

The rogue! He had sent no word that he was coming. But that did not matter now. And surprises were wonderful things—at least *happy* surprises were. He was home!

Eve dashed across the checkered floor of the hall, flung open the door of the visitors' parlor, and hurried inside.

"You wretch!" she cried, pulling undone the ribbon of her hat. And then she stopped dead in her tracks, feeling intense mortification. He was not Percy. He was a stranger.

SLIGHTLY SCANDALOUS

BY THE TIME SHE WENT TO BED, LADY FREYJA Bedwyn was in about as bad a mood as it was possible to be in.

She dismissed her maid though a truckle bed had been set up in her room and the girl had been preparing to sleep on it. But Alice snored, and Freyja had no wish to sleep with a pillow wrapped about her head and pressed to both ears merely so that the proprieties might be observed.

"But his grace gave specific instructions, my lady," the girl reminded her timidly.

"In whose service are you employed?" Freyja asked, her tone quelling. "The Duke of Bewcastle's or mine?"

Alice looked at her anxiously as if she suspected that it was a trick question—as well she might. Although she was Freyja's maid, it was the Duke of Bewcastle, Freyja's eldest brother, who paid her salary.

"Yours, my lady," Alice said.

"Then leave." Freyja pointed at the door.

Alice looked at it dubiously. "There is no lock on it, my lady," she said.

"And if there are intruders during the night, *you* are going to protect *me* from harm?" Freyja asked scornfully. "It would more likely be the other way around."

Alice looked pained, but she had no choice but to leave.

And so Freyja was left in sole possession of a second-rate room in a second-rate inn with no servant in attendance—and no lock on the door. And in possession too of a thoroughly bad temper.

Bath was not a destination to inspire excited anticipation in her bosom. It was a fine spa and had once attracted the crème de la crème of English society. But no longer. It was now the genteel gathering place of the elderly and infirm and those with no better place to go—like her. Under ordinary circumstances Freyja would have politely declined the invitation.

These were not ordinary circumstances.

She had just been in Leicestershire, visiting her ailing grandmother at Grandmaison Park and attending the wedding there of her brother Rannulf to Judith Law. She was to have returned home to Linsey Hall in Hampshire with Wulfric—the duke—and Alleyne and Morgan, her younger brother and sister. But the prospect of being there at this particular time had proved quite intolerable to her and so she had seized upon the only excuse that had presented itself *not* to return home quite yet.

Last year Wulfric and the Earl of Redfield, their neighbor at Alvesley Park, had arranged a match between Lady Freyja Bedwyn and Kit Butler, Viscount Ravensberg, the earl's son. The two of them had known each other all their lives and had fallen passionately in love four years ago during a summer when Kit was home on leave from his regiment in the Peninsula. But Freyja had been all but betrothed to his elder brother, Jerome, at the time and she had allowed herself to be persuaded into doing the proper and dutiful thing—she had let Wulfric announce her engagement to Jerome. Kit had returned to the Peninsula in a royal rage. Jerome had died before the nuptials could take place.

Jerome's death had made Kit the elder son and heir of the Earl of Redfield, and suddenly a marriage between him and Freyja had been both eligible and desirable. Or so everyone in both families had thought—including Freyja.

But *not*, apparently, including Kit.

It had not occurred to Freyja that he might be bound upon revenge. But he had been. When he had arrived home for what everyone expected to be their betrothal celebrations, he had brought a fiancée with him—the oh-so-proper, oh-so-lovely, oh-so-dull Lauren Edgeworth. And after Freyja had boldly called his bluff, he had married Lauren.

Now the new Lady Ravensberg was about to give birth to their first child. Like the dull, dutiful wife she was, she would undoubtedly produce a son. The earl and countess would be ecstatic. The whole neighborhood would doubtless erupt into wild jubilation.

Freyja preferred not to be anywhere near the vicinity of Alvesley when it happened—and Lindsey Hall was near.

Hence this journey to Bath and the prospect of having to amuse herself there for a month or more.

Sometime soon, she thought just before she drifted off to sleep, she really was going to have to start looking seriously at all the gentlemen—and there were many of them despite the fact that she was now five-and-twenty and always had been ugly—who would jump through hoops if she were merely to hint that marriage to her might be the prize. Being single at such an advanced age really was no fun for a lady. The trouble was that she was not wholly convinced that being married would be any better. And it would be too late to discover that it really was not after she had married. Marriage was a life sentence, her brothers were fond of saying— though two of the four had taken on that very sentence within the past few months.

Freyja awoke with a start some indeterminate time later when the door of her room opened suddenly and then shut again with an audible click. She was not even sure she had not dreamed it until she looked and saw a man standing just inside the door, clad in a white, open-necked shirt and dark pantaloons and stockings, a coat over one arm, a pair of boots in the other hand.

Freyja shot out of bed as if ejected from a fired cannon and pointed imperiously at the door.

"Out!" she said.

The man flashed her a grin, which was all too visible in the near-light room.

"I cannot, sweetheart," he said. "That way lies certain doom. I must go out the window or hide somewhere in here."

"*Out!*" She did not lower her arm—or her chin. "I do not harbor felons. Or any other type of male creature. Get out!"

Somewhere beyond the room were the sounds of a small commotion in the form of excited voices all speaking at once and footsteps—all of them approaching nearer.

"No felon, sweetheart," the man said. "Merely an innocent mortal in a ton of trouble if he does not disappear fast. Is the wardrobe empty?"

Freyja's nostrils flared.

"Out!" she commanded once more.

But the man had dashed across the room to the wardrobe, yanked the door open, found it empty, and climbed inside.

"Cover for me, sweetheart," he said just before shutting the door from the inside, "and save me from a fate worse than death."

Almost simultaneously there was a loud rapping on the door. Freyja did not know whether to stalk toward it or the wardrobe first. But the decision was taken from her when the door burst open again to reveal the innkeeper holding a candle aloft, a short, stout, gray-haired gentleman, and a bald, burly individual who was badly in need of a shave.

"Out!" she demanded, totally incensed. She would deal with the man in the wardrobe after this newest outrage had been dealt with. *No one* walked uninvited into Lady Freyja Bedwyn's room, whether that room was at Lindsey Hall or Bedwyn House or a shabby-genteel inn with no locks on the doors.

"Begging your pardon, ma'am, for disturbing you," the gray-haired gentleman said, puffing out his chest and surveying the room by the light of the candle rather than focusing on Freyja, "but I believe a gentleman just ran in here."

Had he awaited an answer to his knock and then addressed her with the proper deference, Freyja might have betrayed the fugitive in the wardrobe without a qualm. But he had made the mistake of bursting in upon her and then treating her as if she did not exist except to offer him information—and his quarry. The unshaven individual, on the other hand, had done nothing *but* look at her—with a doltish leer on his face. And the innkeeper was displaying a lamentable lack of concern for the privacy of his guests.

"Do you indeed believe so?" Feyja asked haughtily. "Do you *see* this gentleman? If not, I suggest you close the door quietly as you leave and allow me and the other guests in this establishment to resume our slumbers."

"If it is all the same to you, ma'am," the gentleman said, eyeing first the closed window and then the bed and then the wardrobe, "I would like to search the room. For your own protection, ma'am. He is a desperate rogue and not at all safe with ladies."

"*Search my room?*" Freyja inhaled slowly and regarded him along the length of her prominent, slightly hooked Bedwyn nose with such chilly hauteur that he finally looked at her—and saw her for the first time, she believed. "Search my *room?*" She turned her eyes on the silent innkeeper, who shrank behind the screen of his candle. "Is *this* the hospitality of the house of which you boasted with such bombastic eloquence upon my arrival here, my man? My brother, the Duke of Bewcastle, will hear about this. He will be interested indeed to learn that you have allowed another guest— if this gentleman *is* a guest—to bang on the door of his sister's room in the middle of the night and burst in upon her without waiting for a reply merely because he *believes* that another gentleman dashed in here. And that you have stood by without a word of protest while he makes the impudent, preposterous suggestion that he be allowed to search the room."

"You were obviously mistaken, sir," the landlord said, half hiding beyond the doorframe though his candle was still held out far enough to shine into the room. "He must have escaped another way or hidden somewhere else. I beg your pardon, ma'am—my lady, that is. I allowed it because I was afraid for your safety, my lady, and thought the duke would want me to protect you at all costs from desperate rogues."

"Out!" Freyja said once more, her arm outstretched imperiously toward the doorway and three men standing there. "Get out!"

The gray-haired gentleman cast one last wistful look about the room, the unshaven lout leered one last time, and then the inn-keeper leaned across them both and pulled the door shut.

Freyja stared at it, her nostrils flared, her arm still outstretched, her finger still pointing. How *dared* they? She had never been so insulted in her life. If the gray-haired gentleman had uttered one more word or the unshaven yokel had leered one more leer, she would have stridden over there and banged their heads together hard enough to have them seeing wheeling stars for the next week.

She was certainly not going to recommend *this* inn to any of her acquaintances.

She had almost forgotten about the man in the wardrobe

until the door squeaked open and he unfolded himself from within it. He was a tall, long-limbed young man, she saw in the ample light from the window. And very blond. He was probably blue-eyed too though there was not quite enough light to enable her to verify that theory. She could see quite enough of him, though, to guess that he was by far too handsome for his own good. He was also looking quite inappropriately merry.

"That was a magnificent performance," he said, setting down his Hessian boots and tossing his coat across the truckle bed. "Are you *really* a sister of the Duke of Bewcastle?"

At the risk of appearing tediously repetitious, Freyja pointed at the door again.

"Out!" she commanded.

But he merely grinned at her and stepped closer.

"But I think not," he said. "Why would a duke's sister be staying at this less-than-grand establishment? And without a maid or chaperon to guard her? It was a wonderful performance, nevertheless."

"I can live without your approval," she said coldly. "I do not know what you have done that is so heinous. I do not *want* to know. I want you out of this room, and I want you out *now*. Find somewhere else to cower in fright."

"Fright?" He laughed and set a hand over his heart. "You wound me, my charmer."

He was standing very close, quite close enough for Freyja to realize that the top of her head reached barely to his chin. But she always had been short. She was accustomed to ruling her world from below the level of much of the action.

"I am neither your sweetheart nor your charmer," she told him. "I shall count to three. *One*."

"For what purpose?" He set his hands on either side of her waist.

"*Two*."

He lowered his head and kissed her. Right on the lips, his own parted slightly so that there was a shocking sensation of warm, moist intimacy.

Freyja inhaled sharply, drew back one arm, and punched him hard in the nose.

"Ouch!" he said, fingering his nose gingerly and flexing his mouth. He drew his hand away and Freyja had the satisfaction of seeing that she had drawn blood. "Did no one ever teach you that any ordinary lady would slap a man's cheek under such scandalous circumstances, not punch him in the nose?"

"I am no ordinary lady," she told him sternly.

*Other titles
in
Mary Balogh's
Bedwyn series,
available
from
Piatkus*

SLIGHTLY TEMPTED

From the moment he spies Lady Morgan Bedwyn across the glittering ballroom, Gervase Ashford, Earl of Rosthorn, knows he has found the perfect instrument of his revenge. But wedlock is not on the mind of the continent's most notorious rake. Nor is it of interest to the fiercely independent Lady Morgan herself . . . until one night of shocking intimacy erupts in a scandal that could make Gervase's vengeance all the sweeter.

There is only one thing standing in his way: Morgan, who has achieved the impossible – she's melted his coolly guarded heart. For Gervase, only the marriage bed will do, but Morgan simply will not have him. Thus begins a sizzling courtship where two wary hearts are about to be undone by the most scandalous passion of all: all-consuming love.

978-0-7499-3786-7

SLIGHTLY
SINFUL

On a Flemish battlefield Lord Alleyne Bedwyn is
thrown from his horse and left for dead, only to awaken
in the bedchamber of a Brussels brothel. The dark,
handsome diplomat has no memory of who he is or how he
got there – yet of one thing he is certain: he owes his life to
the angel of undoubtedly dubious virtue who is nursing
him back to health.

But like him, Rachel York is not who she seems. The havoc
of war has forced Rachel to seek refuge with the 'ladies' of
the house whilst devising a plan to restore her fortunes. The
dashing soldier she rescued from near-death could be her
saviour in disguise. In order to inherit, Rachel needs to be
married and here is a man with no memory – and thus no
ties – willing to do *anything* to help her. However on
returning to England, their marriage charade draws them
both into danger, scandal and a blossoming relationship
that is ever so slightly sinful . . .

978-0-7499-3787-4

SLIGHTLY DANGEROUS

All of London is abuzz over the imminent arrival of Wulfric
Bedwyn – the reclusive, cold-as-ice Duke of Bewcastle – at
the most glittering social event of the season. Some whisper
of a tragic love affair. Others say he is so aloof and
passionless that not even the greatest beauty could capture
his attention. But on this dazzling afternoon, one woman
does catch the duke's eye – and she is the only female in the
room who isn't even trying. Christine Derrick is intrigued
by the handsome duke . . . all the more so when he invites
her to become his mistress.

But Christine has very definite views on men, morals, and
marriage and confounds Wulfric at every turn. Yet even as
the lone wolf of the Bedwyn clan vows to seduce her any
way he can, something strange and wonderful is happening.
Now for a man who thought he'd never lose his heart,
nothing less than love will do.

978-0-7499-3772-0